D1570451

The Fall of Alice K.

Also by Jim Heynen

Fiction

Old Swayback, illustrated by Gaylord Schanilec
The Boys' House: New and Selected Stories
Why Would a Woman Pour Boiling Water on Her Head?, chapbook
Cosmos Coyote and William the Nice
Being Youngest
The One-Room Schoolhouse
You Know What Is Right
The Man Who Kept Cigars in His Cap

Poetry

Standing Naked: New and Selected Poems
A Suitable Church
How the Sow Became a Goddess
The Funeral Parlor, chapbook
Notes From Custer, chapbook
Maedra Poems, chapbook

Nonfiction

Minnesota Schoolhouses, prose poems to accompany photographs
Sunday Afternoon on the Porch, text to accompany photographs by Everett Kuntz
Harker's Barns, prose poems to accompany photographs
One Hundred Over 100
Writing About Home: A Handbook for Writing a Community Encyclopedia

Translations

Sioux Songs, chapbook

The Fall of Alice K.

Jim Heynen

milkweed
editions

© 2012, Text by Jim Heynen
(800) 520-6455
www.milkweed.org

Published 2012 by Milkweed Editions
Printed in Canada
Cover design by Jason Heuer
Cover image © Elizabeth Livermore/Flickr/Getty Images
Author photo by Doug Kurata
Interior design by Connie Kuhnz
The text of this book is set in Garamond Premier Pro.
12 13 14 15 16   5 4 3 2 1
First Edition

Please turn to the back of this book for a list of the sustaining funders of Milkweed Editions.

Library of Congress Cataloging-in-Publication Data

Heynen, Jim, 1940–
    The fall of Alice K. / Jim Heynen. — 1st ed.
        p.   cm.
    ISBN 978-1-57131-089-7 (alk. paper)
    I. Title.
    PS3558.E87F35 2012
    813'.54—dc23

                                                                    2012007805

This book is printed on acid-free paper.

In memory of Anne Paine Williams (1933–2010)
patron of the arts
lover of literature
defender of the natural world

For the body does not consist of one member but of many. If the foot should say, "Because I am not a hand, I do not belong to the body," that would not make it any less a part of the body. And if the ear should say, "Because I am not an eye, I do not belong to the body," that would not make it any less a part of the body.

1 Corinthians 12:14-17

I do not want my house to be walled in on all sides and my windows to be stuffed. I want the cultures of all the lands to be blown about my house as freely as possible.

Mahatma Gandhi

The Fall of Alice K.

PART I

September, 1999

1

Alice Marie Krayenbraak was standing on the screened porch when she heard shots coming from a neighbor's farm—one loud blast after another, the sounds of a twelve gauge. Each time she thought the shooting had stopped, it would start again. Some shots were followed by moments of silence, but others were followed by guttural squeals, like pathetic last-second objections. Sometimes a new blast came before the last squeal stopped. The time between shots got shorter, as if someone was hurrying to get this done.

The kitchen door opened and Alice's father stepped onto the porch with her.

"You don't have to hear this," he said.

The four-foot sections of screens were gray from the summer's dust, giving a hazy view of the feedlots and beyond them the corn and soybean fields that extended in the direction of Ben Van Doods's farm. The buffer of trees and dusty screens might have absorbed the sounds, but instead it caught the blasts and flung them back into the air for a second life, like an echo—or an aftershock. Alice could see the cupolas of Ben's tallest barn and the green domes of trees in his grove, but she could not see the scene on the ground.

"Aldah sure shouldn't hear this," said Alice's father. "Go inside and have her watch some television. Play piano for her or something."

"What's going on?"

"Today's market report."

"What's going on?"

Alice stepped closer to the screen, which prompted her father to move in front of the screen door to keep her from stepping outside and closer to the gunshots.

"Ben must figure it's cheaper to shoot them than truck them to market."

Her father's shoulders twitched with each blast. If Ben was doing this by himself, he was getting faster and faster at it. Now there was squealing before the gun blasts, frantic squeals as if animals were trapped in a corner. The ones that were left must have known what was coming.

"Go take care of Aldah."

Alice didn't move. "She probably can't hear it," she said. "Mother is probably covering Aldah's ears."

"Your mother is covering her own ears," said her father. "Get inside."

Alice obeyed and walked into the kitchen, a space that to Alice felt cluttered in spite of its generous size. The round oak table in the middle was the room's center of gravity, but surrounding it were contradictory images—the brick-patterned linoleum on the floor did not harmonize with the white metal cupboards or the plastic food canisters and cookbooks on the counters. In one corner sat her father's wooden swivel chair, which looked like a respectable piece of antique furniture, but anything respectable was diminished by a scattering of dime-store paintings and plaques with quotations that were supposed to be either edifying or clever on the off-white walls. Some might say the room's decor was eclectic. In Alice's mind, it was a pathetic hodgepodge.

Her mother stood across the round oak table with her back toward Alice. She was leaning over the sink and staring out one of the room's two windows. It was not open, but Alice could almost see the sounds of the gun blasts rapping on the windowpane. As if responding to the sounds of gunfire, all the scattered pieces of the room came together into a harmony that made it feel like a comforting refuge.

"This is just the beginning," said her mother and kept her back to Alice while staring across the lawn toward the gravel road. "Things aren't much better here."

The matter-of-fact coldness in her voice was all too familiar to Alice. The chilly flatness of it.

This was her mother's way of making reference to the millennium. The world was starting to end, one little chunk at a time, one dead hog at a time, one sour thought after another.

Her mother's shoulders looked narrow from behind and sloped

steeply from the edge of her graying hair, which she had let hang loose. She was clearly in one of her dark moods. Alice could not see her hands. Might she have them folded over the sink as she looked out? Alice wondered. Was she praying for Ben? For the hogs? For the Krayenbraak farm?

"Where's Aldah?"

"Watching TV."

"At two o'clock in the afternoon?"

"It doesn't make any difference to her."

Her mother still didn't move. The white cupboards that rose up from both sides of the sink framed her shoulders and made her slim body stand out in sharp relief. The spine of *Joy of Cooking* met Alice's eye where it sat wedged between other cookbooks on the kitchen counter. Alice could almost smile at the irony because her mother's cooking was too much like the perfect storm: it looked bad, it tasted bad, and it was bad for you. The way a lazy doctor might prescribe penicillin for every ailment, her mother prescribed a can of mushroom soup for any dish that needed help. She didn't have those cookbooks because she liked to cook; she had them because she liked to read.

Alice walked to the window that faced the hoglots. "It obviously doesn't make any difference to you," she said and turned to go back onto the porch with her father. He still stood in front of the screen door, all six foot four of him. Alice stepped next to him, all six foot one of her. In her peripheral vision she caught the grim tightness of his lips and thought that her lips looked the same. She had an urge to take his hand but didn't.

"Think we should see if Ben's all right?" she asked.

"He'll be all right."

They stood beside each other, looking out, breathing in unison. "What if he does something terrible to himself?"

"He's too mad for that." Her father took one of his deep breaths that made his shoulders rise. "Maybe we could just drive by," he said and stepped back from the screen door.

Alice drove the Ford 150 pickup with her father beside her, easing off the Krayenbraak farmyard in a reverent manner and driving slowly down the gravel road toward Ben Van Doods's farm. She kept her speed at a steady thirty so she wouldn't draw attention by slowing down when they passed his farm.

What Ben Van Doods had done was all too clear: eighty market-ready 250-pound Chester Whites lay strewn across his cement feedlot like scattered white tombstones. A few were clustered, a whole mound of them, in one corner. These must have been the last ones, the ones that knew what was coming.

Over the next few days, Ben was seen driving to town and getting groceries as if nothing was wrong, but he didn't move the carcasses.

"He's trying to tell the world something," said Alice's father. "He's trying to show what's happening to us."

Alice had the reputation among her friends at Midwest Christian as a straight talker, somebody who faced the facts and looked reality in the eye. She lived up to her reputation a few days later when Ben's Malibu disappeared in the distance and she drove over to his farm to have a closer look at the carnage. She expected to see flies swarming over the white carcasses, but there weren't many. There were more hornets, some hovering like little copters around the snouts and some crawling into the caverns of the ears the way a honeybee goes into a flower. And sparrows, fluttering flocks of them, landing on the bloating bodies and pecking bits of dirt from the forest of bristles.

Numbness swept over Alice at the sight of the bulging pink bellies and all those limbs jutting stiffly out like table legs. She returned a day later, thinking that if she looked again, the horror would diminish. The scene had changed but only for the worse because starlings and crows had moved in and were pecking into the rotting flesh.

She stood with her hands folded and looked at the awful sight. She didn't feel disgusted or angry. She didn't even feel sad. She felt scared. As she stood staring, her clasped hands tightened and her shoulders gave little shudders. The fear that had come over her, as best as she could understand it, was that this was just the beginning. Her mother's dooms-day fantasies might be coming true.

The sound of a car slowing down near Ben's driveway interrupted her quiet and private horror. Alice turned and prepared to be embarrassed by someone who would think she was some kind of pervert who liked to stare at animal carnage. The vehicle, a dark Toyota station wagon, did more than slow down: it stopped, and the heads of three small people stared in her direction. Alice faced them, and for several seconds it was a stare off. Then the vehicle inched forward down the driveway in Alice's direction. As it got closer, she saw that the occupants were foreign—probably Mexican immigrants who worked on one of the big dairies, but the Minnesota license plates didn't make sense. When Mexicans drove in from other states, they usually came from California or Arizona. The driver was a young woman, and she swung the station wagon directly in front of Alice. She was not white, but she didn't look Mexican either.

"Hi," said the young woman, "what on earth happened here?"

She sounded totally American, but she looked Asian. Alice came to a quick realization: these were the Hmong family that had just moved to Dutch Center.

"Are you the Vangs?"

"Whoa-ho!" said the young woman. "Word travels fast around here. Yes, I'm Mai, and this is my brother, Nickson, and that's my mom, Lia. We were just taking a ride and checking things out."

Nickson lifted his hand and nodded. "Hi," he said. The mother, in the backseat, only nodded and smiled.

"I don't live here," said Alice.

"You sound American," said Mai.

"No, I don't live on this farm."

"Looks like you're too late," Mai commented.

"I don't think anybody could have stopped him. They were Ben Van Doods's hogs."

"I meant it looks like it's too late to eat them. They smell rotten! Why didn't he butcher them when he had the chance?"

"I don't know," said Alice.

"Quite a waste there," said Nickson.

They all had such intense eyes and such black hair. Even the mother had those intense eyes, but she was all eyes and no speech.

Alice didn't like the judgment that had been leveled at Ben Van Doods. It felt directed at every farmer around Dutch Center. She didn't like these brazen newcomers, but at the same time, she did. What would it feel like to be that confident and outspoken in an unfamiliar setting?

2

Alice sometimes wondered if she would go to church if she had a choice. In Dutch Center, church was something people did out of habit, sometimes sleeping through the sermon, sometimes gossiping after church in cruel ways. Alice didn't like the way that the people with the most expensive cars parked right outside the front door. Showing off. Wouldn't people do better by staying home and relaxing in a quiet room, reading their Bibles and asking God to help them make the right decisions? Alice didn't have a choice. In Dutch Center, not going to church would have been like having a bumper sticker that said, "God Is Dead."

Compared to some of the real wackos, even her mother, with her doomsday fears of the millennium, seemed relatively sane. One church member thought space travel into the heavens was a Hollywood camera trick created by atheists. There was the millionaire retired farmer who thought global warming was the result of the earth still drying out after Noah's flood, and the even wackier jeweler, Gerrit Vanden Leuvering, whose gray head swaying in the second pew harbored the belief that dinosaur bones were leftovers from an earlier creation because this earth and its creatures were created 6,456 years ago. Around these people Alice knew that it was best to keep her mouth shut. Don't pretend to know more than the next person. If she had spoken up, more people than her mother would be saying she was arrogant, somebody too big for her britches. Alice didn't go to church to argue science. She went to hear the music and to find peace. "Getting centered," some people called it.

She could sing hymns and listen to organ music all day, and often Rev. Prunesma preached sermons that made her think about something other than the judgmental eyes of her mother or the shuffle of hungry steers. Man does not live by bread alone: at its best, that's what church was all about. Going to church also gave her the chance to wear clothes that made her look like somebody who didn't live on a farm. It wasn't as arrogant and pretentious as parking an expensive car in front of church, and it did give her a taste of the future when she planned to be out of here.

The Krayenbraaks walked down the aisle in their usual long-long-short-long order—Father, Mother, Aldah, Alice—and sat in their usual pew: left side, sixth from the front. People said Alice resembled her father more than her mother, and she thought about that as she watched his dignified and stately walk that he reserved for church. Compared to her mother, he looked well groomed when he went out into public. Alice had never known him when he wasn't bald, but he still fussed with the little hair he had left. You could have held a carpenter's level to the edge of his sideburns.

In church, her father did not look like a farmer, and she hoped she did not look like a farmer's daughter. She knew they both looked different when they were on the farm. On the farm, he had an undignified but still controlled, pumping-forward efficiency in his manner. When she was working outside with him, she thought she looked like somebody who was following the mandate of the hymn that said, "Work, for the night is coming."

The church sanctuary was a no-nonsense place of worship. *Simple and huge* is how Alice thought of it—like a large auditorium. The ceiling slanted in straight lines of wooden rafters above them to a peak that was fifty feet over their heads. The smooth oak benches had no cushions, and though narrow arched windows lined the walls, the stained glass patterns were simple designs that did not hint of "graven images." A large wooden cross stood against the wall behind the lectern, which was centered on the raised pulpit—centered to remind everyone that in this church the preaching of The Word was central to the worship service.

The church didn't have a choir, and it didn't have any fresh flowers or stenciled banners. Bright colors of any kind would be a distraction. The congregation didn't want their house of worship cluttered with any New Age garbage. Of all the churches in Dutch Center, this was the one that had the largest number of farmers and the smallest number of the local Redemption College students.

Just as the organ prelude was ending, the Reverend Prunesma walked in from the front of the church, followed by the eight-member consistory of elders and deacons, who seated themselves with their families. At the same time, some young people—probably students who would be starting at Redemption College in a few weeks—also walked in. In her mind, Alice quietly forgave them: they didn't know that you should come early enough to be seated before the minister and consistory arrived. But then, after the ushers had already sat down with their families, there came the Vangs, the very last people to enter—Mai leading with Nickson and Lia close behind. Such short people, but such quick, confident steps. Rev. Prunesma was already standing behind the lectern, but he waited, smiling benevolently, as the Vangs made their way to the front of the church and sat down in what was usually old lady Waltersdorf's pew.

Alice watched the Vangs through the opening benediction and opening hymn. They were familiar with the order of worship, and even recited the Apostle's Creed without having to read it. At least Mai and Nickson did. Their mother kept looking down.

After the long congregational prayer, after the church offering with two collection plates going around—one for the General Fund and one for Christian Education—and after the follow-up hymn, Rev. Prunesma's sermon began. His text was Psalm 23, the familiar "The Lord is my shepherd" passage. Alice knew Psalm 23 as well as she knew the Lord's Prayer. She knew it as well as "Little Bo Peep."

"The Lord is my shepherd, I shall not want," he began. "Brothers and sisters in the Lord, what does that familiar text mean to you? 'Shepherd.' What does that mean to you? Do you see a large bearded man with a heavy staff ready to strike you down? Does a shepherd strike his sheep? Does a shepherd beat his sheep into submission? No! No! That is not what King David is saying in this passage. Shepherds do not strike, they do not whip, they do not poke, they do not abuse. No, shepherds guide their flock lovingly."

He opened his arms as if to embrace the whole congregation.

"What about that big long staff we see in pictures of shepherds? you ask. Does that thing look like a bullwhip? Does it look like a cattle prod? No! This staff is used for giving direction, not for beating. The shepherds of David's time only used their staffs aggressively to ward off lions. For you, His people, the Good Shepherd uses His staff to ward off the lions of temptation. With you, His sheep, He uses His staff as a gentle prod to keep you moving down the path to glory."

The Rev paused, rubbed his hands together, and stepped to the side of the lectern.

"But. But," he went on with sentences that he chopped into questions: "Does this mean?—that He is a cozy companion? Does this mean?—that He is someone?—who has no expectations?—from His people? Is this what it means?—to think of Jesus?—as the Good? Shepherd?"

He shook his head slowly but emphatically. "Oh no. Oh no." He raised his right hand and wagged his forefinger. "Jesus is not your *chum!* Jesus is not your *pal!* Jesus is not your *buddy!* Jesus is the Lord God Almighty, ruler of heaven and earth!"

His voice bounced off the ceiling and reverberated through the sanctuary. Alice loved that energy, even though what he had just said contradicted the soft image of God that he had been extolling a minute earlier. Rev. Prunesma was showing his true colors: he was no softy. He was proclaiming the majesty of a fearsome God. A gentle shepherd and an almighty God—not exactly a Holy Trinity, but a Hefty Duality.

Through the brief silence that followed the reverend's exclamations came the sound of beating wings: the Rev's voice had startled and launched a starling from somewhere in the back of the church, and it flew in short, urgent bursts over the congregation, smacking into one window and then another. When it landed on the baptismal font and started drinking, the Rev continued his sermon as if nothing had happened. The starling sat still, seeming quite content with its current situation.

Thrilling as Rev. Prunesma's exuberant digression and the flight of the wayward starling had been, the duller truths of the world sat next to Alice. Aldah was bored. She may have been the only person over ten in the entire congregation who did not know Psalm 23 by heart. Rev. Prunesma's loud exclamations did not stir her, and, to Alice's surprise, neither did the starling. Her mother had given Aldah two pink peppermints to get her through the sermon. Aldah put them in her white handkerchief and chewed on the prune-sized bundle until sweet pink juice oozed into her mouth. Her mother pretended not to notice, so Alice wasn't about to stop her either.

Rev. Prunesma was going through Psalm 23 line by line, explicating every sentence. It was mostly a dull walk through references to the Hebrew and Greek, but when he got to the "still waters," he had Alice's full attention again.

"'He leadeth me beside the still waters.' When we think of still waters today, we think of tepid water. But here, David is contrasting 'still waters' against the alternative of tempestuous, dangerous waters. This water, we should believe, is clean and calm. *Clean* and *calm*."

His repetition and emphases were puzzling. Rev. Prunesma worked at making the Old Testament relevant to the present, but was he hinting that the clean waters of Psalm 23 were everything that cattle feedlot run-off holding tanks were not? Was the Rev suggesting that farmers were at odds with the message of Psalm 23 by turning calm waters into stinky polluted waters? Was he about to lecture the farmers in the congregation that they were polluting the clean earth that God had created?

She turned her head to catch her father's profile. In church, she could never tell what he was thinking. He had on his stern church look. She wasn't sure what look her mother had on. Maybe it was her let-the-end-come look. Aldah kept chewing on her bag of pink peppermints, and some of the juice ran down her chin and onto her white blouse.

"'Yea, though I walk through the valley of the shadow of death . . .'" the Rev went on. "Here again, we should turn to the Hebrew," he said. "A translation from the Hebrew might read, 'Yea, though I walk through the valley of bottomless darkness.'"

He started pumping his arms. "Yea, though I walk through the valley of disgraceful behavior from our leaders! Yea, though I walk through the valley of falling cattle and hog prices! Yea, though I walk through the valley of self-doubt and mental turmoil. Yea, though I walk through the valley of not knowing what the millennium will bring! People of God!" he shouted. "We are all in the valley of darkness as the millennium creeps toward us like a devouring beast in the night! Are we ready?"

With that, the starling came back into the worship service, this time by plunging into the baptismal font and bathing itself in a furious fluttering of wings and splashing of water, some of it landing on the floor and some of it splattering onto the carpet of the pulpit. The reverend stopped preaching. The starling launched itself energetically into the large open space over the congregation's head, flying even more desperately, as if energized by its recent refueling and bath.

Everyone, including Alice, held their breath. The Rev nodded. Whether this was his acknowledgment that some great Forces of Evil were at work in God's House of Worship or whether it was a signal to the ushers, several men did get up to open all the doors of the sanctuary as a way of showing the starling the light it was probably looking for. The Vangs had their own response to the renegade starling: all three of them held church bulletins over their heads.

Alice's mother stiffened, grasped Aldah's wrist, leaned over to whisper harshly in her ear, then stood up and tugged Aldah to follow her out of church. Alice pulled her knees back in the pew to let them get out. Alice assumed her mother was using Aldah's stained dress as an excuse to get away from a situation that she couldn't bear. Alice hid her alarm at her mother's behavior, and so did her father.

The open doors let in traffic sounds from the busy street outside, along with the distinct and ungodly smell of truck diesel fuel. The starling was still flying aimlessly through the sanctuary, bouncing through the air and against the windows. Then it flew to the front of the church and perched on the right arm of the wooden cross. Its chest was panting madly. Finally, as if in despair, it fluttered to the floor, edged itself between the long cylindrical pipes of the pipe organ that stood next to the wooden cross, and disappeared.

The men closed the doors.

Rev. Prunesma looked down at his notes and picked up where he had left off.

The starling hadn't bothered Alice as much as her mother's behavior. God only knew what crazy ideas were bouncing around randomly in her head until she needed to go off and hide. She was a little bit too much like the starling. Her mother was mentally disturbed and Alice guessed that everybody else must know too.

Alice glued her attention back on the Rev as he made his way to the last line of Psalm 23: "And I will dwell in the house of the Lord forever."

He stepped away from the lectern again.

"We understand 'dwell' to mean 'to take up residence in a place, to abide there, to be at home there.' We think of a place that is stationary and permanent. One who dwells is the opposite of a nomad. Dwellers are the opposite of Seekers. Seekers are unsettled: they do not know where they are going from one moment to the next. They are restless. Seekers are lost in lives of bootless desperation, never satisfied with the green pastures that God offers them, always wanting more: more money, more entertainment, even more knowledge."

Alice sensed that the Rev was looking straight at her. He knew she was a big achiever in school, and he knew how hungry she was for success. He knew she was a Seeker! She felt cornered by his admonitions. She was one of the restless and unsatisfied ones who was outside the fold, a wayward sheep, living a life of bootless desperation. A life of futility. A life as empty as her mother's hopeless declarations.

The defensive shield of Alice's critical mind left her. She felt exposed. She felt pummeled by the sermon. She was not one of God's people as Rev. Prunesma had described them. Not only was she not at peace with the wackos sitting around her, she was not at peace with her parents. And she was not at peace in the presence of the Lord. She was not in his green pastures of contentment. I wish I were stupid, she thought. I wish I could obey every order given to me without asking any questions.

Some farmers were leaving church without going downstairs to the community room for coffee. Were they Seekers too? Were they feeling what she was feeling? Restless outcasts, all of us? Or was it that their farms were in as much trouble as the Krayenbraaks' and they didn't want to hear that awful question, "How are things going?" Her father wasn't moving toward the basement either, but he was probably concerned about Agnes and Aldah—wherever they were.

3

Alice walked out into the parking lot behind church to look for her family. Instead of seeing them, she saw Lydia Laats, her best friend at Midwest Christian. Beautiful Lydia. Witty Lydia. Smart Lydia—and Alice's only academic competition. The attraction was mutual. They sought each other out, especially when they were in school. To be in each other's company was to be free from what both of them saw as the shallowness of so many of the other students. Alone together, they could talk about what they were reading without some airhead saying, "Geez, get a life."

"Hey!" said Alice.

"Hey!" said Lydia.

They flung their arms around each other, Alice's arms around Lydia's shoulders and Lydia's around Alice's waist; then Lydia put her hands on Alice's arms and held her away from herself. "Look at you, look at you," said Lydia. "You look fabulous in that blouse and skirt. Blue is your color, girl. And your hair. I love it down like that."

"Thank you," said Alice, "but look at you!"

Lydia was about six inches shorter than Alice, but Alice always thought she was better proportioned with her larger breasts and more prominent hips—and she had a sophisticated European look about her, which should have been no surprise because her parents were born in Holland and lived in Canada before moving to Dutch Center when Lydia was a little girl. She was wearing a dark dress that had long triangles of bright colors shooting up from the hem and narrowing toward her waist. A delicate gold chain around her neck. Small teardrop gold earrings, dark eyeliner, and dark pink lipstick. Lydia didn't get this look from studying the way other people dressed in Dutch Center.

"You're the one who looks fabulous," said Alice.

Lydia's head turned. "Talk about looks, look at those two," she said.

Two young men across the parking lot were staring at them. Strangers: no doubt early-arrival new students at Redemption College. Alice tried to read their thoughts, wondering if they were staring at her or Lydia, or both of them.

Alice had liked what she saw when she examined herself in the mirror before leaving the farm for church, and now it was more than a slight pleasure to be stared at by living creatures besides hungry steers or a resentful mother.

The two young men saw that they had gotten Lydia and Alice's attention and shot them big toothy grins. They were both blond and handsome, but their grins looked practiced, if not just plain lewd.

"Here they come," said Lydia. "You get the taller one."

They approached at a quick pace, arms swinging and grins getting bigger. These two were more than confident, they were cocky: big-city boys ready to show their stuff to the small-town and country girls. They made Alice feel like a piece of divinity in a candy bowl.

The cuter one with the dimpled chin spoke first. "Hi there."

The taller, athletic one with big teeth was right behind him: "Wow, you're something."

He was looking at Alice when he said that.

The two stopped only a few feet from Alice and Lydia and flung out the lasso of their smirky smiles, but it was the noose of their aroma that caught Alice's breath short—something so sickeningly sweet that both Lydia and Alice's nostrils flared in defense.

"Good grief," said Lydia, "have you guys been at the cologne sample table at Walmart?"

The big-city boys, or whoever they were, withered like thistles under a good blast of 2,4-D. It felt great to see how Lydia had nailed them, but Alice was just a bit disappointed that she couldn't hear what complimenting line might have erupted from their lips. The whole awkward scene with these wannabe Romeos was saved by the voice of Rev. Prunesma, who bounced across the parking lot with the whole Vang family following him.

"Alice and Lydia," said the Rev, "I want you to meet the Vangs."

"Nice meeting you," said big teeth as the two walked away.

"Meeting us?" said Lydia, but the Rev was already upon them with the three newcomers.

"Hi! It's you!" said Mai.

"You've already met?" said the Rev.

"Sort of," said Alice.

Actually, Alice had known more than she had let on when she had met them at the scene of Ben Van Doods's slaughtering pen. Alice knew the Vangs were living in a small house across the street from their church and that they were something of a church missionary project. They had come to Dutch Center because Mai had gotten a scholarship to Redemption College. The son, Nickson, would be going to Midwest Christian High School where Alice and Lydia went. Alice knew very little about the Hmong other than that they supposedly had a big thing about family—and that America owed them gratitude for taking sides against the Communists during the Vietnam War.

The Vangs and the Rev were within hand-shaking distance when Alice noticed the bumper sticker on a van a few feet away: "If You're Not Dutch, You're Not Much!"

Alice felt the sharp edge of the Rev's sermon cutting into her again—and then she felt resentment. How would this stodgy Dweller handle the little bumper-sticker message to their guests? Some missionary project: to slap them with an insult right from the get-go.

The Rev saw the bumper sticker too, but Alice had already covered for him by standing in front of it and putting her legs together. Lydia picked up on what Alice was doing and sidled close beside her.

The Rev wore his big missionary smile, his glad-tidings smile, his everything-is-beautiful-in-its-own-way smile. His huge cheeks mushroomed with good will.

Before the Rev could say anything, Mai held out her hand toward Lydia. "Hi, I'm Mai," she said.

"I'm Lydia Laats," said Lydia. "I am so delighted to meet you."

"And this is my mom, Lia, and my brother, Nickson."

"Mai? Nickson? Lia?"

"You got us," said Mai, and then she turned to Alice: "You know, if you told me your name out there in Dead-Hogville, I forgot it, silly me."

"Alice," said Alice. "Alice Marie Krayenbraak."

"Wow, that's a mouthful," said Mai.

When Alice had first seen the Vangs sitting in their station wagon, they had looked small—but not as small as they looked now. Straightening up to greet them had been a mistake. Alice felt like a giraffe, but Mai's eyes were so bright and confident that she could have been six feet tall.

"This is my mother, Lia, and this is my younger brother, Nickson," she repeated for everyone. The Rev stood by, nodding.

"Wassup?" said Nickson and did a little hand wave that Alice recognized as the same one he had given from the passenger seat in their station wagon. He shuffled a little toward his sister's side, grinned and nodded. He was maybe two inches taller than Mai, about five-five, but his shoulders were broad for his height. All of them had heavy eyelids that lifted their eyebrows high on their foreheads. The mother's face was round, but Mai and Nickson were narrow faced with full lips.

Mother Lia held out her hand and looked somewhere in the area of Alice and Lydia's knees. She was even shorter than her children.

"Thank you," she said.

"So pleased to meet you," said Lydia.

"Same here," said Alice, "I mean to really meet you."

Alice and Lydia stood in place as sentries in front of the humiliating bumper sticker, but Mai moved in closer to Alice and Lydia as if she thought they were the shy ones.

"Are you at Redemption?" she said.

"No, we're still in high school," said Lydia.

"We're both at Midwest Christian," said Alice.

"Oh, just like Nickson."

Mai's eyes looked past them and directly at the bumper sticker. She cocked her head. She read the bumper sticker aloud, but with a question-mark lilt at the end: "If You're Not Dutch, You're Not Much?"

There was a stiff silence.

Alice tried to take a breath but couldn't. "We're kind of weird," came her voice from somewhere.

Alice looked down into Mai's bright eyes and felt ridiculously tall and awkward, but Mai's eyes did not shift and her friendly expression did not change. Their height difference didn't bother her one bit, and neither did Alice's blushing face.

"If you're not Dutch, you're not much? Not much *what*?" said Mai.

"Good question," said the Rev—and they all joined in a relieved ripple of chuckles.

Alice saw a trace of farm dirt under her fingernails as they peeled back the edge of the bumper sticker with its white background and blue printing that imitated the colors of Delft china. "I'll just get rid of that thing," she said and gave it a quick yank. It stuck together on itself as she rolled it into a ball in her palm.

"Good job. Good riddance," said Lydia, and gave Alice a gentle punch.

"Hey, that was the Vander Muiden's van," said the Rev in the voice of Jeremiah.

"Still is," said Lydia.

The Krayenbraaks' Taurus idled impatiently across the parking lot with Alice's father staring in her direction while her mother stared straight ahead through the windshield. Aldah's pink-lipped face looked out smiling from the backseat. Alice excused herself to leave the Rev to clean up the pieces of whatever had been started with the Vangs. Mai kept smiling. She held out her hand to shake Alice's and Lydia's. So did Nickson. Their mother smiled and held out her hand too.

Whatever the bumper sticker had meant to the Vangs, it didn't intimidate them. Unless they really knew how to hide their feelings, it didn't even phase them.

"That was an experience," said Lydia as they walked away.

"Those two guys?"

"We can do better than that," said Lydia. "I meant the Vangs. They're interesting. Did you watch Nickson?"

"He seemed shy," said Alice.

"He wasn't shy about the way he looked at you."

"Give me a break," said Alice. "I must be over a half foot taller than he is."

"We all look up to you, darling."

As Alice walked toward the Taurus, she knew she and Lydia had entered a new circle of energy with the Vangs, a whole different kind of cultural fire than they were used to. These people, especially Mai, were fired up inside and wearing an invisible shield on the outside. They probably would have to tame down that foreign fire in Dutch Center, but the invisible shield? They'd need that.

When Alice got into the car, neither of her parents asked about the Vangs, but Alice sensed an unease. Even if both of her parents would argue vehemently that they held no prejudices against foreigners, Alice knew better. The Mexicans who had moved in to work at the dairies and packing plants attended a Catholic church ten miles from Dutch Center, so no one had to experience the strangeness of seeing them in the next pew. Out of sight, out of mind. Occasionally a missionary convert from Africa would appear in their church, but their visits were always short; and there were a handful of foreign students attending Redemption College, but few of them attended Alice's church. The Vangs were a rarity, and seeing them no doubt stirred the calm waters of her parents' habitual church comforts.

Alice could feel the space around her compact with silence in the backseat of the car with Aldah. It wasn't the kind of silence that suggested her parents had quarreled about the way her mother stormed out of church. This was different—a pressured silence that was building up in the front seat. Alice suspected the silence had everything to do with the Vangs, but she wasn't about to open the conversation on that topic. Instead, she would meet their silence with her own and simply stare out the window.

Which she did: in a casual analytic mode, she categorized the farms as they passed by. Successful farms. Teetering farms. Abandoned farms. Successful farms were like people wearing expensive clothing—not showy, just that confident look of neatly buttoned doors and well-groomed roofs, the kind of farms that would appear on the covers of farm magazines. The teetering farms were like people wearing mismatched clothing—a shining tractor next to a gate that nobody bothered to repair. The abandoned farms had no pretense at all, disheveled but carefree with their tall grass and their splintered doors wagging in the breeze like shirttails that someone didn't bother tucking in. Abandoned farms were like homeless hitchhikers ready to take a ride from anybody who passed.

Alice knew that the Krayenbraak farm was a teetering farm but it didn't have any mismatched clothing. Its troubles were hidden behind a facade of order and tidiness: no loose hinges, no loose barbed wire, no loose shingles.

Three miles from the Krayenbraak farm her father stopped the car at a "cornfield corner," an intersection where the cornfields obstructed the view in all four directions. Alice thought for a moment that he was simply being his cautious self or that he might be stopping to appreciate the beauty of the flourishing cornfields, but then she saw her mother's shoulders tighten and knew this was the moment they had chosen for the dam of silence to be broken.

4

As her father drove slowly through the intersection, the dam broke with her mother's sharp-edged voice from the front seat: "Do those people speak English?"

"Of course," said Alice quickly. "Nickson will be at Midwest and Mai will be at Redemption. You know that. She has a scholarship."

"The mother speaks English?"

"Not much," said Alice. "Not yet."

"What kind of name is Nickson?" asked her mother, and for the first time since they had started driving, she turned toward the backseat. Alice couldn't tell if her expression was genuinely curious or if she was mocking the name.

"Not sure," said Alice.

"Nick-son, Nick-son," repeated Aldah.

"Could they have named their son after President Nixon?" That was her father's voice.

"I could ask him," said Alice. "It didn't seem strange to me."

"They sure are small, aren't they?" said her mother.

"Compared to us, most people are small," said Alice.

That made her father chuckle, but Alice figured he was probably chuckling to keep the conversation from getting into awkward territory where their daughter would turn on them and accuse them of who-knows-what. Alice was in no mood to accuse them of anything. So far the conversation had kept them away from the truly awkward matter of her mother storming out of church. Let me dwell in calm waters for the rest of the ride home, Alice thought.

Beside her, Aldah clenched her pink-stained handkerchief. Pink peppermint stains marked the corners of her lips. Alice unwrapped the wadded-up bumper sticker, took Aldah's stained handkerchief, and re-wrapped the bumper sticker around it.

"Stop," said Aldah when they came to a corner that did have a stop sign.

"Very good," said Alice "Now watch for the 'Slow' sign on the next hill."

"McDonald's."

"No, that's not McDonald's. That mailbox says 'Duh-Duh-Dykstra.'"

"Cheerios."

"You're being silly."

Aldah giggled, then laid her head against Alice. "Nap," she said.

Aldah laid her head onto Alice's lap, but before she could sleep they were home to the Krayenbraak farm. Her mother had the oven set so that her one-dish meal was ready. Her father opened with prayer, and then the language of grim silence began. The stale kitchen air was filled with the gibberish of hogyard smells assailing the odors of a hotdish embellished with Hamburger Helper. The dry joints of the old oak table asked incoherent but shrill questions when Alice's father put his hand down firmly next to his plate. Her mother throttled the slim saltshaker when she picked it up, and then, in movements that were uncharacteristically quick for her, she shook the life out of it in a seeming effort to resuscitate the comatose hotdish.

Alice took small bites, wanting her mouth to be free to utter real words in case she would suddenly have to come to the defense of the Vangs, but it was Aldah's presence that spoke most clearly. She was the canary that went down into the dark well of their family's misery, into the mysteries of the turmoil they tried to deny with silence but which came out sideways, in murky or twisted distortions of what they really meant to say. Alice's parents probably knew their own feelings, but they had never practiced a language that would express them. Aldah didn't have the language either, but when she pulled her head down into her shoulders, her message of distress should have been clear to everyone. The corners of her mouth sagged, and her eyes grew dim. The voice of her whole body said, "Stop. Just stop."

Alice's mother finally did break into actual speech with her usual sense of bad timing: "We are worried about Aldah. She's shutting down more and more."

The trouble with her mother and with the dreadful words that often did bubble out of her mouth was that she was often close to the truth. This may have been one of those moments. If Aldah was a canary measuring the toxins in the atmosphere around the table, she was, as her mother cruelly pointed out, shutting down. She could sit like a frozen icon of something no one could explain.

But after her mother's comment, Alice had to wonder: was Aldah absorbing their moods and showing them what they looked like, or was she developing a new problem? Alice was only two and a half when Aldah was born so she had missed Aldah's early health problems. Alice remembered that Aldah was taking digitalis as a child, and she had terrible ear infections. Alice remembered the screaming and how Aldah held her little hands over her ears. She was a wobbly kid and could hardly walk when Alice started school. By the time Alice was a teenager, her mother had given up on Aldah. Alice hadn't. She did some reading and knew that their family wasn't alone in this journey. Alice would crunch up zinc and selenium and pretend to put some in a glass for herself and some in a glass for Aldah. When Aldah saw her older sister drinking hers, she'd drink too. She'd do anything that she saw Alice doing, so long as Alice smiled at her first. She would have walked over a cliff behind Alice if Alice smiled at her first.

Her parents went on talking about Aldah as if she weren't there. Aldah gave no hints that she was listening or that she understood. Alice knew better: Aldah heard and understood every word. Even her father spoke as if Aldah weren't there.

"Maybe it's time," he said.

"I think so," said her mother.

"We're not specialists," said her father.

"There's state money," said her mother.

"I know," said her father. "I checked that out."

Aldah picked at her food, then reached for the sugar bowl and sprinkled two teaspoons of sugar over the Hamburger Helper. No one stopped her.

The discussion, such as it was, dropped off a cliff. Her father said a quick closing prayer that asked for strength and for the forgiveness of their sins. It was one of his autopilot prayers, predictable and brief. He stood up. Her mother stood up too while Aldah went on eating. They evidently weren't going to talk about Aldah any more—they weren't going to talk about anything. Alice could hear the unspoken message that trickled down through the generations: *Zeg maar niks.* Don't say anything. It was a way of dealing with problems by keeping your mouth shut.

When her mother walked outside to the screen porch after closing devotions, Alice followed her, leaving Aldah alone to digest the sugary hotdish and what had been said about her.

Alice stepped into the porch to find her mother sitting in a metal lawn chair. Alice stood off to the side, not close—but she was there. No matter how much her mother repulsed her much of the time, Alice took the first step in making amends. She had come to smooth things over, to find that little window of hope to connect with her mother, but she kept a good four feet distance.

"Are you still worried about Aldah?"

"Aldah is beyond worry."

"Mother."

"The farm is beyond worry. The world is beyond worry."

Her mother looked relaxed and tense at the same time—like a petrified rag doll.

"Not everything is lost," said Alice. "Dad said cattle and hog prices could go up. You have to believe that something good could happen."

"For somebody who thinks she's so smart, you can't even see the elephant that's stepping on your toes."

"Please stop. I came out here because I was worried about you."

"The only person you worry about is yourself."

"You just walked out of the kitchen. That's not like you."

"How would you know?" said her mother. "Just how would you know what is like me?"

"Why can't you ever believe me?"

"Okay, you were worried about me."

"I was. So what's going on?"

"I was just thinking."

"Okay. About?"

"About you. About your father, about Aldah, about us, about the world. About the grand arcs of history, about the miniature dramas of family, about the futility of our will."

Alice moved a little closer. "Good God, Mother."

Now her mother looked at her. Alice noticed that she had jutted her own left hip out and had her right hand on her right hip. Her mother might see this as an arrogant stance and think that Alice was mocking her. Alice let her arms fall to her sides and leaned humbly forward. Her mother noticed, but her expression was puzzling. She wore an unfamiliar expression, almost an aggressive look, as if she was ready to take on something bigger than Alice or Aldah or anything Alice could understand.

"You okay?"

Her mother turned her eyes from Alice and leaned forward. She tried to turn the metal lawn chair into a rocker, which only made a rhythmic grating sound on the porch floor. "As okay as okay can be." She lifted her head and stared out through the screens, not at Alice. "It's just life," she said. "I don't think my faith can sustain me."

Alice didn't know if her mother was pushing her away with that comment or inviting her in. Alice stepped in: "Sustain you through what? What are you going through?"

"You don't know? Intelligent as you think you are, are you really telling me that you don't know?" There was an edge to her mother's voice, almost disgust—as if she thought the answer was so obvious that only a fool would ask.

Alice paused and took a deep breath. "No, I *don't* know. What *are* you going through?"

A steer moaned mournfully from the feedlot, and Alice worried for a second that she might have missed some ailment when she fed them. Then another steer moaned in response. They were just talking to each other in a sweet eunuchs' conversation.

"What does any person go through when they realize there's no hope," said her mother. "And that there should be no hope. Hope is not a way of honoring the Lord, it's a way of insulting Him. Selfish wishes. Hope is greed disguised."

Never before had Alice imagined that her mother's scattered and so

often scathing thoughts could come together in such chilling generaliza-
tions. "Mother," she said, and she paused and thought before going on.
"How much time do you spend thinking like this? And how do I fit into
your thinking?"

"You?" she said. "You. You'll find your way." She paused even longer
than Alice had paused. "If you can ever find it in your heart to learn humility," she said in a voice of bitter finality.

"All right," Alice said quickly. "Anything else?"

"If you ever stop thinking that the world revolves around you. Stop
acting as if you can go your own way without thinking about other
people. You think you're so clever. I can read that look on your face. I
know you. I know you better than anyone knows you. I know you think
everybody else is stupid."

"Mother." Alice's throat was tightening. "I know *you're* not stupid.
Just confusing. But don't attack me. I don't deserve that."

Alice was not going to show her mother any tears. In Alice's mind,
her mother had lured her into a serious talk only to turn on her when her
guard was down. Is this what they meant by sucker punch? How could
she say Alice went her own way when most of her life was spent trying to
help others? Aldah. Her father. The farm work. At school, she helped stupid, untalented singers who couldn't tell an E-flat from a pig's grunt. And,
Lord knows, she had done more than her fair share of trying to help her
mother by helping Aldah. Even helping her father was helping her mother.
If Alice didn't do the chores, would her mother be doing them? Alice didn't
think so. She pitied her pathetic mother at that moment, but she hated her
mother for making her feel the way she was feeling. Whatever she was going
through, it was not Alice's fault. Her mother put Alice in debate mode.

"I thought you said you were bothered by everything in the world,
not just me. I'm not measuring up to your standards, is that it?"

A taunting blank stare and silence.

"I thought we were having a conversation."

"I've said what needs saying," said her mother.

"What are you saying? Are you saying that I'm not doing my fair
share around here? Is that what you're saying? Just tell me. Is that what
you're saying?"

"I told you," she said coolly. "I'm not sure my faith can sustain me."

"And I asked you, 'Sustain you through what?'" The cold stare turned into a cutting glance that told Alice to speak more quietly.

"Through Y2K," she said. "One grand cycle has completed its arc, and the world as we know it is going to end."

"Oh Mother, don't be one of those people, please."

"I don't think we can be saved."

"Saved from what? Saved from destruction? Saved from a blackout? Saved from hell, fire, and brimstone? Saved from what, I ask!"

"Shush up," her mother said. "I think you know. You seem to think you know everything else. Aldah is the one to watch."

"What on earth does that mean?"

"She is the one who is leading the way down. She is the messenger of what is in store for all of us."

Alice wished there could have been witnesses who could see that her mother was the one who was pulling everything and everybody down, not Aldah. Her mother was a whirlpool of darkness. Even when Aldah reflected their bad feelings back at them, she was still their messenger of hope. She was the one who could teach them how to trust the moment without fear. Alice was convinced that Aldah was a threat to her mother's gloomy view, so her mother had to shoot her down. It was that simple.

"Why do you always have to look at the dark side? Why do you always have to make all of us feel bad?"

Alice waited for her mother to respond, but she just sat there. Alice didn't wait for the ice cube to melt: she walked back into the house. Her father sat in his swivel chair reading the newspaper and seemed unaware of the conversation that had just transpired on the porch. Aldah was still sitting at the table, with that calm expression that suggested she was daydreaming contentedly. Alice went over and combed Aldah's hair, then led her into the living room and told her that she could watch television for an hour. Alice pushed her sister's hair back over her tiny ear, and as the colorful pictures came onto the screen, the calm spread over her cheeks to produce a face of total contentment. If Aldah was a messenger of anything, her message was to live every moment for what it was worth. Looking at Aldah made Alice think of the line from the hymn that went, "It is well, it is well with my soul."

While Aldah watched TV, Alice started a bath.

"There isn't any hot water!" she yelled.

"Come out here," said her father.

"What's going on?"

"I turned off the hot-water heater."

"Say again?"

"Keeping fifty gallons of water hot all day makes as much sense as letting your car run when you're not using it."

"I need a bath."

"It can wait."

"Wait? This dirt can wait?"

"Heat a little water on the stove and wash your face and hands."

"You're kidding."

"I'll turn the hot water heater on for an hour at night. And that's it."

"What's going on?"

"We have to conserve."

"I do conserve."

"You're going to have to conserve a lot more."

"We have plenty of water."

"Water's not the problem. Heating it is. At least a hundred a month."

"This is nuts."

"It's common sense."

"You look like you got cleaned up."

"Not with hot water."

"I'll just wash with cold water then."

"Good idea."

Instead of going to the bathroom, Alice glanced into the living room to see her sister watching cartoons. She walked outside past her mother without speaking. She strolled toward the double garage and backed out the red Ford 150 pickup. Alice started with a bucket of soapy water and a big bristle brush and went to work on the bed of the carriage box. She got on her knees and scrubbed down every groove of the pickup bed. She went after every spec of dirt and manure, every caked-on spilled whatever. Then she hosed it down and went back with a sponge and dry cloth. She got a fresh bucket of water and soaped the entire cab and body. She was an hour into it before she brought out the wax. And then the chamois skin. She scrubbed the tires, and then went back and polished the chrome. She vacuumed the inside. She Windexed the windows— inside and out. People who worked at car washes could have learned something from her. She made that pickup shine. She made it glow like red fingernail polish. She made it so shiny it screamed to the fresh blue sky. Then she parked it out front where anybody driving by would see it. She made the 150 the shining star of their farm. The 150 sat there like a bright plaything of the world, singing, "Look at me! Look at me! Look at me!"

Her father, who stood beside the house looking in her direction, interrupted the glorious moment.

"Any reason you're doing that on The Lord's Day?" he shouted.

5

The smells from Ben Van Doods's feedlot reached the Krayenbraak farm before the county health department declared the rotting carcasses a hazard and had the rendering plant load them up. When Alice looked at the sudden transformation, the clean feedlot was like a taunt that dared her to remember the grim sight that had been there.

The next day notice was published in the paper, and posters went up in stores and on light poles around Dutch Center advertising Ben's farm sale.

"That's that," said Alice's father. "Now let's tend to the work the Lord has given us to do."

Should she feel guilty for starting to think about herself instead of the miseries of someone else? She could spend her senior year pitying herself that their farm was probably in as much trouble as Ben Van Doods's, or she could start thinking of next year, when she could leave her work shoes on the porch and step out with a suitcase, ready for a college dormitory. She could curl up and wither as a pathetic manure-stained farm girl in a manure-stained farm economy or she could shed her farm-girl image like a pair of manure-stained blue jeans. Whatever hope she was going to have for the future would require work, just as her father said, but the work she was determined to do was the kind of work that would save her from being a farm girl forever.

She had learned what she looked like to city people when she visited Sioux City malls. She spent two hours one afternoon on a shopping trip "looking for bargains" but actually looking at city folks looking at farm folks. After an hour of sharp-eyed study, she saw what they saw: that perpetual look of bewilderment or surprise on the farm kids' faces. That dumbfounded expression that said, "Huh? What's that? What's going on?" Farm boys were the most pathetic with their awkward swaggers they thought made them look like tough city kids. Instead, it made them look as if they had spent too much time riding broncos and didn't know how to use their legs for walking. The older farm folks stood out too in the way they always made—or tried to make—eye contact with everyone they met, as if everybody in the world were somebody they knew or who would want to know them. And they were distracted by anything that was going on around them. When they were outside, they looked up if an airplane or helicopter flew overhead. They stared yearningly at passing emergency vehicles. Farm folks had an uncomfortable and gratuitous curiosity about *everything!* And, yes, Alice Marie Krayenbraak knew what "gratuitous" meant. Straight-A Alice knew the meanings of "gratuitous," "exacerbate," "gobsmacked," "syllogism," and a million other words, but she still had that wide-eyed farm-kid look about her, and she knew it—and she knew how hard it would be to shed that look. No matter how hard they tried, farm folks, whether old or young, just didn't have any sophistication. If animals had distinct characteristics of their breed, so did Iowa farm folks. They were their own breed—hicks. It was written all over them. The syllogism stuck in Alice's head: All Iowa farm folks look like hicks. I am an Iowa farm folk. Therefore, I look like a hick. Being over six feet tall didn't help. To city people, she had to look like a gawky hillbilly.

Dealing with dead hogs or her own family's sagging farm was easy compared to smelling like the cattle yards and looking—at best—like the cover girl of *Country Home* magazine. She had dropped out of 4-H when she was fifteen and hidden her one purple and ten blue ribbons in the bottom of her underwear drawer. Grand Champion in Beef Showmanship. Finalist for Junior Livestock Queen. She had the medals, but if she was going to have a life beyond the millennium, it was not going to be as a farm girl.

Alice watched how models on TV walked across the stage, then practiced in front of her bedroom mirror. She stood at the magazine rack in Deweerds' Drug reading *Vogue.* She resolved to erase every smudge of farm life from the person who strutted her lanky presence through the world. A year from now she'd be packing her bags for college and entering a world where she could tell people whatever she wanted. She wouldn't stare at passing ambulances. She wouldn't make eye contact with everyone she met. She wouldn't smile as if she knew or wanted to know everyone who crossed her path. She would walk with a delicate light step that suggested her feet had never touched an unfriendly surface, and certainly no surface as disgusting as cattle hoofprints in their own dried manure. No one would have to know she was a person whose life had been hay bales and John Deere tractors and soybeans and corn silage and weed spray and chemical fertilizers and hogs and steers. A year from now she could invent her past and create her future. She'd burn her work shirts. She'd burn her work shoes. She'd step into the world from the covers of *Glamour* and *Cosmopolitan*. "Who, me?" she'd say, and raise an eyebrow. "Oh, yes, I did grow up in a Midwest farm community. I certainly knew people who lived on farms. I even visited them sometimes. Goodness. How could any civilized human live with those smells!"

At the end of her junior year at Midwest Christian, she had tried to ignore the insults from boys who didn't like her. She might have been all right in their eyes if she were just a star athlete, but she was an A-student star athlete—a combination that they couldn't handle, so they had retaliated with the only weapon they had: name-calling insults. "Ass and a beanpole." She knew she wasn't the first lean female to get the label, and she was sure the labelers didn't have the brains to invent it. At the time, she thought it wasn't bothering her much. She had thought, "At least I have a brain at the top of my beanpole," but over her dateless summer, the label chipped away at her confidence. Maybe I am unattractive. Maybe I look as stupid as they really are.

She granted that there were bigger issues in the fall of 1999 than her pathetic appearance. The dire fantasies about Y2K were not only coming from her mother: the entire Dutch Center community had more than its share of people who were totally convinced that something terrible was going to happen at the turn of the century. "God moves in two-thousand-year increments" was the common declaration. "Something big is going to happen!"

Something big is always happening, Alice thought. How about the collapse of the farm economy? How about a feedlot full of bloating Chester Whites? How about the fact that we are probably going broke on our farm? But her family's money troubles and the money troubles most farm families were having in the fall of '99 were lost in the barrage of Y2K talk, and farm families worrying about their survival made easy prey for the religious fearmongers of Dutch Center who ignored the fact that the stock market was soaring and Microsoft and Apple were breaking records every week. The wild profits told the wackos that the devil was distracting people with filthy lucre while the end drew near. Though some investors somewhere were making millions as the millennium approached, on the farm market-ready hogs were selling for the price of a carton of cigarettes and driving people like Ben Van Doods to his acts of desperation. The wackos had an explanation for bad farm prices too: it meant the Almighty was preparing people for the time when they would no longer have earthly needs.

Alice was smart, and she knew she was smart. Her grades told her she was smart and most of her teachers told her not only that she was smart, but that she was "promising, brilliant, disciplined, focused, goal oriented" and the whole long list of good-student attributes.

The one teacher whom Alice admired more than all the others put together was Miss Den Harmsel who taught the advanced English classes. Miss Den Harmsel rarely reminded Alice that she was smart, and she didn't have to. Her expectations of Alice said it all. Miss Den Harmsel told Alice to read John Steinbeck's *Grapes of Wrath* and Toni Morrison's *Beloved* over the summer. "You've already read the Brontës, Austen, and Dickinson. You must read these Americans before college."

Pleasing Miss Den Harmsel was one of Alice's biggest summer pleasures—and there hadn't been very many. She kept the books stashed in the haymow of the barn, sealed in a plastic bag and behind a bale against the south wall. This way she didn't have to worry about her mother walking in on her while she was reading and telling her to go take care of Aldah. Alice already gave Aldah more time than her mother did, so it seemed only fair that she should steal some reading time while the steers were eating. She deserved private reading time—for her mind, for her education, for her future—and for Miss Den Harmsel who, perhaps even more than Lydia, knew that Alice was destined for bigger and better things than hog and cattle feedlots.

Being a model student was still no defense against the creeping fear that visited her at night when she tried to sleep. Worse than the fear that she looked like a country hick, she couldn't keep the fanatical talk from sinking in: What if those wackos are right? What if the worst is yet to come? What if something really *big* was going to rain down upon them? She pictured clouds of fire coming from nowhere, devouring the wicked but leaving believers untouched as all of their friends and family rose from the grave incorruptible. Did she have to be on the reverend's side to be among the incorruptible?

Alice wasn't sure what she believed. She prayed because it gave her a feeling of relief and acceptance. Her prayers were sometimes pleas for whatever she wanted at the moment, but more often they were prayers of thanksgiving because in spite of everything bad going on in the world, she was the recipient of amazingly good fortune, though she wouldn't use that word around the Rev because he said fortune was a heathen idea. Still she prayed, "Thank you, God, for giving me the strength and mind to deal with this big messy world."

When she finished a prayer like that, she could hear her mother's voice: "Thanking God for your superiority? When will you ever learn humility?"

6

By five in the afternoon of September 1, Alice was in a same-old same-old place in farm-girl hell. The scene was their cattle feedlot. Seventeen years on planet Earth and this is what it added up to: feeding two hundred thousand-pound steers on a sweltering afternoon. Horseflies buzzing through the stench of baked manure. Her copy of *The Grapes of Wrath* sitting on top of the control panel, tightly wrapped in plastic to protect it from corn and feed-supplement dust.

She stood at her workstation, a six-by-six-foot cubicle next to a towering white silo. This was the kitchen, the preparation room with its panel of switches on plywood boards. Switch number one started the rotating arm that scraped the corn silage from the silo, and switch number two started the auger that sent the silage rolling into an elongated mound down the center of a cement feed bunk. The odor of corn silage was not tantalizing but was lemon bath oil compared to the stench cloud that roamed the farmyard.

The moan and clatter of the augers brought the steers lumbering shaggily forward. They nudged themselves into rows to become intimate diners facing each other across the feed bunk. Silage was their first-course salad with its own vinegar dressing of fermented corn juice. The steers flicked each other's ears while their noses smeared each other's cheeks.

Switch number three started a smaller auger that corkscrewed a mixture of minerals into the cracked corn, and switch number four sent the combination streaming like crumbled corn bread over the silage. Enriched cracked corn equaled pounds gained equaled dollars. What she was doing was supposed to create the miracle that could save their farm: thick, juicy, expensive steaks for the rich.

Switches number five, six, and seven turned on the barn light, the silo light, and the big searchlight that could pull the curtain on darkness to expose any sick animals in the far corners of the feedlot. Switch number eight turned on a space heater directed at her feet and legs. She didn't need the lights or the heater. The midday sun had driven the temperatures into the high nineties and was holding them in the mideighties. A scorcher of a day draped in a heavy blanket of humidity.

The churning auger spit bits of cracked corn in her face as it spread the golden color down the bunk. When she wiped her lip on her sleeve, the yellow dust mixed with her sweat looked like the slime collecting on the steers' noses. She pulled at her shirt. Her sweat had plastered it to her neck and shoulders. She wiped her face again, then smeared what she'd gotten from her face onto her jeans. The heat heightened the scent of everything, but the smells of the silage and cracked corn were no defense against the hogyard stench that swam through the thick air and spread its sickening flavor a hundred yards from the hogyards to the cattle feedlots where she worked. A whole farmyard under a dome of bad air. She inhaled a mouthful with every breath. Hot stinky air. The smell would stay in her wet shirt like a bad aftertaste, and her breath would smell like hog crap.

She was quite capable of handling this scene without resentment. The agony came only when she imagined herself being watched by someone her age who attended an Eastern prep school. The preppy would see a gangly country hick, a measly laborer who at best listened to corny religious music and entered the Rice Krispies bar competition at the county fair. She watched her hands working—the grime under her fingernails and the hard calluses on her fingers. No wonder people who worked on farms were called farmhands. The hands said it all: her hands were who she was.

Looking at her hands led her to the rest of the stinky truth of her life. Sweat had turned her light blue shirt into a dark blue. Sweat dripped off her lip and trickled down her neck under her ear. Sweat was a friend and a bother. She gave it credit for opening her pores and keeping her skin cool, but it was also busy soaking things in. Sweat as sponge. It sucked in dust. Dirt dust. Corn dust. Mineral dust. Dried steer manure dust. Steer dandruff dust. And it sucked in smells, the whole barnyard smorgasbord of vaporized manure and silage and tractor diesel fuel. It probably sucked in the smell of steer breath. Then that awful itch when the intense heat slathered them all together. The back of her neck itched. The top of her head itched. She resisted scratching her head because she didn't want her dirty hands to make her hair dirtier. Trying to think of something besides the itch just turned it into a herd of ants moving down her back. The worst thing was that she knew the tracks of sweat were leaving tracks of bad smells all over her body. Her only comfort—and it was an uncomfortable comfort—was knowing she wouldn't be near any Romeo in the next twenty-four hours. Perhaps things would change in the romance department once school started and she'd given herself a good fall cleanup.

The steers had settled down to their slathering and munching. She checked out the long mound of silage mixed with cracked corn and minerals that the feed augers had delivered down the bunks. The steers had kicked up dust when they came toward the grinding sound of the augers, but once they had settled down to their chomping, they were a pleasant sight, a consolation prize for her sweaty efforts. The steers were their own kind of beautiful, even though their mission in life was to gain weight, and gain it fast. All those fat backs lined up on either side of the feed bunk rippled away from her in mounds of prime meat. The strange symmetry of it all. The innocence of it. She didn't harbor a silly love for them. She knew they'd be steaks and hamburgers in a few months, but she didn't fight these moments when, hearing them chew in unison, she could imagine music that would be a perfect complement to the whole scene. She could funnel Bach's *Art of Fugue* played on a harpsichord into the canopy over the feed bunk. Bach would make the steers' hair ruffle. The steers would be so content they'd gain four pounds a day.

She climbed the fence and walked around them looking for the big three—listlessness, runny nose, and cough. The steers were surviving the heat in good form but didn't have the sense to know that a pressure-cooker day like this guaranteed bad weather. These hoof-footed meat carriers. She reached out to rub the shag-carpet back of her favorite tame black steer. A gray mound of dust rose at her touch, then clung to the moisture on her hand. She couldn't find an unsoiled spot left on her jeans, so she dipped her hands into the steers' egg-shaped drinking tank and shook them off.

As she left the swelter of the feedlot, a dozen swallows dove and swirled over the dry alfalfa field. They were doing what swallows do—swallowing—though she couldn't see what insects were on the menu on the first of September.

Swallows were sky dancers who radiated moving color as they flew with their shiny chocolate heads and their maple chests against the background of the pale blue sky. And those sharp-edged tails and wings, the way they made slicing the air look like a spatula swiping through meringue. They were a medley of happiness as they flew, and Alice knew they'd continue to live the good mood of their movements when they weren't flying. They never squabbled or complained like crows or starlings or blue jays. They didn't push each other out of a nest unless they were teaching their young to fly. Swallows made living look so easy. So swift. So graceful. If they could live past their label of barn swallows, maybe she could live past her label of farmhand.

She walked back to the control panels and retrieved *The Grapes of Wrath*. She had already read it once and was almost finished rereading it. The air outside felt too hot and sticky for reading, so she carried the book back up the haymow. Before putting it in its place behind the hay bale, she unzipped the plastic bag and pulled it out. She flipped through the final chapter until she came to her favorite sentence of all: "For a minute Rose of Sharon sat still in the whispering barn." She didn't try to remember what happened next at this point in the novel; she just loved the sound of that sentence, the lilt of it, which was very much like the flight of the swallows.

7

The evening supper table was a sober scene: her stern father offering a stern prayer, her severe mother challenging everything with a menacing stare that never erupted into words, and her soft sister Aldah clinging to Alice's arm when she was not pointing for more food. And more food.

As Alice lay in bed that night, she didn't think about the smoldering discomfort of the dinner table, or the smells she might have taken to bed with her, or about the weather, but she woke to a distant rumbling. Thunder didn't frighten her. It brought back the memory of her kind grandmother saying, "It's just God talking." Thunder as God's comforting voice. It had sunk in. She loved that booming voice.

A bolt of lightning streaked across the sky, followed by a sound of ripping canvas—and then the ba-boom when the bolt bit the dirt within a mile. The sky fluttered with lightning and the clouds murmured with thunder. God was tired of chitchat and getting down to business.

"Alice!" her father yelled up the stairs. "We're getting some weather. It's headed straight at us."

"Yeah, yeah," she said. Tornado season was past. This wouldn't be the first storm their house survived. The approach of a big Midwestern storm could be more exciting than frightening—like watching a bull charge toward you when you're standing safely behind a metal gate.

"Alice!" This time it was the family witch. "Close the windows and get down here."

"In a sec."

"Get down here! Aldah is scared!"

So why wasn't she doing something about it?

"I'm getting dressed."

"Did you hear me?"

"I said I was coming."

"This could be it," she heard her mother say in her practiced ominous voice.

Alice put on her soft fleece sweater and work jeans. She wasn't dressing for the weather; she was dressing to comfort her sister Aldah. When she got downstairs, her father had gone out to lock down any loose doors. She heard the clink of the metal gates in the hog pens. The feeder cattle could find shelter in the sturdy gambrel-roofed barn or the corrugated metal cattle shed that had its back to the wind. Their big block of a house had stood up to a century of Midwest weather, and this storm wasn't about to scare it off its foundation.

Her mother stood in her usual place in front of the kitchen sink, staring out the window at the approaching storm with the family Bible clutched against her stomach. At moments like this, Alice couldn't decide if her mother was a pillar of faith or a pillar of skepticism. How could a person of faith be either so sour or so fearful of everything?

Lightning struck somewhere close with a force Alice could feel in her cheekbones. Blunt fists of wind whacked the house in a syncopated rhythm. This was a stuttery storm—and that was not a good sign. The deep-throated thunder gurgled closer. No longer the voice of God, it sounded like a beast that couldn't make up its mind, sniveling one minute and grunting the next. The lights went out like an exclamation point. Alice swam through the wake of darkness, trying to find Aldah. Her whimpering cries were everywhere—and moving. At Alice's touch, her sister flung her arms around Alice and buried her face in Alice's sweater. If Alice smelled bad, she knew Aldah would never say so. Now the wind leaned against the house with a steady pressure. Twigs and gravel sprayed noisily past the windows, but the house shrugged its shoulders, and Alice thought for an instant: would that the rest of us could be so sure of our place on the planet.

Alice's mother remained standing, her legs apart as if she were getting ready for something. She had laid the Bible down and had both hands on the counter as if she were bracing for whatever was coming at them. This was neither a position of fear nor faith. It looked more like a position of defiance.

Alice turned to Aldah. "We're not going anywhere," she said and stroked Aldah's head.

"Promise?"

"Promise."

A golden light appeared in the doorway from the porch. Her mother turned toward it, and in a voice that sounded like startled relief, she sighed, "Oh, Father," as if she were looking into the face of the Lord of Hosts Himself, but before she could transfigure into the glories of heaven, the light transformed into Alice's father carrying the old kerosene lantern in one hand and a flashlight in the other. Her mother's arms came down in the deliberate slowness of a chicken hawk perching on a fence post. Alice couldn't see her father's face, but she sensed that he wanted to comfort Aldah and her when he shone the flashlight where they huddled next to the kitchen table.

"That's probably the worst of the wind," he said, and no sooner had he spoken than the wind let up. At times like this her father was an Old Testament prophet in his deliberate manner and without a quake in his body or voice. He set the kerosene lantern in the middle of the kitchen table where his father and grandfather no doubt once put it. When he lit the wick and slipped the glass chimney over it, a fist of flame shot up. In his steady way he adjusted the wick until a soft light spread over the round table. He turned off the flashlight, and they all sat down around the yellow tablecloth of light. Aldah kept her face pressed against Alice's soft sweater as Alice smoothed her hair. Their mother stood motionless, a stark shadow in the kitchen doorway. Why, at moments like this, Alice wondered, did she look more like a grim messenger of disaster than like a warm motherly defense against it?

Rain hit like a fire hose against the house.

"Here it comes," her mother rasped.

The crystal ball of her father's bald head glowed in the mellow light. Her mother moved across the kitchen and shoved a pie tin under the lantern with such sharp force that she looked like someone who thought she was saving the day. "Don't burn the table," she said. "That's all we need."

Alice felt tension in the room, but no panic. Aldah stared into the flame with her soft oval eyes. Their father's mouth was like a pencil mark across his face. Alice looked around the room and the steady warm light that the lamp cast on the praying-hands painting and the black-and-white Love Begins At Home plaque. Alice felt as if she was watching a movie in slow motion, a portrait of her family forming and reforming before her eyes, and she couldn't decide if they were scared or relieved to be together like this.

"Will this wind break the cornstalks?" she asked. She didn't put any worry into her voice. She tried to behave as her father behaved at times of crisis—quietly gather the facts and, under all circumstances, stay rational.

"Maybe," he said. The muscles around his mouth tightened.

"What did the weather report say?"

Before he answered, snapping sounds came from the asphalt in front of the garage.

"That."

The first hailstones were large, popping and splattering like eggs, but they were followed by an encore of smaller hailstones. Buckets and buckets of hailstones.

"Horses," said Aldah. Alice saw her satisfied smile.

The hailstones did sound as if they were galloping across the roofs.

"Horsemen of the Apocalypse," said her mother dryly. Alice glanced at her and detected a smirk on her face, as if she were enjoying her own bitter cleverness.

The rest of the family kept their usual silence in response to one of her bizarre proclamations. The hooves of hail became a clatter of pebbles, first on the roof of the house and then amplified on the metal roofs of the cattle shed, the machine shed, the hog feeders, and the corn dryers. Pig squeals cut through the noise of the hail, but they were squeals of life as they fought to get inside out of the storm. A cloudburst of hail. Thirty seconds? Sixty seconds? It was like sitting in the dentist's chair waiting for the drill to stop. Alice clenched her fists. She clenched her jaw. Her mother slumped down into a chair at the table, and they all sat staring into the warm flame, listening.

Alice knew that through his grim expression her father was calculating. What was this hailstorm costing? A hundred dollars a second? A thousand?

Aldah sat between Alice and her mother, with her father across the table. They all stared into the yellow light. Her father could pray at times like this, but he didn't pray. He stared.

A half hour passed before the metal roofs were silent again. Her father stood up. "Well, that's that," he said. "Let's go to bed."

"Y2K," said her mother. "How's that for starters?"

Her mother the conversation stopper.

Her father stood off to the side watching them. No one stirred. For several minutes the family was unanimous in their silence.

Alice could feel the image of that moment make its imprint on her mind: her dear sweet sister leaning into her sweater, the squat egg shape of her, her mouth open slightly with her tongue resting on her lower lip; the chiseled features of her mother, her hair like a helmet, her detached and inscrutable countenance behind the large glowing eyes; and her erect and controlled father, calm and cold as a bronze statue. Alice had no idea what she looked like or whether she resembled any of them in appearance or behavior. It was a vivid photograph of her family, with her as a blur.

When her mother stood up in a manner that was both deliberate and languid, Alice and Aldah rose too, all of them in the dim kerosene light with their shadows casting misshapen figures on the kitchen cabinets and wall. With the kerosene lamp light on her back, her mother followed her own weaving shadow into the living room. She was dressed in jeans and work shirt. She picked up a blanket from the couch and flung it over her shoulder as if she were ready to wander off and away from the whole scene.

All summer the tension had grown in her mother, an edginess that could erupt into sharp words or strange actions at almost any time. She acted as if she was expecting the worst, though Alice didn't know what "the worst" might mean for her mother. She probably didn't either. Sometimes Alice assumed that her mother was afraid of everything and anything the future might bring, whether that was an influx of immigrants or the inevitable change of farm life. The millennium was a magnet that drew all of her unspoken fears together. Now she moved across the living room and became a long silhouette in front of the picture window, then stood motionless again, staring out into the darkness. It was impossible for her to see the hail damage, but she must have known as well as the rest of them that it was there and that it had been devastating.

Aldah's bedroom was a small room, which before the remodeling had been a large pantry off the kitchen. With her father holding the lantern, Alice led Aldah into her pantry-bedroom and tucked her into bed.

"Read to me."

"No light," said Alice. "I'll play something on the piano."

"No light," said Aldah.

Alice knew most of Beethoven's *Moonlight Sonata* by heart, but when she started playing it in the dark, Aldah yelled out, "Not that one! Not that one!"

Alice switched to "Have Thine Own Way, Lord" and played the simple hymn three times to the quiet approval of her sister, who was soon asleep. Alice found her way up to her own room, got in bed, and wondered if she should pray but found her mind was filled with cacophonous sounds of clattering hail and squealing hogs warring against country music and a church organ playing "A Mighty Fortress Is Our God." The Devil's work, she thought to herself, and closed her eyes.

8

Sleep did not come easily. The truth of what had happened to their farm came to her with the weight of the silence. Cool silence, but a silence that was heavy as the sultry silence before the storm. It was the kind of silence her great uncle told about when he spoke of the deathly calm that followed a German bombardment of Rotterdam. Nobody moved because that might have invited more destruction. The old Krayenbraak house had been their bomb shelter while their farmland was machine gunned to death. They had been strafed for an hour, and now the final aftermath was upon them: Silence. Numb silence. Posttraumatic silence.

What was the point of it all? What issue did the sky have with them? Hadn't they suffered enough? She felt battered and defeated like the fields outside. She was wrung out, flat, with neither an urge to pray nor to shake her fist at God and scream, "Why us?"

She thought of her parents and how everything had come to this moment. Her father had been his usual strong self through the storm. She could understand why her mother had fallen in love with him: he was handsome, he was gentle, and he was strong in a crisis. But what did he see in her? True, the pictures of her as a young woman made her look beautiful. She had that wry and sultry look and the hint of a smile, combined with an inscrutable expression coming from her eyes, what Alice had come to regard as an intense blankness. What did her father see? He must have seen somebody who needed rescuing, not from the world but from herself. What did he see in her now? Alice saw a woman who was so erratic in her moods and so unpredictable in her behavior that she'd hate to see what label a certified psychiatrist would give her. Maybe she was only a more sharpened version of the person she had always been. Maybe her father understood her and saw something good, though other people saw what Alice saw: an icy presence who would complain about anything that didn't fit her fancy. Alice absorbed the looks on merchants' faces when her mother walked into a store, the look that said, "Oh no, get ready, here she comes." Her mother was an embarrassment.

People probably talked about her whole family, not just her mother. No other family looked like them. Both of her parents looked older than most parents with teenage kids, and their height made them stand out even more: her mother was over six feet tall like Alice, and her father was a towering several inches above them. Unlike most of the farm folk, the three of them were skinny. Then there was Aldah, who was barely five feet tall and weighed twenty pounds more than Alice. Outward appearances were just a start. Aldah at fifteen had a vocabulary of sixty words, though she was progressing every day—thanks to Alice, not her mother.

Alice was no doctor, but she was convinced that there was something very abnormal about her mother and the way she looked for the darkest possible side of every issue. The approach of the millennium only made things worse: some part of her seemed to relish the most gruesome predictions of what the millennium might bring. That was her mother.

Alice glanced at the clock. She needed sleep. She *had to* get to sleep. The steers would be as hungry in the morning as they were earlier that night. She breathed deeply and tried to relax, but an uninvited guest came into her mind as she was starting to doze. It was her mother from her shoulders up, looking at Alice with eyes that said, "I know you. I know you better than anyone knows you." The face hovered against Alice's closed eyelids. The image of her, yes, perhaps this is what her father saw, a strange warmth. It was love. Alice couldn't fight the feeling. Her mother, bizarre as she was, loved her. She was like a guardian angel, and no one ever said guardian angels had to be nice.

Maybe she was just trying to forgive her mother so she could get some needed sleep, but the feeling was a comfort. As sleep moved toward her, new pictures came into her mind like a shuffling of photographs: pictures of farms, one after another. Dead farms. Dying farms. Farms that hid their sickness. Chronically ill farms that wheezed through the night with sad and drooping fences, with fence posts that looked like contorted spines, farms with thistles on the loose, cocklebur farms, farms with poorly installed culverts that spring floods spit up into the ditches and fields, soil-depleted farms, farms with rutted driveways and flapping barn doors. And the modern transformed farms, megafarms, feedlot confinement farms, polluting farms, farms that stank to high heaven. Eye-watering-stench farms. Sickening smell, gagging farms. Farms whose odors had color and textures and taste, like dense green fog farms, sticky hot mauve farms. Curdling slime farms. The living-dead farms. Monster farms. With the images flooding her mind, so did the smells.

Fading farms, falling off the landscape one broken piece at a time, the old equipment rusting in the grove, the unterraced hillsides giving way to deeper gullies every year, the sway-backed sheds, the leaning mailbox. The slow death, two decades for shingles to wear out, another decade for barn ribs to show, then years of desertion before vandals smashed all the windows. Until the farm looked terminally ill, overburdened with chemicals, on its last breath, exhausted, one finger on the morphine button.

Like the Den Moolen farm two miles away—first the storage sheds, then the chicken coop, then the hog house, then the cow barn, then the lawn and garden, then the seven-gabled white house with its white picket fence and the blood-red rose bushes. The U-shaped grove like a good-luck horseshoe lingering for years—the ash, the box elder, the cottonwoods, the willows, the mulberry, the apple trees, all hanging on like faithful mourners at a wake, until the big Caterpillars shoved and tore and leveled and dug, a brutal preparation for mass burial. Then only the erasure mark where the farm had been, and finally only the long unbroken rows of beans and corn with their indifferent suggestion that nothing had changed, that things had always been this way and were meant to be this way. Rolling endless fields of beans and corn without the jarring images of barns and sack swings and houses and other nuisance reminders of human habitation. Land that imitated what the settlers saw in the endless ocean of prairie grass, waves of it extending toward the horizons. Miles and miles of uniformity. Fields of corn in full uniform, at attention, tasseling bayonets pointing up. All of the undone farms, like the Den Moolens', making what travelers looking at the Iowa landscape called boring boring boring.

"Dear God," she finally prayed, "send a miracle."

Instead of a miracle, more images swept through her mind: fields of sameness, corn of uniform height and color, bean fields of narrow uniform rows, corrugated metal cattle sheds, the uniform silver ridges, the big round bales stacked in perfect rows, the feeder cattle like huge Walmart sales baskets filled with identical cattle figures with glassy plastic eyes, and milk cows all uniformly sized with uniform bland and white spots and with perfectly sized udders and teats, as if shaped for convenience for the cup size of the milking machine, and their uniform cow eyes, all blue-black, shining, perfectly round, rolling across the level screen of her mind. She counted the eyeball marbles as they rolled past, counted and counted until she fell asleep.

When the electricity came back on at 2:00 a.m., it took only the sudden hum of the electric clock to startle her awake. The lights in the cattle and hoglots were back on too—big fluorescent banners that made the whole world outside look as if it should be awake—or at least be on guard. Everything was silver and luminous and resembled neither winter nor summer. She walked around the upstairs and looked out the windows in all directions. The ground had a sandpapery texture, with earth showing through the glowing ice pebbles. The dark lawn was decorated with a million dull lights. Some hailstones had formed elongated mounds along the buildings in the shape of windrows and had the color of the corrugated metal storage bins.

She put her face to the screen in her bedroom window. The air was cool and quiet. She stared at the icy pebbles for a long time. The sight was storybook beautiful: fairy dust, fairy godmother sparkles. Wisps of steam rose up—like afterthoughts, or a ghostly ascension. Like the cloud that hung over the Israelites to guide them as they made their way to the Promised Land. She was with Noah on the ark, and the dove had returned with a leaf in its beak, promising a new beginning. She thought of her mother's fear of the millennium and wondered if this might be a foretaste of what it would mean for the millennium to come and go: destruction followed by the promise of a new world.

9

If Alice thought for a moment that the misty cloud had been a message from heaven that a new and better day was dawning, that hope was erased by the revealing light of the next morning. Hail insurance adjusters in four-by-fours and minivans cruised the sticky gravel roads before seven, stopping every quarter mile to measure the damage.

No insurance adjuster stopped by the Krayenbraak farm.

"Dad? Why aren't they stopping here? Our corn looks worse than anybody's."

He shook his head.

"What?"

"No crop insurance this year. Couldn't afford it."

She stood next to her father and pulled on her boots in unison with him. They walked out into the muddy fields together, shoulder to shoulder, two stalky figures approaching the wounded cornfield. The battered ears of corn drooped from the naked stalks. When her father squeezed one in his large hand, milk from the kernels oozed through his fingers.

"This corn is too damaged to mature," he said. His demeanor was flat and emotionless. It may have been resolute acceptance of what God had given them. The gift of trial. God was seeing if her father could be a Job. He nodded deliberately. "We can harvest it all for silage," he said. "That will at least be something."

Alice looked at the pathetic field of battered corn. Her father's solution would not be that easy. Too much rain had come with the hail, and dark puddles of water glowed between the shattered rows of corn. The dark puddles looked like blood. Which made Alice think of sacrifice. Useless bloodshed of the innocent. Even if the Almighty wasn't thinking of their well-being, why wouldn't He think of the innocent corn, those gorgeous fields that one week ago were an endless celebration of green leaves? Didn't those thousands of stalks declare His glory? Couldn't He have looked down and said, "They are good," and spared them? Alice turned toward her father where he stood majestic and calm. He looked better than the corn. How could anyone accept anything this terrible, just look at it, sigh, and go on? Whatever faith her father had, Alice knew she did not have it. Not yet, anyhow.

The first and only relief of the morning came when Alice went to the cattle feedlot to discover that the steers were unblemished by the hail. They must have found shelter, but they also must have known something was wrong because they took only a couple of nibbles and backed away. It might have been an air pressure thing that made their stomachs feel full. She didn't know. Maybe they needed time to recover the way she did.

In the house, her mother looked shell shocked. Alice tried to impose the image she had of her mother when she had thought of her as a hardened guardian angel, but this was the real thing. Her actual mother looked as if she was "letting herself go," a favorite expression of people from Dutch Center applied to those who were on the skids for one reason or another. Seeing her drooping appearance reminded Alice that nothing looks sadder than a sagging tall woman. She wore the same clothes that she had on the night before, and she had let her hair hang in clumps over her ears and neck. Fists of hair against her narrow face. She still moved like a robot, but she moved more heavily, like a robot with low batteries. Her dark mood made its way into her cooking. She must have been preparing food for the rest of the day so that she wouldn't have to think about cooking again. She was boiling beans, boiling potatoes, boiling cabbage—three pans on the stove at one time.

"Soup," she said when she saw Alice watching her. "We'll be eating lots of soup."

Alice left her alone to do whatever she had to do. She was trying to boil something out of herself. She thought the bubbles on the surfaces of the boiling pots would release her troubles into the air.

When she finished her boiling of vegetables, she brought another pan of water to a boil and dumped in four small packets of instant oatmeal. This was breakfast. Alice wanted to ask her which recipe book she was using, but didn't.

"Merciful Father, we come unto thee with thankful hearts, thanking thee for the abundance thou hast bestowed upon us . . . ," her father prayed.

"Dad," Alice said when he finished, "I'm sorry, but what was that all about? Abundance? You thought, like, maybe God would find that funny?"

"Don't talk like that," said her mother. "If you're going to open your mouth, open it to eat."

Her mother was reprimanding her because commenting on a person's communication with God was sacrilegious. You didn't stick your hand into that fire. You didn't comment on somebody's prayer—unless it was the prayer of somebody with a false religion because they were reaching out to a figment of their imaginations.

Alice's father stared—no, he glowered at her. "As long as we have lips to offer thanks, we will offer thanks."

Alice could feel Aldah absorbing the tension at the table.

"It's all right," said Alice. "Eat, Aldah. Just eat."

Without warning her mother made a bold announcement: "We need to have Aldah go live at Children's Care."

"What?" Alice's response was quick as an "ouch."

"We decided it was best," said her father.

"We?"

"Your mother and I."

Alice leveled her eyes at her mother. "Your mother and I?"

"Your father and I," said her mother.

"The two of you decided this little life-changing event? This little 'Let's break up the family, no questions asked' event?"

Alice pushed her plate away. Her urge was to behave like her mother and bolt from the unpleasant scene, but that would only have left this ridiculous idea unchallenged. "Oh, who cares what Alice thinks about this little decision to shove a family member out the door so we don't have to look at her anymore. Just get rid of her. Vamoose. Is that what you decided? Like what kind of ice cream to buy for dessert or something?"

"As if you didn't know it was coming," said her mother.

"It's a decision that parents have to make, not children," said her father.

Alice stared at her mother, not her father. It had to have been her mother who came up with the idea to dump Aldah. Her mother could get cold and calculating when she wanted to. She had a way of making ideas that were not good ideas sound as if they were. She had worked her father over—and he had caved. If a stare of disdain had any power at all, it would have leveled her mother on the spot.

"It was a hard decision," said her father. "We've been thinking about it for a long time."

"Thinking and *talking* about it," said Alice. "Is that right? *Talking* about it?" She kept her eyes leveled at her mother.

"Yes," said her mother. "Talking about it."

"I didn't hear any talking," said Alice. "Where was I when all of this *talking* was going on? What am I, something you can just ignore and *talk* around? Pretend I don't exist, just shove under the rug and ignore? Like a mouse turd?"

"That kind of talk has to stop," said her father.

"It will be for the best," said her mother.

"That's stupid! An institution won't help her! Look what she's learned from me. You think you can just dump her out of our lives? Export her? Just like that? And the special-ed teachers said she was improving."

"That's not what the scores say," said her mother.

Alice argued, railed, screamed, accused, and finally pleaded.

"I'll come home earlier after school," she said. "I'll spend more time with her after supper. I'll talk to the special-ed teachers about what we can do at home."

Her parents were a stubborn unit. They had clearly planned to let her rant and not budge. Alice was a debater, and both of her parents knew better than to try taking her on with reason and evidence. They just took her on with their mantra: "We've thought about this for a long time, and we believe it is best for everyone." They were even ready on the money issue: evidently, total financial disclosure cleared the way for state aid.

Her calm father was a fully converted accomplice. Aldah would be spending one more week living at home and going to her special-ed classes during the day. After that, she would leave their house and become a full-time resident at Children's Care, fifteen miles away in Groningen City. Her visits home and their visits to Children's Care would be limited. Her sister institutionalized! It was bizarre! It was wrong!

Her mother waited until she could see that Alice felt defeated. Then she gave the final push: "You shouldn't be so possessive of your sister."

Her mother knew how to drop the last straw, but Alice didn't collapse. She walked away and went to bed without speaking.

When Alice came down for breakfast the next morning, her parents were not yet in the kitchen, but there sat Aldah, alone, her hands folded on the oak table. This was not like her to be up without someone waking her, the little sound sleeper, and Alice worried that Aldah might have understood the Children's Care talk a little too well and was so upset by it that she couldn't sleep.

Aldah had chosen to sit in Alice's chair and at her place at the table, but she did not have any food in front of her. She was barefoot and in her underwear but was wearing one of Alice's long-sleeved blue work shirts, which hung down onto the bulge of her stomach. She was humming to herself while staring at one of the framed pictures on the kitchen wall, a mountain scene with a waterfall and deer drinking from a stream. Aldah could dream of being somewhere other than Dutch Center too.

Her sister sitting by herself humming at the kitchen table. It was a lovely thing to see. This was not the image and these were not the sounds of a troubled child who was afraid to go off to an institution.

Alice stood still and listened, trying to hear what song Aldah might be humming, but she was humming a medley of melodies. "Jesus Loves Me" elided with "Three Blind Mice" elided with "Away in a Manger," and each stanza, if she was dividing them into stanzas, ended with the final notes of "Old MacDonald Had a Farm."

Aldah hadn't brushed her hair, and strands swirled in every direction, but she had taken the time to put on her glasses. Her humming continued, almost gleefully. Aldah had found a freedom to live happily in a little fantasy life, free from the other members of her family and even free from the television set. There was a beauty and independence here that an institution would destroy.

Alice did not want to disturb Aldah's sweet contentment, but she couldn't resist moving closer. Aldah turned and looked up at Alice and smiled. Alice put her hands on her sister's shoulders and said, "Keep humming, my angel. It's very pretty."

Aldah did keep humming, louder than before, and when she got to "Old MacDonald," Alice sang along with her sister's humming: "Ee-aye-ee-aye-oh!"

Aldah giggled. "McDonald's," she said and giggled again.

"Yes, my angel. McDonald's."

10

Harvesting the battered corn could not happen until after several days of warm and sunny weather. At first, the shattered leaves looked like green tinsel, but warm weather made the frayed leaves curl and deaden into the familiar beige of what might have been ripe corn. The yellow-green husks turned color too, and the pulpy kernels oozed through the husks to turn the color of dried pus. A tornado would have been kinder. At least it would have picked up what it destroyed and taken it out of their sight. The corn leaves were like flesh that had been lashed until the skin split and dangled in strips, while the slender cornstalks stood like poles to which the tortured leaves and ears had been bound. The fields looked like they were infected. They looked like they had leprosy.

When the big equipment finally rumbled through the fields, disappointment carved its way onto her father's face. They had silage all right, but Alice could see that too much moisture had been lost. They heaped the silage into huge mounds, but it was flaky and it didn't have that pungent vinegar smell. It probably had little more feed value than straw.

For Alice, driving off for the first day of school at Midwest Christian felt like driving off to a much-needed vacation. Already the depleting life on the farm was fading and the delights of advanced placement classes awaited her. She felt as if she were dressed in new expensive clothing, though she wasn't.

The cab of the 150 was a small chamber of peace as Alice drove toward Dutch Center. Better than church. Better even than the haymow where she could escape when she wanted to be by herself on the farm. In the haymow she could wallow alone and content among the hay bales reading or dreaming beneath the cooing pigeons in the cupola, but the 150 gave her a different satisfaction. It gave her privacy but also the good feeling that she was actively in control of something. When she tapped the gas pedal, it jumped. When she put her foot on the brake, it stopped. When she talked, it listened. She chose a long route to school just so that her anticipation of getting there would grow, turning down gravel roads that took her away from the hail-damaged fields and past the healthy fields of ripening corn and soybeans. She kept the speed at forty-five, just fast enough to hear the purr of the engine and the casual rustle of sand against the fenders. Driving to school in the 150 was a meditation.

The high school sat at the end of Midwest Street like a confused experiment in architecture. The original two-story redbrick rectangle rose from its center as a testimony to the school's history, dating to the early 1900s when it was called Midwestern Academy and half of the faculty were ordained ministers. The Latin inscription over the front door in Gothic letters read "COR MEUM TIBI OFFERO DOMINE PROMPTE ET SINCERE." The original structure told Alice that her forefathers respected education and wanted to give the halls of learning some dignity. Since then the school building had expanded randomly, a one-story yellow-brick wing here, a metal-roof Quonset extension there, and a separate hadite block building set back on the edge of campus where the band could sound off without disturbing students in the rest of the school. In comparison to the original structure, the assorted expansions looked like architectural slang, if not downright obscenities.

The 150 glistened along in its red glory and onto the student parking lot where Alice's privacy was lost by faces whirling in her direction. Of course. The 150 was still a sneeze of bright color and people had to stare.

The first day at Midwest this year would be different from the first day last year. Last year she worked on her hair for an hour and spent another hour deciding what to wear, only to feel like someone who was trying too hard to be liked. This year she wore jeans and a blue shirt that hung loose over her hips, and she hadn't thought twice about her long blond hair, which she had given a couple of quick brushes before putting in a clasp and letting the rich bulk of it stream in straight lines over her shoulders. This was the year for brainwork, not bodywork. This was the big one. These were not only the last months of the millennium, this was her last year of high school and her last year as a farm girl. She felt as if her life was a teeter-totter, weighted on one side by the farm and the

other side by school. She intended to weight one side with books and let
the other side fly into the air with its flaky silage.

Although the Dutch Center vicinity was considered a rural community, Alice was one of only a dozen students at Midwest who still
lived on an actual family farm. At least she wouldn't have to listen to
hailstorm talk. Town kids could care less what happened outside their
little worlds of *Army Men* video games and aviator sunglasses. At school,
she could move inconspicuously into their company and leave the whole
home scene behind: the money worries, her weird mother, the impend-
ing loss of her sister to an institution—all of it.

What Alice wasn't expecting on the first day of classes was the on-
slaught from the coaches. They were after her for track, softball, volleyball, and basketball. The basketball coach, Miss Rettsma, who had as
much muscle in her voice as she had in her arms, thought she had first
dibs. Alice had been their team's star forward last year, and Miss Rettsma
thought Alice was the key to Midwest's making it to the state tournament. Alice's real reputation in last year's season had come when the tips
of her fingers nearly touched the rim of the basket just as the ball went
through the net.

"She dunked it!" someone yelled from the bleachers—which was
absolutely not true, but after that, every time Alice got her hands on
the ball somebody yelled, "Dunk it, Alice!" And then, the boys barking,
"Alice K.! Alice K.!" Alice knew she'd make a fool of herself if she really
tried to dunk it, so she didn't.

Why couldn't they yell, "Quit wasting your time on sports, Alice.
Study, Alice, study!"?

Alice didn't waste words with Miss Rettsma. "I want to focus on getting ready for college."

"You could get a sports scholarship to college," Miss Rettsma said in a
voice that sounded like a scolding. "You're a natural athlete."

"I don't want to get a scholarship for what I can do with my arms and
legs," said Alice. "I want to get a scholarship for what I can do with my
brain."

There was actually more to it than that. It wasn't just that sports
took too much time away from her studies, but she thought her nerves
were too brittle for sports—and her temper too short. One of the worst

memories for her was a game last year when they were playing a small school from Saint Michael, a town that was as solidly German Catholic as Dutch Center was Dutch Calvinist. Both Lydia and Alice expressed their disapproval of "Catholic jokes" when one of the airheads around them told one of their lame Catholic jokes before a game with Saint Michael's. Lydia and Alice also offered what they called "intelligent resistance" to the mockery of Catholic girls who crossed themselves before shooting a free throw.

Maybe it was because the coaches and cheerleaders from Saint Michael knew about the Dutch Center Catholic jokes, or maybe they saw and heard the mockery of their girls' crossing themselves before shooting a free throw, or maybe it was because Saint Michael was behind eighteen to fifty-two at half time—but whatever the motive, the Saint Michael cheerleaders led off the second half with this silly cheer:

One, two, three, four, five, six, seven,
Our girls are going to heaven.
When they get there they will say,
Midwest Christian, where are they?

"Yays" and wild whistling and clapping followed this insulting cheer. The cheer lit up the players on the opposing team too. Laughing and high-fiving each other.

When the two teams returned to the basketball court, the girl guarding Alice wore one of those "gotcha" grins.

Alice remembered that moment as one when she became another person, someone who was totally out of control. Reason, common sense, and Christian charity all went to hell in a handbasket in one split second. She wanted to kill.

As the Saint Michael team brought the ball down court, Alice stood in the lane close to the basket. When the gotcha-grin girl got within range, Alice whirled around as if to position herself under the basket, but she used all of her whirling momentum to elbow the girl in the ribs. Hard. Harder than she'd elbow a steer that refused to move. The ref didn't even call a foul, but the girl reeled back with her arms across her ribs. "For Christ's sake, Twenty-four!" she moaned. "We were just joking!"

The girl couldn't go on. She held her arms across her ribs and bent over. The ref called time out. After a few minutes, the game resumed without the elbowed girl. Word circulated on the court that the team trainer diagnosed her with a cracked rib and she was being taken to the Dutch Center hospital.

For Alice, it had been a moment of truth. Using all of her strength to hurt someone was not the person she was. Some athletes were no doubt intelligent, but couldn't she be an athlete without becoming a monster? And if she was going to be a Christian, now or ever, it would be by finding peace, not victory at some silly sport. In that moment, she had become what she despised in others, and she didn't want to go there ever again, not into that arena of madness where she had no control over what she was doing.

As much as Alice regretted losing her temper, she couldn't excuse anyone who would mock her just because she was going to a Christian school. Almost all of the students at Saint Michael's were Catholic, but it was still a public school. Maybe if it had been a Catholic school they would have shown more respect. Maybe the people in charge of public schools thought it was all right to be sacrilegious about heaven, but she couldn't turn into one of them, could she? Going to a Christian school had to mean that there were some differences. Alice thought there were many differences, actually. In her mind, most kids in public schools didn't take life seriously, and they certainly didn't take their studies seriously. Alice imagined that in a school without prayer and chapel, there was nothing to remind students that "Life is real, life is earnest." The teachers in public schools probably didn't take life seriously either. They got paid more than the teachers at Midwest Christian and must have thought life was one big expensive party with summer made up of beer and pretzels. It was a wonder that any students from public schools could get admitted to any college. What would it mean to be the valedictorian in a public school? That you'd learned which direction you had to go to get to Canada and could use a sentence without using "ain't"? "Our girls are going to heaven." You bet. On the issue of defending Midwest Christian, Alice would stand her ground—but not with her elbows. Never again.

You didn't have to elbow anybody in debate and choir. They would be the only extracurricular activities for Alice in her senior year. Lydia was in choir too but wasn't interested in debate. "I don't want to learn to argue both sides of an issue," she said. "I just want to argue the right side. My side."

That was Lydia: funny, quick, and always clear about how she felt. To Alice, debate taught clarity and balance. It taught that there really are two sides to almost every issue. Rev. Prunesma would disagree, but he had a Dweller's tunnel vision on every issue.

Lydia was no Dweller, but she could be stubborn, a real contender in any argument, a fact that, to Alice, just made her more interesting. She was always a challenge, but it was as if Lydia saw in Alice what her parents couldn't see. Lydia constantly reminded Alice how intelligent she was—and how beautiful. "You could make a million dollars as a model if you wanted to," she said.

"Right," Alice said. "A model what? Model string bean for Jolly Green Giant advertisements?"

"And your wit!" Lydia howled.

But Lydia didn't talk about Alice's beauty or wit when they first saw each other in the hallways.

"How are things at home?" she asked.

"Don't ask," said Alice.

"Come on," said Lydia. "I heard the hailstorm hit you hard and that you didn't have hail insurance."

"The rumor mill is alive and well," said Alice.

Alice had dreaded the hailstorm topic because it would be a reminder that living on a farm not only carried bad smells with it, but potential economic disaster as well. Still Lydia was different: she might compete with Alice for grades, but she wasn't the kind of person who found perverse pleasure in a friend's misfortunes. Alice once had a friend like that, and Lydia was not of that kind.

"Not really," said Lydia. "I think my mom talked to one of your neighbors. I don't gossip, you know that."

"I know that."

Lydia looked at Alice with her bright, intelligent eyes. "You don't want to talk about it, do you?"

"My feelings are still pretty raw," said Alice.

"You in Miss Den Harmsel's class with me?" Lydia gracefully changed the subject.

"Yes!"

The mention of Miss Den Harmsel's class put them both in an immediate bright mood. They had an equal admiration for her and love of her classes, and they loved the fact that she didn't change from one year to the next. While her students grew and altered their appearance, one hairstyle this year and another the next and one clothing fashion one year and another the next, Miss Den Harmsel looked exactly the way she looked the previous spring—and the spring before that. It wasn't as if she missed every reference to whatever might be the current most popular music group, but she was like the old Krayenbraak house in the way that she was stable and predictable through all kinds of weather.

In class, Miss Den Harmsel wasn't flashy or funny, but she knew her stuff and was all business. She was almost as tall as Alice, and Alice sometimes imagined that she could be like Miss Den Harmsel someday— except that Alice knew she wanted to get married and have a family. Alice had confused desires, seeing—as was her human lot—through a glass darkly, but she adored Miss Den Harmsel and her unswerving dedication to her work. Her students were her family and she gave them every ounce of energy and knowledge that she had. They'd hear the clicking of her shoes as she approached the classroom, and she'd enter briskly with that wrinkled and serious brow over her long face, lay the textbook down, and say, "Class, we have much to accomplish today"— and then she'd go at it.

"Did she recommend books for you to read over the summer?" Lydia asked as they approached her classroom.

"Of course," said Alice. "I read them both twice. I just finished re-reading *The Grapes of Wrath* last week. I read *Beloved* twice in June."

Lydia looked puzzled. "That's strange," she said. "She had me reading *The Federalist Papers* and Jefferson's *Notes on the State of Virginia*."

"Maybe she thought we'd talk to each other and trade books."

"Maybe she sees us differently," said Lydia.

They walked into the classroom and sat on opposite sides so that they wouldn't be tempted to whisper if Miss Den Harmsel said something that excited them both.

This was Senior Advanced Placement Literature. All sixteen students were preparing for college, several of them to become teachers. Miss Den Harmsel loved Emily Dickinson and William Shakespeare. She said that those two authors would be the focus of the entire semester.

Alice savored the prospect and had both thick texts lying on her desk, used copies that cost only four dollars each and which, for some reason, the bookstore manager had set aside for her.

Alice put her hand on the Shakespeare text and waited for Miss Den Harmsel as she distributed a printed study guide.

Why would anyone want to waste their time on a basketball court with insulting morons from public schools when you could spend time in the presence of a Miss Den Harmsel! Alice thought. Public schools didn't have anybody like Miss Den Harmsel. Miss Den Harmsel was a scholar and elevated students with her high expectations. She acted as if knowing the classics was a birthright that no educated Christian should resist. "Get wisdom. Get understanding," she often said. She was quoting the Bible: Proverbs.

"If you know Dickinson and Shakespeare, you're ready to understand all literature," she began. "Irony is at the heart of both comedy and tragedy," she said. "Shakespeare and Dickinson knew that."

It was strange that Miss Den Harmsel would appreciate irony but never speak ironically herself. Ironically, she probably knew that.

11

Miss Den Harmsel assigned *A Midsummer Night's Dream,* the entire play, for the first week.

"We're starting out with the light stuff," she said. "The only tough part will be the Elizabethan English. Read the footnotes, my diligent ones." She said those words with such respect that even those inclined to be less diligent took note.

After filling their minds with Miss Den Harmsel's passionate rendering of her favorite passages from the play, Lydia and Alice had lunch together.

The cafeteria was a testimonial to Dutch frugality and efficiency. The space served as chapel in the mornings, as theater and choir room in the afternoons or evenings, and, magically, as cafeteria at noon when tables and serving counters appeared at 11:45 and disappeared at 12:45.

Alice and Lydia stood in the honor student line, picked up their pizza, walked over to the honor student table, sat down, and silently said grace.

Alice wanted to read snippets from *A Midsummer Night's Dream* as they ate.

"Yes!" said Lydia. "Let's read it loud and freak everybody out. What ho!"

Her loud and sassy voice carried over to other tables and made heads turn. If Alice's height drew others' attention, Lydia's voice and dress drew even more attention. She was *different* in ways that Alice probably would never be. Even her last name, Laats, separated her from most people in the community. Even though Laats was a Dutch name, there was only one "Laats" in the phone book.

At home Alice had followed her father's interest in the history of the

Dutch in America. The way Alice found private reading time in the hay-mow, her father found it in his basement office. One of his favorite books was a large tattered book that was an early 1900s *Atlas* of Groningen County. It contained historical texts, maps, family photographs, photographs of early churches and schools—and advertisements: pages and pages of advertisements that probably made publication of this huge book possible. Alice had quietly dipped into the book herself and found pictures of her own ancestors. She had studied the picture of her great-great-grandfather and her grandmother Krayenbraak and pondered the grim austerity of their expressions. Variations of that grim expression characterized most of the portraits. Some of the men hid their grimacing faces behind heavy beards and mustaches, but there was a ferocity in the eyes that was chilling. It was impossible to tell if the fierce expressions were the result of straining to keep their eyes open for the camera or if there was something more foreboding in their lives. The women in their long and dark stylish dresses that they must have put on for the photographer looked even more tormented—and always the high collars tight around their necks. Was that to hide necks that might be considered too erotic? But the mouths—so grim, so sad.

If her mother had been alive back then, she would have looked like one of these grim women. There were no more than three detectable smiles among the hundreds of photographs. Maybe the photographer was ugly, Alice had mused to herself, and they felt disgusted to look at him. More likely these people simply were not happy. They looked like a lesson plan in pessimism. Maybe her father was looking for a way to accept the present by viewing the grim legacy recorded in these photographs. Maybe he was using a kind of logic that said: when you look at how bad things must have been back then, the present looks pretty good.

Now her best friend sitting across from her was someone who was the real thing, the living Dutch at the end of the twentieth century. It was hard to imagine that Lydia's family had roots that connected to the Dutch Alice found in the *Atlas*. The Dutch who had come to America in the nineteenth century were evidently a whole different breed from the people like the Laats who had come late in the twentieth century. Theirs was not a name that appeared in the old *Atlas*.

After Lydia's family moved from Canada to Dutch Center, her father became a realtor and insurance salesman, and her mother was the town librarian. Alice knew the whole family spoke Dutch fluently, though Lydia rarely used Dutch words, no doubt because she did not want to break her image of a totally Americanized young woman. Still, there was something different about the Laats: her father always wore a suit and tie, and her mother had a wonderful flair about her that had rubbed off on Lydia. The whole Laats family had a confident manner that made them seem almost foreign, which they actually were, but sometimes their confidence came across as naive. They could act like people who couldn't even imagine that others would be suspicious of them or speak ill of them. Alice envied that confidence in Lydia and hoped that some-day she could equal it.

Lydia's playful wit was also hard to beat. When Alice saw that tell-tale smirk on Lydia's face across the table from her, she knew there'd probably be a Nancy Swifty before they looked at Shakespeare. Nancy Swifties were Lydia's idea and dated back to their sophomore year. She had discovered Tom Swifties ("'Doctor, are you sure the surgery was a complete success?' Tom asked halfheartedly"), but she didn't like the fact that Tom Swifties were always about men.

"What we need are some *Nancy* Swifties."

Alice agreed. That's how it started, and it was Lydia who kept the Nancy Swifty fires burning. She was verging toward a chuckle before she told the one she was storing up. The pizza they were eating was Canadian bacon and pineapple, what kids were calling "sweet swine."

Lydia delivered a Nancy Swifty: "'Where's the pineapple?' Nancy asked *dole*fully."

They leaned toward each other, groaning in unison.

"Not bad," said Alice. "Not Shakespeare, but not bad. Now how about some Shakespeare?"

Lydia held her pizza in one hand and paged through the play with her other. "Here's a sweet passage," she said. "It could be about us." She read in a voice that sounded very much like Miss Den Harmsel's: "'So we grew together, / Like to a double cherry, seeming parted, / But yet an union in partition; / Two lovely berries moulded on one stem; / So, with two seeming bodies, but one heart.'"

"That's between two women?"

"Indeed 'tis, madam, though I don't think the whole speech is sweet."

"Here's one I like," said Alice. "'Lovers and madmen have such seething brains.'"

"Cool. Miss Den Harmsel liked that one too. How about this one? 'A wise prince seeks a woman tall and fair'?" she said in a Miss Den Harmselian voice.

"Where's that?"

Lydia had that look on her face, and then she couldn't hold her laugh. Her cheeks bulged while her shoulders and breasts bounced.

"You made that up, didn't you! Didn't you!"

"Nevah nevah. From the pure of soul the pure of tongue."

"Dos't thy tongue betray thee, lady?"

"I'd smite it off, I would," she said.

Alice held up a half slice of pizza and threatened her. Lydia held up a piece of her pizza in the same manner. "Aye, me lady," she said, "woulds't thou make of me a pizza face?"

"A face of many colors," said Alice. Lydia guffawed. Alice guffawed. Now many faces from other tables turned toward them as if surprised to hear something unexpected from the honor students' table: food fights or any kind of bad behavior.

Lydia did one of her quick mood changes and looked at Alice seriously: "There's something I've got to tell you," she said. "Better from me than from someone else. Word is out there that you're not doing any sports this year. The jocks are pissed, so they're calling you 'Barbie Doll.'"

They united in a mocking, sneering laugh.

"I wish you hadn't told me that," said Alice.

"Better than 'ass and a beanpole.'"

"Not much," said Alice.

"Who cares?" said Lydia. "They're all jerks."

Alice agreed, but she'd still have to look at them every day. "Barbie? Barbie?"

"Sorry," said Lydia.

Alice knew it had to be something other than her physical dimensions that invited the Barbie label. For one thing, she was too tall to fit into a Barbie box, and her biggest bulges were on her biceps and buttocks, not her chest. The tall skinny girl with muscles and buns, that was Alice. Hardly the profile of a Barbie Doll!

So Alice knew the jocks didn't call her Barbie because she looked like Barbie, and they didn't call her Barbie just because she wasn't going out for sports. They called her Barbie because they were scared of her, and they were scared of her because they knew she was both smarter than they were and more than their match in the sports department if she wanted to be. What really got to them was that they knew she did not like or respect them one bit. There were times when she and Lydia would hear them talking in the hallways and chuckled at—correction: mocked—their "I done's" and "We was's." In the case of the jocks, fear transformed into *profound dislike.* Alice skipped over the fear factor and went straight for the *profound dislike:* she thought they were lame-brains, and she didn't need to be scared of them to feel that way. Some truths were self-evident. But she had always kept her feelings to herself and didn't call them names behind their backs. Barbie. How dare they, really! Actually, if even one of them had reminded Alice of Ken, she might have smiled at him and asked him if he'd like to play a game of Scrabble.

"I hope I didn't ruin your first day back at school," said Lydia.

"This isn't exactly what I was hoping for, but, really, it's not your fault."

Alice had known from her dull headache earlier in the day that her period might be starting soon. Now the evidence collected in her abdomen, a slight ache that quickly transformed into a wrenching pain, what Alice imagined as two snakes wrapping themselves together and trying to squeeze the life out of each other.

"Oh, my God," she said. She squinted and folded her arms, each hand clutching the elbow of the other arm.

"Have we just changed the subject?"

"You might say that," Alice groaned. "Have you got a quarter?"

Of all times for a Nancy Swifty, Lydia had one: "'Is that a period I see?' Nancy questioned."

"Stop," said Alice. "This really hurts. Don't make me laugh."

Lydia stared at her and winced too. One of the beauties of her friend-ship with Lydia was that Lydia knew when it was time for the humor to stop and when the quick exchanges of their minds needed to give way to the greater needs of the moment.

"You've got bad cramps, don't you?" Lydia asked without a hint of humor in her voice.

"Really really really bad," said Alice.

Alice saw in Lydia's expression that she was absorbing the misery, maybe from her own memories of this pain, but now her big blue eyes were sending out a steady stream of empathy.

"I'd take half your pain if I could," she said.

"I know," said Alice. "I think you already have."

They exited for the women's room.

"Here's a quarter," said Lydia.

Lydia stood outside the booth to wait for Alice. A minute passed and then Lydia asked, "Are you all right in there?"

"I'm all right," said Alice. "I just want to stay here for a while until the pain lets up a bit. Let's read some Shakespeare."

"You're kidding."

But Alice wasn't kidding: she opened her Shakespeare book and laid it on the floor. She came to a passage that fit the moment. She pounded on the wall of her stall and read, "'Thou wall, O wall, O Sweet and lovely wall, / Show me thy chink to blink through with mine eyne!'"

"You're amazing," said Lydia, "Where's that?"

"Page eighteen." Alice read another line: "'O wicked wall, through whom I see no bliss.'"

"You're funny," said Lydia. "May I laugh now?"

"Laugh all you want," said Alice.

There was a pause on Lydia's side of the wall as she seemed to be paging through her Shakespeare text. Then a sweet but dramatic version of Lydia's stage voice floated through the air: "'Think'st thou this pain upon all womanhood befalls?'"

Alice knew that was a Lydia creation, not Shakespeare's. She quickly considered some follow-up line that would rhyme with "befalls": "beach balls, death shawls, overalls, cat calls, bathroom walls"—and then the perfect line leapt into her mind: "Until the voice of motherhood upon us calls."

"Jackpot! Jackpot!" screamed Lydia. "That was a rhymed couplet!"

Alice stepped smiling from the stall. "'We're a rhymed couplet,' Nancy said identically."

They stood and looked at each other the way mutual winners in a big sports event look at each other after the game. Their glee smothered Alice's pain and they hugged each other tight.

"Do you realize what we just did together?" asked Alice.

"We made some Nancy Swifties and some other funnies."

"And a rhymed couplet à la Shakespeare."

"And we did it fast."

"I know. My brain works like a smooth machine when I'm with you."

"Greased lightning. We inspire each other."

"I know. We're both really smart. I couldn't say that to anyone but you."

"I wouldn't put up with it from anyone but you."

"We're the only two in this school who could have done that."

"I know. Don't tell anyone."

"I won't," said Alice. "Too big a price to pay."

"But there is something else I have to tell you," said Lydia. "Remember how last year we often started our periods on the same day?"

"It was a pretty bizarre coincidence," said Alice. "Sort of a sisterly thing, you think? Are you getting symptoms now? Am I making you start your period?"

"Afraid not," said Lydia. "I'll be on a different schedule this month because I've gone on the pill."

Alice absorbed the announcement. She whispered, as if she was afraid that someone might overhear: "You're going on the pill?"

Alice trusted Lydia more than anyone, but she already knew that Lydia had not been totally open with her about the fact that she had been seeing the same guy since July, a twenty-year-old who was attending the vocational college in Shellhorn about twenty miles from Dutch Center.

"You look shocked," said Lydia.

"I am shocked. I knew you were seeing somebody, but I had no idea you were heading in that direction. Who is it?"

"Randy Ver Sloot."

"Do your folks know?"

"Of course not."

"Are you going to tell them?"

"Of course not."

"What if your mom finds the pills?"

"My mom doesn't snoop in my room."

"What if you forget to take one?"

"I won't," she said.

"Whew," said Alice. "This is a big one."

"You're not going to disown me, are you?"

"I just wasn't expecting anything like this while you were still in high school. And with this guy Ralph."

"Randy. Would you rather I hadn't told you?"

"Is he a Christian?"

"Yes," she said. "He didn't go to Christian schools, but he was raised American Reformed."

"At least he's allowed to go to movies on Sundays," said Alice.

"You've heard of Marvin Ver Sloot, right?"

"Yes," said Alice. "Implement business, right?"

"That's Randy's dad."

Alice didn't know what more to say to the person who had been her best friend since grade school. Alice always assumed Lydia would go on to become something great. A doctor. A college professor. A lawyer or business executive or something. One of her fantasies was that Lydia would one day run for governor and Alice would be her main lawyer / adviser. She couldn't think of Randy as a step in the direction of that future. Going to a vocational college. To be what? The idea of Lydia with Randy made Alice feel nauseated, and it wasn't a menstrual nausea. She had lost her. She had lost Lydia.

"Two lovely berries moulded on one stem?"

Her friendship with Lydia really had been like that, the core of them joined more deeply than anyone else could possibly understand. Their friendship had stood outside the calluses on her farm-girl hands, outside the stench of the cattle and hog feedlots, outside the cold water of the bathroom at home, outside her mother's criticism, even outside the constant needs of her sister Aldah. The way they could laugh together. The way they could challenge each other in playful word games or in understanding difficult passages in literature. Together, each of them was a bigger person than when they were by themselves.

Lydia's announcement made Alice feel as if everything they had given to each other with their friendship might be gone forever. If Lydia was a lovely berry hanging next to Alice on the same stem, one of them had just ripened and fallen to the ground. Her best friend was having sex with somebody who was learning how to fix lawn mowers!

"Tell me again what those two books were that Miss Den Harmsel assigned you for the summer," said Alice.

"History stuff," said Lydia. "I think they'd bore you."

"I could lend you *Beloved* and *The Grapes of Wrath*," said Alice.

"No, that's all right," said Lydia. "I've already read them."

12

Alice wandered into the old redbrick core of the school after lunch, past Miss Den Harmsel's room and down the granite-floored corridors and along the walls that still had the original dark-wood moldings and down the narrower marble stairways with the wooden handrails that were dark and smooth from hands passing over them for almost a hundred years. The old section of the school did not give her the comfort of the hay-mow, or even of the cab of the 150, but it always felt like a good place to put herself together and to get grounded when the ground was shifting beneath her.

The old section with its old classrooms was where the most serious classes were taught—advanced calc, AP English, and senior chem. To leave the old section was to enter the more raucous wider hallways with their slamming steel locker doors and loudmouthed students. As she wound her way through the noisier hallways, she saw a few of the jocks, but they couldn't keep eye contact with her—that shifting unease in their whole body, their feigned attention to something else, anything else. They really *were* scared of her. Losing them was no loss at all. But Lydia. First Aldah, and now Lydia.

In the noisy hallways after sixth period Alice saw the dark hair of Nickson bobbing at shoulder-level of the students around him. She did not see his face, whether it said he was scared, carefree, angry, or totally content. It was hard to imagine contentment for him: the only bird of a feather he might find at Midwest was the adopted Korean girl named Sarah Vande Kamp. Alice tried to imagine a day when half the students at Midwest would have dark hair and tan skin and when a rainbow sea of sounds and colors would obliterate the bigotry of Dutch Center—and probably of her own parents. By that time she would already be gone, away from Dutch Center and swimming in her own sea of many colors.

As she walked alone toward the 150 after school, she saw Nickson again. He was talking to the notorious *bad boys* of Midwest. It looked as if the dopers were reaching out to Nickson. Even worse, he grinned and swayed with them in a little brotherhood circle. These guys were worse than the jocks. They were a little gang that Lydia and Alice had labeled "the Slouchers."

"Hey, Nickson!" Alice yelled.

He stepped away from the Slouchers and walked toward her, the seat of his pants hanging loose as an old sow's jowls.

Alice felt a tantalizing warmth as he walked toward her. She felt as if she was protecting the vulnerable, even though he looked confident in his easy swaying steps. And he looked so different from all the blond hair and white faces swarming out of the swinging front doors of Midwest.

"Sorry I couldn't talk longer after church," said Alice.

"That's all right," he said. "Your folks were waiting."

"Want a ride home?"

The question made his eyebrows jump in surprise, but he said, "Sure." His eyes lit at the sight of the 150: "Yo," he said, "nice wheels," and got in.

"Your Toyota station wagon looks like a good vehicle," said Alice.

"It's all right," he said. "Sits low compared to this baby."

Alice could see his profile in her peripheral vision as she drove. He was looking straight ahead, though he may have had peripheral vision too. Alice glanced down at her knees as she drove and wondered what they looked like from his position. She put her right hand down on the seat between them and turned a corner using only her left hand to steer. She knew she was trying to show off just a bit, though she couldn't tell if he was impressed with her casual driving skill.

A few minutes later Alice pulled up behind the Vangs' Toyota station wagon. She thought she saw an apparition. She refocused her eyes. It was no apparition. Someone had put that awful bumper sticker on the rear bumper of the Vangs' station wagon: "If You're Not Dutch, You're Not Much."

Alice looked over at Nickson, but he just smiled.

"I know it's not funny," said Alice.

"It's pretty lame," he said, but he was still smiling.

They both stepped out. Alice walked around to the front of the pickup, but Nickson walked toward the house.

Feeling her temper rise at a time like this felt perfectly right. She felt righteous indignation and a justifiable feeling that somebody should be punished. She didn't touch the bumper sticker. The police would need it for evidence.

"Alice!" It was Mai, standing on the front steps of their house.

"Mai." Alice pointed at the bumper sticker. "I just can't believe it," she said. "I apologize for whatever jerk did this."

Mai walked toward the evidence. "Oh that?" she said. She was wearing jeans, an oversized gray T-shirt, and flip-flops. Strands of dark hair swirled around her bright face. Everything about her was animated.

The blue-and-white bumper sticker glistened. This time Alice did not stand in front of the evidence, and she didn't rip it off.

"I'm going to get them for doing this," she said. Her lips tightened. She was on the basketball court with nobody to elbow.

"Oh, you don't like it?" said Mai.

"Don't like it?"

"I put it on yesterday before driving to campus," she said. "What a hoot."

"*You* put that bumper sticker on your own station wagon?"

"Yep," she said. "Now all the minority students at Redemption want one—but I'm the only one with a bumper to put it on. Most are putting one on their dorm room doors or wrapping them around their backpacks. They only cost three dollars, two for five."

This was a turnaround Alice wasn't expecting, and she was getting an education in a subject she didn't understand. "Isn't this a little twisted?" she said.

"In a good way?"

"You seem to be enjoying it, so I would say yes," said Alice. "The more I think about it, yes, in a very good way. You have a perverse sense of humor."

"But you get it, huh."

"It caught me off guard, but I get it."

Mai's playful grin had as much sparkle as her eyes. She was probably as smart as she was funny.

"Come inside, see our house."

"If there are more bumper stickers in your house, I'll really think you're twisted."

"No more bumper stickers," said Mai, "but you'll probably find other reasons to think we're twisted."

The screened porch had a small bench-swing suspended on chains from the porch ceiling. Several potted plants sat on the porch sill facing south. Two were in clay pots, but others were in gallon plastic ice cream buckets. There weren't any marigolds or begonias. Next to the door was a heaping scramble of sandals, quite a contrast to the work shoes and rubber boots that cluttered the porch on the farm. Alice took off her shoes and added them to the stack.

The living room furniture was ordinary Goodwill American, but the biggest piece after the dining room table was the TV set, which was so big it blocked one of the living room windows. It was turned on with the sound off. The walls were a dull, rental-house green and beige, but the room came to life with many potted plants that made the place smell like some kind of greenhouse that cheated Midwest weather. Photographs of family members took up most of two walls in the living room. There didn't seem to be a plan in the photo arrangement—except that the older men were in the middle and everyone else was spread out around them like leaves that had grown from the stable trunks of those men. Some of the older men were in army uniforms that were not American. Women were in most of the color photographs and wore elaborate dresses that fluttered with color and necklaces that looked like silver-chain bibs—and the whole dress ensemble was topped off with a purple turban. Not even the wildest getup at the tulip festival could match these colors. God help them if they ever wore clothes like these on the streets of Dutch Center.

The house had a small footprint but surprising space—besides the dining-living-room area, it had three bedrooms, two baths, and a tiny kitchen. One of the bedrooms had been turned into Mother Lia's workroom. She was sitting down and leaning over a humming sewing machine. Stacks of colorful fabric were layered on modular metal shelves around her.

"Here are some story cloths that Mom has finished," said Mai and placed her hand on a stack of rectangular cloths that had red, yellow, and green animal figures stitched onto a blue cloth. At the sound of her daughter's voice, Lia got up and spoke to Mai in a strange voice that made Alice think of a cat meowing.

"Our mother wants to give you something to eat."

Lia was already leading the way to the kitchen. A huge rice cooker sat on the kitchen counter with its little red light glowing. The kitchen didn't smell at all like the farm kitchen, which, more often than not, smelled like mushroom soup or bacon. This kitchen smelled like a spice rack with the caps off. At the kitchen table sat Nickson with the Dutch Center telephone directory. He looked up, and for the first time Alice really looked at his eyes. Dark, bright eyes alert to everything. There was more of his sister Mai in him than she first realized.

"This telephone book is kind of weird," he said. "It's really small but it's got all these V-names. How much Dutch is enough?"

He had Mai's humor too. Alice let out a little laugh but not as loud as Mai's. Mai took the directory from him and paged through it. "Hey, it really is full of V-names! Look, there must be hundreds of them. Vuh vuh vuh vuh vuh," she said in a stuttering voice.

They were right about the Dutch Center directory. It had more than its fair share of names starting with V. All those Vans and Vandes and Vanders and Vandens. You had to know if you were looking for a Vande Griend or a Vanden Griend. Was it Vander Heide or Vande Heide? And did the family use the handle Vanden, one word, or did they use two capitalized words—Van Den?

"Let's see where our name will go," said Mai.

She found the exact spot—Vang would come between Van Essen and Van Gaalen. With all the Van-somethings, it would be among the shortest names on the page, along with Vos and Vonk.

"Van Essen Vang Van Gaalen!" said Mia. "Shouldn't it be Vang, Vang Essen, Vang Gaalen?"

"We better cut the *g* off," said Nickson. "Fit right in."

They were both laughing now. "What a hoot!" said Alice and joined in.

"Don't you have any Smiths or Joneses in Dutch Center?" asked Mai.

"Not unless one slipped through the dyke while we weren't watching," said Alice.

"Here's a Rodriguez," said Nickson.

"Oh, yes," said Alice, "you'll find some Martinezes and Gonzalezes. Lots of Mexicans have moved in."

"What about this name? Moeldema?"

"That's Frisian," said Alice. "The only thing that makes Frieslanders different is their names—their names all end in 'a.' There are the Miedemas, the Osingas, the Hamstras, the Siebesmas, the Fritzmas, the Fiekemas, the Wiersmas, the Tammingas, the Plantingas, the Turbstras, the Boumas, the Bonnemas—on and on like that."

"Oh, here's an Aardema in the A's. And Rev. Prunesma, would he be Frisian?"

"Yes, and if you go to the E's you'll find some Ennemas."

"You're kidding."

"Just look."

"Oh, but it's spelled with two *n*'s—E-n-n-e-m-a."

"Right," said Alice, "but when you say it, it sounds like 'enema.' Most of the Ennemas changed their names to Brennema so people would stop making fun of them—like putting enema syringes in their mailboxes. Or telling jokes like the time this girl introduces herself as Emily Ennema and the other person says, 'Tell me about your family,' and Emily Ennema says 'Oh, we're pretty *regular.*'"

"Too much!" said Nickson and slapped the table.

"You people are really funny," said Mai.

Mother Lia had been standing near the rice cooker, listening but not reacting.

"Now let my mom give you something to eat."

"That's awfully nice of her," said Alice, "but I really have to get home to the farm to do my chores. My parents are expecting me."

Alice didn't want to be rude, but she saw a click in the expression on Mai's face at the mention of parents.

"I understand," said Mai. "We'll feed you some Hmong food another time." She spoke to her mother, who nodded and smiled at Alice.

"Thanks again for that ride," said Nickson as Mai led Alice out.

"Before you go," Mai said, "let me show you what Mom planted out back. It really took off. A farm person will appreciate this."

"Took off already? You've hardly been here for a month."

"Mom's amazing," said Mai. "Wait until you see her sewing. Plants and needles, that's Mom."

A parking spot behind the house was simply two strips of concrete spaced the width of a car's tires. Most people would have been using this spot to park their car, but not the Vangs. Mai pointed at the area between the concrete strips. Small points of green plants sparked from the sandy soil.

"What are those?"

"Those are some of her herbs."

"Amazing." But then Alice saw a metal cage with metal flaps on each end. "What on earth is that?"

"That's a squirrel trap," said Mai. "Put peanut butter on that little tray inside and when a squirrel goes in the trap, pop, the doors on each side flip shut and you've caught your squirrel."

"Who's trapping them?"

"My mom," she said.

"To keep them away from her herbs?"

"Squirrels don't like her herbs," said Mai. "We eat the squirrels. Great soup. And Mom cuts up the hide into tiny pieces. If you mix the pieces of squirrel hide with lemon juice, you can get rid of gallstones. My mom thought she was getting gallstones. Not any more."

As Alice drove home, she felt a thud of sadness about her first day of school. It had not been exactly what she had hoped for when she had set off that morning in the 150. The harangues from the coaches. The Barbie Doll thing. Lydia and her idiot horny boyfriend. The Vangs were hardly a substitute for her friendship with Lydia, but seeing them and their strange world gave some peace to the sadness. The farthest she'd ever been from home was Omaha, Nebraska, and now she had just had a touch of Laos, Thailand, and who knows where and what else. "Toto," she said to herself as the 150 purred toward home, "I've a feeling we're not in Dutch Center anymore."

She drove fast to get home and didn't avoid the war zone of the hailstorm. The white buildings of the Krayenbraak farm rose on the horizon like huge gravestones, and her sadness returned. The stripped fields looked like a manicured cemetery. And the poor survivors: the feedlot of steers that were about to go on survival food. The big white house stood like a huge mausoleum in the center of it all. But she knew the shell of a house had innards that were far more distressed than the fields or livestock. The flickering bolts of menstrual pain were a distraction she could almost welcome.

13

As she drove on the yard, she saw that her father had rolled huge sheets of black plastic over the mounds of bad silage as if somehow to cover it would be to heal it. He was rolling old tractor tires onto the plastic to keep it from flapping around. They were into the stage of covering the truth with an airtight shield of black plastic. Everyone would know theirs was indeed a teetering farm.

Alice couldn't pull a sheet of black plastic over the events of the day as they replayed in her mind. Lydia was the hardest. Alice still didn't want to believe it. What was going on?

She shouldn't have asked. When she walked into the house, her mother was waiting with that telltale pinched grin on her face. She was going to punish her with something. Alice didn't know what—but something.

"Aldah's not going to Children's Care," she said.

"Don't play with my mind," said Alice.

"No, we're delaying it."

"You're delaying it?"

Alice thought for a moment that her parents had decided to listen to the reasons they never gave her a chance to give. This could be the first good news of the day.

"Don't play with my mind," she said again.

"I don't play with anybody's mind. We're not going to send Aldah to Children's Care just yet."

"So state aid got turned down and we don't have the money?"

Her mother ignored that question.

"As you know, Aldah is becoming a woman. And she has the feelings of a woman. Some of those feelings are romantic."

"What are you saying?"

"Aldah has a boyfriend at school. The special-ed people and the people at Children's Care agree that this is an important marker. They feel by having a boyfriend she is starting to define herself. It's her first move toward independence. Pulling her away from school and him right now would be a mistake. They say we should think of this as a transitional phase, a way of preparing her for the bigger step of becoming a resident at Children's Care."

"I've never heard such a crock of bull in my life," said Alice.

"You're not the expert."

"Wait. Let me see if I have this straight. You're not keeping her in school so that she can have a home life. You're keeping her in school because she has a boyfriend there? Did I hear you right?"

"You heard me right."

Alice broke away to go upstairs and change into her work clothes. When she came back down, her mother had more to say: "You should be ready," she said. "Aldah will want to talk about him. Roger. He's like her, but he's more verbal."

First Lydia and now Aldah. Not Aldah. Not her innocent one. The very idea of it was unreal. Only two years ago she had taught Aldah about the realities of becoming a woman. Aldah still didn't really understand that she was a woman. She could hardly remember from one month to the next about keeping herself clean.

Over dinner that night, Alice followed the family practice of talking about Aldah while she was sitting right there. "Is this normal?" she said. "Is this normal?"

"People at school say it is. Very normal, they say."

"What on earth are you going to do about it?"

At this point her father mildly stepped into the conversation, looking at Alice. He had his instructive look. "The people at school said we should be supportive, just listen, and let her and Roger talk to each other on the phone. That's what was recommended by the special-ed teachers and that's what Aldah and Roger want to do."

"Mother," said Alice, "where is this going to lead?"

"We'll have to trust in the Lord," she said.

Alice wanted to say, "What's going on, Mother—has your faith taken an optimistic turn?" She didn't. She looked at her mother, studying her.

Her mother didn't look depleted for a change. She looked strangely steady, like a strong woman surmounting a difficult and challenging situation. Her mother was the most together, the most deliberate and rational, when there was a problem bigger than the problems in her own head.

"All right," said Alice. "I can handle this."

Finally, her mother turned to Aldah. Alice had noticed Aldah's puckish little smile as they talked about her. She had enjoyed it.

"Aldah," her mother said, "don't you have something you want to tell Alice? You can tell her."

Alice was the only person that Aldah typically looked in the eyes when she spoke. She didn't look at her now. "I have a boyfriend," she said. "Some things are private."

"I know," said Alice. "Some things are very private."

Her teachers must have prompted that last comment about privacy. Over the years Aldah had accumulated a list of comments that could be applied to various situations—"This is very special," "Friends are good," or "We must be kind." "Some things are private" was a new one.

Aldah leaned toward Alice and whispered, "He is a special friend."

Alice whispered back, "That is very nice. It is good to have a special friend."

"Some things are private," she said to no one in particular.

"I won't tell anybody."

Aldah folded her hands under her chin, tilted her head, and looked at Alice coyly. She was posing, giving Alice the look she would give her boyfriend. Her little sister was in love, and Alice didn't know how to be happy for her.

After supper, Alice tried to draw Aldah into their routine of reading, chatting, and tapping out a tune on the piano. "Come over here, my angel," said Alice.

Aldah looked directly at Alice. "I'm not an angel," she said, "I'm a person."

Transformation. Was falling in love transforming her little sister? Or was this another phrase the teachers had programmed into her with constant repetition? But did the teachers even know she called Aldah "my angel"?

"Come to me, my special person."

This pleased Aldah. She had won an argument, really. Maybe she *was* becoming a person. If love could do this, love was doing more than all the surgery and drugs in the world had done so far. They sat down on the couch together and opened a book. Alice pointed to the words as she read, but Aldah's eyes were elsewhere. She was staring off into space.

"You're thinking about Roger, aren't you?" Alice said gently.

"Yes."

Alice closed the book and sang to her while rubbing her head:

Rock-a-bye, baby
In the treetop
When the wind blows,
The cradle will rock.

She left Aldah sitting where she was, still staring off, but when Alice got to her room and tried to go online to research the year's debate topic, Aldah had tied up the phone line with a call to Roger.

Something didn't quite seem fair about what was going on. Alice went downstairs to talk to her parents. They were both watching TV, and Aldah had taken the phone into the screen porch. Alice's best eaves-dropping spot would be from outside. Slipping out was easy, and it wasn't hard to find a shadowed spot behind the honeysuckle that protected her from the yard lights. The September evening was warm and the air was still. Alice heard the whispery love talk as she edged closer but couldn't make out what Aldah was saying. She was not facing in Alice's direction, so when she spoke, Alice moved closer. It was one of the few times that the hearing loss in Aldah's right ear worked to Alice's advantage. Aldah held the receiver to her left ear, her good ear. While Roger talked, Alice edged up closer from the direction of her sister's weak ear.

Then the words came clearly, though her mother was right: he was more verbal, so most of the time that Alice listened, she was listening to silence. When Aldah did speak, her words were not exactly earthshaking. "You are very special," she said, a comment that must have prompted a long countercompliment from Roger. Alice could see Aldah's squinting eyes smile as Roger spoke. "You are my very favor," she said a little later. Then she giggled. "Yes, you are," she said. "You are my very very very very favor in the whole world."

This declaration brought on an extended monologue from Roger. It went on and on and on and on. Alice wished she could have heard his voice. Whatever he was saying was lulling Aldah to sway slowly from side to side, as if rocked in the soft, sweet cradle of love.

This was how it could be, Alice thought, as she watched and listened: the beauty of innocent romance. Aldah had the trust of a baby. Never in the many times that she had sung "Rock-a-bye, Baby" to Aldah did she ever sing the last two lines. It would have been cruel to have the bough break. Aldah saw none of the dangers of love, and Alice didn't want her to. Lydia's romance was a mockery of love compared to what she was witnessing here. Lydia was taking a cheap ride at the carnival of love, and her cleverness would protect her when the bough broke. At that moment Alice couldn't envy whatever it was Lydia was into. But she envied what Aldah had.

14

It was a Monday night and Alice was studying when the phone rang. This was Roger's time to call Aldah, and Alice still hadn't heard his voice and wanted to, but it wasn't Aldah's lover boy. It was Mai, and her voice was panicked: "Something terrible just happened!"

Alice thought of Mai's mother, even though she had heard that Asian mountain people didn't have heart attacks or strokes—and why wouldn't Mai call 911 if there was a medical emergency?

"What's wrong?"

"They beat up Nickson!" Mai sucked two loud breaths of air. "They beat him up good!"

Sometimes the sounds of ambulance or fire engine sirens in Dutch Center carried to the Krayenbraak farm, and when something really bad happened they'd hear the wuff-wuffing sounds of a medical helicopter flying in from Sioux Falls, South Dakota. Alice hadn't heard any sirens or helicopter, but she could see Nickson's small bloody body lying on a gurney in the Dutch Center hospital with puzzled white faces looking down on him.

"Where is he?"

"He's here. Mom's working on him."

That had to be good news. A bloody nose. A scraped elbow.

"Did somebody from school do it?"

"Nobody from Midwest," Mai said quickly. "Nickson didn't know them. He said they looked kind of funny, kind of nasty he said, not like most people you see in Dutch Center. It happened about an hour ago."

"Were they Mexicans?"

"No, white guys, but it was close to the Mexican restaurant. He went out for a couple tacos and was taking a shortcut home through an alley.

These three guys followed him, yelled at him and called him a spic. Nickson said he took off, but they caught him and shoved him down and hit and kicked him. They were like animals, he said. They just piled on him like dogs. He almost passed out."

"I'm coming over," said Alice.

"You'd do that?"

"I'm on my way."

Alice hung up the phone and yelled, "I need to run! Friend's in trouble. Explain later. Don't worry." Alice ran out of the house so fast that she wouldn't be able to hear her parents if they did try to stop her.

Alice thought of a sleeping dog when she ran up to the 150 where it rested peacefully in the garage. When she turned the key and touched the gas pedal, it took off with a leap. It sprayed gravel as it left the driveway and within thirty seconds was going so fast down the gravel road that Alice didn't take the time to glance at the speedometer, but knew she was going much faster than usual when they were airborne over the railroad track and came down with a slush of gravel under the fenders. They laid rubber when they wheeled onto Highway 75 toward Dutch Center. They were flying. They were a red streak.

The front door to the Vangs' house was unlocked, and Alice ran in with her shoes on. Nickson was leaning over the kitchen table with one elbow propped on his calculus book, which made no sense—but there it was: a beat-up kid with his elbow on his calc book. His right eye looked like a prune, but Lia had applied some gelatinous concoction that looked as if it might drip into his eye. His dark hair was speckled with bits of hamburger, grated cheese, and a sliver of taco shell. His right arm looked as if someone had gone to work on it with a cheese grater. He had been shoved down hard all right. His chest had a bootheel bruise that glowed maroon through his tan skin. He sat there, without a shirt, his shoulders glowing like a matte-finish photo. Lia was working on him, with Mai at her side. Nickson looked up.

"Yo," he said.

His mother didn't look toward Alice but kept working, rubbing on spots that looked bruised and spots that didn't. Open containers of Bengay and Tiger Balm sat on the table. She held one hand on top of his head and rubbed with the other in a regular and smooth motion, like somebody going after a stubborn spot on a pan with a scrub brush. With every sweep of her hand, Nickson gave a little growl.

He looked up again. "You didn't have to come," he said. "You didn't have to."

"I wanted to."

"Thanks," he said, then focused again on his mother's rubbing and responded with little grunts.

"You're welcome."

It looked as if Lia was trying to rub away all the miseries of poor Nickson's flesh. Mai picked up the open container of Tiger Balm and held it to her mother to reload onto her fingers. Lia's face was all business. Her hands weren't shaking, and Alice could tell she had done this sort of thing before. She was following some kind of system with her rubbing, some kind of routine. With all the aromas swirling through the air, the kitchen didn't smell like a hospital emergency room. It smelled like a combination of a barbershop and a compost pile.

"The hospital's only a few blocks away," said Alice.

Mai's response was a quick and sharp look. "Let's go out to the porch so Mom can concentrate," she said.

On the porch Alice said, "He could be hurt bad. What if he has internal bleeding?"

"Mom saw a lot worse in Laos," said Mai. "Mom used whatever she had strapped to her back or could find in the jungle and put people back together who were all shot up, full of shrapnel, bones sticking through the skin. Some of them were at the refugee camp. Should have heard them talking about her. Mom's seen it all. My uncle told me that when the spirits of the dead saw my mom coming, they turned tail and flew off."

If Nickson was bleeding internally and died, Alice would never be able to forgive herself. She was a witness. She should have been calling someone.

"What are the police doing?"

"No police," said Mai. "We can take care of this."

Alice looked around the porch and out the window, as if expecting help to arrive. "Does anybody else even know about this?" she asked.

"He was cutting through the alley, taking a shortcut home. He would never have walked through an alley in Saint Paul, but it's supposed to be so safe here, right? A couple of Midwest kids came out of the restaurant and heard him moaning. They helped him up and offered to take him to the emergency room. Nickson said to just take him home."

"What did your mom say?"

"She told him he shouldn't go down an alley by himself again."

A car slowed down as it approached the Vangs' house, slowed down and started angling toward the curb to park behind the Toyota station wagon. Alice expected it to be the police. The Midwest kids who found Nickson would have gone to the police and they were no doubt coming now for a report and to get a description of the thugs who beat him up. But it wasn't the police: it was Lydia and a young man. Alice knew it had to be the guy she was shacking up with. This was the last circumstance under which she wanted to meet Lydia's lawn-mower repairman.

They approached the porch door like people who were uncertain either of the address or of what they were doing here.

"It's my friend Lydia," said Alice. "You remember her from church?"

"Of course," said Mai.

"And I don't know the guy with her."

Mai held the screen door open. "Hello," she said in her hostess voice.

Lydia didn't look surprised to see Alice at the Vangs' house. Mai greeted her by name, then looked at Lydia's friend.

"This is my friend Randy," said Lydia. "We know about your brother and have something to tell you. Randy, this is the Alice I'm always talking about."

"Hi." Alice held out her hand stiffly. She studied his hand as it came toward her and saw surprisingly clean fingers. She studied the rest of him. On first impression, he looked like a wholesome, decent young man—tall, slender, blond—and dressed in jeans and a short-sleeved, blue shirt with some kind of brand insignia on the left pocket. But his lips were the advertisement of the face: big wing-shaped lips that, when he smiled, didn't look wholesome or innocent. The lips were sly and scheming. Lips that showed practice. Dishonest lips. When he turned to shake hands with Mai, Alice saw only his buttocks bulging indecently in his tight jeans. Alice had been afraid this would be exactly the way she'd feel when she met him. She did not like her best friend's boyfriend one bit.

"Is Nickson going to be all right?" said Lydia. The question seemed to come straight from her heart. Of course. This was her dear Lydia who, when she wasn't using her big brain to joke around, was using her big heart to look out for others.

"Yes," said Mai. "He's banged up pretty bad, but he'll be all right."

"We know who did it," said Randy. Ah, so he was assertive too. Maybe Lydia had found somebody as confident as she was. The big difference would be that Lydia had reason to be confident. But this guy? This grease monkey?

Alice saw flames shooting from Mai's eyes as clearly as the streetlight outside. "You know who did it?"

"They're at Perfect Pizza in the mini-mall downtown right now," said Lydia. "We heard them bragging and laughing about it. They thought they beat up a Mexican kid who dissed one of their friends."

"Mistaken identity," said know-it-all Randy.

"We'd just seen the boys from Midwest who found Nickson . . . ," started Lydia.

"So we knew what these jerks were talking about," interrupted Randy.

"We thought you should come with us to the police," said Lydia.

"No police," said Mai. This comment stopped the conversation. They all stared at her. "Did you say they were still at Perfect Pizza?" asked Mai in a cool, inquiring voice. Mai was acting too collected for comfort. Alice sensed a calm before the storm.

"They had just ordered when we left," said Randy. "We thought you could get the police over there by the time the order was ready."

"You really should call the police," said Lydia.

Alice was watching Mai. It was clear to her that Lydia and Randy were not. They weren't noticing the gathering tightness behind Mai's relaxed exterior. Alice was. It wasn't a familiar tightening. It was foreign, but it was obvious, and Alice knew it was real.

"I don't want any of you involved in this," said Mai. She was talking to Lydia and Randy. "You've done more than enough, and I thank you for it. But you can go now."

"I wouldn't feel right," said Lydia. "There must be something we can do."

"Come on," said Randy. "We're not needed here."

"Are you sure?" she said to Mai.

"Absolutely," said Mai. "One thing—what do they look like?"

"Can't miss them," said Randy. "They're all about eighteen or so, all wearing black caps that they have on backwards. The little one has cowboy boots."

"Thanks," said Mai.

"Alice?" said Lydia.

"It's all right, it's all right," Alice assured her. "Just go. It's all right."

Randy and Lydia left and drove slowly off, the car wavering a little in its lane, as if it were as hesitant and confused as its occupants.

Mai's calm reserve transformed into quick action. She stomped back inside the house and returned in a moment carrying a woven handbag.

"Mai," said Alice, "what is going on? What are you planning to do?" Then she saw a flash of metal in the handbag. "What on earth is that?"

Mai pulled it out and held it up. "It was my grandfather's," she said. Whatever it was, it looked like something that belonged in the props for the fight scene in a high school production of *Macbeth*. It was a strange looking thing with a shining silver blade over a foot long that angled in two edges from the point. "For special occasions," said Mai. "It was passed down to my father."

"What on earth are you going to do with that thing?"

"What do you *think* I'm going to do with it?" she said. "He's my brother. Do you understand that? Nobody beats up my brother."

"You can't be serious."

Alice felt as if she was seeing the world from inside her mother. This is what her mother saw: a world in which solutions were no longer a choice. It wasn't a fear for herself or for Mai exactly. It was a bigger fear, a fear so big that it didn't feel like fear. Not fear for themselves as individuals, but fear at the image of what humans could become. When violence began to feed on itself, a self-perpetuating monster. It was a pure, detached fear of the *terrible* coming to earth.

Mai held the dagger like someone who was ready to use it. When Alice locked eyes with her, she saw more than fire. Mai was approaching a precipice and could ruin her life in one crazy mindless moment. But Alice had signed on to something, and now something large and powerful in her was rising against her will to join in collusion with Mai's rage. It was a rush of energy. She could double Mai's strength, maybe triple it. Her teeth clenched involuntarily as she imagined grabbing one of the thugs, jerking his head back, while Mai slit his throat—or at least beat him into unconsciousness with that strange weapon. One after another, a heap of thugs bleeding like pigs on the floor of the restaurant.

"You shouldn't come along," said Mai. "This is family. My grandfather and father are dead, and my uncles and cousins aren't around. I don't expect you to understand this. You stay here. It wouldn't be good for you to be there. You stay."

"We've got to stop and think," said Alice. She reached toward the hand that held the dagger. Mai jerked it back. "We've got to call the police."

"No. I'm going. Now. Before they leave. You stay."

Mai started toward the front door and Alice followed. She grabbed Mai's shoulders from behind. Mai was stronger than Alice could have guessed, but Alice was stronger than Mai could have guessed. Alice held Mai's shoulders in her grip. The shoulders were like small barbells, but she wasn't squirming to get away. "If you go I go," said Alice, "but you've got to leave the dagger behind. No cutting. No killing. I'm with you, but no dagger. Please, Mai. Please!"

They stood speechless, locked in their rigidity for several seconds. "All right," said Mai.

Alice let go, and Mai handed her the dagger. "You can put it back in my bag."

The dagger was heavier than it looked, but the blade was duller than it looked. Stabbing somebody with this thing would have been like shoving a crowbar into them. Alice dropped the dagger into Mai's handbag, and threw it onto the porch swing. "Come on," said Alice, "we'll take the 150."

"One-fifty?"

"You'll see."

The mood of the 150 had changed when Alice started it up. It didn't feel wild and eager, it felt deliberate and cautious. It had a rescue feature perking through the memory of its cylinders and moved deliberately down the streets as if it were looking for stranded cows. It eased stealthily onto the mini-mall parking lot and into a parking spot.

The 150's rational behavior made its way into Alice. She did not want the next fifteen minutes to ruin the lives of Mai and herself forever. "There's one way we can win this one," she said as they pounded the asphalt toward the Perfect Pizza.

"There's no way we can lose," said Mai.

"Going to jail would be losing."

"No it wouldn't."

The image of the three thugs was like an ink stain on the restaurant window. They were obvious, total losers, with their ridiculous posturing and their caps on backwards. The little one probably threw the first punch. He was smaller than Nickson. He'd be the one with the cowboy boots.

The waitress set their pizza down in front of the three as Mai and Alice entered.

"Let's just expose them," said Alice.

"We'll expose them all right" said Mai and charged in.

"Mai! Think!"

Mai didn't falter in her step. Alice stayed with her and saw a blur of faces—families with kids, young couples, a group of five boys who looked as if they were in some sport together. A fairly big, decent crowd—except for the object of Mai's—and now Alice's—intentions. When they reached their target table, Alice was ready for anything. She kept her hands open. If she was going to hit them, it would be with the heel of her hand. She would also bite. She could feel the urge in her jaw. She would bite until the blood ran down her chin.

Mai stopped two feet from the losers' table. She put her hands on her hips and yelled, "You beat up my brother!"

First came smirky, badass grins, followed quickly by that what-the-hell-is-this look of surprise, followed by desperate help-me-buddy glances at each other, followed by that oh-shit-this-is-bad look of the cowardly losers that they were.

The jury of customers came to a quick verdict. "Did those guys beat up that Hmong kid?" came a steady male voice from somewhere in the background.

The three looked around at the other tables and saw that those around them had already come to a conclusion. None of the onlookers moved to prevent what might happen next, but the cold verdict was in the eyes of the adults, and the children looked more excited than afraid.

"You," said Mai in a sharp voice. "Yeah you, shorty. I'm talking to you. You the one who kicked my brother when he was down?" A pissed-off chihuahua confronted a pit bull.

He looked down and started to smile. Big mistake.

Alice had a quick image of the Chinese World Champion Ping-Pong player when she saw Mai's arm come around in a greased-lightning swing. If she were taller, those fast hands would also have been devastating in volleyball. She hit him so fast that it would not have been possible to know how hard the slap was if his cap hadn't left his head as if a firecracker had exploded under it. This was no ordinary energy. This energy was coming from a place and delivering a force that ordinary physics would not be able to explain.

So this is what Coach Rittsema meant by "a demoralizing blow on the first play."

Neither one of the other two thugs moved after the cap launching.

Now the reaction of the people in the restaurant came out in sighs, "whoas," and "yeses" that reverberated around them and told the three that the judgment was complete and the verdict announced.

Alice stepped behind the biggest. "How about you? You the one who punched him in the eye?"

At that moment, it wasn't just the image of Nickson and Mai's ancestors that came to her mind—all those men in army uniforms hanging on the Vangs' living room wall—but also all the rational and strong-willed energy of her own ancestors, those silent Dwellers and agitated Seekers. Whatever the confluence of energies that made this a moment of truth, Alice felt no fear for the present or the future. Her hands were not shaking. She could feel the thunking of her pulse in her temples and a swimming determination in her brain.

Alice jammed her thumb down into the soft spot in his collarbone area. His butt slid forward on his chair and his face turned toward the ceiling, his eyes wide and expressionless, making him look as if he had just been hit by a 50,000-watt charge of electricity.

"Good grief," came a woman's voice from one of the tables. "Somebody better call the police."

"What's going on?" yelled the voice of management.

"I think everything's going to be all right," said the kindly voice of a father type as his wife led their children from the restaurant. "I think we've got the situation under control."

Mai had kept her warrior stance, feet planted firmly apart, her arms at her sides. She was staring at the one Alice had thumbed down. In his slouched position, he watched her right hand, but it was her left hand that flashed from her side. He didn't see it coming. Alice wouldn't have seen it either if his head hadn't jerked suddenly to the side. Mai had hit him high and hard. She was decrowning them.

"Would you like to call the police?" Her voice was a sarcastic snarl. "Shall we call your mommy and tell her about everything that happened tonight?"

The only response he gave was a red-faced look of embarrassment.

There was now only one boy at the table wearing a cap. Mai stood in front of him. He knew what was coming and started raising both hands to protect his face and cap. His eyes were so wide and pathetic he might have been facing a firing squad. Alice stood behind him and hauled back and whacked him so hard that his cap landed on the next table.

"Whoah!" yelled somebody from the assembled.

"This has to stop! Now!" the voice of management yelled.

The capless, red-eared boys were surrounded by what could have turned into a lynch mob, and the three creeps knew it. Alice couldn't resist: she hauled back once more and slapped the face of the biggest one who did not yet look very penitent.

"Say you're sorry," said Alice. "Say it."

"Yeah, we're sorry," he said.

"Not 'we,' 'I,'" said Alice. "Say it to her. Tell her you're sorry you beat up her brother."

"Sorry we beat up your brother."

"Are you deaf?" said Alice. She raised her right hand from her side. "Not 'we,' 'I.'"

"Sorry I beat up your brother."

"Now the rest of you," said Alice. "Say 'I,' not 'we.'"

"I'm sorry," said one.

"Sure," said the other. "I'm sorry. All right?"

"I'll tell my brother you're sorry," said Mai. "Now get out of here."

The three staggered to their feet. One reached for his cap.

"Leave the caps," said Alice.

The three obeyed and walked toward the door with their heads lunging ahead of them as if they were afraid of being hit from behind.

Alice picked up the three caps and stacked them one on top of the other. "Evidence if we ever need it," she said.

Someone started clapping, and then, like a repeated bad memory, came the grating sound of boys chanting, "Alice K.! Alice K.! Alice K.!"

Everyone in the restaurant was standing.

Outside, the defeated thugs wavered down the street, leaving a trail of black shadows behind them.

"If you're not Dutch, you're not much," said Mai and gave Alice a high five as they walked out.

"This probably isn't over," said Alice as she felt a wave of terror making its way through her.

"It never is," said Mai.

15

It started with her fingers tightening on the steering wheel as she drove back toward the Vangs' house. Claws on a snake. Her shoulders stiffened. A mouth full of ash. She licked her dry lips.

That wasn't me, that wasn't me, that wasn't me, repeated itself in Alice's mind.

The 150 tightened up. In the passenger seat a smiling Mai rubbed her hands together. The 150 stuttered at a stop sign.

A demon was with them. Not fear of the capless boys. Not fear of people talking about them. Scarier than that.

Question: What is your only comfort in life and death?

Alice saw the face of Rev. Prunesma and heard his voice. She knew the answer as well as she knew Psalm 23. Would that Psalm 23 had played through her head instead of the answer: That I, with body and soul, both in life and death, am not my own, but belong unto my faithful Savior Jesus Christ; who with His precious blood has fully satisfied for all my sins, and delivered me from all the power of the devil.

There was more to the answer, but that was enough.

She never thought about what the questions or answers meant when she was fifteen and preparing to make Confession of Faith. Delivered from the power of the devil? She and Mai had been possessed by the power of the devil.

That wasn't me, that wasn't me.

"How are you feeling?"

"Great," said Mai.

"You don't feel weird?"

"For what?"

"You're right."

Alice glanced at Mai again. There was nothing on her guilt plate.

"What was Lydia's boyfriend's name again?"

"I forget. Elmer, I think."

"No, that wasn't it." Mai tugged at her seat belt and gave a shrug of her shoulders. "He sure is cute. I wonder where he goes to school."

"Lawn-mower repair school."

The caps sat between them on the front seat. Limp, pathetic, dead. When the 150 took a corner too sharply, the caps squirmed in their death throes.

Question: How many things are necessary for you to know, that you in this comfort may live and die happily?

Answer: Three; the first, how great my sins and misery are; the second, how I am delivered from all my sins and misery; the third, how I am to be thankful to God for such deliverance.

No thankfulness. No deliverance.

That wasn't me, that wasn't me.

Mai stared at Alice as if she could hear what her head was reciting. "You all right? Those caps freak me out."

"At least the freaks aren't inside them."

A heart as black, hard, and cold as the anvil in the toolshed bolted to the two-by-ten bench.

"Maybe not, but their spirits are."

"I'm going to keep the caps. Trophies. I could stuff them with straw and put them in the garden next spring as scarecrows."

Words like ice chips.

"I remember. His name was Randy. Where did you get *Elmer?*"

"Just came to me. Out of the dead-letter box, I guess."

"Is that a local expression?"

"It is now."

"Something's wrong. I shouldn't have let you come along."

"I can't understand how you can think about guys right now."

"I'm trying to think about good ones after those three. Randy looks like a good one, don't you think?"

"He's a real Ken."

"I'm sure it was Randy."

Alice passed gas. Mushroom onion hamburger hotdish.

"Okay, keep the caps—if you're all right with that. I don't want to see them again. This chapter is over. Case closed. Turn the page."

A stench in the cab. Mai stared at the caps.

"They stink."

The 150 pulled to the curb and shone its lights at the bumper sticker. They sat silently for a moment.

"If you take them home, you might be inviting their bad spirits into your house."

"They'd have plenty of company."

"I liked the way you made them say 'I' instead of 'we.' You made them *own* it. *Own* it. That was good."

"As good as it gets," said Alice.

Mai studied her. "I feel terrible you had to get involved in this."

"Wouldn't have missed it for anything."

"Good," said Mai. "Please come back in the house."

"I should call my folks. I ran out without telling them where I was going."

Alice looked at her watch. She had left home only an hour ago.

When they got to the porch, Alice picked up the bag with the dagger and pulled it out. It was heavier than she remembered. She felt relieved to hold it, as if it were giving her the assurance that it could have been worse if they had brought it with them. "What would you have done with this thing?"

Mai paused for a long moment, then said, "That was a ceremonial dagger—*rab ntaj neeb.* It's not used to cut people. It's used to chase away bad spirits. I probably shouldn't have been using it."

"Better this than one of your kitchen knives. Those suckers look like they could kill a steer."

"They've got heft, all right: you can use them to club or cut."

They went inside and started toward the kitchen, but Lia's voice stopped them. The voice made Mai hold Alice back.

"She needs ten more minutes. She's just gotten to the important part." Nickson's little groans expanded through the house.

Alice walked around the living room looking at the pictures that hung on the wall. They didn't look like violent people, but there was something in the eyes. If she could have translated what the eyes said, it would have been "Don't cross me."

"Where are all these people now?" asked Alice. "Do any of them come to visit?"

"They're all dead," said Mai.

Alice looked again. "Even this one?" she asked. "She looks so young."

"She's dead, all right," said Mai. "A real fighter."

"She died in the war?"

"Not exactly," said Mai. "She died killing herself and the man who betrayed her."

They stood in silence with the sounds of Lia and Nickson coming faintly from the kitchen.

Alice kept studying the pictures, always returning to the young woman. She didn't know what to say.

"All the women in my family are fighters," said Mai. "Drives the old patriarchs nuts."

And then she told Alice the story of her aunt and what some would call the murder-suicide that ended her life.

"It was in Laos," said Mai. "This guy had a really big crush on my aunt but she wasn't interested in him. When it was clear to him that she wanted nothing to do with him and wouldn't marry him, even though his family was from a different clan and had plenty of silver bars for a good bride price, he started bad-mouthing her to everyone. Ruined her reputation. Called her a slut."

"I don't understand," said Alice. "Why would you kill yourself and the other person just because he bad-mouthed you?"

"No, you don't understand," said Mai. "It's an honor thing."

Alice looked at her red hands and rubbed her thumbs across her palms. "How did she do it?"

"You really want to know?"

"I'm not sure."

"She invited him over like she was going to make up to him, but she planted a trip-wire bomb between two trees, ten times the powder that goes into a hand grenade. She opened her arms to him, but when the jerk's foot caught the trip wire, they were both blown to smithereens. That's how women in my family handle men who do them wrong."

"But she killed herself too," said Alice and looked back at the picture, the sweet, round, smiling face.

"Of course she killed herself. He had bad-mouthed her so bad that her life was ruined anyhow. It was the only honorable thing for her to do. A no-brainer, really."

"This makes sense to you?"

"Perfect sense."

"If that had been a cutting dagger, you would have used it."

"I would rather have set a booby trap and been ten miles away."

How odd: that such a story could be a comfort to Alice just then. Maybe what they had done was not as terrible as she was feeling. Alice wondered how soon Mai would tell this story to a guy she was dating.

Lia had finished her work on Nickson and invited Mai and Alice back to the kitchen. Nickson sat with his left arm resting on the table, and the calculus book had been shoved aside. He still had his shirt off and the big heel mark, now blue, had been covered with a paste that had dried to a chalky color. One eye was swollen to leave only a slit. At the sight of him, Alice felt a comforting relief moving through her. They had avenged this crime at Perfect Pizza. Perfect justice.

"You're looking better," said Mai.

"I don't feel so good," he said. "I'll be all right."

He looked at Alice and opened his good eye wider. Alice could see his chest while staring at his face. His lips were lavender. It was hard to tell if that was their natural color or if they were bruised. Her right palm was still warm and it wanted to reach out and touch his shoulder. Mai's hand reached out to his shoulder instead. "Does this hurt?"

"Not much. Where you guys been?"

"Long story," said Mai.

Nickson turned both eyes toward Alice. "Stay a while. Those calc problems were hurting my eyes already before I went out."

"Thanks. I can't—and I've got to call my folks."

"You hungry?" Mai said to Nickson.

"I could eat a pig. My dinner is in a million pieces in that alley."

"I could comb some out of your hair," said Mai. "You go call your folks. I'll get Nickson some food."

Alice prepared excuses to her mother. She'd fudge by saying she'd explain when she got home and then get her story straight in the company of the 150.

Busy signal. Her mother was phoning around, trying to find out where she was. She looked at her watch. No. No. It wasn't even that late. This was Roger's time to call: Aldah was on the phone with her sweetheart.

Alice hung up the phone to say good-bye to the Vangs. Nickson was eating rice with a spoon. He paused between bites, looked up at Alice, and said, "I'd like to join the debate team."

Alice nodded to hide her gulp. Her emotions were going through a series of such quick changes that she couldn't keep up with them. "You can't be serious! I mean, there's an awful lot of research." The words jumped out of her mouth. They must have sounded like a challenge. They must have sounded as if she didn't trust him to do the hard work, but anybody who could ask that question with his body all banged up had to have something going for him.

"I've already started," he said. "I did some research to see if this was something I'd like to do. I'd like to do it. I need speaking experience, you know, and I want to learn how to argue." His words did not come out very clearly, but it was a wonder he could talk at all.

While Alice still struggled to pull her mind and emotions into some kind of equilibrium, into a place where she could think clearly, Nickson pulled his beat-up body up straight and said, "Resolved: That the federal government should establish an education policy to significantly increase academic achievement in secondary schools in the United States."

Those were the exact words of the year's debate topic. Now she felt challenged to regain her composure. This young man could be beat up, go through the pain of his mother's field-tested remedies, and come back into the world ready to debate?

"You're amazing," she said. "Let's talk to the coach when you're healed a little more. I don't have a partner yet." Had she really said that?

Alice stared at his lips. They were fuller, larger, darker, and no doubt softer than her own. At that moment she felt overwhelmingly attracted to Nickson, and even as she had the powerful feeling, some part of her told her that it was a perfectly safe attraction because he was a head shorter than she was and from a culture so foreign to her that being his debate partner would never cross over into anything dangerous or foolish. Anything romantic.

As the 150 took her cautiously out of town, the voice of Rev. Prunesma threatened to come back with the next catechism questions. If his voice started speaking, she'd drown it out with country western music. The caps sat next to her like sleeping rats. Without thinking, she rolled down the window and flung them out. In the rearview mirror, she watched them flup-flup down the road until darkness swallowed them.

She turned off Highway 75 onto the gravel road that led toward their farm. Another car turned onto the gravel road behind her. She didn't remember seeing that car behind her and wondered if a patrolman had seen her throw the caps out the window. Just what she needed to top off the evening: a ticket for littering. She kept her speed at forty. The car stayed back a safe distance but had the eyes of something that was stalking her. When she turned for the last quarter mile to their farm, the car turned too. She accelerated to the driveway and watched for the glint of gun barrels from the windows of the car. The 150 made a right-angle turn onto their yard and scampered toward the garage. The car sped up and whizzed on by. She looked to see if she recognized the car as one of their neighbor's. It was not a familiar car, but it had three people in the front seat. She parked the 150 and stood outside the garage listening to hear if the car was turning around. When the sound of it faded in the distance, she walked to the house.

Aldah was still on the phone, and her parents were still watching TV. She wondered if they even knew she had been gone. She had just had a more varied, exciting, frightening, and confusing experience in the past two hours than she had in the past five years—and no one in her family even noticed she was gone?

When she walked into the kitchen, it felt oddly normal. "Aldah, it's time for bed, my special person."

Aldah didn't hear her, so she went to her bedroom to review the year's debate topic. Her arms felt too tired to lift to the keyboard. She looked at her right hand. Except for the calluses, it was as red as the 150. She put it to her cheek to feel its comforting warmth.

She felt like someone who had wandered onto a strange road in a strange neighborhood where there were no familiar road signs telling her where she was or where she might be going. She thought of trying to pray as a way of finding her way back to something familiar, but the idea of trying to pray while she was in this strange place felt sacrilegious.

PART II

October, 1999

16

Dutch Center was not like an Amish or Mennonite Colony that tried to carry on its traditional ways and images. It made no pretense of preservation when it eliminated the old family storefronts on Main Street. Vander Leike's Furniture, Monnema's Hardware, Kolenberg's Bakery, Vaank's Grocery, and DeBloom's Clothing were all wiped out and replaced by a mini-mall and a Hy-Vee. Dutch Center had its Dairy Queen, its Hardee's, and its Kentucky Fried Chicken. Strangers driving through town might miss the windmill in the city park and see only the usual assortment of ostentatious billboards and advertisements. If this was a distinctly religious community, the only visible indicators were the skyline that bristled with steeples and the Good Shepherd Bookstore in the mini-mall.

This was hardly the uniform community that Alice saw in her father's old *Atlas*. Nor was it the island of believers depicted in another book that her father kept in his office. Her father's hero was a Rev. Hendrik de Cock who, in 1834, led conservative country people away from the Dutch Reformed Church of Holland, the official state church that, over the years, had been poisoned by "the invasive effects of the Enlightenment." Sometimes that war against the Enlightenment came out in Rev. Prunesma's sermons. The boogeyman was Humanism, a way of thinking that diminished God's place in the universe and made man "the measure of all things." Alice loved those sermons, not so much because she agreed with everything that the Rev said but because they pulled her into the comfortable territory of her mind. They made her think about something other than feeding the steers or maneuvering around her mother's constant assaults.

The forces that chipped away at Dutch Center so that it no longer looked like a little City of God were not so abstract as a belief in Humanism. They were grounded in practical matters of making money, and through the transformation that accompanied money-making enterprises, Dutch Center had lost its uniformity. Not only the businesses but the faces on the streets had changed with the influx of Mexicans to work in the big dairies and meatpacking and ethanol plants and with the international students that Redemption College brought in.

Strangers passing through town would catch few signals that they were, in spite of outward appearances, still entering a place that harbored an old and stubborn identity, that beneath the facade of modernity and diversity was a core of interrelated majority. If someone wasn't an uncle or aunt, they were probably related by marriage to someone who was; so when the sheriff and his deputy called Alice out of class, she was looking at one of her second cousins and someone who was married to her mother's second cousins—whatever that would make him. They didn't want to talk about what happened at Perfect Pizza so much as what might happen next.

"We maybe should have arrested those three," said Sheriff Bloemsema.

"Would'na made no differ'nce," said his deputy. "Some people's just got haturd in 'em. Three days in jail would'na jailed the haturd out've 'em."

At the very sound of the deputy's voice, Alice thought of the losers at Midwest Christian. So this is what became of C- students who were nursed through school. Law enforcement!

The sheriff knew who the three thugs were and had talked to the Vangs.

"It's not those three small-timers that we're worried about," said Sheriff Bloemsma. "It's their connections, you see. They have very, very bad connections as far away as Omaha. Chicago maybe. When you see lowlife white fellows like those three talking with the bad apples among your Mexicans, you've got trouble. There are some Mexican criminals who come up here to mix in with the good Mexicans. We're talking drugs. And we're not talking your cannabis. We're talking methamphetamines and crack cocaine and heroin. We're talking dangerous people."

The sheriff's manner was more refined and his speech more acceptable to Alice's ears, but then there was the deputy: "With all them thar aliens now-days, ya cain't tell what's soybean and what's a milkweed."

"They do stick together like weeds," said Sheriff Bloemsma. "They stick together and multiply until you've got a whole patch of them."

"You wouldn' believe the stink of them meth labs," said the deputy. "Man, oh man, I tell you!"

Of course, he didn't tell her. Thank goodness.

These criminals were loyal to each other, the sheriff said, because they didn't dare not to be. The sheriff figured the attack on Nickson was a mistake. The thugs probably mistook him for a bad Mexican who was moving in on the turf of their bosses.

"They's got themselves their own rule book," said the deputy, "an it ain't the Bible."

"What we're saying," said the sheriff, "is that you better be real careful. You better call us right away if something don't look right. If some strangers are following or watching you or one of them Vangs. We can't guess what those three are telling their friends."

"Wouldn' want to neither, tell you that," said the deputy.

Alice thought of the car that seemed to follow her after the Perfect Pizza scene. Was she now a marked person? Was her whole farm in danger? Could they hurt Aldah?

No sooner had the sheriff and his deputy left when Alice countered her fears with the proposition that she had just listened to some small-town cops who needed to imagine big-time criminals to make their lives more exciting and to make themselves feel more important. Big crime in Dutch Center? At least a third of the residents were retired farmers with their wives, and most of the town was peacefully asleep by nine o'clock. Sheriff Bloemsma and his deputy had been watching too many episodes of *Cops* and were concocting a dangerous world that couldn't exist anyplace but between their ears. Not in Dutch Center with its culture of peonies and doilies, not here in macramé and bake-sale heaven.

There had to be worse things to worry about than a few losers who probably wouldn't dare show their faces again anyhow. Most folks were worried about the economy, what with farm sales and foreclosures all over Groningen County—and especially last year when hog and cattle prices dropped through the cellar and put dozens of farmers out of business. With few exceptions, they were putting their hope in the election of George W. Bush because, they believed, he would be a defender of individual liberty. And he was a Christian.

At school Nickson favored his scraped-up right arm, holding it at an angle as if he had it in an invisible sling. In his other arm, he carried his books. Whatever Lia had done for his swollen eye had worked. Except for a dark ring on the lower eyelid, it looked normal. He had been working on the debate topic and had talked to the coach who told him that if Alice wanted him as a debate partner, it was fine with him.

"That's it, then," said Alice. "You're my debate partner." They shook on it, and Alice's long fingers enveloped his whole hand. Just the touch of his hand had a warm and strange feeling to it, as if she had just extended her life into an unexplored world.

Nothing that the police had said changed how Alice thought of the Vangs. They fascinated her for reasons she did not try to understand. She tried to question her desire to know all of them better and wondered if they had to put up with this kind of attraction all the time from white people, a friendliness that was really no more than curiosity. Curiosity that probably harbored suspicion and disrespect. She worried that they might see her as the stereotypical white person whose interest wasn't that different from their interest in animals in the zoo. She rejected her own suspicions of herself: her desire to help Nickson at Midwest could not be bad. It could not be suspect. It simply couldn't be. It was such a pure urge and filled her chest with a joy she could only think of as Christian: "Let us love one another."

She asked Miss Den Harmsel if they could use her room during the noon hour to work on debate. Miss Den Harmsel not only agreed but had a table cleared for them where they could lay out their materials.

Nickson looked uncomfortable, sitting across from her, his hands clasped on the table. When his eyes met hers, she sensed that his discomfort was not about seeing her.

"The sheriff talked to you, didn't he?"

"Oh yeah. And that deputy. He's a trip." Now Nickson was smiling.

The sheriff and his deputy's visit with the Vangs had been quite different from their visit with Alice.

"They thought I was dealing," said Nickson. "They thought I got beat up for not delivering."

"You're kidding," said Alice. "They told me they were worried about what might happen to you if those three wanted revenge—or if their friends would take revenge on you for them."

"Sounded more like they were worried about what I would do, not what somebody else might do to me. They didn't like me much."

"And Mai was right there?"

"Oh yeah. They had some questions for her too, like why would she come all the way over here to go to college. Mai let them have it on that one."

"I can't believe they talked to you like that. Get beat up and then get accused?"

"Don't worry," said Nickson. "We're used to that sort of thing. It wasn't so bad in Saint Paul anymore. Too many of us and they can't get away with it anymore. And a lot of the Hmong up there are lawyers! Well, over a dozen at last count."

"Your mother heard the way they were talking to you?"

"We didn't translate any of it for Mom, but she understands more than she lets on. She gets almost everything. She just doesn't like to talk."

Nickson knew more than Alice did about the three thugs. They were high school dropouts from a town just outside Gronigen County, not far from Sioux City, which had its own history of crime and once had the distinction as the one city in the United States that had more people on the FBI's Ten Most Wanted list than any other city in the nation: two! The three small-time thugs had never been arrested for anything worse than stealing car parts from a junkyard, but they were already working as a brainless unit. When the sheriff had finished questioning Nickson, he warned him that these three were connected to bigger trouble and more dangerous people.

"I think they thought I was mixed up with these guys," said Nickson, "and they were warning me to stay away from them if I knew what was good for me. I think they thought they were warning a small-time criminal—me—against big-time criminals."

Nickson said that the whole ordeal hadn't frightened any of his family—especially not his mother—but that she'd move them all back to Saint Paul if necessary.

"Mom's not afraid of trouble and she'll stand up to anything if she has to," said Nickson. "But she'll try to step out of the way if she sees trouble coming. Sort of a Hmong thing."

"And you and Mai? Does all this talk scare you?"

"I'll be ready next time," he said, "and if they ever lay a hand on Mai I'll call family in Saint Paul to come down here. We know how to defend ourselves, and we would."

Nickson's tough talk made Alice uneasy. She couldn't even imagine thinking about personal retaliation and revenge, but Nickson's people had known death and bloodshed beyond Alice's small range of experience, and what she really heard Nickson saying was how important family was to him and that he loved his sister. She'd known this in theory before, but now it was real. What he was really saying was that he would look out for Mai the way Mai looked out for him. At that moment, Alice realized she would do the same for Aldah.

Nickson handed Alice an article on school vouchers.

"Personally, I don't think school vouchers are a good idea," he said.

"But that's beside the point," said Alice.

"You got it," he said. "This is debate."

They read and took notes for a half hour, shuffling articles to each other and highlighting main points. He had the discipline to get ready for debate. How he would perform in an actual debate was another question. But that was not what mattered. What mattered was that she was helping him.

"Should we get together tonight to work on this some more?" Alice asked.

"At my house?"

"At your house," she said. "Any particular time?"

"Any time."

While he was finishing the last article, she watched him. He didn't read as fast as she did, but that didn't matter so long as he understood what he read. And he did. When he finished and looked up, Alice was struck again by the mild intensity of his eyes. She noticed his lips again too. Their color was different from the lips of other boys at Midwest, a deep but subtle purple. His lips were the color of a steer's nose but had the curving edge of an iris. She always noticed little things, whether a painting hanging in someone's room or the length of someone's fingernails. An eye for detail. So noticing Nickson's lips was not such a strange thing for her. What was strange was that she couldn't keep from rubbing her own lips together when she looked at his. There was something so different about him—and so wonderful.

17

Alice came home that afternoon to a house that looked ransacked—papers strewn around the kitchen, dirt on the floor, dishes on the table, unfolded clothes stacked on chairs—but nobody was there. A messy silence. The groaning refrigerator and humming electric clock were discussing the situation.

Her father had left a note on the kitchen table: "We had to take Aldah to the doctor. Nothing serious. Hogs are fed. Do your regular chores. Check silage mounds. Mother has hotdish in oven. We'll be home for supper. Dad."

Alice knew Aldah's little acts. She probably wanted attention and faked an earache. Stomachaches worked too. Aldah didn't try her attention-getters on Alice, but why did she need more attention now that she had a boyfriend?

Instead of hurrying out to do her chores, Alice decided to check her parents' bedroom. On Saturdays, Alice cleaned the house—except for their bedroom, which her mother would never let her clean. For some reason, she wanted their bedroom to be her space and no one else's. Before going into their bedroom, Alice tidied things up in the kitchen. This way, if she got caught in their bedroom, she could say that the house was such a mess that she couldn't stop herself from cleaning their bedroom too. She cleared off the kitchen counter and folded some towels. Then she headed for her parents' bedroom. If her father's basement office was his little chamber of secrets, her parents' bedroom was her mother's. Alice knew how deceptive her mother could be about almost everything, including information about the farm's money problems. Going into their bedroom felt like an investigation in pursuit of the truth. She checked her mother's big box of greeting cards. She put her hand in every pocket of the dresses and coats and sorted through the makeup drawer. This was promising. There was more than makeup here; there were assorted medications. Aspirin and Motrin, of course. She had allergy medicine for her allergies—but Alice expected these. Then she picked up a surprise, a dark prescription bottle: Valium. Ten milligram Valium.

As she started to put everything away, she noticed a rectangular bulge in a blanket that was folded on top of the clothes hamper. When she unfolded the blanket, she found several books:

Why It's Never Too Late: Final Thoughts on the Millennium
God's Countdown
Don't Be Left Behind: God's People Prepare for the Millennium
From Creation Until Now: the 2,000-year Cycles in God's Plan.

No wonder she needed Valium.

When Alice left the bedroom, she saw Aldah's pink purse lying on the living room couch. The purse had a clean handkerchief. Alice had taught her that: always have a clean handkerchief to wipe your nose or lips. The purse contained Aldah's glasses case and her tiny coin pouch, but in the side pocket was a three-by-five-inch picture of a young man. If his hair had been longer and his lips a bit thinner, he would have looked like Aldah's twin. This had to be her Roger. Alice was certain of this: she could learn more about her family when they weren't around than when they were.

The kitchen clock told Alice that she had been on her mission for a half hour. She would have to move quickly to finish her farm chores before her family got home from the doctor's office.

The cattle feedlot calmed her. The wind was in her favor and blew the smell of the hogyards in the opposite direction, but it was also the comforting rhythm of the process: the measuring of the minerals, the throwing of switches, the eager response of the steers as they came galumphing toward the sound of the augers. She liked the subtle, almost muted aroma of corn dust and the wafting sweeter smells of alfalfa hay. She liked the buffed, dusty smell of the steers and the busy sounds of sparrows everywhere. Just as she was tiring of considering the steers' well-being, she heard the Taurus drive onto the yard.

Aldah hopped out of the backseat and walked away from the car in her proud, swaying swagger. Alice was right: Aldah gave no indication of being sick.

"So what was wrong with you, my special person?" she asked Aldah at the supper table. "Were you sick?"

"She needs to drink more water," said her mother.

"You need to drink more water?"

"I need to drink more water," said Aldah. She gave Alice her *proud* smile.

"Constipation," said her mother.

That was the last word of the conversation before closing prayer. Oh God, Alice prayed as her father mouthed one of his habitual prayers, let it be constipation. Don't let it be more than constipation.

Nothing seemed to be bothering Aldah when Alice put her to bed, but her mother was waiting in the living room. The tight skin on her hard cheekbones glowed like linoleum.

"We need to talk." Her words relieved her body into its familiar sag from the shoulders down. From totem pole to willow branch in seconds. Alice braced herself for worse news about Aldah.

"I'm right here."

"I knew those people would be trouble." She sounded disheartened more than angry. She sighed pathetically. "Things can only get worse. And they will. But we have a role in this, in this downward direction. We bring much of it upon ourselves."

"I assume you're talking about the Vangs."

"You know who I'm talking about."

"They're good people, Mother. They go to our church."

"I know why the sheriff was talking to you."

The Perfect Pizza scene had not been a topic of conversation in the Krayenbraak house, though Alice knew from others that her mother had been talking about it. Her mother had in fact doctored up the story by telling a neighbor that Alice had not slapped anyone. Only the Hmong girl did that. The Hmong girl was beside herself. No one had ever seen anything like it. She had gone wild until people in the restaurant stopped her. Her mother the guardian angel, lying to protect her reputation.

Alice didn't know how her mother had heard about the visit from the sheriff and his deputy.

"I guess people finally have something to talk about. May I go now?"

"I'm not through," she said. "Why did you snoop through my things in the bedroom?"

"I wasn't snooping, I was cleaning up."

"Right. Right. You have hands of mischief. Hands of mischief can work as much ill in the world as tongues of deception."

"Somebody's got to do some cleaning around here."

Her mother put her hand to her pointed chin; she cocked her head and raised her eyebrows quizzically. "I've been suspecting you for a long time," she said. "You're a snoop. You are developing the profile of an un-, trustworthy person. A little deception here, a little deception there—eventually, you will become a polished master of deception. The body is the Temple of the Holy Spirit. What you do with your hands can defile or purify that temple. I don't know that I can trust you anymore."

"I don't have time for this, Mother. I need to leave for a few hours."

"Leave? Really? You have to leave? On a school night?"

"I need to work on debate."

"And why, pray tell, can't you work on debate at home? Especially since we've gone through the trouble of making such a good work space for you in your room."

"I have to meet with my debate partner."

"Your debate partner. And who might that be?"

"Nickson."

"Did I hear you right? That Hmong boy is your debate partner? After all this trouble, he's your debate partner?"

"Yes. He's really smart."

Her mother moved her lips as if there were something lodged behind them. "I am hearing more than you are saying," she said, "and I don't like what I'm hearing."

"What?"

"I am detecting something," she said. "That young man is a trouble magnet."

"We're a debate team, Mother. We have to get started."

"Get started," she said. "Get started?"

"He joined the debate team and we have to get started."

"Sit down."

Alice sat. Her mother nodded her head knowingly. "Aldah is on to you too," she said. "You should know that. You think you're such a good influence on her? Well, she's getting onto you too."

"Onto what?"

"Your lies, your wayward snooping hands. She told me how you stood outside the porch listening to her and Roger."

"I needed some air that night."

"You need more than air," she said. "And you're not going to drive into town tonight. You think we don't know what the sheriff told you? You think we don't know that we should be locking our doors from now on? We need motion detectors."

"We need the National Guard."

"Sooner or later you'll have to get serious about *something,* young lady."

Alice picked up the phone and left the room to call the Vangs. Mai answered. Nickson was studying. "Don't bother him," said Alice. "Tell him that I can't make it tonight to work on debate. I'll talk to him tomorrow. And Mai? Tell him I'm sorry. Tell him my mom needs me to stay home."

"All right," said Mai. "He'll be really disappointed."

When Alice got to her room, her first feeling was anger toward her mother, but then she had a surge of disappointment, an aching disappointment that she didn't know how to interpret, and didn't want to.

She lay down on her bed to work on *Macbeth.* Miss Den Harmsel's study guide showed exactly what would happen in each act, so she knew the story before she started reading.

"I don't want you reading Shakespeare's plays as if they were whodunit thrillers. I want you to know the story in advance so that you can appreciate the beauty of the language."

Alice did read to appreciate the language. She didn't check the footnotes to understand the strange Elizabethan words, but she read aloud in her mind to hear the wonderful sounds and to get a sense of the characters. Lady Macbeth quickly became one of her favorites. How could such an evil person be adorned in such lovely language? She underlined "screw your courage to the sticking place, / And we'll not fail." She wouldn't seek courage to hurt someone the way Lady Macbeth was doing, but she would seek courage to deal with whatever the year might challenge her with. And she would enjoy Shakespeare, both to please herself and to please Miss Den Harmsel. And Lydia! She thought of a Nancy Swifty when she got to the witches' brew passage: "'Double, double, toil and trouble,' Nancy bubbled."

If she had nothing else left of her friendship with Lydia, at least they might be able to come together around Nancy Swifties.

That night Alice heard her mother move through the house. It was 2:00 a.m. When the floor squeaked, the movements stopped for several seconds. She was listening to hear if she had awakened anyone. Alice heard her leave the house and then a sound that might have been the opening of the trunk on the Taurus. Minutes later the front door opened slowly, stopping when the hinges squeaked. A few minutes later a muffled thunk came all the way from the basement. The next morning when her father went out to feed the hogs and before her mother got out of bed, Alice went to the basement. The storage room had empty boxes, but when Alice pulled one back, she found that the box behind it was not empty. Inside the box she found ten large bars of chocolate and a half dozen cans of Spam. Her mother's idea of survival food. It looked as good as the stuff she served for supper.

18

Lydia was wearing a rather silly outfit to school the next day, a multi-colored plaid skirt and knee-length yellow socks. What was this look? Something that her supercool friends in Canada had sent her? When Alice asked her about her clothing, she said she was just getting into the comic spirit of Shakespeare's play. Then she landed a Nancy Swifty: "'I Bottomed out on *A Midsummer Night's Dream,*' Nancy said Puckishly."

When Lydia was on, she was hard to beat, but Alice reminded her that they were reading *Macbeth* now.

"So give me a *Macbeth* Nancy Swifty," said Lydia.

Alice was ready: "'Is this a dagger which I see before me?' Nancy asked with a cutting edge to her voice."

Ah, but Lydia was ready too: "'Out, out brief candle,' Nancy said flickeringly."

"How about this?" said Alice: "'It is full o' the milk of human kindness,' Nancy uddered."

"Good one, farm girl. "'Double, double, toil and trouble,' Nancy bubbled."

"Hey! That's mine! I thought that one up last night."

"Sure you did."

"I honest to God did. I'm not kidding, Lydia, I thought up that exact same one last night right before I went to sleep."

"In your dreams."

It was an unkind remark, and Lydia knew it. "Sorry," she said. "Let's have lunch today."

"I'm sorry but I'll be working on debate. And why are you wearing an Al Gore button? The election's not until next year and Bill Bradley will probably beat him out anyhow."

"What's going on between you and Nickson?"

"Why are you changing the subject? Don't you get a lot of flack wearing a Gore button?"

"Wouldn't know why. Once people's minds can separate him from Bill Clinton, they'll see that what Gore says about the environment is what we all should be thinking about."

"People are more concerned about character after Bill Clinton," said Alice, "and that's why I think Gary Bauer has a chance."

"Get real," said Lydia.

"I don't think who's president makes any difference," said Alice.

"So what's going on between you and Nickson?"

Hearing the question come back a second time sent that familiar flush of shame across Alice's face.

"Why did you ask that?"

"People are talking."

"People are talking? People are talking? I'm helping him with debate."

"And driving him home from school, and hanging out with his sister, and slapping those creeps who jumped him, and locking yourselves in Miss Den Harmsel's room during noon hour."

"It's about debate," said Alice. "Plain and simple. Debate."

"So you and Nickson are having private little debate ceremonies in Miss Den Harmsel's room?"

"We don't lock the door," Alice said quickly, but her voice sounded frantic and she knew it. "I'm trying to help him."

Lydia reached and took Alice's wrist. The grip felt like her mother's. Alice's pulse throbbed in her ears, and now she felt the way she had when she was eleven years old and accidentally discovered the pleasure of touching herself and did not stop after the first good sensation and continued until her mother walked into the room and looked at her with that look of horror. Found out about a truth she hadn't begun to admit to herself. Found out at doing something that could only lead to humiliation.

Lydia had been cruel, but the glaring truth had a cruel sting to it: what if people were so dense that they simply couldn't understand how perfectly good her friendship with Nickson was? They won't understand, and then they'll talk behind our backs, and then they'll start making jokes about us, and then they'll mock us to our faces, and then they'll pick on Nickson. The little fears were dominoes clattering through her mind. I don't care if they pick on me, she thought, but why couldn't they, including Lydia, understand that her friendship with Nickson was the most interesting thing—no, it was the best thing—that was happening in her life? It had such an innocent beauty to it. It felt so pure. It felt so beautiful. The only person who could understand the innocence and beauty of this friendship was Nickson himself, and if that's the way things were, so be it.

"I can see on your face that I'm right," said Lydia.

"Whatever look you see on my face is telling you how nuts you are."

"Remember when we first saw his head bobbing along at about shoulder level with the other students? Remember? We called him 'the Little Bobber.'"

"Right. The Little Bobber. How could you be so stupid as to think anything was going on between us?"

"You're jealous that I have a boyfriend and you're trying to make up for it with the Little Bobber."

"You call him that again and I'm going to haul back and smack you Lydia, I really am."

"Whoa. Sorry to touch a nerve."

"You have the nerve to insult both of us. He's my debate partner."

"Careful. *Partner's* a pretty big word."

"You're the one who's shacking up."

"Oh, sorry Rev. Krayenbraak. We used to say we wouldn't judge each other."

"You could use some judging, judging by your bad judgment."

"At least he can see over most people's heads. Good grief, Alice, Nickson is eight inches shorter than you are!"

"Do you actually love that creep you're with, Lydia? Is he going to follow you off to college? Maybe fix lawn mowers for the college where you go to school?"

"I'm not going to listen to these insults."

"Insults? Insults? Who's been hurling the insults?"

"I'm not going to stand for this!"

"Neither am I!"

"That's it then."

"That's it.

"I've had enough!"

"You've had enough? I've had enough!"

Everything that Alice admired about Lydia dissolved. Lydia was more than confident, she was a spoiled and arrogant brat. And those stupid Canadian pronunciations she could give to some words! Pronouncing *been* so that it rhymed with *seen?* Was that supposed to sound sophisticated? Was that supposed to make her sound just a tad bit English? And the way she could pronounce *house* to sound like *hoose!*

Alice stomped down the hallways, stewing about that person who posed as her best friend.

It took no more than ten minutes of good stewing for Alice to realize that the trouble with ending a friendship in a small town and in a small school was that there was nowhere to hide from each other. And when the sky cleared, the truth was that Lydia—and maybe now Nickson—was the only person she could really talk to.

As Alice walked toward Miss Den Harmsel's room for her noon meeting with Nickson, she was still simmering about Lydia, but she was also resolute that her time with Nickson would be like a classroom discussion when a teacher is present. Like her mother, Lydia could come close to the truth in her cruelest moments. Alice knew all too well that there was something crazy about her friendship with Nickson. She knew it had to cool down. It had to be a friendship that was about debate and nothing more than debate—if for no other reason than to prove how wrong Lydia was.

An outline of topics formed in Alice's mind—federal block grants; standardized national testing; cooperative budgeting between local, state, and federal agencies—and then two steps from the top step on the beautiful granite staircase of the old part of Midwest, she was eye-level with him where he stood facing her at the top of the stairs—those lips, those eyes, and now—oh, how could they be so clear?—those eyebrows that pulsed like dark butterfly wings in sunlight. Their faces were two feet apart when Alice stopped short on that second-to-last step, and the people behind her veered around her. Her face muscles contracted so that she would not smile.

"Debate?" she said in a voice that she forced to sound earnest.

"Resolved," he said, and then she took the final two steps as he stepped back and she rose to her eight inches above him and his eyes did not rise to her eyes but stopped on her breasts, and she realized she was wearing her tight rose sweater that Lydia once said made her look like an advertisement that would sell a million sweaters. She had actually gone after this sweater in the morning, digging it out from the bottom of her dresser drawer—her sexiest sweater—but this was before she talked to Lydia and made her resolution to prove how wrong she was.

Miss Den Harmsel was leaving when they arrived at her classroom door.

"Here's how you lock the door from the inside," she said, "if you want to make sure nobody disturbs you. Just don't tell anybody," she said. "School rules say we're never supposed to lock our classrooms during the day."

Alice locked the door.

Nickson looked totally healed in his tan shirt and dark brown pants, which together set off his skin and hair.

To Alice, her own fingers looked wiry as she spread the materials out on the table neatly in stacks. Nickson watched her every move. He watched those fingers when she touched things. He followed them to her wrists and arms, and then her face. His eyes moved from her hair to her lips to her chin. He was studying her like a map. His attention didn't make Alice tenser—it did just the opposite, the muscles in her shoulders relaxing and her whole body becoming fluid, her fingers like taffeta, her arms conducting a largo movement. His curious eyes were eyes of approval, not judgment, and as he was studying her, she studied him. She stared at his knuckles. She looked at the eye that had been swollen. Then at his eyebrows that moved so beautifully when he talked, then his cheeks, then his hair, that beautiful dark, thick hair that had a natural glisten to it. She took him apart piece by piece, and she saw in his face that he was finding the same comfort in her attention that she found in his. She couldn't be feeling this way, but she was.

In a minute, as they sat across from each other, their hands brushed as they moved papers. Immediately, Alice set up the opportunity for their hands to brush again.

Alice didn't have much experience with this feeling. Last year, when she was a junior, she'd had her one and first serious boyfriend. Her parents had approved when they were seeing each other every Friday night—always with specific plans for the evening, like choir or debate research. Yes, he had been her debate partner last year. The young man was a senior and from a good family. He was an excellent student and was not only on the debate team with her but also the a cappella choir. Alice knew how much her parents had approved of him, but what they didn't know is that when he was alone with her, he was interested in only one thing. Mr. Octopus-hands was all over her, and there wasn't an ounce of gentleness in him. He even drove his car recklessly, accelerating from stop signs much faster than necessary, taking corners stupidly fast, and when he talked he was one exaggeration after another. Everything about him was an overstatement of what was necessary. When she was ready to be physically intimate, she knew that this was not how it would start. Alice cut him off, and within a week she saw him with flashy Madeline with the tight jeans and plunging neckline. He was going to get what he wanted without Alice—and no doubt do it as fast as he could.

How different Nickson was. He had a way of making her feel his energy without flexing his muscles or trying to put on a sexy smile the way Lydia's Randy had done when she first met him.

She and Nickson did work through the noon hour. They worked in perfect harmony, and there were moments when Alice felt as if she had known him for a very long time and that they were natural work partners, people who understood what the other one was doing and knew exactly what to do next.

"Is that hand still hurting you?"

She held out her hand, and he laid his on hers. She turned it over, and couldn't resist using her other hand to stroke it with her long fingers. When he gave a slight squeeze in response, she had the urge to bring his hand to her lips. With her holding his hand, they looked into each other's eyes, steadily. They were relaxed, deeply relaxed, and totally content to look into each other's eyes without saying a word. Alice knew, he knew, they both knew.

With such a deep longing growing in her heart, Alice couldn't hate anyone. Not even Lydia, and now she needed Lydia more than ever. She found her after school.

"How are you doing?" Lydia asked. "Still mad?"

"Not really. You?"

"Not really." She walked over, stood in front of Alice. "We need to be more careful with each other's feelings."

"Agreed," said Alice. "Sorry things got tense earlier today."

"That's all right," said Lydia. "My fault too."

"I need to ask a favor." Lydia waited. "If my mom calls your house tonight, would you cover for me by pretending to be my debate partner? Tell her I was there but just left—and then call the Vangs and ask for me so I can get home before she knows that I wasn't at your house."

"I can do that, but could it be a bit complicated?"

"I'm sorry. You don't want to be dishonest."

"That's not it," said Lydia. "It's our moms."

"Our moms?" said Alice, totally puzzled.

"Our moms talk a lot, you know. Your mom is a regular at the library so my mom sees her a lot. And they talk."

"No, I didn't know," said Alice. "Most people run when they see my mother coming. I'd run too if I had anywhere to go."

"I know how you feel about your mom," said Lydia. "From what you've told me, I don't blame you. But she must be different with my mom. My mom says she has a huge intellect. That she's very philosophical, actually. And very well read. 'An abstract thinker' is what my mom calls her."

Hearing someone talk about her mother the way Lydia was talking about her was like hearing someone talk about the sweetness of a weasel.

"You wouldn't believe the crap she reads," said Alice. "It's all this weird end-of-the-world stuff."

"I don't know about that," said Lydia. "She must read other stuff too or my mother wouldn't find her interesting—and very intelligent."

"My mother, intelligent? My mother has a dark-cloud foggy brain that she uses to beat me up and pretty much bring everybody down. 'Wet blanket' is the kindest thing I can say about her. And her cooking! Gads!"

"Hey, girlfriend, you got your brilliant mind from somebody."

"All right, all right," said Alice. "Let's stop. I won't tell my mom that I'm at your house if she's friends with your mom. I'll have to figure something else out."

Lydia had her own solution: she'd stay near the phone in case Alice's mom called. "I could tell her you're in the bathroom or something—and then I'll call the Vangs to warn you."

"But what if our moms talk at another time about our being in debate together?"

"Don't worry," said Lydia. "I'll tell my mom about your situation. She'll cover for you, too. I know she will."

"I'm never going to get angry with you again," said Alice.

"I like Nickson," said Lydia. "You should know that."

"I believe you," said Alice. "Thank you."

After school, the same bad boys Alice had seen Nickson with before were there, surrounding him with nodding respect. The Slouchers may have been friendly, but Alice thought of them as leeches. Nickson led the way down the sidewalk, and the other two imitated his walk. Then he fell back, following one of them to a beat-up blue car. One of the Slouchers opened the door and Nickson leaned down inside the car, his head hidden under the dash. In a moment the old car started, Nickson got out, gave the Sloucher a highfive, and walked away. Nickson's association with them made no sense, but Alice figured it was a matter of the bad boys seeking out the minority kid as a way of looking supercool. When Nickson saw Alice, he gave his friendly wave—holding his arm out at a right angle and moving his hand. They had forgotten to talk about a ride home, maybe because they had already agreed to meet that night. But he walked toward Alice, and already she understood that they knew what the other one wanted without having to say anything.

"What was that all about?" asked Alice.

"He lost his keys," said Nickson. "I started his car for him. He's got another set of keys at home."

"Oh," said Alice, not having the slightest idea of what had just happened.

"See you guys," said Lydia as Nickson and Alice started off toward the 150.

Nickson held out a folder of papers. "Debate?" he said and moved his eyebrows.

Debate? It was becoming Alice's favorite word.

19

Alice was bald-face lying to her parents by saying that Nickson had dropped debate, that Lydia was her new partner, and that she had to go into town to work on the topic with her. Alice's mother emitted smug approval at the news: she must have felt she had won a major victory by driving Alice away from Nickson. Her mother was so pleased with the announcement that she didn't question the truthfulness of it, so pleased that Alice could sense an unfamiliar wave of affection.

The successful deception was delicious. It made Alice feel giddy. And energetic. And confident. It filled her with a strange joy that was only briefly interrupted by twinges of fear and guilt, but they were no more than little sour spots in a delectable helping of strawberry shortcake. That's exactly how she thought of this feeling—a generous helping of strawberry shortcake, even though in her actual life she did not feel like eating anything.

Part of her giddy joy was realizing that lying to her mother was the only safe path to getting her approval. Killing two birds with one stone! She was getting her mother's approval and protecting Nickson from her mother's insults at the same time.

It was unfortunate that Lydia had to be conscripted into her deception, but Lydia already had practice by deceiving her parents about Randy. She could forgive Lydia for that: after all, sex should be a private matter. Her own lies had even better moral footing because her mother had been so totally wrong in telling Alice that she couldn't go to the Vangs' house when she first announced that Nickson was her debate partner. Lying to her mother was a way of erasing her mother's error, or at least balancing it. Two negatives made a positive, and the positive feedback she was getting from her mother proved the logic of it. It probably proved the morality of it too. Life was good.

Lying had another little side-benefit for both Alice and Lydia. A bonus. Putting a couple of lies into their lives was a generous thing to do for their lame-brain classmates. It broke her and Lydia's perfect honor-role image and gave them at least one way in which they were now no better than the rest of them. Just one of the crowd, like everybody else.

The air was full of Monica Lewinsky and Bill Clinton talk. Lydia and Alice had agreed from the start that they wouldn't tell Monica jokes, but they couldn't help but talk about Bill Clinton and his deceptions to his family and the whole country. That didn't mean they were imitating Bill Clinton—and they certainly weren't imitating Monica Lewinsky. Still, the new bond of deception was bringing them back together just when the friendship had been navigating through some rocky shoals. This was better than a white lie: this lie was golden.

"We should be worrying about Georgie Bush instead of Billy Clinton," said Lydia. "Billy should have a better zipper on his pants, but Georgie should have a better zipper on his mouth to keep the nonsense of his brain from dribbling out. And big money folks are still throwing money at him. Breaking records! They should be embarrassed!"

"You have a mean streak, girlfriend," said Alice.

"You're the only person around here that I can talk politics with," said Lydia.

"Talk all you want," said Alice, "but you know I'm not very political. I don't want to waste my time on politics any more than I want to waste it on sports this year."

"But you're pouring a lot of time into debate."

"Yes. Debate is very important to me. It's great preparation for a lot of things, don't you think?"

"I see," said Lydia, and Alice could tell from Lydia's "I see" that she was seeing more than Alice meant to reveal.

Nickson and Alice planned to meet only once a week at night and twice a week in Miss Den Harmsel's room. Like Alice, Nickson seemed to sense the dangers of excess and how it could lead to exposure not just to Alice's parents but also to his mother who, as Nickson had hinted to Alice, would disapprove of their relationship if she suspected it was about something more than debate.

"Hmong parents think if a guy and girl are together that they're together for only one reason."

Alice didn't ask him to explain.

Most of the time when Nickson and Alice were together, they did no more than share notes with each other until they felt they had accomplished enough, and then they reached for each other's hands the way they did the first time in Miss Den Harmsel's room and swam in each other's eyes. Anyone looking at them would have seen wax statues, their eyes locked as if they were hypnotized. It all felt so safe, and it was nothing that her parents or his mother could disapprove of even if they did see it. How different they were from the silly couples at school that were always giggling and groping each other. Alice and Nickson did none of that in the first weeks of their realization.

But something huge and fragile hovered between them, like a presence that was bigger than both of them, and neither did anything to break it. The flower of romance had budded, and they could not resist watering it with kind words and total attentiveness. They heard each other say, "That's what I was thinking too" and "I know exactly what you mean." Often their harmony went beyond agreeing with each other, and they would say the exact same words at the same time.

In Alice's mind, what she and Nickson were nurturing was mutual respect, and it was only natural that the roots of mutual respect would reach for the sunlight of their touch. Alice ran the tips of her fingers lightly over his arms, and when she did, she watched the excited goose bumps sparkle to the surface like budding leaves opening and trembling in the breeze. His hands moved naturally to her cheekbones. He'd run his fingers lightly down to the point of her chin, and when he touched her neck lightly, a small tremor moved down her back.

When they left Miss Den Harmsel's room, Alice would assure herself that when she moved back into the rest of her life, everything would be the same and she would be back in her old familiar world, but Nickson didn't really leave her when they parted company. Her body and mind remained charged up all day as she replayed every moment that they had spent together and anticipated the next moments when they would

be together again. Everything she looked at, whether the dull tan of the
school hallways or the falling oak leaves along the streets of Dutch Center,
had a bright intensity. Her senses were hyper-alert.

"Have you been watching a lot of TV?" Lydia asked her.

"That's a silly question. Why on earth did you ask that?"

"You ought to see the way you walk lately."

"What?"

"You're starting to walk more like a model than a farm girl."

"Like a model?" she said and tried to put a tone of disgust in her
voice.

"Yes," said Lydia, "like a model who is trying to show off her ass."

That night when Alice went to the Vangs' house for debate, she wore
a disguise of modest slacks and a modest blouse, and she didn't wear
lipstick or a smile that suggested she was too happy to see Nickson.
She tried to walk like neither a farm girl nor a model but like a serious
student—one with a folder of debate material in her hand. As usual,
Lia nodded and said "Hello, Alice," and retreated quietly to her sewing
room.

Alice suspected Mai knew that Nickson and she had more going on
between them than folders of research papers. Her smile and enthusiasm
when Alice came into their house told Alice that Mai not only knew but
approved.

Another night when Alice arrived, Mai was cleaning up in the
kitchen. The kitchen looked different from the last time: now some of
Lia's herbs hung by rubber bands on a wire strung over the sink. The
sight of the bulky kitchen knives made Alice shudder, though the items
Mai had out on the counter didn't—but they did look strange: fish
sauce, oyster sauce, ground chili pepper, ginger, a package of MSG, and
sriracha. What was *sriracha*?

"You hungry?" asked Mai.

"No thanks, just ate," said Alice.

"I'm going to go to the Redemption Library," said Mai. "Don't work
too hard, you guys." A minute later Alice heard their Toyota drive away.
At the same time, from Lia's workroom came the soft whirring sound
of her sewing machine. This had become Mai and Lia's regular routine:
they cleared out.

Alice laid her folder on the table, sat down, and started her close study of Nickson.

"Let's go for a walk first," he said.

His eyebrows took flight in her chest. She couldn't keep her lips from smiling.

"Why not," she said.

They were kissing before they got past the squirrel trap. In her mind, Alice had practiced this moment, and now that it was happening, it was easier than she thought it would be, with her bending down and his reaching up. Alice didn't have much experience kissing a man, but she knew this was good. She knew this was as good as it could be. His kiss had the life of his eyebrows, the intensity of his eyes, and the warmth of his voice. When they paused, she held him with his chin between her breasts and her chin on top of his smooth thick hair. In this pause, they noticed that the kitchen light shone on them through the window and that they were risking exposure to Lia from inside the house and to the whole world outside.

"You smell so good," he said.

Alice put her face down into his thick dark hair. "So do you," she said.

"Let's walk," he said.

They walked away from Main Street and toward the outskirts of town. There wasn't much traffic on the wide asphalt side streets, but every car that passed them slowed down. Small-town curiosity, but each time it happened, Alice tensed up. Then one car that met them did a U-turn at the intersection behind them. It came speeding back and someone in the backseat rolled down his window and yelled, "Goddamn spic!"

In one quick reflexive move Nickson thrust his fist in their direction: "Go to hell!"

The car did not slow down.

The movement from heaven to hell had been quick. "Don't swear," said Alice without thinking, and the voice she heard coming from her mouth was her mother's.

"I'll never run from those bastards again," he said. "Never."

"Those weren't the same guys," said Alice, though she hadn't seen them clearly enough to know for sure. But of course they weren't: some jerks were just jerks who needed an outlet for their ignorance and stupidity.

"I don't care who they were," he said. "They're all the same."

Alice still did not see any anger or panic in his face and his breathing had not quickened, but there was a deliberate movement in his steps. His feet were coming down especially hard.

"Just jerks," said Alice. "Don't let them get to you." She reached for his arm. "Let's go back to your house."

When her hand touched his forearm, it was rock hard. His whole body was ready to act.

When they sat down at the kitchen table again, Alice's feet kept moving under the table, but Nickson looked calm. Steady but coiled, she thought. His brow was furrowed and his eyebrows were not moving. Although she did not know what he was thinking or feeling, and she had never before seen the Nickson who had exploded outside, she felt her own discomfort transform into a feeling of allegiance. This was no ordinary person. He had a quiet and mysterious depth, but he was also a man of action when he needed to be. No hesitation. He was so sure of himself, and this was a comfort. She could feel protected with him, and she would be his ally in any way she had to. Yes, she understood that anger. She knew that anger, perhaps better than Nickson could have realized. If she was going to align herself with someone who was always in danger of outside attacks, she should learn to prepare herself too to protect him as much as he would protect her. She could do push-ups in her room. She could carry bales of hay with only one hand. She could practice kicking when she was doing chores. If she prepared her body, she wouldn't need her anger, only her controlled strength. That's what she saw in Nickson: controlled strength.

They tried focusing on the debate papers they had laid out. They sat quietly for a while, their arms resting on top of the papers. The sweet vibrations between them were not there.

"We have to stop what we're doing," said Nickson.

"Debate?"

"No. This other part. We have to stop."

"What other part? We haven't really started anything," she said.

They sat staring without reaching to touch. Tension filled the space between, and Alice did not know what feelings might be living inside the tension. Was Nickson feeling that he had to protect her from more scenes like the one on the street? Was he losing his feelings for her because she had talked like a prude outside?

"What's wrong?" she said and put her hand down on the table where he could reach to touch it.

"You're too good for me," he said.

"Don't say that," she said in a hushed voice. "Don't ever say that."

He hesitated, looking at her hand. He did not look up. His hand reached out for hers, and for a moment its gentleness had returned.

"I feel ashamed," he said.

"No," said Alice. "No. Not ever."

"All right," he said, but Alice couldn't tell if he meant it.

20

A near-full moon was rising and the sky was clear as Alice set off for home in the 150. Instead of going down Highway 75 and taking the most direct route home, she chose the gravel roads—and she chose to take them slowly. She needed to decompress. She needed to assure and comfort herself that something essential had not been lost between her and Nickson, and what better way to do it than under the golden light of the moon?

She rolled down her window and looked out at the farmland and buildings that lay before her. The countryside around Dutch Center was like a patchwork quilt, laid out in 640-acre sections with an intersection every mile. She could count miles by counting the spaces between clusters of farm lights spread out across the landscape, layer upon layer, for the seven miles that she could see to the horizon. The moonlight still cast its own version of light, a blue and soft illumination that made the distant barns appear as silhouettes and the corn and soybean fields closer to her look like a sea of frozen ripples. She would be able to see the road in this light, so she turned off the headlights.

As she drove down the first mile of gravel road outside town, she couldn't help but imagine that Nickson was beside her, absorbing the half-light with her. This was the kind of light they needed, just enough so that they could see out but no one would be able to see in. Like a one-way mirror. What she and Nickson needed was a one-way mirror to look out at all the people of Dutch Center without the burden of having them look back. This was the kind of privacy that would save them from another scene of fools yelling insults at them.

Driving with her lights turned off also saved her from the dangers of cornfield corners because she'd be able to see the headlights of any cross-traffic at what could otherwise be dangerous intersections. But what if there was another driver on the road, enjoying the moonlight with the headlights turned off the way she was? The question struck her as a joke, but she still stopped at the next intersection where cornfields obstructed the view.

When her grandfather was a child, there would have been a one-room schoolhouse at this intersection, the way there were once one-room schoolhouses every two miles. The schoolhouses had long since been torn down and the one-acre school grounds plowed up and turned into fields of corn or soybeans, but she saw a landscape echo of that one-acre plot—or thought she did. The corn grew taller on the one-acre school ground that was only grass for all those decades that children played on them.

It wasn't only her moonlit view that told her where she was. She smelled the ethanol plant before she saw it. She smelled the distinct difference between approaching cattle feedlots and approaching hog feedlots—and, worst of all, an approaching turkey-raising operation. It was even worse than the large chicken factories with their thousands of defecating chickens. She zigzagged home, turning every mile and, at one point, choosing a mile where all of the farm buildings had been removed. This gave her a whole mile of nothing but the odors of ripening corn and roadside grass.

She turned down another road that would add two miles to her drive home, but at this point she knew she was delaying the moment when she would enter the hailstorm zone. When she did enter that zone, she saw that other farmers had done what her father had done—harvested the battered corn and turned it into silage. These fields were nothing but corn stubble now. Barren fields, and at the sight of them her mood changed.

She hated the reminder of the hailstorm, but instead of images of her father sternly and quietly accepting what the Almighty had delivered to them, Bible quotations started blasting at her like scoldings, but they were scoldings directed at Rev. Prunesma. "Seek and ye shall find!" Why didn't Rev. Prunesma use that text when he was talking about Seekers and Dwellers? Wasn't "seek and ye shall find" a commandment from God? And what about "Seek ye the Lord while He may be found?" The Bible was full of orders to *seek*. The Rev just chose to emphasize what fit his narrow-minded agenda. The Rev's mind could be a cave dweller. Why am I getting angry now? she asked herself. Why?

When she took the last gravel-road corner to their farm, her foot hit the gas pedal hard. She put the spurs to the 150 just to hear its terrific groan of acceleration, a sound and rush of speed that would set her troubled spirit free. Even if the reverend and her mother would try to control her, even if the cowardly racists on the streets of Dutch Center tried to ruin her friendship with Nickson, she had this. She swerved as she accelerated, just to show herself and the moonlight that she could fishtail without losing control. Gravel sprayed from the rear tires, and the front end of the 150 pointed toward the ditch for a split-second before she whipped the wheel and brought it easily back on-center. Alice knew how *not* to overcorrect. A controlled recklessness, yes! Oh, she had practiced this stunt before, though the first time had been with her father's supervision on snow in the middle of the farmyard. He taught her how to bring the pickup out of a skid. Gravel was easier than snow, and she gunned it one more time just to hear the big tires spit gravel.

Her mind weaved toward Miss Den Harmsel's class as she drove on the yard and parked the 150. Miss Den Harmsel had talked about metaphors in *Macbeth*. She had looked straight at Alice when she read the lines, "I have begun to plant thee, and will labor / To make thee full of growing." Alice had gotten another A on a quiz. She knew Miss Den Harmsel was proud of her, and Alice loved the fact that Miss Den Harmsel was taking some credit for her success.

Alice thought of Nickson as she remembered those lines. She was falling in love, really falling in love, for the first time in her life, but the night had shown how fragile everything could be and how easily the perfect could be soiled by the ugly world around them. Now he was ashamed of what she admired in him. It was all so complicated, but the feeling she had in her chest was a pure and throbbing ache with no shades of doubt in it. She would live up to her heart's demand and shower him with so much approval and admiration that all of his fears would disappear.

She turned the headlights back on as she drove onto the yard. The dangers of the drive home had not been the dangers of driving in the dark. Driving in the dark had turned some lights on in her mind. She needed to be brave and take some risks. She would honor her love for Nickson. They would be driving in the dark together, but her love was clear-sighted. All she needed was control over what she was doing, whatever maneuvering was necessary to show him how much she cared about him without frightening him away.

Aldah was asleep and her parents were watching TV when she walked into the kitchen. Her father usually cleaned up around his swivel chair, but he had left a glossy brochure sitting out. *Raising Chinchillas for Fun and Profit.* The brochure had it all, including order forms for cages and chinchilla food, which appeared to be a combination of alfalfa hay cubes, whole grain supplements, and pellets. Inside the brochure, her father had a sheet of paper. In his orderly manner, he had made columns of "expenses" and "reasonable expectation." In temperament, chinchillas were supposed to be exceptionally friendly, gentle, and curious. He had highlighted those three words. Chinchillas had other irresistible virtues: because their fur was so thick they were free of parasites, and because their diet was vegetarian, they didn't create bad odors. Alice pondered that logic: cattle and pigs were vegetarians too, but the hog and cattle yards didn't exactly smell like lavender bubble bath.

Under his calculation columns in which he concluded that he could make forty thousand dollars a year on chinchillas, her father had written the names of chinchilla fur retailers: Neiman Marcus, Bloomingdale's, and Kaufman Furs. He was hoping to go big-time. A chinchilla fur poncho sold for $7,495. A scarf sold for $349. How could he go wrong?

Alice laid the brochure back where she had found it and said goodnight to her parents. When she went to the bathroom, she found her father's wet work socks drying on the toilet lid. She lifted the lid and saw the muddy water. He had washed his work socks in the toilet water and laid them on the lid to dry. Just how far was he going to go to save a buck? She flushed the toilet and bent over the tub to start a cold bath for herself.

The events of the night faded from the stage of her mind. Give me a stage with only one person on it, she thought. Give me a simple world where I can love Nickson and he can love me back without all the foolish nonsense of the rest of the world cluttering things up.

The next morning the chinchilla brochure and her father's calculations were in the garbage. It was a start: at least one ridiculous item had been taken from the stage. But her father. How many false illusions was his brain holding? Or were chinchillas her mother's idea?

21

Seeing Nickson moving through the hallways the next day, Alice couldn't tell whether he was returning to his loving self. He looked beautiful and content in Miss Den Harmsel's room, but he was more reserved. Still, he had an amazing ability to wear an expression that gave no signals as to how he felt. But this was always true of him: it was hard to tell if he was happy, or worried, or scared, or sad—but, like now, he always looked attentive, like someone listening to and watching the world without judgment.

Miss Den Harmsel had put up black-and-white photographs along the top of the chalkboard—an entire row of the actress Judi Dench as Lady Macbeth in different scenes from the play. The look in her eyes in every photograph was cold and detached. Alice looked at Nickson and offered him what she hoped he would see as a loving and accepting expression. He touched her hands when he passed debate materials across the desk, but there was no hint that he was feeling what she felt. His eyes did not look into hers and his lips did not look like lips that were eager to meet hers. The emptiness between them felt like a missed opportunity: Miss Den Harmsel's room had as much privacy as she had felt driving the 150 through the moonlit countryside.

She didn't push him, though an ache in her chest could easily have moved up into her eyes. If she cried now he might withdraw even more. She would control her attraction and move slowly and patiently. He was not cold in response to her measured movements, but he seemed to imitate them. At one point, he looked up and smiled, but he did not try to touch her. His eyebrows did not dance when he looked at her. He was being very, very careful.

When she left school that afternoon the ache in her chest felt like a vacancy that Nickson was unwilling to fill right now. It was a dull, sad ache—but she would not let this bad feeling grow. Nickson hadn't dumped her, after all, and she had no good reason to let her heart break.

At home, she faced a different vacancy. If their house was not empty, it was hollow.

It was not as if her mother had stopped functioning, but Alice had noticed that she was working like somebody who was getting her house in order. She had paid the bills. She had put the spices in alphabetical order. Alice saw a stack of envelopes addressed to various relatives. Alice had no idea what she was writing, but it no doubt had something to do with her fear of what the new millennium would bring. Meanwhile, her father was like cement that was setting harder every day. Watching his increasing rigidity made Alice feel rigid. Aldah played with her dolls. She watched television; she coaxed Alice to read to her. She ate.

But now Alice was alone in this soundless space, like a place abandoned. Was this a foretaste of what lay ahead for their farm? Again, there was a note written by her father: Aldah's health once again. But Alice smelled a rat. Her parents were off doing something that they didn't want her to know about, most likely looking for ways to earn extra money. This time the note told her to check the hogs' water. That was suspicious too. The hoglots were her father's territory, and she guessed that he wanted her to get used to dealing with the hogs as well as the steers. He was expanding her chores so that he could work elsewhere.

Alice stood in front of the bathroom mirror before going outside and looked at the face that Nickson looked at. She looked at the lips that Nickson had kissed only last night. Her lips were swollen, and she wondered if anyone at school had noticed. Lydia of course would have noticed, but she had not said anything. Nickson must have noticed and remembered, but he hadn't given any indication that he remembered that delicious moment as much as she did. Of course, he was being sensible and cautious, and she knew she should be too. She could let her heart rampage with desire, but she should keep her hands firmly on the wheel of self-control.

She tried to imagine what Nickson must have been going through as a foreigner in this jungle of white faces and blond hair. She couldn't even imagine being in a community of Baptists or Mormons or Catholics.

How much tougher it would be to be the only blond, white person in a community of Asians. Or African Americans. Or Mexicans. Nickson was much more confident as the only male Asian at Midwest than she could fathom being if the tables were turned. Coping skills, that's what they were. Nickson had major coping skills as the shortest, darkest-skinned, darkest-haired guy at Midwest. Oh, but there had to be a vulnerable person behind his outward confidence. He had to fear the judgment of the whole community if they thought he, the total outsider, was stealing the heart of one of their own.

She tried to assure herself that Nickson's feelings for her had not changed. He was just afraid of showing them. She would honor that fear by concentrating on debate when she was with him. If he was thinking about debate and not worrying about her feelings, his own fears would have a chance to calm down. Together they would study and practice until they were an unbeatable team. She would help him. She would teach him everything she knew, and slowly he would relax and show his love for her again. She knew it was there. It had to be there.

In the meantime, they would still have their respect for each other. They would have what no other couples at Midwest had: that beautiful synchronicity when they'd say the same thing at the same time.

Right now, doing chores would be a perfect way to take away her own worries. She remembered how her father used work to cleanse himself of distress. When her grandmother, her father's mother, died, her father went out after the funeral with a hand scythe and swiped away weeds from the fences for three hours without pausing. He had come back with blistered hands and a comforted heart.

Alice slipped on her tennis shoes and headed out the door, already feeling the head-and-heart-clearing power of work.

The late-afternoon October air on the farm was quiet but moist. She walked toward the hog feedlots with a stealthy determination. The modernized feedlots were probably not fully paid for, but they were state-of-the-art facilities that had big cement slabs with metal grates suspended a few inches over the concrete. The slabs sloped slightly so that, as the pigs walked around, the manure under their feet oozed through the grates and muddled its way downhill toward the huge holding tank.

These modern feedlots were the scene of their biggest money loss in 1998, but her father had reinvested in hogs on a smaller, safer scale. They no longer had sows with baby pigs. Instead, her father had bought isowean pigs when they were fourteen pounds, and now they were being fattened for market. Her father would have done the math and calculated that feeding little pigs for market could be more profitable than raising sows and overseeing the births of all those litters. The feeder hogs were babcocks, white and lean animals that would produce the tasteless pork that everybody wanted. They were now at about one hundred fifty pounds—another hundred pounds to go before market. The hogs spoke in friendly little grunts as Alice approached. "Oi, oi, oi, oi," they said.

"Oi, oi, oi, oi," she answered. "Why aren't you oi-eating eating eating and making us lots of oi-money money money?"

"Oi, oi, oi, oi," they said agreeably and looked up at her from under their flapped ears.

The hog feeding operation included three separate concrete slabs, each forty feet by thirty feet with a corrugated metal shed at one end where they could find shelter from bad weather. Alice walked down to the far lot, the one where her father had thrown a few old tires and a log chain. These were materials for the mean chewers to chew on. There were some cannibals in that far lot. Getting some cannibals in the mix was the risk of buying pigs instead of raising them. Her father probably hadn't put this possibility into his calculations, but here they were. Something had gone awry in the breeding, some York blood where it didn't belong or something, and the result was an assortment of renegade hogs interspersed among the mild-mannered ones. A few bad apples, but these bad apples had teeth and no qualms about eating their peaceful neighbors rather than eating with them.

Giving the chewers something to chew on was a workable solution. Alice didn't think of the cannibals as evil. They just had a compulsion to chew things to bits. Her father called them chewers, though somebody else might have called them shredders. The Krayenbraaks weren't the only hog feeders who had to deal with cannibals, and different farmers used different distractions to keep them from killing each other. One farmer put bowling balls in his pen because it was hard for the hogs to cannibalize a bowling ball. Hard and round, the bowling balls kept slipping away as they tried to bite them. The evasive and slimy globes interested the cannibals so much that they practically turned the hoglot into a bowling alley. The rolling balls also forced the gooey manure through the grates to hasten its journey to the manure holding tank. Her father didn't have any bowling balls, but he did have these old tires and a log chain.

Alice leaned against the fence of the hoglot. Most of the animals looked peaceful and content, but two chewers were going at an old truck tire, ripping at it like a couple of toddlers with a magazine. Alice had to admire their energy and wondered if they had been doing this all day. Then she saw one sickly smaller pig lying against the fencing in a puddle of manure that had not worked its way through the grates. His skinny white body was totally slathered with manure. The animal looked disgusting, but she couldn't take her eyes off him as his chest kept moving in steady breaths. She was not about to let this sickly pig turn into another corpse. She was not about to give in to the forces that were descending on the world.

She leaned over the fence and looked more closely into the eyes of the pig. The part of any pig that looked most like a human being was the eyes—those big lashes and the shape. The eyes of this pig were very much alive, almost as if it were sending her a message. His eyes shone like little beacons of hope from the grim reality of the rest of his body.

Two chewers were still chomping at the old tire some distance away, but then the biggest of them looked in Alice's direction where she stood studying the manure-covered pig. The chewer started in their direction. At first, Alice thought it was simply curious about her and expecting that she might be delivering some special feed, but when it got closer Alice saw that it was interested only in the sickly pig. There was something ominous in the slushy thunking of its approaching feet on the murky grate. It didn't look angry or aggressive, but it did have a clear purpose. Alice didn't have anything handy to bat the threat away, but she thought the army-green glaze on the sickly pig would be enough protection. The chewer walked over, nudged the sickly pig for a response, and then took a nasty chomp at the rear flank. The muscles in the hindquarter contracted, but the victim didn't squeal. He looked back over his shoulder. He was ready to let the chewer devour him from the hindquarter forward, just give up and be done with it.

Alice regretted that she wasn't wearing her ankle-high work shoes instead of her old tennies, but she wasn't going to stand by and watch. She flung a leg over the fence and spun into the pen. As she landed, the cool moisture of the manure moved up her ankles. The sensation shot new energy into her legs, and she gave a full roundhouse kick to the chewer's grimy jowl. "Go! Go!" she yelled. She spun around again, manure flying through the air, and smacked the bottom of her tennie against the chewer's ribs. "Go!" she yelled, and kicked it hard. And kicked it again! The chewer skidded and scrambled on the slimy grates and stumbled away in the direction of the other hogs.

Alice looked down at her reward. She had saved the pig's life, but he was still a very pathetic animal. He was a runt and weighed no more than seventy pounds. Why hadn't her father removed this helpless animal from this pen? He had gone out into the fields and harvested the damaged corn, even though its silage was practically useless. This was a breathing, living thing and deserved to survive like everything and everyone else. She was determined to get this pig over the fence, safely away from the chewers, but she didn't have any gloves. She wasn't afraid of getting pig manure on her hands, but she wasn't sure she could get a grip on the slimy legs. She looked toward the house and thought she might be able to run to the porch and grab a pair of gloves, but she was not about to leave now and give the cannibals a second chance. The sickly pig's flank was bleeding, a red stain working through the grime. If the cannibals smelled blood, they'd finish the job before she got back.

Thinking about doing something like what she was about to do was always worse than actually doing it. She stooped down and slid her hands through the manure and under the bony rib cage. When she lifted, the animal squirmed and kicked. She wasn't going to turn back. She went down in the manure and felt the knobby grate on her knees. She pulled the kicking pig toward her stomach. She stood up, holding him like a squirming child in her arms. She leaned over the fence and placed him on the ground outside the pen. The pig stopped his kicking and squirming. He didn't try to get up. He lay motionless but safe, then stared up at her with eyes that were all too human, but if there was gratitude in his eyes, she couldn't detect it.

The chewer was watching. It acted as if it could care less about what

Alice had done. If it could talk, it would have said, "Don't you have any-thing better to do?"

A particle of manure had lodged in Alice's left nostril. She couldn't even smell it—only detect its cool presence. A gentle northwest breeze brushed Alice's cheek, and it was if she were suddenly nowhere and everywhere at once, and the moment—if it was a moment because time stood still—was a moment of peaceful neutrality when nothing mat-tered but everything was beautiful or, at least, not harmful. She could have been anywhere, suspended and free of time and space, free of pride or shame, free of fear or ambition. She could, in her suspended state, see herself covered with hogyard filth, but she could not smell the stench, and the dung-colored slime that covered everything that met her eye was not ugly. She was totally part of it all, one with it, and felt no urge to judge or reject any of it. Dreamily, her eyes moved to the chewer that had slashed the flank of the sick pig she had saved. The chewer looked nei-ther content nor aggressive but stood in its dung-covered being in a state of peaceful indifference. We really are all in this together, she thought as she stood in her stunned state of acceptance.

A burning sensation stung her left nostril. She put the back of her hand to her right nostril and blew the lodged particle of hog manure from her left. With her shoulder she wiped hog manure from her right eyebrow. Her sweatshirt and jeans were so filthy that she didn't bother with them. She bent down and washed her hands in the hog water trough.

She walked to the hydrant and attached the hose to wash off the pig. She sprayed at the grime until the pig's white bristles and pink flesh came back into view. She sprayed that white pig until it was spotless. She looked at what she had done and felt clean. This is what it meant to care for something or someone other than herself.

The Taurus with her parents and Aldah drove onto the yard. Aldah hopped out of the backseat. Again she gave no indication of being sick. Aldah and her mother disappeared into the house, but her father saw Alice and walked across the yard.

He looked at her, then at the pig. "I don't think that one was worth it," he said.

Alice stared at him. "What *is* worth it?" she said.

Alice walked away.

"You'd better get cleaned up," her father said.

"After I feed the cattle," said Alice and glowered at him the way he could glower at her.

Alice did go to feed the cattle, and she walked out among them where they were feeding in their long rows. She squeezed between the steers, rubbing her body against their hairy ribs. She imagined a car wash where the large rotating brushes washed the grime from the sides of a vehicle. The steers' hairy ribs were her brushes and she rolled her body past them. If she rubbed hard enough the hog manure smell would be removed, and, at worst, be replaced by the mild smell of dusty steer hair. She scooped up handfuls of useless silage, sniffed it, and rubbed it against herself.

When she got to the house, she showered until her father shouted, "That had better be cold water you're using!"

How were you going to bathe your chinchillas? she thought.

When she came into the kitchen for supper, she saw everyone's nostrils respond when they looked at her.

"You didn't get it all off," said her mother and couldn't repress an expression of satisfaction.

"It'll wear off," she said and sat down.

Whatever odor she was emitting turned everyone's stomachs. The overcooked hotdish her mother had in the oven turned her stomach—so Alice guessed they were even.

"I got new glasses," said Aldah.

So she had, thicker ones that made her eyes look larger. Constipation one day and new glasses the next.

"I need to drink more water," said Aldah.

"I know," said Alice. "We could all use more water."

Miss Den Harmsel had talked about symbols in Shakespeare's plays. It was strange to hear talk about blood as a symbol of guilt in *Macbeth* and then to come home and see an innocent runt pig exuding blood from the teeth of an animal that had no control over its own impulses. Blood stains equaled the stain of guilt? What did the manure stains that infused her body say about her?

Actually, Alice thought, if anyone wanted to have symbols for what was happening in her family, hog manure stench combined with constipation and magnified perception would have been good candidates. Symbols for what, she wasn't sure.

Alice knew Nickson would never be able to understand that hogyard scene, but she liked the thought of his seeing her now. If he actually thought he wasn't good enough for her, he might change his mind at the sight and stench of her. He was ashamed for cursing at some jerks? If he could have seen her in the hogyard, she could match his feelings of shame and one-up him big-time. Her mother seemed to detect the satisfying fantasy on Alice's face and stared at her with eyes that were more malevolent than any chewer's. Her father sighed a few times as they nibbled at their food. He read from Psalm 118 before his closing prayer, and stopped with verse 24: "This is the day which the Lord hath made; we will rejoice and be glad in it."

22

The next day the hog manure smell still oozed from Alice's body when Lydia sniffed like a beagle in her direction. "There's something rotten in the state of Denmark," she said. Wasn't that from *Hamlet*? Lydia had been reading ahead but so had Alice.

"You could better have said, 'Out out, damned spot.' I had the ultimate farm girl experience yesterday. The ultimate. I'll tell you about it if you think you have the stomach for it."

"No thanks," said Lydia. "I already have the nose for it."

What a topsy-turvy world. Alice's heart—what she wanted to trust as the grand informer of all things good in the world, her guiding light, her connection to God—where was it now as the stink of her body overwhelmed everything beautiful? Whatever moment of freedom she had felt when she stood in the heart of the stench, being freed from it by being one with it, was gone. What was that anyhow, that strange moment when the worst part of farm life had swallowed her so totally that all fear and disgust of what was really happening was gone? So strange. That feeling must have been what Jonah felt when he was in the belly of the whale. That whale of the hoglot had spewed her back out into the real world but lingered as a malevolent odor that stood between her and her friend.

Lydia didn't draw away. She actually stepped closer.

"Wear this," she said. "Build a little buffer zone."

Lydia's suede coat had come below the knee on Lydia but was an inch above the knee on Alice. "Wear it," said Lydia. "I was going to get it cleaned anyhow."

Alice didn't like to build up a debt to Lydia, but she put on the coat. She'd build another buffer zone by faking a sneeze anytime somebody got close. Meeting Nickson at noon in Miss Den Harmsel's class would be the biggest challenge. She got through her morning classes, though a few of the town girls turned toward her and wore the kind of smirk that showed they relished the fact that even though Alice did well in school she could still smell like a farm hick. No doubt about it: the smell was seeping through the coat. Alice saw it on their faces—that odd combination of disgust and smugness. Those spoiled brats whose cheap drugstore products made them smell like raspberry Kool-Aid.

When Alice met Nickson in Miss Den Harmsel's room, he trapped the smell in midsniff and didn't inhale any further.

"Something terrible happened," Alice blurted out. "I feel terrible. I stink. Don't get close to me. I smell like hog crap."

Nickson squinted, as if trying to understand a puzzling mystery, and Alice wasn't sure if the mystery was for him a rational problem or a sensory one. He grinned, not so much playfully as forgivingly. "It's not so bad," he said.

For Alice, this was one of those moments when the best possible thing could come from the worst possible situation. His playful smile. The bright spark in his eyes. She wanted to leap up and hug him, but that would be the very kind of impulse that could bring his fear back and push him away.

"I know it's bad," said Alice. "Lydia told me it's bad. The looks on people's faces tell me it's bad. I would have gone home sick but. . . ." She stopped herself, and then she said, "But I wanted to see you."

Those final words were not ones that Alice had planned. Her bad smell could so conveniently have eased the way into a comfort zone of focusing on debate. It could have been a safety net, something that kept Nickson just far enough away that he would have time—slowly, increment by increment—to realize how wonderful their friendship could be, and then they would be able to restore their closeness. She'd be able to embrace and kiss him every time they were alone together. Now she feared she might be rushing him, and doing it through the repulsive fog of her farm girl odor.

"I'm glad you came anyway," he said. "I really wanted to see you too."

Alice was afraid he might have said that out of pity. Pity was better than nothing, but pity was not the kind of affection she was trying to find.

"I don't want you to think of me the way I must be smelling," she said.

Alice rose from their debate table, walked slowly across the classroom to the window and looked out at the Iowa countryside beyond the school grounds. The glass in this old classroom window had a shimmering and distorting quality. In the distance, two figures in orange vests and orange caps were walking across a harvested cornfield. When she swayed to the side, their orange clothing grew brighter or dimmer with the window's varied magnification. A cock pheasant, with its distinct shiny brown color and long tail feathers, flushed from the corn stubble in front of the two figures. Their shotguns rose quickly to their shoulders and the ends of the barrels jumped with accompanying puffs of blue smoke. A second later the distant blasts reached Alice's ears. The pheasant soared on, swooping down over a distant hill, and the men in orange walked on, the barrels of their shotguns pointing up.

"Smells," came Nickson's voice from behind her. "I don't really hate any smells. I have a high tolerance, you know."

He pointed his nose in her direction to prove his point. If he heard the distant shotguns, he wasn't letting on.

"You don't have to humor me," she said, and walked back to sit across from him at their debate table.

"No," he said. "I have a lot of memories of smells, you know. I mean, I can smell Laos and Thailand in some of my mom's stuff."

She dared to lean closer toward him across the table. "Are you serious? Even now? So long after that war?"

"Oh, yeah," he said. He leaned back in his chair and turned his head. Alice wondered if he was trying to avoid her smell, but he looked more like someone who was trying not to be distracted from the memories he was calling to his mind. "You can't get rid of those smells," he said. "And you can't forget them. Mom's got some pieces of old parachutes that probably smell like dead American pilots. There's gunpowder smell in some of Mom's old clothes from when she was taking care of wounded people. From their clothes maybe, or maybe the smell of gunpowder in the air got into things."

"You can actually smell that?" Her surprise at what he was saying was enough to make her unaware of her own stench for the moment.

"Some of the smells just stick around," he said, "and then there's smells that you just remember, you know. I can't remember the refugee camp so good, but when we took a ride last week, just Mai and Mom and me, out in the country—the way we like to do—past these big chicken farms, I got a funny feeling about the smell; it just hit me like something sad, you know, and I told Mom, I said I didn't like the smell, and she said, '*qaib ntub dej.*' I was remembering that awful wet chicken smell from camp when I was a baby."

He turned and put his hands toward Alice like the first time. "You don't smell so bad," he said. "I can smell right through it to the real you."

Alice entered another one of those moments when she felt set free from the ordinary ways of life into something different, foreign, and exhilarating. She held out her hands to meet his. She blinked against the blur of tears that were rising. He squeezed her hands gently, but he did not lean over to kiss her.

She thought about what he had just said. "So you think the person under this smell is still worth knowing?" she asked.

"Yes," he said.

"I'm glad," she said. "I'm glad."

Increment by increment, she reminded herself. He had reached out to her with his own story. It had to be his way of rebuilding their friendship.

"We'd better stick to debate, though," he said.

"I know," she said.

"I like working on debate with you,"

"I like working with you too. You seem to understand the issues totally."

"Studying is easy for me," he said. She wondered if he was really telling her what *wasn't* easy for him.

She opened her hand on top of the table. He took it, looked up at her, then reached for a stack of cards where he had rebuttal notes. "We'd better get started," he said.

"Yes, yes, of course," said Alice. "We have a lot of work to do."

Alice met Lydia after school and handed her the coat. The look on Lydia's face told Alice that she was still picking up the odor.

"Why don't you wear it home?" said Lydia. "Bring it back in a plastic bag."

"What a strange day," said Alice.

"How were things with Nickson in your debate session? Did you bring some room freshener?"

"Very funny, but I didn't have to," said Alice. "He understood. He seems to understand everything."

"You two have something big going."

"It's you and Randy who've got something big going."

No," said Lydia. "No. What Randy and I have is not about anything big. It's not about love."

"Aboot?" said Alice. "Aboot anything big?"

"You're getting passive-aggressive again," said Lydia. "Don't tell me you're mad about my little air freshener comment. I'll say 'abow-wowt' if you prefer."

Lydia was smiling. It seemed that even she could forget the smell for a few seconds. But how could she say that what she had going with Randy was not big? What could be bigger than having sex with someone? Alice wanted her talk with Lydia to go on, but other students were walking near them, and she was not about to mention sex in front of them.

"You want to talk, don't you?" said Lydia. "I can see it in your face."

"Very much. Yes. I really need to talk to you."

"Drive me home," said Lydia.

"But the smell in the 150 will be as bad as it is in my clothes."

"I'm almost used to it already. Let's go."

Lydia got into the passenger seat of the 150, and immediately it felt strange to have her there. Even though Lydia was her best friend, at moments like this Alice realized how much they *didn't* share with each other. Lydia hadn't told Alice about her boyfriend for weeks after they'd started up. That was a big omission, but Alice didn't share everything with Lydia either—not even the 150. This was the first time that Lydia had ever sat in the 150, and there was something so unfarmlike about her that had never come out so strongly as it did now. They were such equals when they were playing word games or talking Shakespeare and they were so mutually equal in contrast to the giggling airheads they had to put up with at Midwest, but Lydia and the 150 were a bad fit. Both Mai and Nickson looked more like people who belonged in a farm pickup than Lydia did.

The stench of pig manure was right where Alice had left it stranded inside the cab. She opened the windows and turned the blower on full blast. "Sorry," she said. "I'm afraid this thing has bad breath."

"I can handle it. Let's talk."

Lydia lived only eight blocks from Midwest, so Alice knew she'd have to take a few detours if they were going to get any serious talk in. "All right," said Alice, "how can you say you and Randy don't have a big thing going when you're having sex with him?"

"Minor League sex," said Lydia. "I don't want to be in love with the first guy I have sex with. I won't be ready for Major League sex until I'm through college and ready to get married to somebody I love."

"I can't believe you can talk about a boyfriend like that. I could never talk about Nickson like that—and we're not having sex."

"Not yet," said Lydia, "but what you have is big. It's written all over you, and I think it's written all over him too, though I'm not sure I can read him as clearly as I can read you."

Alice turned down a quiet side street and idled along at ten miles an hour through the drifting fallen leaves.

"I don't want you to be disappointed in me," Lydia went on, "but I think it's time I'm more honest with you. You know that being born in Holland means my parents are a lot more tolerant than the folks around here. The Dutch in Canada were more tolerant too, at least about matters like sex. My mother knows I'm on the pill."

"What?" said Alice. "Why did you lie to me about that? I thought we could trust each other about these sorts of things."

"Sorry, but I didn't want to shock you. My mother also knows I'm not really serious about Randy."

"And your mother can handle that?"

"Pretty much," said Lydia. "She says I should be careful with my heart and anybody else's heart, but she says she trusts me not to get too reckless. I can live with that."

"But we've been going to the same church and Bible classes all these years," said Alice. "How can your folks be all that different from most of the people in our church? You dress a little differently, but you can't be all that different."

"Appearances," said Lydia.

"I'm supposed to know what that means?"

"Maybe people are what they appear to be. Maybe they appear as they would like to be."

"That's not Shakespeare," said Alice. "What have you been reading?"

"Just talking to my mother," said Lydia. "I like the way my mother puts it when she says that going to church fills a real need in our lives. Say, what happened to the stink? I don't smell it at all anymore."

"That's because you've become one with it. Like me."

"'I can't get enough of this great air,' Nancy inhaled piggishly."

Finally, they were laughing together again.

Alice wanted to talk about Nickson before they arrived at Lydia's house, but she wasn't sure where to start. "Why do you say Nickson and I have something big?" she asked.

"I don't know that much about him," said Lydia, "but I know you. You don't do anything halfway. You're an all-or-nothing sort of gal."

Alice thought about that, not sure if it was true. "I think it's best that I'm just Nickson's friend," she said. "I think we should stick to debate. He's so new and alone in Dutch Center, but he's *so* smart and *so, so* open about things. He's *so* willing to try something new."

"You can hide behind your little debate screen if you want to," said Lydia, "but you're obsessed with him, Alice. Question: Can you remember even one hour in the past two weeks when you weren't thinking *abow-wowt* him?"

"I think about a lot of things every hour," said Alice.

"Hey, it's all right to be obsessed with him. You have my blessing. I just hope you don't get hurt."

Alice stopped at an intersection and looked both ways for cars, though it was clear that none were approaching. "Nickson would never try to hurt me," she said.

"Maybe not," said Lydia, "but there's the rest of our Dutch Center world. You'll see some heads turning and some suspicious stares when people figure out that something big is going on behind your debate act."

"It's not an act," said Alice. "We're working hard on it. We'll be tough competition, you'll see."

Alice pulled the 150 to the curb and stopped.

"I have had enough *terrible*," she said through a throat that was tightening. "I want some *beautiful*."

When Alice looked at Lydia, she saw that her eyes were glassy too.

"You're a beautiful person, Alice," she said. "Without you at Midwest, I'm not sure I could stand it." She slid over and flung her arms around Alice. Alice hugged her back but then saw a car of staring faces approaching from the opposite direction. Alice pushed Lydia away.

"Those people are staring at us," she said. "They probably think we're lesbians."

"Stop worrying about what people think," said Lydia. She pulled Alice even closer and pressed her face against Alice's cheek.

Alice's face brightened. "All right, all right, I won't worry *aboot* it," she said. "Now I've got to get you to your *hoose* so I can go home to do my chores."

The house where Lydia lived was on a cul-de-sac on land that, when Alice was in grade school, had been the Van Haverhorsts' farm. Now it was cleared land with many new houses and small maple trees, a few that still had faltering blood-colored leaves. The Laats' home went up when Alice was in junior high and was the largest on the cul-de-sac, what some people would call a minimansion with its staggered high gables and an enormous picture window facing the street. The house was made of brick and had an arched entryway that shaded a large wooden door with a stained glass window in its upper section. A gray Lexus was parked in front of one of the three garage doors that faced the street.

Alice had seen the house often and had spent many hours after church when they were in junior high listening to music in Lydia's room. Her farm girl schedule never allowed her to spend weekends with the Laats, though the invitation had been made many times. But through all those years, Lydia had never been in the Krayenbraak farmhouse. It just never seemed to work out: too many chores to do, too many demands from Aldah—and what person in her right mind would invite somebody over to eat her mother's cooking?

Looking at the Laats' house, Alice saw it as she had never seen it before: it screamed *wealth,* which not only made the Laats *look* different but probably made them different in a host of other ways too. Inviting Lydia over to her world of hog and cattle feedlots and her mother's bad cooking would have been embarrassing in the past. It would be even more embarrassing now that the farm was teetering and there wasn't even warm water in the cold white house with its even colder atmosphere.

More than a Lexus, what faced the street from the Laats' house was a bold Al Gore lawn sign. It was the first such sign that Alice had seen in Dutch Center and added one more piece of evidence: *The Laats are not one of us!*

"I see you're not alone in your support of Gore," said Alice.

"Indeedy," said Lydia. "Especially my mom, but my dad too. My mom thinks Gore will be the candidate—and she reads *everything*. I like that she practices what she preaches: she started a recycling program at the library and is setting up classes for grade school kids on the environment."

Except, perhaps, for a couple of Redemption College professors, there probably was not another Al Gore lawn sign in all of Dutch Center. If the Mexicans had Gore sentiments, they would be savvy enough not to put them on their lawns. But the Laats? These Dutch Canadian settlers, they dared to do it. They dared show their hand a year before the election!

"You're really behind Al Gore, aren't you?" Alice said.

"Oh, yeah," said Lydia. "But I'm worried. Too much money on Georgie's side."

"If a rich guy is going to win, why don't you think it will be Steve Forbes? Talk about money!"

"Flat-tax Forbes," said Lydia. "I doubt it. One-act pony, that guy. And have you looked at his eyes on television? The guy doesn't blink. He's scary. But Georgie is just enough of a good old boy that the fat cats will love him. Corporation George. Just watch," said Lydia.

"Looks like your folks are doing all right," said Alice. "I mean, maybe not super rich, but, I mean, looks like your dad knows how to work the system."

"Dad has done very well here," said Lydia, "but he says he'd be happy to pay more taxes."

Alice didn't know where to take the conversation after that. Money talk could only lead to pain. The very idea that somebody could have enough money not to worry about more taxes seemed, at that moment, simply bizarre.

"I don't want you to take my awful smell with you into your nice house," she said as Lydia opened the passenger door to get out. "What will your mom and dad think?" She grabbed Lydia's smelly coat and pulled it toward her, but Lydia yanked it out of Alice's hands.

"Stop it," said Lydia. She briskly put the coat on and stood defiantly wearing it. "You forget they're the real Dutch? They can handle shit."

The conversation had not really ended, and Alice had not really talked about what she wanted to talk about. She wanted to talk more about their moms' friendship and if maybe Lydia's mother was as crazy as Alice's. Birds of a feather and all. And Nickson. She wanted to tell Lydia that she was in love with Nickson and afraid that she'd drive him away if she moved too fast. She wanted Lydia's advice about how to charm him without scaring him.

As she drove home, Alice thought about Lydia and her family. In spite of their occasional spats, Lydia had always seemed like a refuge from their fellow students whom Alice could not respect, and she had seemed like a refuge from Alice's family. She had not exactly been a refuge of peace. Maybe sometimes church could be that, maybe sometimes Aldah, maybe sometimes Miss Den Harmsel's class, but Lydia had been a real soul mate. She had been a safe place for the Seeker in Alice to find friendly company. But now it felt as if Lydia might be outside comfortable boundaries for even the Seeker in Alice.

23

The bad hogyard smell followed Alice back to the Krayenbraak farm where it had begun. It was less strong than it had been in the morning, like a fading headache—almost gone but not quite, a lingering dull throb of hog manure.

After parking the 150, her first stop was the basement. She opened the washing machine where she had thrown her dirty clothes the night before. She reached up and felt the hot water pipe, then walked over to the hot water heater and threw the switch. She waited until she heard the water bubbling in the quick-recovery unit and turned off the switch before her father would have a chance to notice that she had defiantly sucked up one more dollar's worth of energy. She threw her school clothes in with the work clothes that had already been washed once in cold water. She put them all on one more super-cycle with two cups of laundry soap. She'd dry them with a triple application of scented fabric softener.

"'What these clothes need is some good fabric softener,' Nancy said Bouncily."

That gave her a chuckle, even though Lydia was not around to enjoy that Nancy Swifty. Then she turned grimly back to the work that she had to do. She felt as if she was sprinkling perfume on a murky green sea from the rotting pit of hell itself. "Purify!" she commanded and pointed her finger at the dryer. And then she laughed at herself. "I am one piece of work."

While she waited in the basement, she decided to see if her mother had added any survival food to her supplies. Two more heavy boxes had been added. Inside were quart-sized cans of pork-and-beans, and twenty more cans of Spam. Alice considered taking a can of Spam upstairs to see what life after the end of the world would be like.

But she still needed deeper cleansing than she needed food of any kind and decided to use whatever hot water might be left to take a good bath.

She added a heavy dose of bubble bath to the water that was fast becoming lukewarm. Would this do it? She wanted to be sure. She took a full bottle of hydrogen peroxide and emptied it into the bathtub. If her father could use it for a mouthwash, it had to be safe for the rest of a person's body. She crawled into the tub that was hissing with bubbles and could feel the hydrogen peroxide solution sizzling the filth from the pores of her skin.

"Will all great Neptune's ocean?" she said—but couldn't think of a Nancy Swifty to complete it.

She soaked in the cleansing solution and, as the cleansing bubbles bubbled around her, she sang in a way that Handel himself would have appreciated: "And it shall pur-i-fy-aye-aye-aye-aye-aye-aye-aye-aye."

When she got out of the tub, she sniffed her armpits and hands. She sniffed her shoulders. So far as she could tell, she was scentless. What a glorious condition for the human body! A sweet neutrality of air. Odorlessness! What a fine word! Her Dutch ancestors were right about one thing: cleanliness really was next to godliness! To remove the stench of the body was to set the spirit free! She started drying herself but remembered what her social studies teacher said: "Every solution creates a new problem." The new problem was her hair. The hydrogen peroxide had taken issue with her hair's natural color. She was normally a darkish blond, with her pubic hair quite a bit darker. Now her pubic hair was the color of the cigarette stain on her great uncle's fingers. And her head—what color was this? Her normally long blond hair had turned a color not found in nature—at least not found in nature until now.

No one ever thought or said Alice Marie Krayenbraak was stupid. Until now. And she was first in line. "Alice Marie Krayenbraak, how could you have been so stupid!"

She did not understand the force that drove her to do what she did next, but she invited Aldah to go with her to feed the steers. It felt like an attraction to peace, an urge not unlike the urge she sometimes felt on Sunday mornings when she walked into church in search of Something or Someone soothing and forgiving. Her sister's company as sedative against the trials of the world?

"I don't think it would be a good idea for Aldah to go out there with all those moving gears," said her mother.

"Aldah is becoming a woman, remember?" Alice argued. "She needs to learn how to keep herself safe in the world."

"What have you done with your hair!" Aldah looked too, but did not show her mother's shock.

"It doesn't stink anymore," said Alice.

"Another one of your brainy solutions? Well, live with it."

Alice held out her hand to Aldah. "Come," she said.

"You'd better take better care of her than you take care of yourself," said her mother. "If anything happens, you're responsible."

"Agreed," said Alice and led Aldah toward the cattle feedlot. As they walked, Aldah stared at Alice's hair. She reached toward it.

"You may touch it when we get to the silo," said Alice. And she did let Aldah touch her hair. Alice sat down on a hay bale so that Aldah could come close, look close, and touch the transformed straw stack on Alice's head. Aldah touched it gently at first, then put both hands into it and ran her fingers through it as if she were looking for the secret of the transformation.

"You like it?" asked Alice, raising her eyebrows to indicate to Aldah that she was looking for approval rather than judgment.

"Yes," said Aldah. "Nice hair," she said. "Pritty hair."

"Thank you, my special person," said Alice and pulled her sister sweetly to her chest.

"Aldah?" said Aldah, pointing at Alice's hair. "Aldah?" she said again, still pointing.

"You want hair like this?"

"Yes. Aldah hair."

"You have your own hair. But you may touch my hair whenever you want to, all right?"

"All right," said Aldah and touched Alice's hair.

When Alice put her own hand to her hair, she thought it felt like steel wool. She wondered if it would get brittle and break off in tiny shreds. "My hair is funny," said Alice. "Don't you think my hair looks funny?"

Aldah touched it again. "Yes," she said. "Funny hair," and giggled.

When they came in from chores, her father stared at her hair but didn't say anything. Alice assumed that her mother had warned him, not to excuse Alice for what she had done, but to make a case for how foolish her behavior could be. She knew her mother: she would secretly celebrate the little hair debacle by talking about it behind her back.

"Nothing serious," said her father.

He wasn't talking about her hair. He was still talking about Aldah, and Aldah knew it: she put her hand over her stomach and groaned a little. Aldah was performing for her parents' attention.

"Drink this," said her mother.

Aldah took a few sips, then looked up at Alice and smiled the smile she knew would get sympathy—or was it simply a conspiratorial smile of understanding?

"I drink more water," said Aldah. She took another small sip.

"So I heard. Good for you."

"I can read," she said.

"Of course you can, my special person."

"Let me sit on your lap."

Alice pulled her big body up. Aldah stroked Alice's hair without comment. This was as normal as their house would ever get. Alice sniffed the air around her and liked what she didn't smell.

After supper Alice told her parents that she needed to work on debate. Both her mother and father looked limp and exhausted, so her timing was good. Her mother was sagging again. Her father looked as if he was sagging with her. Alice left the three of them with the TV set holding them in numb communion.

But by the time she tried to get online, Aldah must have deserted her parents and had the phone line tied up with her usual talk with Roger. Alice waited fifteen minutes before going down to ask her to please finish her conversation.

When her mother heard the gentle request, she stomped into the room.

"What's the problem?" she demanded.

"I need to use my computer," said Alice. "I have a lot of work to do."

"It's time for you to stay away from that computer," she said. "You are spending too much time with that thing. It will ruin your brain."

"You don't even know how to use a computer," said Alice.

"And you can be sure I never will. You need to stay away from that thing. Get used to getting along without it. Get used to getting along without a lot of things."

Alice was actually hoping to see something more in her mother than the usual simpleminded naysayer. After all, she'd already had her put-down fun of the day around the little issue of her oats-straw hair! Was this a woman whom Lydia's mom could regard as intelligent? It made her worry about Lydia's mom, that well-read librarian!

"Computers hardly take any electricity," said Alice. "I can show you the data."

"Data. Don't tell me about data. Half the scientists in the world are worried that computers won't work when the clock strikes twelve, you know when."

"We talked about that in school, Mother. They've worked through that problem. It's not going to happen."

"Maybe not at a literal level," she said. "Maybe not at a literal level."

"Whatever that's supposed to mean."

"There are bigger issues around computers, what they do to your brain. Computers can distort your sense of space and time. They're a pathway to a life of unrealities."

Her mother talking about unrealities? That was a joke.

"They're a shortcut to reality. A paradise of knowledge at our fingertips."

"A false prophet's idea of paradise."

Aldah heard their exchange and hung up the phone. She looked at Alice, not at her mother, to see if everything was all right.

"All done," said Aldah and walked quietly into the living room and sat with her father in front of the TV. Her mother joined them. Alice looked at them, all three of them taken in by a rerun of a *Hogan's Heroes*. Now there's an unreality for you, Alice thought, and set off for her bedroom to deal with the reality of Miss Den Harmsel's assignment.

Someone had been spending time at Alice's computer—papers on her desk moved, the mouse in a different place, and the user's manual with a paperclip marking a page. Whoever had been up here had put things away neatly—but not exactly as she had left them. She booted up and checked the history of sites visited. Agriculture sites. Her father had been upstairs at the computer. Alice didn't know what he was looking for, but she knew he was up to something.

Later when she tried to sleep she lay awake and watched the minutes change on her clock. Then the hour changed. It was 1:00 a.m. She got out of bed, looked at her long naked self with its new color highlights in the mirror, and got dressed. If her father was doing his own research on-line without telling her, there must have been something that he wasn't talking about. The most likely place to discover anything was in his basement office.

Alice was Spider-Woman making her way downstairs. She stretched her arms to put equal pressure on both banisters. She put her stockinged feet down slowly on the spot that was least likely to squeak on the outer edge of each step. She whispered her way down to her father's office.

The overhead fluorescent lighting in her father's office did not reveal one speck of dust on the oak schoolhouse desk and sturdy chair, not one speck of dust on the two black metal filing cabinets or the one lonely metal folding chair. Even here, her father was Spartan and tidy.

Beneath this sheen, she would look for the truth, no matter how messy that truth might be. If her father was doing research, he was doing research to protect the family from something.

The top drawer of one filing cabinet had folders dating back to the early nineties. Alice picked out a 1992 folder labeled "Dairy." She was ten when they went out of the dairy business. The twenty Holstein cows whose milk had been what her father called their "social security"—a steady though modest income they could count on through long periods of no income while the cattle and hogs were fattened for market.

Her father's calculations told the story. The "costs" and "income" columns showed that they lost $5,600 by milking twenty cows back in 1992—and that didn't figure in any labor costs.

Looking at these columns was like watching her childhood walk up the chute onto that large semi when those beautiful Holsteins were loaded. Her father had said that the big milk-processing companies no longer would drive out to their farm, that their milking operation was just too small and that the big company only served much larger dairies. As a ten-year-old she had believed her father, but now she saw a bigger reason—and probably the real one—why they had gone out of the dairy business. It was no longer their social security, it was a money-sucking leech.

She imagined her father's hands as she neatly put back one folder and opened another. She opened the "Hog" folder. She was a doctor studying x-rays of someone with a progressive disease. Her father had calculated that it cost him 37½ cents a pound to fatten a hog to a 250-pound market weight. He had written ninety-five dollars as the total cost of fattening a hog. When the market prices dropped to eight cents a pound in December of 1998, he was losing seventy-five dollars for every market hog he sold.

The prices had led to the shotgun blasts on Ben Van Doods's farm. Her father didn't shoot his hogs. He took his losses—and he hadn't sold the farm. He had fattened two thousand hogs in 1998. The calculations were clear. They were bold. They were shocking. While President Clinton had been diddling in the Oval Office, her father had quietly suffered the loss of $150,000 for his labor and money. He had worked with his usual diligence even though he must have seen all too clearly that the dark night was coming.

The news was not much better in the cattle folder. The columns of costs and returns for the steers had the final outcome of a $42,000 loss.

Another envelope was labeled "Medical." Medical bills for Aldah totaled $203,000. Why hadn't the government paid for problems like Aldah's? Alice knew it was possible that her father might have avoided "handouts" on principle. It appeared that insurance had paid for some but not all of her medical expenses over the years. Her father was paying off the medical bills to a collection agency at the rate of $400 a month.

Sweat was forming under Alice's arms and breasts. She pushed her hair back and wiped her forehead. This house, this farm—everything she always counted on as a given—everything was teetering on the edge. Maybe her mother was not so crazy in stockpiling survival food.

This still wasn't the end of the story. Alice found mortgage papers on the Krayenbraak land, and her mother was a cosigner on the mortgage agreement. She had given Alice the impression that they at least owned

the land clear and free. She had said "not to worry." Her mother probably thought that worrying made no sense because not even worrying
could save them.

Alice had assumed that even through the bad years they were still
rich the way big landowners were rich. They owned 320 acres of land,
and with land prices at $2,500 to $3,000 an acre, they were worth practically one million dollars in land value alone. The loan was for $460,000
with annual payments of $34,000. And there was another loan applica-
tion ready to go: this one for another $100,000 with annual payments of
$15,000. This must have been her father's response to the hailstorm. At
this point, Alice was surprised that a bank would even give them another
loan. They were mortgaged to the hilt!

There was even more. In the top drawer of his desk she found his
calculations on what it would have cost to take out hail insurance. Seven
dollars an acre for $200 per acre coverage on corn. With their 220
acres of corn, hail insurance would have cost over $1,500. "Reasonable
expectation," he noted: "160 bu/acre @ 220 acre=35M bu @ $4.00
bu=$140,000." The two hundred dollars per acre protection would only
have guaranteed forty-four thousand dollars, which would still have left
him ninety-six thousand dollars short of "reasonable expectation." To
him, hail insurance must have looked like a bad investment.

Putting it all together, Alice saw what her father was doing. He was
preparing for the end, not the way her mother was preparing for The
End: her father was preparing for the end of the Krayenbraak farming
operation. They were going broke—if they weren't broke already. His
generous payment to Alice last summer of five thousand dollars in wages
plus another three thousand dollars for the computer and printer made
even less sense. It looked like a death wish now. Then Alice discovered
something even more astonishing. In an envelope on his desk, she saw
the familiar windmill logo of their bank, Holland Savings and Loan of
Dutch Center. Here she found the accounting of his and her munici-
pal bond fund account—with some major surprises. The account was
no longer joint registered in both of their names—it had only her name
on it. And the accumulated amount was not the five thousand dollars or
so she expected to be there. The total amount was thirty-two thousand
dollars. He had attached the paperwork showing that he had paid the

Social Security taxes on this money, which he had recorded as wages. This must have been his way of protecting what was labeled as her money from creditors. He was trying to buy Alice a future at his own—or the farm's—expense. He was protecting her from what he must have feared would be the collapse of their farm.

A moment of truth: Her father's wise farming practices had not protected them. His faith had not protected them. The long Krayenbraak tradition had not protected them. With or without God, her father was no Superman. But through all of his cold calculating, he was thinking of her. She didn't feel like a spoiled daughter. She felt like a spoiled son. She was David, her parents' first child—David, "the beloved," who died of rubella when he was three days old.

It had been last May—May, 1999—in one of those rare moments when her mother did speak openly to her. She let the conversation drift toward the past. It was a day when Alice's father was in an especially crusty mood. "He's still angry that God took David from us," she said, "and I think he blames it on me."

She might have been right, even though Aldah was a much greater and current emotional drain. "That was nearly twenty years ago, Mother," Alice had reminded her.

"It doesn't matter," she answered. "People think you can't love a baby who is only three days old. We loved that baby so much. We still do. It was just as sad as if he had lived to be a grown-up and then was taken from us. We prayed so hard for God to spare that baby."

They no doubt had prayed hard. Alice had done her own share of praying without results.

"It's sad. I know it's sad," Alice had said. "I wish I had an older brother, but it happened. It happened twenty years ago. It wasn't anybody's fault. It just happened."

"Sometimes you can be so cold."

Alice hadn't answered. She didn't know what she might have said, but she wondered if there would ever be a time when her mother opened up to her again.

Her father had responded to the divine insult of having his son snatched away by working harder to make the farming operation succeed. His expanded feeding operations became his new baby. When she,

Alice Marie Krayenbraak, was born three years later, having a girl was probably not their first choice. Her mother said they were happy that this way they wouldn't be comparing her to what they imagined David might have become. Maybe that wasn't a lie. But how many farmers with hundreds of animals to care for and 320 acres of land to till wouldn't rather have a baby boy than a baby girl? Alice grew into a tall skinny kid—Leggsy in grade school, Leggo in junior high, and, of course, "ass and a beanpole" in high school. But no one—including her father—had ever said she couldn't pull her own weight. And then some.

Now Alice was looking at a big nest egg that would help her through college, especially since she would almost certainly be offered scholarships. But had she failed her father? Would a son have been able to help save them from the disaster that was so clearly upon them?

Alice felt she had just eaten from a tree of bitter knowledge. When she turned to go quietly back to her room, her father was standing in his office door.

"What are you doing in my office?"

"Sorry," she said.

"Sorry?" There was a sharp edge to his voice. "Sorry? Your mother is right about you. You are deceptive."

"I'm sorry," she said again.

"I've tried to protect you," he said. "Just go to bed and live with what you know."

"I can do that," said Alice and walked quietly out of his office and up to her bedroom. When she tried to pray, she found she could not. She tried to get into a prayerful state of mind; but instead of feeling the merciful hand of God reaching down to her, she felt rigid and cold and her mind closed so tightly that no clear thoughts could either enter or leave it.

PART III

November, 1999

24

Whatever physical features Lydia had that were more attractive than Alice's, Lydia's complexion was not one of them. Alice's smooth skin could not be matched by anyone, including Lydia, who had, in fact, had major problems with acne in their junior year. When Alice isolated her own face in the bathroom mirror—the darker-than-blond eyelashes over the bluest of blue eyes and the perfectly sloped cheeks over prominent cheekbones like her mother's—she knew that it was her face more than her lean body that deserved admiration, whether from males or females. Lydia might have been teasing in her flattery of Alice as a potential model, but Alice knew it was her beautiful and unblemished face that was the crowning jewel of her body.

Until that morning.

Out of nowhere, red domes of pimples had burst through the polished smoothness of her cheeks, not so much like weeds on a newly plowed field, more like pocket-gopher mounds disrupting an unblemished expanse of alfalfa. When she gently rubbed the corrugated terrain of her newly sullied face, her fingers were like the tires of the 150 on the bumpy washboards of a gravel road.

Acne! she thought. Acne! Why me?

For the first time in her life she covered her cheeks and lips with makeup before going to school.

"You look fabulous!" said Lydia as they stood next to each other in front of the ladies' room mirrors.

"Thank you," said Alice, but she wasn't sure whether Lydia had told her that because she meant it or whether she was trying to help Alice feel good about herself.

Perceptive Lydia must have read Alice's suspicion. "You do look fabulous," she said, "but I know what you're fighting. I had the same problem last year, remember?"

"I do," said Alice and felt relieved that Lydia was opening the door to the kind of honesty Alice craved from her. "But you look fine now. You look great, even without makeup."

"Thanks," said Lydia, "but the real thanks goes to this kick-ass medication I took. I've got over a month's worth left. I'll give it to you if you'd like."

"I'd like," said Alice. "In the meantime, I hope I don't look too gross with all this makeup."

"Let people's reactions be the judge of that!" said Lydia. "I suspect you'll do just fine."

Of course, Alice thought, she was thinking of Nickson's possible reaction.

Miss Den Harmsel was especially congenial when Alice saw her in the break after chapel. Was everybody going to be friendly to her so that she would not be embarrassed by her complexion? Miss Den Harmsel had a way of giving dignity to every moment, no matter how informal, but Alice wondered if she suspected anything between her and Nickson while they were supposedly working on debate in her classroom, especially now that she had all this makeup on her face. Maybe not. Miss Den Harmsel was such a guileless person herself that she probably couldn't fathom anyone having motives other than the ones they gave.

"You're doing wonderfully well in my class," she said.

"Thank you," said Alice. Getting As was one thing, but having Miss Den Harmsel actually say she was doing well was rare and even better.

"When my sister and I go for a drive on weekends, it pleases me to imagine you in that big old Krayenbraak farmhouse reading Shakespeare," said Miss Den Harmsel.

"You drive past our farm?"

The idea of Miss Den Harmsel having any interest in anyone or anything except what Alice saw of her in the classroom seemed very strange. A misplacement or something—like seeing Rev. Prunesma at a cattle auction.

"Oh yes," she said. "Hilda drives and I just stare out the windows, relaxing. I understand your mother was an exceptional student too. Do you read Shakespeare together?"

"My mother is too busy taking care of my sister Aldah," said Alice. "Aldah needs special care, you know."

"Yes, of course," said Miss Den Harmsel. Hilda was Miss Den Harmsel's older sister, a nurse at the hospital. They were both single and lived together. Alice had always thought of these two—whom many people dared to refer to as "the old-maid sisters"—as one of the community's great gifts, as a selfless unit of service.

Hearing of a link between Lydia's mother and her own mother was bad enough, but the very idea that Miss Den Harmsel could have a good impression of her mother was surprising. It was downright shocking! At least Miss Den Harmsel was going on hearsay and didn't actually know her mother. Alice quietly congratulated herself for stopping the conversation short with that little lie about her mother caring for Aldah. Miss Den Harmsel was everything that her mother wasn't: rational, a good listener, concerned about others, and capable of praise! She did not like having them both in the same brain space.

When she met Nickson for debate, he looked at her sweetly but gave no hint in his expression that he was noticing either her makeup or her acne. To keep her focus on debate, Alice tried not to look at Nickson's eyebrows—and she didn't—but she couldn't close off the smell of him, not aftershave or some disgusting deodorant, just a pleasant human smell, like the smell of a meadow on a warm day. Before she took her sandwich out of the to-go bag, she folded her hands to say grace. When she opened her eyes, he was staring at her face. If he was reading her lips, he would know that she had used the rote words that her father often used: "Forgive us our many sins and keep us from sinning."

As she opened her eyes to the sight of the beautiful man across from her, a small tremor moved through her chest, not unlike the tremor that would come if she forgot to lock a gate or turn off a water hydrant. It was just there: a startling disturbance beneath the calm surface, the shame of the farm's collapse. Right now, that possibility was a little secret, just barely hidden from the world, but it was evidently there, always, and at any moment could threaten to erupt and say, "Remember me?"

For ten minutes Alice and Nickson quietly highlighted important information in what they were reading—yellow for negative and red for affirmative. They did focus on their work, but often they would make the same suggestion at the same time. They were so much in sync that it registered as a pleasant pain for Alice. This was the kind of painful distraction she invited her mind to make. They'd stare at each other, though neither would say with their voices what thoughts lay behind the eyes. They started to smile at each other, and then checked themselves. They were breathing like two metronomes set at the same speed.

When he reached for an article, their hands brushed and his energy scurried up her arm like a centipede.

"We've really been getting a lot done," she said.

He laid his hand on her palm.

"That's because I love you."

"Don't," she said before she could understand what he had said and long before she could understand how her body and mind were reacting to words she so rarely had heard in her life, not even from her grand-parents who, if they did say anything like that, she didn't remember it. She never heard those words from her parents, though she used them with Aldah, so she must have heard them somewhere, but from her parents? If her parents ever did say those words, they would have been used as a weapon to get her to do or not do something and she had re-pressed the memory long ago. Behind the absence of those words, she knew there was history, more than family history—a long tradition of *zeg maar niks*—better to be silent than cheapen what were nearly sacred words by using them over something as preposterous as having a crush on somebody who was of a different tradition, from a different race, and who was eight inches shorter than she was.

She stared at him. "I love you too," she said.

Her eyes looked down. Her eyes looked out the window. Her eyes looked up at the clock. "I feel cold," she said. "Is it cold in here?"

"It's chilly," he said.

"We'd better go."

He nodded, and his eyes said nothing. "Okay."

She sat on her hands as he gathered strewn articles from the table. His eyebrows fluttered when he glanced at her, but she didn't move. She stood up, and he walked around the table toward her. If he was uncomfortable, he was hiding his discomfort behind that easy shuffle with the shoulders giving a small twist with each step. When he stopped in front of her, she didn't reach out for him, but she didn't move either. She stood towering over him, his eyes level with her breasts, and he did not turn his eyes from them. The idea of kissing him just then seemed painful. It seemed ludicrous. She would be a large mother bird bending her neck to feed her young.

"That word," she said. "Love." But she couldn't think of anything more to say.

He looked up at her eyes and grinned his small gentle grin.

"I didn't know I was going to say that," he said. She saw how beautiful his face was, his complexion smoother than hers had ever been, his dark eyes more intense—and probably sincere—than her own. And those lips, those gorgeous full lips.

"I didn't either," said Alice.

"I think I meant it. Is that all right?"

His unease told Alice that he wasn't afraid that he didn't really mean it. His discomfort told Alice that he knew he did mean it.

"I think I meant it too," she said. They both stood silent, as if stunned by the implications of their mutual declaration. Finally, Alice said, "Love isn't a bad thing."

"I know it," he said.

Alice's mind tried to find a rational framework to process the meaning of what they had said to each other. It needed to fit inside a notion of herself as living normally, not as someone who was losing her bearings and skidding in directions over which she no longer had control.

"It doesn't really have to change anything, does it?" she said.

"I don't think so," he said.

"We can still be friends too," she said.

"Even better friends," he said.

"We could meet for debate again," she said before she knew she was going to say it. "Is that all right? I mean after school? Like tonight?" but after she said those words they didn't sound innocent as they played back in her mind.

"I wish we could," he said.

Alice felt a wave of relief fighting with a wave of disappointment. "You can't?"

"No. I have to be with my family tonight. Big family thing," he said. "Lots of folks. I have to help get ready."

"Is November first a Hmong holiday?"

"Not sure," said Nickson, "but lots of folks are coming because my mom is sick."

"Oh no!" said Alice. "Something serious?"

"She's depressed. Really depressed." He stared at Alice for a moment. "You've got to keep this secret."

"I don't think you can keep a big family gathering secret in Dutch Center," said Alice.

"No. You've got to keep the secret that she's not really sick. Just depressed. I don't think we could have gotten a shaman to come down here just because our mom was feeling depressed. So we lied. Mai and I did. We told our family that she's had a bad fever and has been vomiting. We lied quite a bit, but it got the gang together. They're all coming down. A big deal. A clan thing."

"A clan thing?"

"Yeah, a clan thing. We're going to do an old-fashioned healing ritual for my mom."

Alice did not want to show her ignorance by asking for an explanation.

"I won't talk about it," said Alice.

"Thanks."

After school, Lydia caught Alice exiting the front door. She had the magic medication that would supposedly make Alice's excessive makeup unnecessary.

"Here," she said, and held out a baggie of pills. "I went home at noon to get them. Start taking them immediately and give them a few weeks to do their work. That's how long they took for me."

She handed Alice the baggie, which Alice took quickly and put in her pocket. This must look like a drug deal, she thought. Even worse, she was accepting *charity* from her wealthy friend. What next? Lydia was going through her purse, and Alice soon learned *what next.*

"These would look better on you than they do on me," said Lydia, and handed Alice another baggie, this one filled with facial creams and lipsticks.

"You deserve to look like your glamorous self, even through this pimply time," she said. "Use these to get you through the next few weeks."

Yet one more gift from her friend. Alice didn't like to have others see Lydia giving her handouts, but she quickly took this baggie too and slipped it under her arm.

Beggars can't be choosers, she thought to herself as she drove away.

25

It was as if the love Alice felt for Nickson had invited God's love to come into her heart, and praying came easily for her that night. A pure and purifying heavenly love moved through her, a wave of joy that carried with it beautiful images—and among them was the image of Miss Den Harmsel. Alice could see her face and hear her voice, and Alice realized how much joy Miss Den Harmsel had given to her and to her life. Not only in the classroom but in the memories she carried from the classroom, and even into the haymow where she kept the books that Miss Den Harmsel had recommended for summer reading.

The advanced placement lit class was the third class Alice had taken with her—one her sophomore year, one last year, and now the most challenging of all. It wasn't just her tall and stately presence in the classroom that came to Alice's mind but the elegant and unpretentious steady beauty of her mind: her devotion to something bigger and less concrete than any petty bodily needs. When she thought of Miss Den Harmsel, she thought of her desire for knowing the world, the way she aspired toward a paradise of knowledge.

Even when sitting in the classroom with Nickson working on debate, Miss Den Harmsel's presence was always there. A glance at her handwriting on the chalkboard. The model of the Globe Theatre. Miss Den Harmsel was what God was showing Alice of the unsoiled in the world. Her love of knowledge was a broad umbrella of love, and as Alice found her prayer flowing through her mind, it was a prayer of thanksgiving for God's love and a request for knowledge to understand the world and to know what was right.

She credited the prayer when she woke up the next morning with a warm sense of peacefulness: the efficacy of prayer. But when she got to school the big Vang gathering of the night before had the grapevine sizzling. Town kids were talking about how the Vang house had been surrounded by cars with Minnesota license plates.

"It looked like a used Honda and Toyota car lot," one of them said.

There wouldn't have been much of a fuss—even the most reserved people in Dutch Center had a high tolerance for noisy family reunions—if it hadn't been for the pig. The laughing and loud talking didn't bother the neighbors. Even the gong and drumming and rattling that people said sounded like a first grader's hand rattle hadn't troubled them enough to sound any alarms. It was only when they had heard a gurgling pig squeal coming from the back entrance of the Vang house that they called the police.

No one was arrested. Fortunately for the Vangs, two of the regulars on the Dutch Center police force had grown up on farms, so the puddle of pig blood on the back steps did not alarm them. The police were also accustomed to calls that might involve charges of animal cruelty. They warned the Vangs that it was not legal to slaughter an animal within the city limits without a special permit, and that if they did get a permit for the next celebration, they would have to use a stungun to knock the pig out before cutting its throat. They could borrow or rent a stungun from one of the area slaughterhouses.

The police had less trouble with the event than Alice's mother did. She chose the kitchen as her usual place to strike.

"Just like in the Old Testament," she said, "these people were sacrificing animals to a pagan god." The dull, heavy chisel of her voice. Alice couldn't tell if she was in a drugged state or menacingly alert.

This might have been a good time to side with her mother. Siding with her would have helped create a safety zone between her and the Vangs. It would have helped her keep a lid on a relationship that was getting increasingly sticky: with so many little complications at every turn, some part of her knew that she was, as her mother might say, "courting disaster." The peace of last night's prayer could not be a prelude to a shouting match with her mother.

Alice's head and heart spun in many directions at once. If she joined her mother in her sentiments against the Vangs, it would be so much easier for her heart to begin the great release that might be necessary. She could love Nickson the way she loved Lydia, as a friend. Wasn't friend-ship love the least dangerous and most lasting of all? Equilibrium is what she needed. She needed a heart whose desires were balanced, not one that moved blindly in only one direction.

But her mother was being so unfair in her attack. "What you say is simply not true!" Alice said. "It's their tradition—like us and our pig roasts."

"We don't cut pig throats on the steps of our back porch."

There was a slicing quickness to her mother's responses that triggered in Alice a quick change into debate mode: "It's not as if they have a barn where they could to it."

"You should be able to see trouble brewing. I see it." Her mother walked across the room. Her walk was confident, her movements sharp. "Waves of disastrous implications are surrounding you. You'd have to be blind not to see trouble brewing."

"You always see something brewing. You didn't see anything brewing when they started coming to our church."

"That's before they started making a party out of killing a pig. That's godless, heathen behavior." She put her hands on her hips and faced Alice. "Nobody heard any hymn singing coming from that house."

"Maybe God's a good interpreter," said Alice.

"Don't get smart with me," she said and gave Alice her cold stare. She pulled out the big guns of the Scripture: "'No one comes to the Father except through Me,'" she said with a ministerial finality.

"Right," said Alice. "But the 'me' in that text is not *you*." She lifted a finger to her mother on the *you*. "Judge not that ye be not judged."

"Oh, you're so clever, clever, clever, aren't you?" she said. "Even the Devil can quote Scriptures."

"You ought to know."

Alice saw her mother's eyes pick an aiming spot on her face. Her mother wanted to slap her, but she had seen Alice often enough on the volleyball and basketball courts. Her mother would know that the long arms hanging at Alice's sides had springs in them. She would know that Alice wouldn't hit her back, but she also would know that Alice could catch any slap she threw.

Alice could feel bile burning in her throat. It no longer made sense to worry about skidding with her affection for Nickson when the real evil of her life—the dark hopelessness—was not coming from Nickson and his family but from her mother. Nobody could make her think bad thoughts and speak harsh words the way her mother could.

Through the resentment came the awful thought that her mother might be right. Did Lydia's mother see wisdom as well as intelligence in her mother? And what had Miss Den Harmsel heard about her mother? Alice already knew part of her mother's educational background: she had graduated from college, all right, and become a grade school teacher before she met Alice's father. The cold voice that Alice heard from her mother was hardly the voice of a kind grade school teacher. Still, that didn't mean she was wrong about the foolishness of Alice's relationship with Nickson. Of course, just because her mother was cruel didn't mean she was wrong. Trouble *was* brewing but it had not yet reached the boiling point, and continuing with Nickson in anything but a safe friendship would lead to the disaster her mother warned about.

Do I have a choice? Alice asked herself. Yes, she thought, yes, and her answer to herself was like another prayer, and this one said, "Yes, with God's help."

Thinking of Miss Den Harmsel again led her to seek refuge in Shakespeare. She took out her copy of *Hamlet*.

She came upon Hamlet's soliloquy that began with "To be or not to be—that is the question."

The famous quotation struck her as one of the stupidest questions she had ever read in literature. To be or not to be? What an indecisive loser. What had Miss Den Harmsel said about melancholia? Hamlet didn't need her mother's Valium; he needed a perker-upper!

Then she came across a quotation that was as good as anything she might have found in the Bible. "Refrain to-night, and that shall lend a kind of easiness to the next abstinence: the next more easy."

That sounded like something Miss Den Harmsel might quote. Why couldn't her mother put it like that? She didn't need her mother to make her keep her relationship with Nickson in safe territory. She had restrained herself with him for over a week. The rest would be easy.

Alice intended her next conversation with Lydia to be about Shakespeare first, and then she'd use talk of Shakespeare to make a transition to Nickson. She would ask Lydia if she had any advice about how to keep a friendship with a guy in safe territory, even if Lydia didn't know how to do that herself. Unfortunately, Lydia was less interested in talking about Shakespeare—or Nickson, for that matter. She wanted to talk politics!

When she started ranting about how terrible things would get if George Bush became the next president, Alice interrupted her. "You sound like my mother! All my mother can do is talk about how bad things are going to get, but she thinks it's the millennium. She thinks the world is going to end!"

"It will end if George Bush and his buddies buy the presidency!" Lydia bellowed.

"You're sounding as crazy as my mother in your talk about how bad things are going to get," said Alice. "My mother thinks our computers will rot our brains if they don't make airplanes crash and clocks stop. You two are fellow doomsayers!"

Lydia straightened her back and turned to Alice in what one could only call her snippy way: "Bad things *are* going to happen," she said. "Your mother is not entirely wrong about that. Some of it will have everything to do with the millennium. I read that some crazy cult people will commit suicide the way they did with the last millennium. And the government's a lot more worried than they let on. National Guard troops are going to be ready in case major power outages actually happen."

"My mother is hoarding cans of Spam, Lydia!" Alice yelled at her. "It's nuts!"

"Stockpiling food is not such a bad idea either," said Lydia. "Especially if George Bush becomes our next president."

"Have you gone bonkers?" Alice stared at her. Was this her dear friend in whom she confided and in whom she would like to confide a lot more in talking about Nickson? "I don't think things will be much different whether Bush or Gore or Elizabeth Dole or Steve Forbes or Bill Bradley or anyone else is president."

"Yes, they will," said Lydia. "Yes, they will."

"Have you turned into one of these conspiracy-theory nuts?" said Alice, still staring in disbelief at her dear friend who looked as if she was possessed by some strange power that was making her mad. She was practically hyperventilating.

Lydia read Alice's dumbfounded expression. "Sorry," she said. "Sometimes I get carried away."

"Me too," said Alice, "but not about George Bush."

When Alice and Lydia parted, the fear that Alice had was that Lydia's vision of the future put her in the same camp as her mother.

26

The next afternoon Alice's father called a family meeting without Aldah present. Something bad was coming down. It started with her mother criticizing Alice for not spending more time with Aldah. That set Alice off: "Aldah is the one who doesn't have time for *me*," she said. "She's always on the phone with her boyfriend."

"We put a stop to that," said her mother. "We're going to be putting a stop to a lot of things. Albert, tell her."

Her father pursed his lips and nodded his head.

"Things are bad," he said. "We're going to have to do something different. You didn't tell her anything about this, Agnes?"

"She doesn't listen to me, why should I tell her anything?"

"Because we're going to have to work together as a family. No sense beating around the bush. Things are bad."

"They'll get worse," said her mother.

"Your mother and I had to find jobs."

The surprise that wasn't a surprise. Her parents going off to work, leaving the whole farm stranded, uninhabited, halfway toward total abandonment? Even though Alice had fantasized about this scenario, she wasn't ready for it.

"Dad, don't do it. If you and Mom go off to work, everybody will know how bad things are. Let me give the summer money back." She kept control of herself. She wouldn't let her mother know about the thirty-two thousand dollars.

"That money is not on the table," he said. "Your mother and I will bring in some money."

"And Aldah will have to go to Children's Care now," her mother said.

Another surprise that shouldn't have been a surprise!

"And Aldah in Children's Care? Now? You're dumping everything! You're just dumping it—Aldah, the farm, me! You're just dumping everything!"

"The world is narrowing," said her mother. "Things are closing in. We have only one path to follow."

"An empty house is a pretty dumb path," said Alice. "And a deserted farm doesn't earn money."

"Your mother has been offered a job at the Bylersma Chicken Farm. There are 180,000 chickens in that operation."

"Chicken farm?" said Alice. "Chicken farm?"

"I grew up with chickens," said her mother. "I know chickens. There are so many things you don't know about me."

"So you're going to walk around all day with a bag of chicken feed saying, 'Here, chicky chicky chicky'?"

"Stop it," said her father. "Your mother will be overseeing the grading of eggs."

"And you?" said Alice. "What are you going to do while Mother stands around with her grade book? By the way," she said, turning to her mother, "What's a passing grade for an egg, C-?"

The face of her mother: large blank eyes beneath her high forehead, eyes that refused to say what the mind might be thinking. Inscrutable eyes.

"Stop it," said her father. "I am going to work for the Vander Myer Dairy. Three hundred cows milked three times a day. We'll be on the same schedule—thirty hours a week."

Her mother continued her blank stare, though she was barely able to control her distorted grin. This had to be one of her parents' conspiracies: they'd worked things out together and now were laying it all out on Alice, one puzzling piece at a time.

"We'll be working nights," he said. "We're giving you a lot of responsibility because we respect you for how responsible you can be about work. And we were sure you would understand why this is absolutely necessary for the family right now."

Alice held her tongue while her father laid out the plan. They'd go to bed shortly after Alice got home from school and get up at midnight to work until six in the morning. Her father would be around to help her with the morning chores, though she'd have to do all the chores alone in the afternoons when she got home from school. She'd have from five in the afternoon until eleven thirty to have supper and study while they were sleeping.

"Our work will be supervisory," said her father. "It shouldn't take too much out of us. We're lucky to get these jobs."

All of Alice's suspicions about what they were up to were coming true. He had just recited a whole life-changing program. Alice let it sink in before asking for clarification. Was he really saying that they would sleep the whole while she was home after school, only to get up just before midnight and not be home again until early the next morning? Did he really say that? And did he really say Aldah would be leaving the house, going to live in one of those—those homes? Did he really say all that?

He really had said all that. When Alice shuffled the information in her head a few times, it still didn't make sense.

"I thought those were all Mexicans working at the dairy and chicken factories," she said.

"They are. That's why our roles will be supervisory."

"Um, shouldn't you both be able to speak, like, Spanish if you're going to supervise Mexicans?"

"Not necessary," he said. "The important thing is that we're able to speak English to the owner to tell him what is going on, who is doing their work, and what needs improving. He has people who can translate to the Mexicans what needs doing that isn't being done."

"Louis Vander Myer actually owns that big dairy?" asked Alice. Only a few years ago he had looked like your ordinary farmer scraping by.

"His father and uncle in California have had big dairies out there for years. They're just expanding the family operation out here."

"So Louis is more like a manager than owner?"

Her father saw where Alice was going with her analysis. He didn't want to admit it: he was going to work for a corporation, even if it was a family corporation. A family corporation with California money.

Alice had fooled herself into believing that she could outsmart any situation. She was a problem solver who could look at the information, figure it out, and come to some workable solution. Not this time. She understood the expression, "Things were getting desperate."

"I really don't get it," she said. "What about things here? We can't just stop feeding the hogs and cattle!"

"Of course not," said her father, and his voice had gotten louder. "I'll do some of the chores before you get home from school, and I'll be home before seven in the morning to help you finish morning chores."

"To help *me*? To help *me*? Don't we have something turned around here? I thought it was I helping *you*."

"See what I mean about her?" said her mother. "Listen to the way she talks: always me, me, me! That's all she can talk about! Me, me, me! Me, me, me!"

Where was a good hailstorm when they needed one? Maybe some lightning or a flood. At least they had their own little earthquake going: their chairs were moving even though no one had gotten up.

Like an apparition, Aldah appeared in the kitchen doorway. She was wearing her bathrobe with the little white sheep against a blue background. It was a soft flannel and fit her loosely. She had everyone's attention.

"Aldah took bath by myself," she said.

"Very good, my special person," said Alice.

Her hair was moppy over her ears. She had slipped into her soft bunny slippers and put on her new thick glasses. The living room behind her was shadowed, and she really did look like a guardian angel, eyes glowing, coming to rescue them all from themselves. When she looked at them, all Alice saw were those big magnified eyes.

"Where's David?" said Aldah.

Did Aldah know what she was doing? It's not as if she and Alice had never talked about the brother she never had, and when Alice talked about David, Aldah had seemed to understand that he had died as a little baby. When Alice talked about David, she tried to make Aldah feel that she had something that most people didn't have, like a secret that was to be treasured. "David" was one of the words that Aldah could read. Maybe she had seen David in her mind and went looking for him to see him again. Alice thought this was possible—one of God's gifts to those whom he had shortchanged.

"David is not here," said her father.

"Now you get ready for bed," said her mother. "Alice, you take her to her room."

Alice was in no mood to take orders from her mother, but she preferred leaving the room to staying there, so she took Aldah to her room and tucked her in. When Alice walked back through the kitchen on the way to the stairs and her own room, her father said, "We're not finished."

Alice rejoined them.

"Because we'll be going to bed right after you get home from school, you'll always have to be here by four o'clock. I'll show you what needs to be done with the hogs, but this does mean you'll have to cut out all extracurricular activities."

"I'm in choir and debate. Sometimes I'll have to stay after. Not often but sometimes."

"No extracurricular activities. This is family survival we're talking."

"Drop them both," said her mother.

"She's right," said her father. "Drop them both."

Her parents were emptying everything. They were taking it all. What exactly did they think she'd have left? Alice didn't understand the emotion that filled her as her father dropped the last bombshell, but it was not a feeling of defeat. It wasn't anger either. If this feeling had a voice, it would be a war cry. A powerful voice in her chest that screamed for justice.

Her parents were depriving Alice of everything that mattered. Did they really understand what they were doing? Did they even care? Did they have one inkling of how cruel they were being? No! And they were trying to act as if they were the ones who were making a sacrifice. They didn't care about anything that was important to her. They wanted to use her as a free grunt. Less than minimum wage. They were turning their daughter into a slave!

Given what was happening in her family, holding back on her relationship with Nickson made no sense. What was there to fear? She had absolutely nothing to lose. The whole situation was totally unfair. What her parents were doing was the most unjust thing that had ever happened to her in her entire life. If they were going to slam one door shut, she'd open another one. She would open every door that she could open and invite Nickson inside. She would pursue him. She would seek out his company every second she could. Oh, she'd study. She'd be a star student. She'd study hard and jerk the valedictorian honor right out from under Lydia's nose. Scholarship offers would come at her from everywhere like a platter of goodies. But she would have Nickson too. She'd sneak away to be with him at night. She would love him. She did love him. She would give all her love to him. She would give him everything she had. She would go for it!

In her bedroom, she took a second look at Hamlet's soliloquy. "To be or not to be." He still sounded like a loser. God gave people minds to make decisions, not to avoid them. She would take back the life that her parents were so recklessly determined to steal from her.

27

The next morning Alice's resolutions were still clear, but her complexion was not. She would follow Lydia's instructions to take these orange capsules with their clear mark of where to break them in half. They were sixty milligrams of something-or-other and she was to split them in half and take one half in the morning and another half at night. With lots of water "or they'll burn your throat."

Taking these things made her feel as much like a druggy as her mother, but she took them—aggressively because more crimson pimples had sprung full bloom onto the field of her once smooth and flawless skin. Is it my diet? she wondered. Is it nerves? She thought of how President Clinton's impeachment fanatics talked about how "the truth always comes to the surface sooner or later." No, she would not believe that her deceptions were a dark cloud that had unleashed this storm of acne on her face. She slathered her face in makeup.

When she got to school, she was looking for Nickson but found Lydia.

"I think Hamlet is a jerk," said Lydia.

That was a relief. At least Lydia was thinking about Shakespeare instead of George Bush.

"I know," said Alice. "I thought the same thing."

"I mean, why couldn't that guy get a life already? Sometimes I felt like kicking his butt."

"Exactly," said Alice.

"Especially when he is talking to Ophelia. You know what I think? I think Hamlet is gay and doesn't know how to come out."

"I hadn't thought of that," said Alice.

"You know what I think?"

"Not really."

"I think what Hamlet needs is a couple of weeks working with you on the farm. Get a little pig crap on his hands."

"Thanks a lot," said Alice. "Maybe a couple of weeks fixing lawn mowers might help him."

"Hey!" said Lydia. "Let's not go at each other."

"You started it."

"Okay, I'll stop it," said Lydia.

Alice noticed that they were both wearing tight sweaters. Alice knew she was wearing hers for Nickson but had no idea why Lydia would be showing her goods at Midwest when lover boy was off somewhere getting his hands greasy.

Lydia was a 36-28-34. Alice was a 34-28-37—but the 37 was her legs, not her hips. If she got 28X36 jeans, her ankles poked out into the wide-open spaces. Lydia had great hips and boys stared at her butt when she walked in front of them. Alice wasn't sure what the boys saw when they walked behind her. Something tall and lean with buns and arms of steel. Some guys, like the creeps she had met briefly at church, would start to hit on her until they realized she was smarter than they were. One of the beautiful things about Nickson was that he was attracted to her mind as much as he was attracted to her body, though she wasn't sure what Nickson actually thought of her body: given how short he was, he really had no choice but to stare at her breasts.

"What's with the sexy sweater?" asked Alice. "Your lover boy isn't at Midwest."

"I dumped him."

Good riddance, Alice thought, but said, "Oh no, I'm so sorry."

"Don't be," said Lydia.

"So who's the sweater for?" said Alice.

"For me," said Lydia. "I want to feel good about myself."

"No new prospects?"

"I've been dating another guy. He goes to Redemption."

"You quit taking the pill?"

"You kidding?" said Lydia.

"You wearing the sweater for him?"

"And any other cool guy who takes an interest," she said. "There has to be at least one guy at Midwest who has the mind of an Einstein and the looks of Tom Cruise."

"I like the Einstein part," said Alice.

An excited sad feeling. A delicious but painful realization. Crosscurrents of envy and resentment. Lydia seemed so free, but she was talking like a slut.

Alice still wasn't sure what Lydia suspected about Nickson and her. There actually hadn't been much to suspect, but right now she wished she had at least a little bit of Lydia's experience with which to fight back.

"You look great in that sweater," said Lydia, "and my makeup looks better on you than it did on me."

"Thanks," said Alice. "I'm not trying to look alluring; I'm just trying not to look disgusting. Now I've really got to run."

"Debate?"

"Yeah," said Alice. "We're just getting to the real meat."

Even after that exchange, Lydia was ready with a Nancy Swifty: "'More matter, with less art,' Nancy said matter-of-factly."

But Alice was ready too, and she had practiced this one: "'Brevity is the soul of wit,' Nancy said in as few words as were humanly possible in order to make what she had to say really, really funny."

"Oh, come on," said Lydia. "You practiced that one. You didn't just think that one up on the spot."

"So what? I'll bet you practiced yours too."

"Did not."

"Did so."

"Did not."

In Miss Den Harmsel's office Alice didn't waste time with Nickson. She told him about the big changes at her house. She told him what would be her new home schedule.

"That's big," he said. "That will change your life. That's really, really big."

"My parents will be asleep from about four-thirty in the afternoon until eleven-thirty at night when they'll get up to go to work," she said. Nickson watched and listened. He seemed puzzled, but maybe he was finding what she was saying more exciting than troubling.

"I could leave the farm before six and be back home any time before eleven-thirty and they'd never know I'd been gone," she said.

At this point, it was clear that Nickson understood where she was going with this. His shoulders tightened in a way that was unusual for him.

"You're thinking that we could get together while your parents are sleeping? And you wouldn't even tell them?"

"It would be easy," she said. "I could drive over, maybe pick you up and go for a ride. They'd never have to know."

"But my mom would know. She wouldn't like it if we went off together alone."

"Can't you get out of the house, just tell her something? I could park a little ways away so she wouldn't see you get in the car."

Nickson rarely looked uncomfortable with anything that Alice said, but he did now. "I don't want to get caught lying to my mom," he said. "Mai is always going off on dates and telling Mom that she's going to the library; my mom doesn't trust me the way she trusts Mai."

Some part of Alice knew she was doing something bad, not only in deceiving her own parents, but even worse in getting Nickson to deceive his mother. She sensed there was some kind of slippery slope here, but if sliding down this slippery slope meant more private time with Nickson, it was worth it. The expression "Sometimes a person does what a person has to do" played through her mind.

"So tell your mom you're going off to the library. Wouldn't she believe that?"

"Maybe. I'll have to practice. She always seems to know when I'm lying. I'm glad she's not a cop."

"Don't you want to see me?"

"See you? Oh yes, I really want to see you. A lot."

"Nickson, this is our chance."

"I know," he said. "I know."

Silence felt like the appropriate pressure to put on him. She sat silently. She sat silently and waited.

After a minute of stillness, Nickson slowly nodded his head. "Maybe I could do it," he said. "I'll watch the way Mai does it. I could tell Mom I'm going off to the Redemption library to work on debate. I wouldn't even mention you."

"Now we're talking," said Alice. Alice looked at him. His eyebrows danced.

Tomorrow would be the great house emptying at the Kayenbraak farm, with Aldah going off to Children's Care and her parents starting their midnight shifts. Alice would fill the vacuum with Nickson. She would wait one night, giving her parents a chance to learn how to fall asleep so early. Then, on the second night, she would pick Nickson up at six while her parents were asleep.

The more she thought about it, the more it felt like it was all quite fair and balanced: her parents doing what they decided to do and she deciding what she deserved in exchange. Being deprived of Aldah's presence in the house was the final justification.

Aldah's face showed no sadness the next morning as she got ready to leave for Children's Care. She helped Alice fold her jeans and roll her socks, and she counted the number of shirts up to five, as if she knew how many days there would be between washings. The way Aldah cooperated in packing her suitcases told Alice how much her sister did not need to be institutionalized, but it was happening, and there was no stopping it now.

Alice tried to give support to Aldah by imitating her excitement. For Aldah, going to the new school was like going on a picnic. She hummed "Old Macdonald" as they packed her little mirror and her special crayons. Aldah didn't realize how this was anything *but* a picnic; she didn't know how permanent this would be and that she'd be staying overnight night after night after night. She didn't know this would mean separation from her parents, from her house, from Alice.

Alice's own emotions were so overfed with everything that was suddenly happening in her life that she couldn't sort one feeling from another. Sadness and joy volleyed in her heart and mind. Watching Aldah get into the Taurus registered a moment of terror: her sister really was being institutionalized. Then a moment of chest-tightening guilt: she, Alice, had failed. Not her mother, not her father—Alice! She was the one who had pretended to be the authority. She taught Aldah to speak clearly and never loudly. She taught her to keep her lips together when she wasn't eating or talking. She taught her to read many words that she could now recognize without hints or prompting. Anyone who knew anything about what happened at their house knew Alice was the one who had been *educating* Aldah. She was the only real teacher, the only effective teacher, Aldah had ever had. But she, Alice, had failed to keep her out of an institution.

According to Alice's mother, the family should not make a big fuss about the departure. They were supposed to celebrate it for Aldah's sake and not show too much sadness in her leaving. Alice didn't know whether that was professional advice that had been given to her mother or something she had made up, but Alice did control her emotions as she watched Aldah being driven off with her suitcases in the back of the car. An innocent lamb was being led to the slaughter. Aldah couldn't fight back against injustice the way Alice could, but maybe her innocence would save her. That glimmer of hope: all might be well. Alice waved to her as she sat smiling in her big-buttoned pink dress, her hair held away from her face with a pink barrette, her seat belt fastened snugly across her shoulder. Alice kept smiling. Aldah, my angel, my special person, your life is beginning anew. Like mine.

When she walked into the house, she went to Aldah's deserted little bedroom. Aldah's favorite flowered blanket had been packed, along with her mirror and the purse that always lay on top of her dresser. Alice closed the door and walked over to Aldah's bed. She knelt down beside it and rubbed her hands over the sheet where Aldah would not be sleeping. She remade the bed without taking off the sheets and puffed her pillow. Aldah would not have to see what she did next as she leaned over the pillow and tried to breathe in the last scent her sister's head might have left on the pillow. When she stood up, her eyes blurred and then the tears flowed freely onto her sister's empty bed.

28

That evening Alice's parents started their midnight jobs. It was as if the Krayenbraaks had their first big garage sale, and the first items to go were the people.

When she got home from school at three thirty, her parents were starting the new work routine by getting ready for bed. Her mother was in one of her up moods—whether through medication or the challenge of circumstances, Alice didn't care.

"I have the oven set to go on at five. It will be ready by five-thirty." Alice opened the oven and saw a tuna hotdish. Tuna and mushroom soup?

"Try not to wake us," said her father.

"I won't."

Doing chores that first evening, Alice found that her father had over-prepared for this transition: feeder wagons full of hog feed were parked in the alleyway of the corncrib, the tractor had been filled with gas, he had mown the grass and weeds around the entire farmyard, and he had put boxes of lightbulbs on little shelves inside the buildings. She had already gone through the routine of checking the hoglots and hog feeders, but her father still left her notes about proper levels in the feeders and about nutrient ratios. And one final note: "If that runt in pen 3 dies, just drag her to the north side of the hog units out of the sun." She spotted the runt. At least this one was not in the pen with the chewers. But if it died, of course, she could drag it away. There was not a job on the farm that she couldn't do—except think of a way that it could make enough money for them to survive the winter without the humiliation of having her parents working midnight shifts. The freedom from them and the weight of the family's money problems. Oh, the mixed blessing of it all. The mixed curse.

Little fears nipped at her as she did her chores. This was a dress re-
hearsal for tomorrow night when she would be seeing Nickson as soon
as she was sure that her parents were asleep. What if something happened to her while she was doing chores? What if she sprained an ankle
and wouldn't be able to drive off to see him? What if she smeared herself
with so much hog manure that she wouldn't be able to wash the stench
away? There was no wet chicken in any refugee camp that could smell as
bad as Iowa hog manure.

Tonight was practice in how to do this right. Her plan was to be sys-
tematic about this chores enterprise. She'd have an efficiency formula.
She'd make to-do lists for the first week and stick to a schedule. She'd
take note of the tasks she had to do and think of them as station stops.
She'd find the most efficient route. She could learn what it takes to fatten
a bunch of hogs for market and to do it without exhausting herself. If
only she had control of the market prices. Somebody somewhere probably did have control of the market prices, but that somebody somewhere
also probably could have given two hoots for the Krayenbraak farm.

She'd still do her job, and she'd do it well—and she wouldn't leave a
mess anywhere. Slovenliness was often an early sign of a farm that was
going under—but untidiness was the first thing old-timers in the community noticed about anything. Tidiness, the pretense of cleanliness,
she thought to herself. That she could do. As she worked, she knew she
was imitating her father. Something about him said that if he just had all
the pieces lined up, everything else would line up too. She was imitating him, as if she too believed that a neat framework could give meaning to it all. They were looking for order when the truth of the matter
was everything was falling apart. Was it his faith that order would bring
prosperity, an image of God's blessing? If this was faith, then faith was
pretense in action.

If the hailstorm had broken the back of their faltering farm, and if
it was now in its final stages before collapsing to its knees, Alice knew
it was her father who would feel like the failure. Everything he did, he
did with such deliberate certainty: he sat erect at the table, he enunciated
with exaggerated clarity when he read the Bible and offered prayers at
the table. He never spilled feed, and when he put a feed scoop away, he
always brushed it clean and hung it on the same hook. So much control.

So much determination to keep things in order. He was wound so tight that if he ever did break, he would break like a twig overburdened with ice. Her mother was so bent already in her dark vision of the future that if total failure came to rest on the Krayenbraak farm operation, she probably would go on in a slightly more bent version of what she was already. As to herself, she didn't think the collapse of the farm would ruin her place in the world, except that she probably wouldn't be able to buy any new clothes. She'd probably be ashamed that they couldn't make it as a farm family, but she'd probably feel the greatest shame at seeing that her parents had failed.

The further she progressed with the evening chores the more she let go of the thoughts of her parents and the farm. When she looked at her hands as she worked, she thought of how thoroughly she would wash them before she saw Nickson tomorrow night. She wondered what Nickson would think of her flexing muscles as she lifted hay bales, one in each hand.

The more she thought of Nickson the happier she felt. She sang hymns to the hogs: "And the trumpet, the trumpet shall sound! And the dead shall be raised incorruptible!" she shouted to their indifferent slobbering snouts.

When she got to the steers, she playfully recited lines from *Hamlet*: "Number 77," she said to the dangling ear tag of a big black, "What would you do if your 'too too solid flesh would melt, fade and resolve into a dew'? And number 154, are you sure you want to crap right there next to the feed bunk? 'Foul deeds will rise.'"

She felt giddy. She augered the useless hailstorm silage into the bunks, grabbed a handful of it, squeezed it, and brought it to her nose, then tossed it into the air and watched it drift down onto the steers' backs like huge green snowflakes. She turned to number 88 with a handful of the worthless silage and tossed it in front of his nose. "Sweets to the sweet," she said.

The steers weren't as uniform as the Big Macs that would come out of them. They were a mixture of exotics—all sorts of colors. They came from ranches in South Dakota and Wyoming, and her father bought them in little bunches at sales barns where they had been shipped. Alice liked the Limousin breed. Her father had bought several, though few showed the true golden-red colors of the purebreds. Most of these were tan, but they had the short head and wide forehead of the purebreds. Alice liked their spunk even more than their looks. "Back-kickers" her father liked to call them. They usually weren't aggressive, but they did not like sudden noises one bit. Alice felt like bringing out their wild spirits. When she had started up the augers, the Limousins twitched and lifted their heads like startled deer. When they were sure they were safe, they joined the other steers at the bunks. Alice sneaked around behind them, and as they were munching away, she reached over and gave one Limousin a quick tickle on its rump while saying, "Cootchie-cootchie-coo!"

He was a back-kicker, all right. His back heels flew level with her eyes and his brisket whacked against the feed bunk. "Humph," he said, and spit out a mouthful of dry silage. She gave three more Limousins the same tickle on the rump and got more good kicking responses. When one of them backed out of his place at the bunk after he'd kicked, she knew this game might have consequences. He turned toward her like a bull and lowered his head.

"Not so fast," she said, "no offense," and backpedaled away as he watched her. Fear had led to anger in this one, but it only intensified the thrill for Alice. "Come on, come on," she said, daring him to charge her. The Limousin looked at her warily. Alice didn't doubt for a second that she'd be able to get over the fence before he could get his thousand-pound body in gear. "Come on, come on," she teased again, but the animal stared nervously and did not move.

While the steers were eating, Alice went into the empty barn. Checking the barn to make sure there weren't any sick steers inside and that all of the doors were secure was the last step in her evening chores. But no sooner had she stepped into the barn than a wave of nostalgia came over her. This was part of her world that Nickson had never known. She not only wished she could show it to him; she wished she could show it to him the way it was when she was a little girl. Back when they still had milk cows, the barn felt like the most wonderful place on earth, the safest and most comforting refuge a girl could ever hope to have. When she was eight and playing outside in the winter, sometimes her fingers and toes got so cold that being outside wasn't fun anymore. But she didn't like going to the house to warm up because as soon as she

stepped into the porch her mother would yell, "Take your boots off! I
don't want all that snow melting on the rug!" Once Alice had her boots
off, she wouldn't want the bother of putting them back on to go outside.
As a little girl, she knew the barn was the one place where she could
warm up without having to take her boots off.

If she had known Nickson when he was a little boy, she could have
shown him the barn as she knew it as a little girl: the cows, chewing their
cud and looking out with their mild dark eyes and spreading peacefulness around them. The swallows in their nests tucked against the beams
overhead, the dark heads of the babies peering over the edge of the nest
with their little yellow beaks open.

When her father sold the milk cows, all the stanchions that covered
one half of the barn were removed. The small calf and pony pens that
broke up the other side into cozy compartments were removed too.
There were no longer any mangers. There was no alleyway. The whole
ground floor was turned into one big open area that had no character at
all, just a big space for fat steers to sleep and defecate. Who would want
to come to a place like this to get away from anything? She stared at the
open space of their barn with the steers starting to come in after feeding.
If she ever did have a chance to show Nickson the barn, she would tell
him how it once was.

She started back to the house, her stomach growling for the food that
would be waiting for her. These free hours when the chores were finished stood before her like a wall of time. Her parents were indeed asleep
when she came in to find the hotdish ready. She did her homework while
she ate, and when she finished she quietly cleaned up the kitchen. Then
she sat down at the table to face the wall of silence. The silence was like
a presence, a thing alive that was closing in. She missed the sound of
Aldah's eating and her enlarged eyes smiling through her thick glasses.
She missed the sound of her father's voice saying grace. She even missed
her mother's critical surveillance of everything that was happening. She
missed the tension of the supper table. Without the tension of knowing that any moment her mother might launch an attack or that Aldah
might tip her milk or cough after taking too large a bite—without something real around her to keep her on guard, her energy was being sucked
from her. She could feel it go, bit by bit, starting in her head and working

its way down to her feet, and out into that vacuum, swallowed by silence. This was worse than the awful silence that followed the hailstorm. When she felt her neck sagging forward, she had an image of what she looked like. She took a deep breath and sat up. She was starting to look like her mother.

This was the greatest injustice of all. This curse of silence that her parents were subjecting her to. She could have made loud noises to wake them up, but waking them was the last thing she wanted to do. She moved quietly in the kitchen. Then she went outside and started the Taurus, which was quieter than the 150. She drove it to the end of the driveway with the lights off. Then she drove it back and parked it. She went into the living room and walked toward her parents' bedroom door to see if they had stirred. They hadn't.

Out of habit she walked over to Aldah's small bedroom, opened the door and turned on the light. She could smell her sister's presence, a pleasant and subtle smell, like clean flannel. She decided to leave her door open, not to prove to herself that Aldah was really gone but to allow whatever was left of Aldah's presence to come into the kitchen and keep her company. She would read down here tonight, with Aldah's bedroom door open.

Tomorrow night would be different. Tomorrow night she would close Aldah's bedroom door before quietly slipping outside and driving off to see Nickson.

29

The plan was to pick Nickson up at six o'clock and go for a ride. No big deal. Nothing that any normal parent would object to, even if they did know about it.

Alice finished her chores in half the time it had taken her the night before. She had an apple for supper, took the meatloaf out of the oven, and put it in a plastic container in case Nickson was hungry. It was only five o'clock and already she could hear the soft duet of her parents' breathing.

Whatever the midnight work schedule was doing to them, they weren't losing sleep over it.

She didn't take any risks about waking them: she worked quietly to get ready. She brought a kettle of water to a boil, added it to cold water in the bathtub and took a slow lukewarm bubble bath. She put on some of Lydia's lip gloss and used a touch of Lydia's eyeliner. Then she gave hydrogen peroxide a second chance: she dabbed her field of blooming pimples with it. For good measure, she gave them a second soaking with rubbing alcohol, thinking that she would "suck these suckers dry" before applying makeup. When she did put on her makeup, she turned to Lydia's gift again, using a base cream that filled in the gaps on her corrugated face, before putting on a final application that gave her face some color. She brushed her teeth twice and rinsed with Listerine. She shaved her armpits, but she did a sniffing double check against odor. She put on scent-free deodorant. Her hair looked like something you'd see sticking straight out from the backside of a runaway palomino. This was not the lingering effect of the hydrogen peroxide; she planned this new look. She put the dryer to it until she saw that it didn't need fluffing, but it did need pasting. She wet it down, but it sprang back. It looked wild, and she left it that way. But what to wear? She wanted to be layered enough to stay warm if they ventured outside, but not so layered that she'd hide everything. She put on tight jeans and a cashmere sweater with a V-neckline. She'd put on a coat if she had to. When she looked in the mirror, she thought she looked like a woman who was trying to get picked up, but since she was doing the picking up she had no problem with it.

She had decided to take the Taurus because people were accustomed to seeing her in the 150. She knew why she didn't want to call attention to herself: if the Hmong, as Nickson had told her, assumed that a teenage boy and girl alone together were up to no good, the people of Dutch Center were not far behind. The old guard assumed that anybody who stepped outside the norm in one way was stepping outside the norm in many other ways. A teenager who had tattoos probably also used drugs. Male-female couples that had tattoos and rode a motorcycle were also taking drugs, drinking, having sex, and stealing. If somebody dared to step so far outside the norm that they dated someone from a different race, they were going out of bounds in ways that would be too numerous to count. That's how the old-timers of Dutch Center thought. They probably wouldn't say anything directly to her face. *Zeg maar niks*— they'd look at her, say nothing, and think the worst.

If she and Nickson could slip out of town without being noticed, they could ride through the countryside talking. They'd go outside the Dutch community, where the names on the mailboxes changed from Van-this and Van-that or De-this and De-that, out of the culture of "yah shures" into the land of "hell yeses" and "damn rights," where the mailboxes had names like Brekken, Holm, and Rezmerski. Maybe they'd drive across the river into South Dakota to the forlorn town of Ludson where the abnormal was normal and no one would stare at them. They'd drive to a dirt road leading to the river, the one her father used to drive down when he took her fishing. Nickson would hold her hand and they'd stand on a bank under an oak tree and look at the water passing by. He'd tell her how happy he was that he had moved to Dutch Center and met her. She'd tell him that he was the most interesting person at Midwest. She'd tell him that he was attractive, that she thought he had a gorgeous face.

She'd tell him his lips were beautiful and he'd say that hers were too. She wouldn't tell him that his eyebrows made her go wild because she did not want him to become self-conscious.

When she started the Taurus to drive away, it made no more noise than the refrigerator starting. She kept the lights off, slipped the car into drive and eased off the yard. She arrived at the Vangs' house fifteen minutes earlier than she had said, and pulled up with her headlights pointed away from their house. Nickson was already outside and walked toward the car, casually carrying his backpack.

He got in and immediately told Alice that he had to revise his story for his mother. When he had told her that he was going to the Redemption Library, she suggested that he ride with Mai, who also said she was going there. So he had to tell his mom that Alice was picking him up to go to the Redemption Library. Now both of Lia's trusted children were off on dates instead of at the library. The Redemption Library was working overtime that night in providing alibis.

Alice's stomach knotted when she heard the story. There was no regret that this was happening, but she had a vision of being caught.

"I'll drive past the Redemption Library. Maybe some people will see us and think that's where we went. Then if your mother talks to somebody. . . ."

"Mom doesn't talk to anybody about where we are," said Nickson. "She just asks us. She trusts us."

"Are you feeling bad about doing this?"

"It would be hard if my mom figured out what I was doing," he said. "Lying to my mom is tricky. It's all right," he added. "That's my thing and you shouldn't worry about it."

Alice picked up an aroma coming from Nickson. Something musky but sweet. He put on his seat belt and turned toward her as she drove slowly away from the Vangs' house.

"Looks like you're ready to argue with that backpack of material," she said.

"Resolved," he said.

"No rebuttal," she said.

"I love your hair," he said.

"Thank you. You look great."

Alice felt herself relax as she sensed that he was relaxing too. This felt even better than she hoped it would—a plan that was working to a T.

She did drive past the Redemption Library but then out of Dutch Center on the blacktop road that led toward South Dakota. She turned on the radio and asked Nickson to find some music. He cruised the dials and stopped on soft rock when he saw her turn and smile. He was learning to read her. She liked that a lot. She would learn to read him too.

After ten miles, the Dutch names started mixing with non-Dutch names on the mailboxes. Ookstra followed by Sutter followed by Vanden Boom followed by Jenkins followed by Den Broelekamp followed by Wanek until they were out of the mixed neighborhood and all mailbox names were non-Dutch. They had crossed into the land of freedom. No one but no one would recognize them out here.

Alice pulled over at the next intersection, put the Taurus in park, and turned off the headlights. She turned toward him. He loosened his seat belt, slid over, and they kissed and kissed and kissed in the land of "hell yeses" and "damn rights."

When they saw headlights approaching in the distance, he slid back into his place and Alice drove on slowly until they came to the rickety bridge over the Sioux River. Ahead lay the forlorn little town of Ludson.

Just over the border she pulled over again, and again they kissed, even more intensely, more lavishly, than before, and reaching around him she found a spot between his shoulder blades that when she touched it his whole body arched, and she pulled him against herself, hard, to feel his chest against her breasts. Their breathing filled the Taurus with warm moist air that covered the windows with a soft mist.

When headlights of another car approached, she drove on. The sun had set and darkness pushed some stars into the sky. A crescent moon hung low to their left, and then they moved under the dull yellow streetlights of Ludson. The sad little town had one deteriorating small business after another. No malls in Ludson. She drove past the Lariat Restaurant where pickups and minivans had moseyed up to the curb, and then drove into the residential area.

Sweet and disheveled little Ludson was free of judgment, free of ostentation, free of anything familiar. If there were any churches, they were in hiding. The town catered to neither Seekers nor Dwellers. No one here looked as if they were on the treadmill of bootless desperation or stuck in the ruts of contentment. Ludson showed the peacefulness of failure. Under the dim, single-bulb streetlights innocent but tough-looking kids on old bicycles swerved from one side of the street to another, while in the houses the colors from TV sets filled the windows. The kids hardly looked like achievers with their thin faces and unkempt hair, but they did look like a new generation of freedom addicts. Maybe they were restless. Maybe they were their own kind of Seekers, swerving over people's lawns and turning roadside curbs into ramps that sent them and their bicycles briefly into the air.

"I like this place," said Nickson. "Feels like a place that doesn't care what the next person is doing."

"I like it too," said Alice. She reached toward him with her right hand, which he took in his, easily and gently, almost as if to give a soothing afterglow to their intense kissing. He rubbed the heel of her hand, then the palm and slid each of her fingers through his fingers, easily and gently, and she could feel the cares of the day easing from each finger as he slid it through his, and then the relaxed feeling spread up into her arm and farther to her shoulders and neck and back and down into her legs. He let go as she started to turn left at the next intersection and needed both hands.

She drove back past the Lariat, where a group of young men had gathered in a circle, all dressed like hard working farmhands with their seed corn caps and denim work jackets. They did not look up as the Taurus drove by, but Nickson's shoulders jolted back.

"What?"

"It's them," he said. "It's those guys."

"What guys?"

"Those guys that jumped me. All three of them. They're standing next to each other in that bunch of guys there."

"I'm getting out of here," she said, and accelerated.

"No," he said. "Drive by again. I want to make sure. Come on, they won't see us—they're busy talking."

All the tension reentered her body, but she accepted Nickson's reading of the situation. Those young men were so busy with each other that they'd have no reason to look at two people in a Taurus driving by. She did a U-turn at the next intersection and started back, but Nickson was busy in his backpack. They were almost back to the Lariat when she saw what he had been looking for—in his right hand he held a black L-shaped thing, and with his left hand he shoved a flat rectangular tube into the handle. The streetlights made the barrel glow.

"Just in case," he said before she could utter her horror. "It's okay," he said and laid the gun on the floor between his feet, the muzzle pointed away from them.

She did not slow down as they passed the Lariat. She kept her eyes straight ahead and did not say a word.

"It's them, all right. It's them. They're dealing."

She didn't have to announce that she was going to get the two of them out of there. She aimed the car out of town and did not speak until they had crossed the bridge out of South Dakota.

"Nickson," she said. "Where did you get that gun?"

"One of my uncles," he said. "When folks back in Saint Paul heard I got jumped, my uncle brought me this nine millimeter the night of the healing ceremony. He's just a year older than me and knows about these things. He taught me how to use it."

"That thing really scares me.".

"I got caught off guard once," he said. "Never again. Don't worry."

"You wouldn't use that thing. You wouldn't shoot somebody."

He sat silent, then picked up the gun, took the clip of bullets back out of the handle, and dropped the gun and clip into his backpack. "If they were trying to kill me or hurt you, I'd have to," he said.

Alice kept her speed under the speed limit. She wondered how Nickson could suddenly be so calm again. As if nothing had happened. They passed the turn-off to the dirt road that would have led them down to the river, to the place she remembered where her father took her fishing as a little girl. She had imagined standing on the riverbank with Nickson, but she let that fantasy go. "We'd better get back to Dutch Center," she said.

"Yeah," he said. "I'm real sorry about this."

They rode in silence for a few miles, both staring out the front window as the white centerline stripes flashed rhythmically by. Then Alice said, "I've got a little bit of a nicer surprise in my backpack. Reach back. It's in the main compartment."

Nickson pulled out the container of meatloaf. "You hungry?" Alice asked.

"This looks good," he said. He took out the thick slice of meatloaf and bit into it. "Wow," he said, "this *is* good. You make it?"

"My mom made it."

"This is really good. She's a great cook."

"No she isn't."

"I like it," said Nickson. "I like your mom."

"You what?" Alice lifted her foot from the acceerator.

"I do. I like her. She's a straight shooter."

"You don't even know her."

"I watch her in church. I've seen her downtown. She knows who I am. She always says hi, and sometimes we chat for a couple minutes. She's kind of uptight, but she really seems to want to hear what I have to say."

"My mother?"

"Sure. You tell me everything she says to you, and I can see that she might talk to you like that. A person knows where they stand with your mother. She doesn't sugarcoat anything. I like that."

No, not again, Alice thought. Was a distorted version of her mother seeping out into the universe like a vicious virus, infecting people's minds?

"I can't believe what you're saying."

"There's a lot of her in you—the way you cut through things and see the way things really are. You look a little bit like her too."

"People say I look like my father. I still can't believe what you're saying."

"You look like both of them. You have your father's strong chin and his stretchy walk. You have your mother's beauty, that long back, that slim waist and those sharp hips."

"You've been looking at my mother's ass?" Alice did more than slow down more; she pulled off the road. She turned in her seat and stared at him.

"No! Not like that," he said. "I just notice those things about your mother that remind me of you."

Alice did not put the car back in gear. She kept looking at him. "What about those blank eyes? Do I have her blank eyes?"

"I don't see that. I don't see blankness. I see the eyes of somebody who's kind of puzzled by things and trying to figure them out."

"She's puzzled, all right. She's downright bewildered. She's certifiably nuts is what she is. I can't believe she snowed you like this."

Alice put the car back in gear and pulled onto the road.

After a mile of riding in silence, Nickson said, "I love you, Alice, and that means your family is in the picture. Your mom is who she is. Mine too."

Alice looked at the speedometer. She was going only thirty miles an hour.

"Could you find some music?" she asked.

She drove without talking to the sound of soft rock. She was with a man who thought her mother was a straight shooter. Strange choice of words for somebody who carried a weapon that could kill people. This would have been the time to tell him that she never wanted to see him again, but that was not what she felt. She felt the opposite. She wanted to protect him from a world that would make him carry a gun. She wanted to be his shield against everything that was unfair. And if he could find a place in his heart to accept her mother, he had to be the most generous-spirited person in the world. She wanted to give herself to him, although her silence as she drove did not tell him that.

She dropped Nickson off at nine thirty. She turned the lights off to give him one last good-night kiss.

"I'm sorry," he said.

"I want to see you again," she said. "Soon. And I'm sorry I smeared so much makeup on you. I was trying to hide my pimples."

"I know," he said, "but you don't have to hide anything from me."

When he walked toward the house, she turned the headlights back on, only to see Mai in the kitchen window with her big friendly smile giving her a friendly wave. Alice waved back and drove off.

30

Alice fed the hogs and cattle and read her Shakespeare and generally showed the world that she was someone who was bravely carrying on, even with her parents going off to work at night and her sister Aldah becoming a resident at Children's Care. What others couldn't see was that Alice was caught in the swirl of it all, driven by a force that didn't let her mind pause and evaluate. Nothing made sense and yet everything was clear: she would do everything necessary to see Nickson.

Her life became a series of calculations. Doing her homework quickly cleared the path to see Nickson. Doing her chores efficiently cleared the path. She fell asleep thinking of him and got up thinking of him. She couldn't look at anything without thinking of what he might say about it. She couldn't speak to anyone without wondering what Nickson would think if he heard her voice. She couldn't listen to anyone without thinking of his voice in its place.

Except those times when the unwelcome voice of her mother came out of nowhere and replayed itself in her mind: "I see trouble brewing." Alice hated that voice and would repress it quickly by turning to the tasks that stood between her and seeing Nickson. If Nickson heard her mother's voice, he might feel different about her too. But if Nickson actually liked her mother, Alice fantasized the possibility that Nickson's acceptance of her might mean that he could reason with her if and when that became necessary. One good thing Alice could say about her mother: she tended to accept, or at least tolerate, people who showed her respect, and Nickson apparently had done that.

Lydia was guessing that Alice's relationship with Nickson was progressing nicely, which indeed it was. She would ask indirect questions, like "Did you know that Nickson is taking advanced calc and is at the top of his class?" and "Nickson looks more and more at home at Midwest all the time, don't you think?"

Alice usually changed the subject. For some reason, her relationship with Nickson was not something that she wanted to discuss with Lydia. Not yet, anyhow. She was afraid that Lydia would start asking the tough questions, like "Do you really think this thing with Nickson can go anywhere?"

Alice kept her focus on efficient planning so that she could get together with Nickson almost every night. She saved money by skipping school lunches and eating her supper leftovers. She alternated between using the Taurus and the 150 and used her lunch money for gas—one or two dollars at a time so no one would notice a suspicious change on the gas gauges.

The farmland around Dutch Center became the setting for their private hours. They had the radio and the starlit sky, they had the concealing curtains of abandoned barns and corncribs, and they had the sight, smell, and warm touch of each other.

They started taking items of clothing off and exploring each other's flesh. Each night brought a cautious advancement of intimacy, and one night's restraint led to the excitement of the next. She held his hardness in her hand. He kissed her breasts. They knew where this was leading and never talked about stopping it. It felt right. It was meant to be. He said when they found the right time and place, he would bring condoms so she would not have to worry about that. Instead of frightening her, his preparations deepened her trust. She could not feel guilt for what was happening. She did not pray for God's blessing on what they were doing, but she felt Nickson's and her love for each had something to do with God's love for everyone.

Lydia's magic medication was showing no signs of improving Alice's face, but Nickson told her that she didn't have to worry about the acne. She didn't even have to put on makeup if she didn't want to.

"There isn't a blemish in the world that could hide your beauty," he said. "And everything about you is beautiful, not just your lovely face."

On an evening when she wore no makeup and on which she felt totally free to be her natural self, she and Nickson made love for the first time. It was in an alfalfa field, behind a grove, under the stars, and it did not feel like a big change from what they had been doing for several nights of exploring each other's naked bodies. The final step was a natural step, not just to join their bodies but to join their bodies with the cool green plants of the earth against them. To make love while being connected to the earth itself. Earth and sky around them and the cool breeze on their flesh, his easy caution with a condom, the ease and then the intense pleasure of coming together. Everything was in harmony. It was Paradise before the Fall. They took turns positioning themselves, first one getting to stare into the star-filled heavens and then the other. Sometimes she felt they were doing things to and for each other that no other lovers had ever thought of.

One night as she drove him home, he cruised the radio stations and stopped on the classic western radio station. They listened to "Heaven's Just a Sin Away." When the chorus came around the second time, they sang it together.

"Do you like country western?" he asked.

"Not until now," she said.

"I really like country western," he said, "but I can't play it when Mai is around. She thinks it's corny."

Alice had always thought of herself as a planner, but she never planned for this adventure of love. She had not planned on meeting the most incredible human being on the face of the earth during her senior year in high school. Now that the unplanned had happened, she was determined to make plans inside this new unplanned world. It was like a game with its own rules and problems. One of her favorite challenges was determining when and where. She was constantly watching for new and private places. New love nests. Low-maintenance dirt roads were good, but too often other young lovers would be there too, and she'd have to drive elsewhere. She liked fields that were hidden behind groves on abandoned farms, ones that had little private dirt farm roads leading up to them and that she could drive down with the lights turned off. They did not return to Ludson, though she never asked Nickson after that if he had his gun with him, but since he always had his backpack, she assumed he did. He said he would never carry it loaded, and she would make sure he would never be tempted to use it. She now knew that he loaded the gun by slipping the clip of bullets into the handle grip. He said there was one more step before he could fire the gun. She didn't ask what that was. She trusted him.

One night of lovemaking, Nickson introduced another new element into her life. He had a little tube the size of a cigarette. She thought it *was* a cigarette.

"What's that?"

"A little one-hitter," he said. "Want to try it?" He had a small green bag of what looked like alfalfa leaves. "This is very mellow," he said.

"Is that marijuana?"

"This is marijuana," he said. "You don't have to try it, but do you mind if I do?"

"Marijuana is not addictive," she said with an authority that she had not earned.

"Of course not," he said.

"Sure, I'll try a little," she said, "but I don't know how to inhale."

They both took only one puff from his one-hitter. She inhaled only a little bit and didn't think she felt anything. She just felt like talking, and then like touching his face, first with her fingers, and then her lips, and then she wanted to make love—but she had wanted that before the marijuana.

After that, the one-hitter was a regular partner. On a night when Alice took the 150, they decided to use the cargo bed. All they had was an old blanket, but they still had the moon and stars above, and she parked in a spot where the only smells were of mulching leaves and drying cornstalks.

Alice lay naked on her back in the cargo bed, staring up into the dark and glittering universe. Nickson's warm lips and hands roamed warmly across her body, touching gently, kissing as he explored. His face stopped between her opened legs, kissing her, but then his lips stopped and he inhaled her intimate scents. Am I clean? she wondered but did not tense up. He lifted his face in the starlight. "If there is a heaven," he said, "every flower will smell like that."

The suspension system of the 150 adjusted quietly to their presence. The hard-ridged cargo bed felt cushioned. The springs of the 150 did not squeak.

Another time they went out into a cow pasture, found a place where the cows had not defecated, and spread out a blanket on the short grass. Some cows gathered around them curiously but offered only sighs of

mild approval. When it rained, she took the Taurus and pulled off into
a private place and they stayed in the car, put the front seats back against
the backseats and adjusted to the various humps and slopes.

Nickson was always very careful with his protection. One night they
used four condoms, and she started worrying about the expense.

"I should be helping pay for those," she said.

"No way," he said.

"Where do you buy them?"

"I don't buy them," he said. "Mai buys them for me."

"What? So she knows what we are doing and how often we're doing it?"

"I guess," he said.

"Doesn't she ask any questions?"

"Of course not," he said, "she's my sister."

Alice decided that other people should not be an issue, but the
November nights were getting colder, and outdoor loving could soon
be a problem. Although the barn had changed in ways she did not
like, the haymow was still intact the way it was in the old days when
they still had cows. Taking Nickson to the haymow would com-
bine her childhood love of the barn with her new and larger love of
Nickson. With her parents sleeping soundly, there was no reason why
they couldn't drive back to the farm. She could park the car and they
could quietly walk to the barn. They could move around the steers
and climb up into the haymow that held all the sweet memories of
her childhood.

Sometimes Alice did wonder what it would be like to make love in a
bed with box springs and a soft, level mattress. Would the soft convenience
of everything make the pleasure greater? She couldn't imagine how or why.
It was true that having a door you could close and curtains you could pull
down would give privacy, but she would miss the sight of the moon and
stars and the fresh air on their skin. She would miss the smell of alfalfa or
grass. She would miss the sounds of night birds and the smell of animals.
Did the people who made love in beds with closed doors even know what
they were missing? She wondered if Lydia had ever known this kind of
pleasure with a man. She wondered but hesitated to talk to her about it.
She was afraid that Lydia would make sex seem like something that was
much less magnificent than it really was.

31

Of all the buildings on the Krayenbraak farm, the big gambrel-roofed red barn was still Alice's favorite, in spite of all the changes it had gone through. It was over a hundred years old, but it did not have the tired swayback look of some aging barns in the neighborhood, the ones with flaking skin and creaking joints. The Krayenbraak barn had kept its luster over the years. Its windows were free from cataracts of caked dust, and the rooster weather vane on top of the metal cupola still spun like a ballerina in the wind.

To Alice, the old barn had more character than their house—and it had more pleasant memories. When she was ten, she had thought of it as her private refuge. When she was troubled, she would leave the confusing energy of the house and go to the barn to see the animals, and often to talk to them. She would think of all the animals that must have been born here: not just the calves but all of the birds—pigeons, sparrows, swallows—some of them appearing without warning after migrating hundreds of miles and choosing to build their nests here. What guided them? she wondered. What strange forces of nature sent out a welcoming signal in the sky, saying, "Here here here, this is the place for you to find your home?" At ten, Alice thought that the new birds arrived and stayed because they knew she was waiting for them, but, at ten, she also thought that the swaying trees caused the wind. That magical year—and even now the barn felt like a guardian of that old magic.

Some things were terribly different now that the ground floor had been turned into one large open space for the feeder cattle, but the haymow had not changed. It still held its old magic for her, and she still found it to be a place of peace. No other place on the farm gave so much space and privacy at the same time, with open space rising up thirty feet and the walls separated by forty feet—and yet the silence, the safety, the privacy. In the haymow she could sit and listen to the hushed whispering of the wind and the choir of pigeons and sparrows. Sometimes she thought the cupola was like a steeple with its spinning weather vane pointing to heaven.

The haymow offered food for her spirit and hay for the animals. Almost all the hay that was stored in the haymow was fed to the animals every year—but never all of it. The haymow was like a big cauldron that would have more added to it before the original ingredients were gone, so it was never totally empty. Some of the hay dust could have been from the days of her grandfather and great-grandfather, when Dutch would have been the only human language spoken here in the presence of the varied songs of sparrows and pigeons and starlings and swallows—and the rare and beautiful barn owls.

Her ancestors must have loved this haymow as much as she did. Some of them would have made love here. It was impossible that they would not have. The smells of the alfalfa hay were sweet and musky. Alfalfa that was matted when wet and then dried out had this rich and lusty smell. She imagined that in the good years her parents might have made love in the haymow. In the years before Aldah. In the years before they both lost their dreams to expense columns and balance sheets. And her great-grandfather—the one who thought a radio show called *Father Knows Best* was a blasphemy because only the Heavenly Father knew best—him with his handlebar moustache and hawk eyes, he must have had his way with his lady in this haymow. Alice could forgive her ancestors for their hardnosed Calvinism when she imagined them making love here. She could love them for loving here.

There were hay bales now instead of the old loose hay, but the haymow still had the lush smells and the privacy. If there was anything else on earth that she would want to share with Nickson, it was this space— and immediately her mind started working on how she might make that possible. It was such a grand desire that she could hardly believe how simple it would be to make the wish come true. She would simply pick him up as usual and come back to the farm and to this very haymow while her parents slept. If she picked Nickson up at their usual time, they could be together in the haymow for at least an hour and she'd still have the 150 back home before nine, giving it plenty of time to cool down before her father drove it to work.

When she told Nickson of her desire to take him back to the farm and to the haymow, he looked worried, but when she told him how simple and safe it would be, he agreed. When she drove up that night, Nickson came out of the Vang house without his backpack. There would be no gun. This was the perfect beginning to a beautiful evening. She turned off the headlights as she came onto the farmyard and let the 150 swoop slowly toward the barn. She went in first and coaxed the cattle outside. Then she took Nickson's hand and led him to the ladder up into the haymow and to the spot where she had hidden a blanket under a bale of hay. She scattered loose alfalfa over a raised platform of bales on a spot where the moonlight came through a haymow window and gave them a rectangle of light. She put the blanket over the loose hay and patted their mattress.

Nickson stood and stared. He looked up at the barn rope that hung just below the rail that once conveyed huge fist-shaped sling loads of hay through the large haymow door. He stared up at the opening into the metal cupola with its terraced bands of moonlight.

"This is something," he said simply. "This is really something."

"Yes."

He stared at the window frame of light on the raised column of hay bales.

"It looks like a throne," he said.

"We don't have to hurry," she said. He followed her up onto the bales. On their knees and holding each other's faces in their hands, they kissed gently, then lay down on the blanket and undressed each other.

"I've never been in a place like this before," he said.

She ran her hand through the forest of his hair and put her lips to the paradise of his moonlit flesh. Alice was lost in the history they were adding to this haymow because she did not hear what was most immediate—not the sounds of steers walking below them, not the sounds of the wind rattling the windows, but the sounds of someone on the ladder.

"I thought so."

The sound could have been nothing. It could have been an auditory phantom, but it was a real human voice cutting through their lovemaking breaths. They startled, stopped, listened, and then looked quickly in the direction of the voice, and there it was: the pop-up silhouette of her mother's head and shoulders, the black cutout like something propped up at the entrance to a Halloween party. The tragic thrust of it. Its comic silliness.

Only her head and shoulders were showing, but she saw everything. And as quickly as it had appeared, it was gone.

"Conscience does make cowards of us all," Shakespeare wrote. When Alice saw her mother's head and shoulders, her conscience did not make her feel like a coward.

"Get out of here!" she yelled.

Nickson rolled over quickly, as if he thought she was talking to him.

Nickson and Alice were Adam and Eve grabbing the fig leaves of their clothing, but the face and shoulders were gone faster than the serpent into its hole. A jack-in-the-box performance.

Scrambling cattle sounds from below, the slamming of the barn door, like a shotgun blast—and then silence.

The empty space that surrounded them was larger than Alice could ever have remembered it.

"Oh my God oh my God oh my God."

A moment of pounding silence, both frozen in place as if fearing that the phantom would reappear.

"That was really her, wasn't it?"

"Yes, that was really her."

Again they froze in silence.

Nickson brushed alfalfa leaves from his knee. "Is she gone?"

"Not far enough."

Nickson took a deep, resolute breath, and then he said, "That wasn't right."

More anger than fear, more excitement than horror, more defiance than despair. Alice looked at Nickson, and when she saw that he had not faded, she put her hands on his shoulders, pushed him onto his back, and lunged on him.

Afterwards, he said, "Now what should we do?"

"You're so calm," she said.

"I know it."

He laid her shirt over her shoulders. She sat trembling on their blanket with her arms clutching her knees to her chin. Nickson rubbed her head gently.

"It could have been worse," he said.

"How?"

"It could have been *my* mother."

They grabbed each other, pulled themselves hard against each other's bodies and giggled like crazy people, her tears bouncing from his shoulder like drops of uncontrollable laughter.

"Well, that's that," said Alice.

"You said that right," said Nickson.

Nickson had told Alice that a person should never feel totally trapped. Even if people think they have you cornered, don't let them believe that they do. Act as if you're not trapped. You're trapped only when you act trapped. He said when he ran from the thugs in the alley, he was just looking for a place to set the tacos before he turned around and kicked their asses. She was ready to believe him. "Just kidding," he had said. "I was running for the streetlight so they could see I wasn't what they wanted to see."

"They called you a spic."

"Yeah, I'm not a spic."

"Nobody should be called a spic," she had said.

"Right," he had said, "but I still wanted them to see who and what they thought they were going to beat up. They knew as soon as they had me down, you know, but then they couldn't stop. They had to show off to each other, and when something like that gets started it doesn't know how to stop. When I never said 'ouch' and I just kept looking them in the face while they beat on me, they knew they weren't winning. They knew if they ever tried it again they'd be dead."

Alice had reached over and pulled Nickson against her breasts. "Oh Nickson, please," she had said. "Don't talk like that." Then she had asked him, "Why were they so stupid as to go to Perfect Pizza afterwards?"

"They had to show how brave they were, you know. They didn't prove it to me, and they knew it."

The times Alice saw Nickson in tough fixes he would startle and then immediately calm down—his whole body looking comfortable and

relaxed and his breathing slow and deep. Something in him was a warrior. He was as controlled as she was when she was debating in front of
an audience.

Nickson was calm now as they dressed. Alice tried to absorb his composure, the way his hands took each item of clothing so carefully, the way
he examined it before putting it on, and then how he turned to her to see
if she needed help.

"I guess we don't have much to be afraid of after that, do we?" she
said.

"Think she'll be waiting with your dad outside? We better be ready
for that."

"No, no," said Alice. "That's not how my mother operates."

She wasn't waiting for them when they left the barn. They got into
the 150 and drove slowly off the yard with the headlights on. It was all
over. The worst had happened. It was a relief that gave Alice a feeling of
invulnerability.

After she dropped Nickson off and was driving back to the farm,
she no longer felt invulnerable. Her leg muscles tightened and she felt
chilled. This was going to be a bad scene. It wasn't her mother she was
afraid of so much as her father. She could already hear his voice. He
would say, "I can't tell you how disappointed I am in you."

Her father's disappointment—that would be the deepest cut.

But her mother wasn't waiting up for her. Nor was her father. So far
as she could tell, they were both asleep and would be until they got up
to go to work.

Alice took her half tablet of medication and went up to her room
with a practiced normalcy to her step, took one long look at herself in
the mirror to see if she was still the same person, and fell into bed, leaving her clothes a wrinkled puddle on the floor.

She lay in bed awake and heard her parents get up at eleven thirty
to go to work. They didn't call her downstairs. She knew her mother's
tactics: she'd give Alice the silent treatment until she got so upset with
herself that she'd crumble. Seeing Alice disintegrate in shame would
give her mother a sense of accomplishment. But Alice was not about to
crumble. No matter what happened, she had Nickson's love, and nothing her mother did could threaten that. She fell asleep with a renewed

feeling of calm. There was nothing to pray about. She felt no need to confess anything to anyone, not even God.

The next morning when her parents got home from their evening of work neither of them talked to Alice, and neither of them acted as if anything unusual had happened. Her mother had breakfast on the table but was not in the kitchen when Alice finished morning chores with her father. She left for school without seeing her mother again—and she wouldn't, until that evening.

32

When Alice came in from afternoon chores it was after five o'clock. Her mother should have been asleep, but she was wide awake and sitting on a chair in the kitchen, her arms folded across her chest, her feet planted on the floor. She was waiting like a patient cougar on a branch. Her eyes did not look blank but had an attack intensity. She wore a loose denim gray shirt with long sleeves and sloppy loose black slacks. She had nothing on her feet and her toes looked like knobby claws. Still, she looked tired and depleted, like someone who was worn out but still ready to take her last stand against someone—and Alice knew that someone was Alice Marie Krayenbraak.

"I haven't been sleeping," she said in a taunting voice, "and I think you know why not."

"I'm sorry to hear that."

"You've given me too much pain."

"I'm sorry to hear that."

The taunting voice became accusatory: "You're not sorry anything."

"Anything that keeps you awake makes me sorry."

"You're the sorry one."

Her mother's lips were dry, with little flakes of skin peeling back where they came together. The wrinkles in her upper lip had gotten deeper. The look on her face was one of total revulsion.

"How stupid do you think we are?"

"I never said you were stupid."

"You're stupid if you thought we wouldn't notice how somebody always rolls up the seat belt on the passenger side. Looks like somebody doesn't know what to do with his hands. Looks like somebody is pretty nervous about what he is doing. Looks like somebody has a guilty conscience. Not the driver. The passenger."

"Dad didn't say anything about rolled-up seat belts."

"Your father's worries are bigger than rolled-up seat belts."

"Why don't you just spit it out, get it over with?"

"All right." She stood up and faced Alice. "I started staying awake when I knew you were driving away after we went to bed. I've been listening to you drive off every night and come back home two or three hours later. I lie awake every night praying for you, praying that you'll change your ways before it's too late."

Alice looked up at the praying-hands painting on the wall, then at the plaque that was left over from when her grandparents lived there: "We Get Too Soon Old And Too Late Smart." She walked into the living room and sat down on the couch. It was almost six o'clock and she could hear her father's deep breathing coming from her parents' bedroom.

Her mother followed her and stood facing her. "Don't you have a conscience anymore?"

"Yes, I do."

"I am quitting my job," said her mother. "The smell is killing me, and so is your behavior. I'll be home at night from now on." She pointed her finger at Alice and said, "And so will you."

"Whatever you have to do," said Alice. Her mother was watching Alice's face.

"I was not surprised at what I saw last night," she said. "I know what kind of girl you've become. I don't want you hanging out with those people. None of them."

"It's not their fault."

"So you're that kind of girl now?"

"Whatever you need to think, Mother. Just don't blame Nickson."

"He doesn't look like us and he doesn't think like us. At least he must be squirming about what he's doing. Rolling up seat belts."

"He said you're friendly to him when he sees you downtown."

"I don't judge people until they do something that deserves judging. At least he seems to be uncomfortable about what you're doing. Or is that just a Hmong thing?"

Alice looked up at her mother. "Don't go there, Mother."

"You think I'm a bigot."

"I told you not to go there."

"I'm a realist. The surface of things says a lot about what's going on under the surface. Realists look for the deeper reality."

"Realists don't quit work when things are bad."

"The money I was making was not enough to save us. Your father is preparing to sell everything. Now are you satisfied?"

"Satisfied? I'm not the reason this farm is in trouble!"

"Things will get worse. The prophets foretold these bad days."

"What prophet, Al Gore?"

"You really have made no progress, have you?"

"I don't see that you believe in progress."

"I believe in progress, all right." She transformed into her formal mode, lifting her chin as if she were about to address a multitude. "The natural progress of actions bringing results. We all make our own beds. Do you understand that kind of progress? Progress, progression, one thing leading to another. You should progress in your seeing what your behavior will lead to, not submit to your uncontrollable, uncontrollable—"

"Stop it, Mother! You're a stuck record."

"You should get ready for things to get worse—because they will."

"'Things will get worse, things will get worse.' All right, things have gotten worse. So what's worse than worse?"

Her parents' bedroom door opened and her father stepped into the living room. He wore his long white nightgown and looked like a bedraggled ghost.

"Agnes, what are you doing out of bed?"

"I needed to tell Alice that I was quitting work," she said in a voice that was suddenly and surprisingly pleasant.

Her father appeared to have no idea of the topic of their discussion. Had Alice's mother not told her father about last night? Could she possibly be keeping her knowledge of Nickson and her from him?

"Oh," he said, and headed toward the bathroom.

Alice stood up and looked at her mother with what must have been the most quizzical look her mother had ever seen on her face. "Mother," she whispered, "didn't you tell him?"

"I was too ashamed of you to tell him. Things are tough enough for him already."

"Mother? Is this our secret?"

"It's our secret, and I have no intention of hurting him with it. But secrets have their own way of unwrapping themselves. You can smother it now before it finds its own life. Smother it. Just stop. Don't honor that young man's destructive hunger."

"Mother, don't blame Nickson."

"You and that young man are in the process of bringing shame to both of your families."

Her father returned from the bathroom and looked at them with a puzzled look on his face. "We'll be all right," he said. "I don't want either one of you worrying. Now, Agnes, I hope you come to bed soon. You look awfully tired."

"I'll be there in a minute."

In a few minutes Alice could hear her father's deep breathing as he fell back to sleep. Alice and her mother seated themselves across the living room from each other and sat in silence. The electric clock on the wall looked tired of passing the time. Steers coughed in the feedlot—that rough cough, like a smoker's cough. The hog-feeder metal lids clanked down when hogs pulled their heads back. Her mother kept staring at her, and it occurred to Alice that Valium might not be enough to keep her mother under control. She might be mentally ill and dangerous. Alice stood up and started toward the stairway to her room. Her mother didn't stop her, but Alice heard her go into the kitchen and sit down. She was guarding the front door to keep Alice from leaving the house.

Alice took her medication, went to her room, and lay in bed planning her escape. There had to be ways to continue seeing Nickson at night, even with her mother on vigilant duty like a prison guard.

The next day she told Nickson about her mother's behavior.

"She's mad and she had to blame somebody," he said. "Give her some time to cool off."

"My mother's not normal," said Alice. "She doesn't cool off. She just stews inside her sick head until the lid blows."

"We still have to respect her," said Nickson. "She's still your mother."

The barriers that her mother had set up to prevent her from ever

seeing Nickson again were no more than a harmless little whirlpool to
Nickson. The way he saw things, Alice's mother had to be who she was,
they couldn't stop that—but that didn't mean that she should stop what
they were. Alice agreed with him in her head, but her feelings were tied to
a stake while her mother turned loose the hyenas. Her mother was doing
more than turning loose the hyenas, she *was* the hyena.

"We can find a way without hurting her," said Nickson, and when he
said that Alice knew he was right. Of course, they could get around her:
even hyenas had to sleep.

Dealing with her mother and her new attack-dog vigilance was just
a game, and it was a game Alice knew she and Nickson could win. If
prisoners could break out of Alcatraz, she could find a way through the
walls her mother was trying to build around her. She brainstormed playfully in her mind: dig a tunnel out through the basement, crawl out of
the chimney, buy an "invisibility dress" on the Internet, put padding on
her feet and jump out of the upstairs window.

Her mother was now on a schedule of staying up until after the ten
o'clock news. Alice knew what she was thinking: if she stayed up that
late, Alice wouldn't have time to sneak away and see Nickson and be
back before 11:30 when her father got up to go to work. She essentially had Alice under house arrest. Alice got rational. Every would-be
escapee had to start by studying the guard, learn her habits and weak-
nesses, find her vulnerabilities.

The vulnerability in her mother's prison was a short timeslot between 10:15 when her mother went to bed and 11:30 when her father
got up for work. Her mother must have calculated that an hour and
fifteen minutes was not enough time for Alice to rendezvous with
Nickson. Alice accepted the challenge. They had a window of just over
an hour when they would have to get out of their houses and meet and
then get back to their houses. The problem to solve was how to steal
that little satchel of time and fill it with sweet loving without anyone
noticing.

Alice presented the problem to Nickson.

"I know," he said without hesitation, "I could run to your house and
we could meet in a field somewhere."

"Don't be ridiculous," said Alice. "We live seven miles from your house."

"I can run eight-minute miles forever," he said. "I could be there in less than an hour, and my mom isn't watching the clock on my side. We'd have to meet close to your house somewhere, someplace where you could get to real quick without starting a car."

"You're serious?"

"Try me," he said.

Alice studied Nickson's hands, watching them for any sign of the nervousness her mother thought was the reason Nickson rolled up the seat belts in the Taurus and 150. Again, it was clear just how wrong her mother could be: Nickson's hands were as calm as the praying hands on their kitchen wall.

The evenings were getting cold, but Alice knew a bridge on the gravel road south of their farm that had a big open space beneath it. She told Nickson exactly how to get there—even recommending that he jog down the railroad track for a few miles so he wouldn't attract any attention. Then he could easily cut across fields and meet her under the bridge. They'd be a quarter mile from the farmhouse. She'd put a blanket under the bridge, tuck it up next to the pigeon nests. This would be simple. If they met at 10:25, they could have at least a half hour together and she could be back home in bed before 11:30 when her father got up to go to work. Since she could easily run the short distance from their farm to the bridge in a few minutes, she wouldn't have to start a car with the chance of waking her mother. No one would know she was out of the house. Nickson said no one at his house would notice that he was gone either, or he could say he was walking to the Redemption Library on well-lit streets where nobody would mug him.

They arranged for a 10:20 rendezvous. When she thought about it, Alice loved the possibility that their bodies would be warm by the time they reached each other.

Alice stopped on the bridge on her way home from school and planted the haymow blanket for them to use. Once again she was filled with the joy of anticipation. She chatted with the pigs. She sang hymns to the steers as she fed them.

She tried not to act too happy when she came into the house after chores. She ate dinner quietly and then got out her books. She made sure she did not wear the kind of grin that would tell the guard that her prisoner was planning an escape. Before Alice went to sleep, she did not try to pray, but she did take her medication. If there were blemishes in her life, they would not be on her face.

33

Alice first saw him when he was a half mile away, an apostrophe on the shining line of railroad tracks. He came angling down the embankment, a slither of dark movement. He disappeared briefly, the way night-moving animals do, following the path that raccoons and foxes made through the drying grass, then reappearing briefly, his dark clothes reflecting moonlight, a glint of shadow, only to disappear again at the fence where he crawled under to emerge onto the moonlit field of mulched corn stubble. He stayed close to the fence and hardly looked human, his pace more a lope than a walk or jog, but moving evenly and steadily, a dark fluid figure rippling across the moonlit field. The world came alive with a vivid intensity, the sharp clarity of the cradle-shaped moon and the myriad stars making the dark harvested fields look like a calm, dark sea, and the faint hint of straight rows where the corn had been shorn looking like deliberate paths through the night that led him toward her.

And then the muted rhythmic sound of his feet coming down as he got closer, a sound disguised, as if it were not human, as if it were a creature whose presence the earth had never received before.

"I'm here, over here," she whispered. She followed the sound of his breath as he made his way more noisily through the weeds, which she parted for him, spreading her arms like wings to open the space into which he moved to receive her embrace. They had done it. They were together again.

"I was watching," she said. "You looked so sure of yourself, as if you had come this way many times."

"I didn't feel that way," he said. "I didn't like it when I got off the railroad tracks and had to go down through that brush. I kept thinking of wild animals."

Already his breath was coming more slowly. She put her hand on his chest and felt it rise and fall against her palm. "We don't have tigers out here," she said. "Nothing that will bite you except the barbed wire—and I saw how you slipped right under that."

"In my head I knew there weren't any mean critters out there, but my grandfather's stories about tigers kept popping into my head, you know. Every noise was like something pouncing at me."

"There are some pretty mean tigers in your mother's pictures too."

"I know it."

She led him under the bridge and unfolded the blanket. They were practiced lovers, following and knowing each other's moves, undressing as they embraced. The chilly air washed over their perspiring bodies. Beneath them, the creek bed breathed its long-stored summer warmth. It was soft, sandy earth, the nearest thing to a mattress that they'd ever had. They did not say but knew how short this moment would be. Intense. Beautiful. Brief.

After they dressed, Alice looked up at the pigeons and saw their dark forms lined up like rocks. Some were on nests, but most had settled on bridge pilings for the night. A waking signal passed among them, and, one after another, their heads rose from under their wings to watch. The birds' heads swiveled like turrets and their beaks pecked in Alice and Nickson's direction like fingers repeatedly pointing at them. One pigeon ruffled, and another, and then they started flapping off into the night. The first dived in their direction to get clearance from the underside of the bridge. Nickson reached for the blanket and tried to pull it over his head as if he really were under attack. The startled pigeon veered away from the movement but left a white dollop on Nickson's shoulder.

"No, not bird crap!"

Alice grabbed a handful of dry grass and swiped it away.

"At least it didn't land on my head. That would have been really bad."

"Hair can be washed," she said.

"You don't understand," said Nickson.

Alice did not know that bird droppings falling on a person was a bad omen. If there were other bad omens in the air that night, she was not seeing them either.

Nickson picked up the blanket for her, shook the sand out of it, and then his hands did look nervous, pulling the corners of the blanket together and then pulling and putting them together again so that the edges were perfectly even, then folding and refolding, all of his attention focused on the exactness of the edges, and finally he had folded it as evenly as she had seen an American flag folded in a ceremony. He handed the neatly folded rectangle to her. Folding the blanket had taken as long as their lovemaking, but she took it and placed it where they could reach it if and when they used it again.

She watched him jog easily away from the bridge, worried briefly about his safety, and then turned and sprinted for home, slowing down as she got close, then walking slowly to catch her breath. There were no signs that the guard had awakened in her absence. She imitated Nickson's easy and stealthy movements, and then assured herself that even if her mother did catch her coming back into the house, she would never guess that she had been off with Nickson. Unless it was written on her face. Unless she looked so happy that her mother would regard her suspiciously. As she moved through the house, she heard only her own movements.

The door to Aldah's bedroom was closed. Alice opened it slowly and turned on the light. Her normally slovenly mother had cleaned the room up. She had removed the bedsheets and pillowcases to leave the sad spectacle of a bare, striped mattress. She had even polished the floor to leave its tan speckled surface glowing in the light. Even Aldah's bureau had been cleared and its pine finish polished. The tiny room did not have the look of a motel room that was being readied for the next guest; it looked more like someone preparing for a home sale. The room smelled like bleach and wax, not like Aldah. Her mother had sanitized Aldah out of the house; she had erased her.

As the pain of Aldah's absence dug into Alice, she countered the pain with an even greater resolution to see Nickson again. As often as possible.

When Alice got to her room, the clock told her that it had been exactly an hour. More rendezvous with Nickson would be easy—at least until the snows came and made it impossible for Nickson to run across the field to meet her as he had done on that most beautiful November night. Not every night, but maybe three nights a week. When snow and freezing cold came, they would find another way. Love like theirs knew no barriers that they couldn't get past.

As she went through the motions of the next few days at school, Alice's heart and mind were elsewhere. She sealed them in a vacuum of bliss. As she went through the routines of her day, the universe gave her an abundance of happiness. Even some of her old teammates from basketball were friendly to her again. She must have had a welcoming aura around her, and every daily task was easier. Doing chores at night was easier. The hogs and steers were friendlier. When she fed them, the hogs looked up at her as if they knew something good was happening in her life. She kept singing and talking to them, and they responded with sounds that could have been the sweetest of human words. She could see the pork chops growing on them the day she sang "What a Friend We Have in Jesus." The whole world smiled at her. Everything that needed doing passed through her life without encumbrance.

The only exception was her first B on a quiz in Miss Den Harmsel's class. Yes, it was a B, but it had an assuring note: "Alice. I assume the demands at home have been very great for you. Don't worry about this one B; I'm certain you'll make up for it on the next quiz."

The morning market report announced that hog and cattle prices were going up. The world was sending messages of hope: she was in love and their farm was going to be saved from ruin.

How different her life was from other people's. Her mother's wrinkled misery. Her father's cold resolve to press forward, press forward. Other students at Midwest were so often tied in knots of trivial encounters, kicking their stuck lockers, sneering at cafeteria food, snapping at their friends for the slightest of insults. Whatever Lydia had with her new boyfriend or boyfriends, she didn't have what Alice and Nickson had. Lydia's eyes looked so empty that Alice guessed she had already grown tired of her own reckless life, though Lydia was more than eager to show Alice that she had gotten an A+ on the quiz on which Alice had gotten a B.

"Good for you," said Alice. "Me? I just got my first B of the year."

Lydia repressed her glee over her own A+. "One B won't destroy your grade," she said, "any more than one pimple would destroy your beautiful complexion."

"Still not much change," said Alice and pointed at her cheeks that were covered with their usual heavy makeup.

"It takes a while," said Lydia, "but your face is an A+ and I'm sure your grades will soon be A+ again too."

They stood smiling at each other, and Alice hoped Lydia wouldn't use the pause as a transition to go on a political rant. She didn't. Instead, she asked, "Have you been hearing from any of the colleges where we applied?"

"Oh, yes," said Alice, "but I haven't followed up on anything yet. There's plenty of time."

"Not really," said Lydia.

There was another pause, but this one was not filled with mutual smiling.

"You're putting it off because of Nickson, aren't you?" said Lydia. She must have seen Alice's intense squinting at the question. "Don't look at me like that: I'm happy for you and Nickson."

"You're right," said Alice. "I've got to get at that. I didn't even open the letter from Stanford, but I don't think I'd want to live in earthquake country."

"At least answer them," said Lydia. "Major League love shouldn't hold you back, you know."

Lydia was peeling back too many layers with her comments, and Alice couldn't decide if Lydia was trying to warn her that her "Major League love," as she called it, was a choice that was interfering with her determination to be somebody in the world, someone bigger and more accomplished than the bonds of Dutch Center would ever allow her. Loving Nickson had to be a better choice than the way Lydia was playing the field. How was she managing to keep her academic focus while dillydallying around with every Tom, Dick, and Harry who crossed her seductive path! But, no, she would not confront Lydia. She wouldn't even argue with her. As uncomfortable as Lydia had just made her, something told Alice that she needed Lydia more now than ever. To keep her heart in balance. To keep her mind focused. And to cover for her if the need arose.

That Sunday Alice read the church bulletin to see the interesting coincidence that the title of Rev. Prunesma's sermon was "Love Love Love."

His text was John 15:12, "This is my commandment, That ye love one another, as I have loved you." Alice watched the Vangs come in and sit in their usual pew and felt that her love joined them all together.

The Rev chose to complicate the topic by talking about three different kinds of love. He liked to demonstrate his knowledge of Greek and Latin, defining each word as a way of explicating the text.

He gave the least time to *Eros,* which, he said, of course gave us the word *erotic.*

"Eros, if left to its own designs," he declared, "is destructive. Fleshly love. Bodily desire. Eros is like a young and untrained horse that is turned loose. If there is no bridle, if there are no fences, Eros will gallop out of control to its own destruction."

Alice felt relieved: her and Nickson's love was much more than unbridled desire.

The Rev went on to *Filial,* which, he explained, was inside our word for *family* and was probably what God meant by *brotherly love.* He talked for several minutes about the brotherly love of Jesus's disciples and of the brotherly love that members of the church showed with mutual concern for each other. "Filial love is what children show by obeying their parents," he concluded.

Yes, Alice thought. This is the kind of love Nickson had for his mother.

But what Rev. Prunesma really wanted to celebrate was the third kind of love, *Caritas,* the kind of love that Jesus brought to earth. Selfless love. This was the grandest love of them all, and his gestures became broader and broader and his face redder and redder as he extolled this greatest of Christian virtues. "But," he warned, "it is only through God's love that we depraved sinners can even imagine the beauty of *caritas.* If we show it to others, it is only because the Lord God Almighty, through the sacrifice of his only begotten son, Jesus Christ, has instilled that love within us."

Love love love, Alice thought as the Rev preached on. She and Nickson had the gift of all three kinds.

There was no intimidation in the sermon and no triggers for remorse or guilt. The whole sermon was an invitation to celebrate the beauty of love and to accept the deep comfort and security it could give against all the torments of the world.

Out of respect for her parents, Alice did not try to talk with Nickson after church. This was his time to be with family too. It had been some time since she felt so good about one of Rev. Prunesma's sermons.

She was buoyed by the feeling of abundant love until the next morning, when, for no reason she could name, she felt bushwhacked. At first it was a mere twinge of fear: if her love for Nickson was so wonderful, why couldn't she talk to anyone about it? Why was it such a secret? She tried to imagine telling people that she was in love with Nickson but could only imagine mocking and scornful responses, and the imagined voices made her angry.

That morning when she arrived at school, her fear turned into a dark sadness that started when she saw Nickson with the "bad boys." The days when she was seeing Nickson had been filled with explosive moments of seeing the beautiful, but, at that moment, she had an implosive moment of seeing the ugly: the Slouchers must have been where the marijuana was coming from. What if Nickson was the dealer? What if he had brought a large supply with him from Saint Paul? And their big celebration: what if other members of his clan had brought huge supplies of marijuana that Nickson was now selling? What if Lia's story cloth business was just a cover for Nickson's drug operation? What if Nickson was giving Mai drug money to buy condoms? What if this whole romance thing was a sham and she was a fool? What if she and Nickson were the wild colts of Eros intent on their own destruction? What if her mother was right?

And what if this awful change of mood is what her mother experienced all the time, chemicals running wild in her body, making her need Valium just to remain calm enough to function in the world? No matter how much she vowed never to be like her mother, the curse of being her offspring was like having wiring that channeled every impulse in her being to imitate her.

No, she thought. No—but she could feel her body temperature drop, and with it her good mood plunged. When she saw her classmates, she had no desire to talk to them. Her neck muscles were tightening, and she could hardly swallow. She stood in front of the women's room mirror, and her own face scared her. Her face looked like a fun-house mirror had distorted her features. Her cheeks moved in dizzying waves and her eyes looked unfamiliar and blank. She felt as if she was looking into the eyes of a stranger in a face that was malleable and changing, with her flesh swimming on her cheekbones. Looking at herself made her want to vomit. It was even worse than that: some force inside her was erupting and she felt as if she was being disemboweled, and it was all happening so fast. Only twenty-four hours ago her heart had been riding through the sky on a soft cloud of love.

Her body's eruptions rose from her stomach to her heart and continued upward to lodge in her mind, screaming: look what you have done with your life! She was seventeen and having sex with a man from a different race who carried a gun, who hung out with shady characters, and who had introduced her to drugs! She had been so busy with the desires of her flesh that she had neglected the life of her mind! As Lydia had reminded her with an innocent enough question, she had not even followed up on her college applications!

Alice came to the terror of full realization: something had forced common sense right out of her and she had veered out of control. No, it was not the wide path of destruction that Rev. Prunesma could talk about, and it wasn't the narrow path of salvation. Worse than Shakespeare's "primrose path of dalliance," she had followed a pathless path of confusion and selfishness. This was worse than being thrown into a den of lions. This was bootless desperation.

But why should she entirely blame herself? Her mother had successfully trapped her with her sickness and smothered her with her pessimism. Oh, and her father, good old controlled Albert, with his neat little rows of failure. Rigid as her father was, there was something limp about him. She wouldn't blame Aldah, but raising her as Alice had done didn't give her much of a chance for friendships with normal boyfriends. Bubbly Mai didn't help either. She was probably a Linda Tripp, blabbing the news of Nickson and Alice's sexual adventures to anyone who would listen: "Four condoms a night! That's my brother! And how about that Dutch princess!" Har har har: "If you're not Dutch, you're not much."

She wrapped her hands around her shoulders and pulled. I will pull myself together, she thought. I will, and this will pass. I'll hit bottom and then come back up. But her dark thoughts kept digging in and shaping her day. She avoided Nickson and asked to be excused from the last class, but being alone in the women's room only made her feel worse. The terrible way she was feeling—she couldn't hide this from Lydia. If she ever needed her best friend's support, she needed it now.

She caught Lydia after school and told her that she was feeling terrible. "I just can't shake it," she said. "I just can't shake it."

"I should have told you," said Lydia. "This happens on the medication. Don't blame yourself; it's just a chemical thing and your bad mood will pass. Trust me."

34

Alice drove the 150 slowly, waiting for some comfort from the sad and purring engine. Oh yes, Miss Den Harmsel, she thought to herself, I am quite aware of the irony of seeking comfort from a combustion engine rather than from God or Shakespeare, or even a sensible life.

Her unemployed mother was home. Her mother's chronic anger always filled the house, sometimes mildly like a thin layer of dust that Alice could brush off easily, but more often like anhydrous ammonia—so astringent that it hurt to breathe in her presence. If she was in her astringent mode now, Alice would be ready to match her. But her mother chose not to show what form of anger lurked behind her eyes. She just studied Alice like a hog buyer looking for flaws. The punishment of silence had not stopped, but her mother looked like the victim of her own agenda: her black mood had made black circles under her eyes. The only white was the pale skin that was emerging in the early winter weather. She looked thinner every day. Occasionally in the past week Alice had seen her out in the roadside ditch, wearing dark sunglasses and snipping dead flowers and weeds for a winter bouquet which she'd then stuff, crackling, into large vases in the living room. Was she creating images of herself? More likely she was growing more and more silent and looking darker and darker as a way to punish Alice. Mostly, she appeared to be celebrating the death of things. Alice felt like giving her a serving of her own hoarded Spam.

Whether sensing Alice's dark mood and wanting to escape it or wanting to guard her own darkness in the privacy of her own company, her mother announced that she needed to run to town and would be right back. Her father was gone too, though he'd be back soon to go to bed. Alice was suddenly alone in the house, with only her own dark mood to keep her company. She imagined that the way she felt was probably how her mother felt most of the time. Without a second's thought, she went into her parents' bedroom and straight to her mother's drug supply. She shook out four Valium and put three in her pocket in case she'd need them later, walked to the kitchen and swallowed one, along with another half tablet of her acne medication. She'd level a chemical assault on the outer and inner blemishes in one fell swoop.

When Alice started to get dressed for her evening chores, her dark mood was upstaged by a painful constriction on the skin of her breasts. She looked down to see the bulging presence of her breasts forcing themselves over her brassiere. This had to be part of her anguish for the day, but then she realized that not only were her breasts swollen, but she was a week overdue.

Or was she? She walked to her wall calendar and paged back to the previous month. She stared long and hard at the Sunday her period had begun. No mistake: she was eight days overdue. This had never happened before: she was as regular as her and Lydia's clock before Lydia went on the pill. The thought that she might be pregnant was a call back to reality. The dark mood left and she went into clear-thinking mode. Nickson was too careful for this to happen. Then she remembered the night the condom almost slipped off and how they hadn't worried at the time, but now she tried to remember exactly which night that was. She thought she did remember it and checked the date to see when in her cycle that might have occurred. Thanks mostly to Lydia's mother whose sex education of Lydia had been passed on directly to Alice, they both knew about *mittelschmerz*. They both knew about ovulation and when it was likely to occur.

Yes, she and Nickson had sex on the twelfth day. Oh, but they also had sex on the fourteenth. She wasn't going to panic: this was part of the shock treatment she needed to come back to reality. When she felt a sharp cramp the next day, she thought her worries were over, but then nothing happened. To put her fears to rest, she decided to get a pregnancy test kit, but she couldn't decide where to buy one. She couldn't go to the drug store in the Dutch Center mini-mall because it was owned and operated by a deacon in their church. She couldn't go to Corner Drug in Brummel City either because everybody who worked there had kids at Midwest Christian. She couldn't think of anyplace nearby where people wouldn't have some connection to her parents or to students at MC. She was not terribly anxious. In truth, she felt quite optimistic. She was back in problem-solving mode.

She thought of the Walmart that had opened on the outskirts of Brummel City. They had several Mexican workers who were not likely to recognize her and who most likely went to the River Valley Catholic Church.

She drove to Walmart on that Saturday morning under the pretense that she was going to visit Aldah at Children's Care. She was right: the person at the Walmart register was Hispanic. Alice looked around, saw no one she knew, and quickly purchased the self-test kit. Alone in the Walmart bathroom, she watched the little spot where she put a drop of her urine and waited for it to turn green. The green light would actually be like a yellow light of warning: she and Nickson had to stop having sex. They had to cool down, which was inevitable anyhow because the realities of winter weather would be stronger than her fantasies of outmaneuvering them. How did she really think they were going to get together in midwinter: Public restrooms? The backseats of unlocked snow-covered cars in parking lots? Her late period no doubt was the result of the stress she was under and was the warning that would help her come back to her senses: she would stop having sex with Nickson, and they would have the debate-partner relationship that she originally intended. No *eros*. All *caritas*. The little dot on the test sheet didn't hesitate. It turned pink. Alone in the Walmart bathroom that Saturday morning, she learned that she was pregnant. She stared at the gray toilet-stall walls. Numb. Alice Marie Krayenbraak had conceived with Nickson Vang.

Or had she? She reread the instructions, especially the section about reliability. It warned that the results would not be one hundred percent accurate. Of course not. This was just a fluke, and she had gotten a false positive. With Nickson's caution, there was no way she could be pregnant. She checked her wallet to see if she had enough money to purchase another kit. She would be spending all of her lunch money on pregnancy tests, but so be it. Skipping a few meals could be no worse than bathing in cold water. She went up to the cash register with a second pregnancy test.

The Hispanic woman—and this time Alice looked at her more

closely—saw her coming and saw what she was carrying. The woman was about forty-five, her hair pulled back and clipped with a shiny plastic barrette. Her face looked kind but worn, a gentle toughness. She started smiling sympathetically when Alice laid the kit down.

She reached out and took Alice's arm. Alice would never forget the woman's dark, kind eyes.

"You didn't like what it said, did you?"

Alice didn't want this familiarity. She didn't want anyone to feel they knew this much about her, but the woman looked so kind. Alice wanted to lean over the counter and put her face onto the woman's large bosom and cry.

"I just think I'd better do it again to make sure. I think I got a false positive. I mean, it was pink but not all *that* pink."

The woman blinked her big sympathetic eyes. "Don't bother, darling, these tests don't lie."

"Maybe this one did. It's possible. It says right on the package that the results aren't one hundred percent."

The woman shook her head slowly, still offering her kind smile. "*Chica bonita,*" she said, "you will make a beautiful mother."

Alice left and got into the 150 to hear the pronounced and familiar double click of the driver's door closing. She held the steering wheel and looked out to see the world moving in slow motion in much the same way it did after Nickson gave her some marijuana.

She put the 150 in drive and idled toward the parking lot exit. Instead of turning toward home, the 150 turned toward Children's Care.

Family members were not supposed to visit without prior arrangements, but the supervisor looked relieved. "Your sister talks about you all the time. Let me tell her you're coming so she won't be shocked."

Aldah had lost weight, a fact that didn't make her look healthier, just thinner. But her face: her spirit had gotten thinner too.

Alice moved toward Aldah slowly, as if in a dream. Aldah pretended not to recognize her, but Alice walked over and wrapped her arms around her sister. She was giving Aldah the assuring embrace that she needed herself, and she needed to feel that assurance coming back to her. Aldah tightened up in a way that felt more like the very tension Alice was feeling in herself, but Alice didn't let go. Then Aldah's body started to shake, and she whimpered in Alice's arms until her tears soaked into Alice's shirt at the shoulder. Alice tried to hold her own tears, but when she blinked, large drops spattered on Aldah's unwashed hair. The two of them were together, but they were together in sorrow more than in the comfortable assurance Alice craved.

"Let's take a little walk," said Alice. Holding hands, they walked to the recreation area where other children played with clay and wooden blocks.

"Is this your sister, Aldah?" asked the attendant.

"Alice," she said. Finally, Aldah smiled and leaned against Alice, clutching her arm and leaning her head against her side. This was the sweet-mannered Aldah who could get anyone to adore her, and it was behavior now that caused smiles to spread through the room.

Hand in hand, Alice and Aldah walked over to an open area on the floor where two speechless children were rolling balls of clay over and over, one mirroring the other's actions and neither of them saying anything.

Alice sat down and started forming an egg-shaped figure. "Pig," said Aldah.

"Yes. Pig. Now you make the tail, all right?"

"All right."

Aldah picked up a piece of clay and rolled it between her palms. The piece of clay broke in two, but she picked it up again and started rolling the clay into the shape of a thin pencil. The attendant watched. "Something's working," she said.

Alice took Aldah's pig tail and attached it to the round body of the clay pig. "There!" said Alice, and Aldah clapped.

"Would it be all right if I took her for a ride?" Alice asked. "Aldah likes to take rides in the pickup."

"One-fifty," said Aldah

"It's a Ford 150 pickup."

"That would be fine. Just be sure to give the information at the desk, and say when you'll be back. Maybe Aldah would like to bring her new friend."

This news about Aldah could have been good or bad. Alice's own mood was shifting toward the very comfort she was hoping to find by driving to Children's Care, but she didn't want to meet a new boyfriend, if that's what this was all about.

"Aldah will tell you all about him, you can be sure of that." The attendant had a milky caretaker's voice that made Alice cringe.

Aldah's new friend was not flesh and blood at all. Aldah pointed to an empty space in the corner of her room next to her bed. Aldah's new friend was imaginary.

"What is his name?" Alice asked in an earnest and sincere voice.

"David."

"David?"

Aldah nodded.

An imaginary friend named David? The people at Children's Care seemed to believe that an imaginary friend was good for Aldah, but they didn't know the whole story. Alice wondered if she had made a mistake a long time ago in telling Aldah about David, the brother she never really had. A dead brother. It had seemed like a good idea at the time, but now Alice wondered.

"How do you know his name is David?"

"He told me."

"He told you? He said, 'Hi, my name is David'?"

"Yes."

Imaginary David had become Aldah's playmate at Children's Care. She showed Alice some of the clay figures David had made. David specialized in cats, cats with round middles, pointed heads, and round marble feet.

"Where's the tail?"

"No tail."

"No tail? David doesn't make tails?"

"No. Aldah makes tails."

When they got back to her room, Alice pointed to the clothes strewn on the floor.

"David did this?"

"Yes. David did it." Aldah picked up the clothes like a disgruntled mother cleaning up behind her child.

"I think David's real name is John," said Alice. "I think he wants to be called by his real name. Let's call him John."

"No," said Aldah. "This David."

"Are you sure, Aldah?"

"Yes. This is David." She was staring at the wall next to the door where David had evidently moved.

"Aldah, I am going to have a baby."

Aldah kept staring at her David but she had heard Alice. "Have a baby?"

"Yes. I am going to be a mommy."

"I am your mommy," said Aldah.

"No, Aldah, you are my sister. I am going to be a mommy. You are going to be an aunt."

Aldah looked to see David's reaction.

"I am going to be a mommy," said Aldah.

"No. Don't tell people that. I am the one who is going to be a mommy."

Aldah walked over and hugged Alice.

"It's a secret."

"A secret," said Aldah. "Shhhh."

"Let's leave David here while we go for our ride," said Alice. "David needs to spend some time by himself."

"Okay," Aldah said.

Instead of taking Aldah downtown, Alice drove back to Dutch Center and to the Vangs' house. When they got out of the 150, Aldah waited outside, holding the pickup door. She waited several seconds and made a "come on" gesture with her hand. David had decided to come along and now was being stubborn about getting out of the 150.

New planters with leafy growth sat in the windows. Lia had covered her little herb garden with plastic to protect against frost, but the mound of flip-flops and sandals at the back door had not been replaced with warmer shoes.

Mai saw Alice and Aldah through the kitchen window and bubbled out of the back door to greet them. *My sister-in-law.*

Mai invited them in to eat something, though the kitchen table featured a stack of Nickson's textbooks.

"My brother's junk," said Mai. "He was up at six this morning. Studying."

"On a Saturday morning?"

"He's always studying."

Aldah saw the bowl that Mai was carrying to the kitchen table and pulled back a chair to sit down and eat.

As they all ate bowls of rice with cooked broccoli, carrots, and spicy bits of pork, Alice could hear the soft sounds of Lia working. *My mother-in-law.*

Nickson walked in dressed in baggy brown pants and a faded green sweatshirt. His hair was messy and his feet were bare. There was no way he could undo his natural beauty. *My husband. My beautiful husband.*

"Yo," he said and sat down next to Aldah. They looked at each other closely, and Alice knew how rare it was for Aldah to make eye contact with strangers. Alice often judged people by Aldah's reaction to them. Nickson was passing with flying colors. *Aldah's brother-in-law.*

When they finished eating, Mai asked Aldah to come with her to see what Lia was doing.

"Come see the pretty pictures," she said. Mai held out her hand to Aldah. Two small hands. The beautiful way the color of their skin contrasted.

Aldah was ready to go with Mai, but she paused to look around the kitchen. She was drawn to the enormous pot hanging on the wall, the bunches of herbs tied in little bundles and drying, and all the planters spewing green leaves. She probably noticed the spicy smell too. Alone in the kitchen, Alice sat across from Nickson and embraced him with her eyes.

"Really glad you stopped by," he said.

"Me too."

They walked over to the sewing room where Lia was showing Aldah her story cloths. Now it was Lia who connected with Aldah. She held Aldah's hand and rubbed it over the figures on the story cloth, as if helping to read it through her fingers. Short little stitching needles stood out on the working tables. Colorful threads and scraps of cloth were everywhere, and a stack of finished eyeglass cases, story cloths, and bookmarkers rose in neat stacks on metal shelving along the wall. This was a high-functioning workroom—and warehouse.

"Pretty," said Aldah.

"Thank you," said Lia. Her round face was a sunbeam, and Aldah was not afraid to look at it. Then she looked into a space next to Lia and gave a separate smile to acknowledge David's presence in the sewing room. Lia followed Aldah's eyes and looked into the same blank space. Lia smiled into the blank space too, and for a moment it seemed that they were both seeing David.

"Let's go downtown," Alice interrupted. She looked at Mai: "You, me, Aldah, and Nickson."

Agreement with the suggestion came quickly, and both Mai and Nickson got dressed for the excursion, Nickson appearing in denim slacks and a beige shirt with subtle ruffles along the buttons. Mai soon appeared in black jeans and a beige shirt close to the color of Nickson's.

Alice swung up the consul of the 150 so that it became part of the seat. Mai hopped behind the seat, and Aldah slid between Alice and Nickson. *A family outing.*

35

When they walked through the mini-mall food court, they strolled past Perfect Pizza, but Alice didn't glance inside.

Mai wanted to go to Variety Paradise where her mother's work was sold. Alice didn't even know about this. Hmong products in Dutch Center? Why not?—half of the things she bought in Dutch Center were made in China.

"Mom has been pumping it out," said Mai.

The owner of Variety Paradise had put up a sign:

******* Authentic Hmong Needlework *******
Mrs. Lia Vang, currently of Dutch Center, is a native of Laos. She learned her traditional Hmong needlework as a small girl and perfected her techniques while in a refugee camp in Thailand. All of these colorful items are made from highly durable fabric. The story cloths make ideal end-table covers or can be hung on the wall as art pieces.

"During the first two weeks, they hardly sold anything," said Mai. "Then Mom started making bookmarks out of pieces of old parachutes that she has. And she started making eyeglass cases. Then she started doing some story cloths that weren't traditional Hmong."

The Vang products were the first visible items inside Variety Paradise. The prominent piece was a large story cloth four feet square with thirty separate little scenes. The owner had it displayed on an enormous easel.

Mai pointed to the scenes: "Look, here is a shaman—see the altar—and over here they're cooking a pig for a celebration. Look how big the pig is—it's too big for the pot they're cooking it in! And over here, this is a wedding celebration. Wow. I don't know what Mother was thinking of

over here—I think this is a war thing, but over here, look, this is a plant-
ing scene, and over here the harvest. Uh, look at these tigers over here.
Mom likes to do tigers. Aren't these amazing?"

It was Aldah who leaned in most closely.

"Don't touch," said Alice.

"Don't touch, David," she said. She did not touch the fabric with her
fingers, but she did lean in so closely that she touched it with her nose.
Mai leaned toward the images too. Like Aldah, she seemed transfixed by
them, and didn't pull back. Alice followed their example and leaned in
to look closely too.

"She must have worked on this a month before we came to Dutch
Center," said Mai, "but a lot of this stuff she finished after we moved
here. Dutch Center has been good for all of us."

It was as if Mai already knew and was inviting Alice into her family.

The owner of Variety Paradise walked over with a salesperson smile.
Mai and Nickson recognized her and smiled over their extended
hands. Alice kept looking at the Vang display. On a small table was a
stack of more, smaller story cloths, but these were not Hmong scenes.
Some depicted tulips, windmills, pigs, and gambrel-roofed barns—and
churches, one of them strangely resembling the First Reformation
Church of Dutch Center.

The owner told them she had sold six of the new story cloths depict-
ing Dutch and rural scenes. "People are gobbling them up. I'm not sure
what she's showing with this one over here—this huge sun rising over a
dark foreground. Is it religious?"

"I'm not sure," said Mai. "She told me it was supposed to represent a
new day coming. Maybe the millennium? I'm not sure."

Lia obviously worked with great speed—but—as Nickson had told
Alice—she also worked on Sundays to the voiced displeasure of some
people in the church.

"I can't wait for the nativity scenes and Christmas tree designs she's
finishing now," said the owner. "They will be very popular. I'm sure I'll
sell them as fast as your mother can make them—and if she ever gets
enough of them made so that she can take them to the annual craft show,
oh boy, look out." *Community acceptance.*

Alice grappled with contradictory notions in her mind: was Mai trying to show that her family was capable of being a private enterprise success story, or was she showing Alice just how high a fence she would have to climb to enter their world? Or, Alice wondered, am I just reading too much into an enthusiastic person celebrating the work of her mother?

Some peccaries of resentment also nipped at Alice: Weren't the Vangs a charity case of their church? Wasn't it the church that was making their well-being possible? Free house, free tuition, free house furnishings, and now were they making bundles of money on the side?

"Your mother does beautiful work. You must be very proud."

"She's the best," said Nickson.

"Oh, come on," said Mai, "you said Alice was the best."

They both chuckled nervously at that remark, but then Mai saw Alice's unease. "We're just teasing, Alice. I think you're just as wonderful as Nickson does." She put an arm around Nickson and gave him a pull toward Alice.

Aldah was leaning over a stack of story cloths. Before Alice could stop her, she picked one up. "Buy," she said.

It was a forty-dollar choice. "I can't. We just came to look."

"Mom will give her something," said Mai. "You don't have to buy anything from us."

It was happening: she was becoming part of their family. She was part of them and they were part of her. She looked at Nickson and felt that it would be beautiful to tell him right then and there, before going back to the Vang house to tell Lia too. Alice was part of their family and they didn't even know it—but she couldn't tell them just then. She couldn't. She would have to tell Nickson alone, but not now. She would need to be alone with him, and it would have to be the right time and place. It would be a ritualistic moment, a grand announcement that would be the beginning of their life together. The comfortable feeling she found when she went to see Aldah at Children's Care was happening again. How could I ever have imagined that getting pregnant before I was married would be an unimaginable horror? It wasn't. As she stood with Aldah and Nickson and Mai, she felt deeply at peace with herself and the world—even though she knew that some tough conversations lay ahead. She'd have to adjust her plans for the future, of course. None of this worried her at that moment. She could not imagine an unhappy outcome from the news of the day.

The attendant was waiting with her senseless smile when Alice dropped Aldah off at Children's Care. Alice sensed her inadequacy as a caretaker and distrusted her easy acceptance of Aldah's David. A real professional should have been able to extract that phantom the way a good dentist might extract somebody's extra tooth.

The 150 did not offer its usual comfort as Alice drove toward home. She had constructed a beautiful fantasy in seeing Aldah and the Vangs, but the sweet fantasy was fading quickly. It's just the medication, she assured herself, the mood swings Lydia had warned her about, but she couldn't stop the dark feelings from descending around her. Pieces of herself turned against her. First her throat, which gave little gasps. Her forehead started to swim away. Her hands grew limp but vibrated. A rock replaced her stomach.

The day was turning into a roller coaster of emotions. Alice aimed the 150 straight for the refuge of the barn.

She moved past the steers and looked up at the swallows' cup-shaped nests made of mud and grass that were empty though still firmly in place on the large beams. They looked like the most permanent and stable things in her world right now—and they were empty. She climbed up into the haymow where, immediately, two sparrows came like fluttering dust balls past her face, landed on windowsills and were gone again, bouncing through the air and disappearing somewhere beyond a stack of bales. Then they reappeared as if to give Alice a second look. She recognized one as a male, with the black patch on its throat, and the other smaller one as a female. It was not courting season and Alice wondered if she was standing close to their nest and they were trying to draw her away. She walked through a corridor of stacked bales and looked for what might be their nest, but she knew they could nest almost anywhere in the haymow, sometimes burrowing between bales and calling it a home until the bales were moved.

She sat down on a hay bale and the grim truth of her life settled on her: she was pregnant, and only the woman at Walmart and Aldah knew it. She got up and climbed onto the bales where she and Nickson had made love, put her hands over her uterus, and began to tremble.

She no longer felt like sharing the news with anyone. She didn't want to talk to anyone, she didn't want to see anyone. She wanted to find a box, crawl inside, wrap herself up and pretend that she had never been born, that she would float around in friendly silent fluid forever. She wished she were her own fetus, and she didn't want to talk to any human beings, not even Nickson, and least of all her parents.

She forced herself to stop the self-pity and to think about what she should do next, but her mind betrayed her and snagged her in vile thoughts. There was nothing beautiful about her life. There was nothing beautiful about her pregnant body. She hated the long, skinny nuisance of it. She hated the life she was living inside this long and skinny contraption. As she held her hands over the silent stranger inside her, she hated it too. She felt *benauwd,* boxed in. Trapped and scared. It didn't feel like fear of her parents' punishment or fear of her classmates' ridicule. It wasn't even fear of what the church would do. It was horror of what she was. Crying would be such a cheap response. Babies cried. She felt more like lashing out at somebody or something. No crying, but her body shook like somebody naked in the snow. She stood erect on the platform of bales and imagined that she was Joan of Arc about to be consumed by flames.

She was interrupted by the return of the sparrows, the short bursting sounds of their bursting flight as they bounced through the air and then landed and perched on the long draping rope beneath the peak. They studied her in their twitchy way. The muted vibration of their ruffling and the quick nodding of their little heads. They were such harmless sojourners on earth, little messengers of goodwill, equipped with nothing so attractive as the brilliant colors of butterflies, but with such a simple and uncomplicated existence. One chirped what to Alice sounded like an ironically cheerful chirp.

She raised her hand and waved to them. "Got any good ideas?" she asked.

They rocked jerkily on the rope, the male chirped a few quick chirps, and they both flew off.

When she sat back down on the hay, she reached for one of the stalks of alfalfa and started nibbling its leaves. She tried to focus on the smells and sounds of the barn, which was probably all that the sparrows knew of their simple world; but lines from *Hamlet* came parading through her mind. The fat king, Claudius, spoke to her. His insufferable wife, Gertrude, spoke to her. Claudius because he was a hypocrite like Alice Marie Krayenbraak. She was her own "smiling, damned villain." Oh yes, she was indeed her own villain, but not a smiling one. She thought of Claudius's wisdom in his villainy: "Oh Gertrude, Gertrude, / When sorrows come they come not single spies, But in battalions."

"'Aye, there's the rub,' Nancy chafed."

Alice laughed the deep and pathetic laugh of someone who saw her own foolishness, but she was her only audience. She thought of Claudius's battalion of sorrows. The collapse of her family's farm was a mere foot soldier in this battalion. Her mother's screwed-up mental state was barely a drill sergeant. But, oh the truth of her womb: this was a veritable Napoléon's army and what she had in defense was the unarmed peasant of her flimsy self.

In her blissful blindness she had not prayed sincerely for two weeks. Was what was happening to her God's idea of tough love? Had he sent her mother to catch them in the haymow as a final warning? Her mother as the archangel Gabriel. Or her mother as Amos, the prophet of doom with his declaration that their sins would catch up with them.

Alice wanted to argue with God. Resolved: That Alice Krayenbraak should discover God's love in her life through the earthly means that God provides her.

"Mock not that ye be not mocked" came spiking into her mind. Her proposition was a mockery of God's love and she knew it. If you want to find God's love, the counterarguments began, feed the poor, visit the sick, honor your father and mother, care for the planet, visit the homeless, deny the needs of your own sinful flesh. Obey the Ten Commandments! She could see the judge's scorecards, and she was not in the winner's column.

If she couldn't pray in this sacred space, where could she pray? She did not want to pray for forgiveness for actions that were the most beautiful and loving moments of her life. Praying to deny love seemed wrong. She wanted to pray in a detached and thoughtful way. She wanted to have a conversation with God. Alone in the haymow, she folded her hands and closed her eyes. She waited for the right words to come to her. Instead, her mind gave her more words of the villainous king Claudius: "My words fly up, my thoughts remain below: / Words without thoughts never to heaven go."

She looked up and around the haymow for a message. She stood and listened, but there was no movement and not a flutter of sound.

PART IV

December, 1999

36

It was cold and getting colder. When Alice looked outside at the brutal winds whipping topsoil off the barren fields across the road from the Krayenbraak farm, she could almost see the broad and ruthless arm of the Lord sweeping the earth clean for the millennium. She took another one of her mother's Valium before going outside to do the morning chores and coming to the table for breakfast.

The thermostat in the house was set at fifty, and it felt as if even their old and sturdy farmhouse was preparing for a time when familiar warmth would no longer be an option. Her mother wore her down parka in the kitchen and had her gloves on at the breakfast table, and, while her father wore his sober and inscrutable expression that suggested nothing was abnormal, he still had on a sweatshirt. Alice defied the circumstantial evidence of a cold world by washing her hands and face in cold water and wearing only her jeans and a light cotton shirt to the table.

Alice had read that people being prepared for surgery were often kept in cool rooms and that the operating room itself could be downright chilly. She felt as if she was preparing for a major operation: the announcement of her pregnancy to everyone concerned. The person she told should be cool, and the place where she told them should be cool, anything to keep her own cool composure against the possible heat of the moment. Making the announcements would be major surgery, and she planned to be the surgeon, not the patient.

Aldah's cradle of love had been a safe haven for the first announcement, and her acceptance a comforting precedent for what might follow. The rest made easy, cool and easy. The muscles in Alice's arms felt relaxed and her mind felt at peace. The Valium was working.

Nickson first, then her parents, and next Monday Lydia. And, sometime soon, Rev. Prunesma before the rumor mill told him. Not to tell the Rev would in his eyes deepen the gravity of her offense. Not to tell him would be denial of what she had done. A cover-up.

Telling any and all of them would not be a confession, it would be an announcement: *I am going to have a baby.*

To be ready meant being ready for it all: for the surprise, for the anger, and, no doubt, for the follow-up questions. What about college? Are you going to get married at seventeen? How are your parents taking it? How are the Vangs taking it? What does Nickson want to do? Have you told everybody? Are you going to give it up for adoption? You wouldn't abort, would you? And the biggest question: How can you handle the fact that this changes everything for the rest of your life? In that peaceful but temporary state of mind immediately after learning she was pregnant, the question didn't cross her mind. Something inside her had put the question on hold, but now it hovered over everything. Everything.

But along with the question came the gift of resolve from somewhere, and it didn't matter where: God, her own heart, her mind, or the Valium—it didn't matter, but she felt it like a gift from an anonymous giver. What she felt was a cool and collected resolve that had calm hands and an expressionless face.

Resolve left no place for guilt, and how could anyone ever feel guilt for an accident of love?

If a person felt guilty for what she had done wrong, a person felt shame for something over which she had no control, shame for how others looked at her. Resolve was a less sturdy defense against shame, and she could not shut out the question to herself: How will you deal with the scornful faces of the lesser students at Midwest? High and mighty Alice Krayenbraak brought down to size. Shame from her mother's harsh judgment. Shame from her father's disappointment in her.

I am going to have a baby. Keep it simple. *I am going to have a baby.* That was the premise from which all else would follow.

That Saturday was the day for announcements. Nickson first. Whatever she and Nickson did after the announcement, she was sure the pregnancy would deepen his love for her—but telling him would not be easy.

At 9:00 a.m. on Saturday when she picked Nickson up, he read her tension. "What's wrong? Your mother?"

"We need to talk."

She drove to the city park. The day was sunny but cold—a crisp, decisive day. Fallen leaves fluttered nervously along the ground and crows weaved awkwardly against the gusty winds. They had never taken a walk quite like this one before, freely strolling through the open space of the park, exposed to everyone, and now their footsteps through the fallen leaves reminded Alice of their perfect harmony, the synchronized swishing of their feet through the fallen leaves. When her hand touched his elbow, his hand came up and took hers, and it was as if some part of him already knew that from now on their love for each other would be a secret to no one.

They walked to the cold picnic table behind the windmill whose huge arms like big white fans were locked and stationary. They sat down together with their backs to the tabletop.

An old adversary, sheer fright, had not visited her for many years, but here it was, trying valiantly to challenge her resolve. The last time fright had visited her in this way was when she was a sophomore at Midwest and in her first debate tournament. Fright had such a firm grip as she stood up for her first rebuttal that the five-by-eight note cards quivered in her hand, but what she had learned in the next few seconds was that she could trust the sound of her voice by letting the words pour out and finding that the flow of the sound would carry her along. The rest made easy. At the first sound of her voice the right words had come to her then and her resolve assured her that they would again.

"Nickson," her clear voice now said. She held his hand in hers and looked at him squarely. "I am going to have a baby. I'm pregnant."

There was a quick shocked expression on his face, followed by a slow nodding of his head. Then his neck seemed to flush and his face reddened. His eyes met hers. "You're kidding."

He slowly pulled his hands free from hers and crossed them between his knees.

"I took the test," said Alice. "I've got all the signs."

She put her hands under her breasts. He looked at her hands with an expression that was more curious than alarmed. "It's not your fault," she said. "You did what you could."

His breathing grew measured and deep. She watched the squint of his eyes. She watched for signs of alarm. She watched for signs of anger. She saw none.

"How long, do you think?"

"A month, I think."

He glanced down at her stomach and then at her face. His eyes glazed. "I knew it. When that pigeon," he said, and stopped.

They sat silently in the cold air.

She leaned her shoulder against his. "I think it happened before that," she said. She watched his clasped hands. They were not clenched tightly, but he was rubbing his thumbs over each other.

The large windmill groaned as if it wanted to start turning, and they both turned to look at it. How did other teenagers handle this moment? She reached for his clasped hands.

"I'm sorry," she said, "but I'm happy too. I probably shouldn't be, but I am. Our baby."

"This is a big one." He unclasped his hands and took hers.

She pulled. "Be close."

"Oh boy." He leaned his head forward, as if he were about to put it to her chest, then stopped, looking over her shoulder.

"We can handle this," said Alice.

"I am not worthy of you or your baby," he said. "I'm not. You are so beautiful—and so intelligent."

"Don't say that," she said. "You are so very worthy. You're everything I could dream of."

"Alice," he sighed, "you hardly know me. I am such an empty man."

"Stop," she said. "I know how well you're doing at Midwest."

"Trying to fill myself with something," he said. "Trying to be somebody you could be proud of."

"Please stop, Nickson." She put both hands on his arm and gripped him tightly. "You are everything to me."

"I wonder if it's a boy," he said. He stared at the ground. He clasped his hands over his knees and rocked slowly on the bench as the cold breeze ruffled his hair.

"That doesn't matter," said Alice.

He still didn't look at her. "I need some time," he said. "Figure out what it means, you know. I need time."

"Of course, of course," she said. She rubbed his shoulder. He had stiffened up. "We can handle this."

"I know it."

Their walk back to the 150 was slower, but he did take her hand again. Alice listened for the synchronized swish of their feet through the leaves. They were still in step with each other. It was now *their* news.

"I just didn't think this would happen," said Nickson.

"I know," said Alice, "but don't blame yourself. I'm as responsible as you are."

"Do you hate yourself for this?" he said.

"No, no," she said. "This is no time for hatred of anyone."

"I'll try," he said. "I really need some time."

He needed time. She understood that because she had needed time too, simultaneously to try to understand what was happening and what would happen next. She would let him digest the news in private. If she could have taken all of his pain, she would have, but it was his pain and she would honor his need to work through it himself. When she dropped him off at the Vang house, he wasn't able to hug her: he'd start and then withdraw. She thought he was suddenly afraid people were watching, but the two of them didn't need secrecy any longer. Their private lives would soon be public, so why not start now, and if others saw them they would know that they loved each other and that their child would truly be a love-child.

She pulled him toward herself, but he was a large spring that started to uncoil and then sprang back.

"I'm sorry," he said. "I love you."

She softly let him go. "I love you too. And don't ever say you are not worthy. You are a wonderful man. It's I who should worry about being worthy."

She knew his love was there and as strong as always, but right now loving him back meant giving him the time and space that he needed.

"Do you want me to come with you to tell your mom and Mai? We could do it together. They could see that we're together on this. It's our news."

"It's best I tell them," he said. "Don't worry. Have you told your folks?"

"Not yet."

"Have you told anybody?"

"Just you," said Alice. "No, that's not right. I told Aldah."

"You told your sister?"

"Yes," said Alice. She realized how strange that might seem to him. Tell a sister before the father? She watched his face to see if he was disturbed. He looked puzzled, but not angry. "I think I was practicing," she said. "Aldah won't talk about it. I'm not sure she really understands. I just needed her comfort. Do you understand that?"

He looked at her, and then he nodded. "Yes, actually I do. That makes sense. I might tell Mai first too."

"Do you think your mother will reject me when she finds out?"

"She couldn't do that." He opened the pickup door and slid out. He stood with the door open, looking at her.

"You are so beautiful," he said.

"I'm sorry," she said.

"No."

Alice felt the tears coming to her eyes. Nickson saw her expression and stepped back into the 150. He slid across the seat and took her in his arms. He put his hand behind her head and pulled her face to his neck.

"You have not brought me shame," she said. "Don't ever say that again."

"I want to believe you," he said.

"I only hope I haven't brought you shame."

"My family is strong," he said.

"Nobody's losing anything, all right?"

"All right," he said and turned to walk toward the Vang house with the weight of the news she had given him.

37

Only three months ago, the future had seemed so clear as Alice left the farmhouse for school. She would be a college-bound super student who did not go out for sports. It had been a ten-ton-boulder decision that nothing could budge—not her parents, not her friendships, nothing. It was the kind of rock-hard clarity she often thought her father had when he laid out his tables showing investments in livestock or crops with their corresponding tables of "reasonable expectations." Create a reasonable framework and then work relentlessly to fill it.

Oh, how strong she had been when she told the coaches with rock-hard clarity, "I'm not going out for sports this year." Her clear mind had been its own defense against naysayers who were never able to pierce or find a flaw in the armor of her clear decision.

She needed to sustain that kind of clarity again. She would do what had to be done, and the only thing she needed to think about was the telling: the clear telling.

It was time to tell her parents.

Dad, I'm going to have a baby. Mom, I'm going to have a baby.

As she drove onto the driveway, she saw more clearly, more exactly, than usual: her father's obsession with order declared itself everywhere. Whenever her father finished using a piece of machinery, he lined it up neatly—everything in a row. The machinery was aligned as evenly as cornrows, and green sat next to green and red next to red. When tires of worn-out wagons started sagging, he pumped them up to make the wagons look ready to go. No matter what swerving sadness lay under the surface, her father's was a parallel and perpendicular world.

In the middle of the farmyard appearances had broken down. Her father was standing with the repairman next to his John Deere 4240 tractor—one of his farm-sale steals. The 4240 had the muscle for most farmwork, but it was now over twenty years old and arthritic. Her father always defended it with the story that he had bought it for a quarter of its original price when it had only six hundred hours on it. Alice looked at her troubled father and his troubled tractor. A mixer-grinder load of corn and soybean meal was attached to the tractor, which had stalled en route to the hog feeders.

Alice parked next to the men. Rodney Ver Mayr was a friend of the family and a lanky man like her father. He had his black work cap pulled down, making his dark protective glasses look even darker. Rodney had the expression she'd expect on a policeman's face if he had just driven up to tell her one of her dearest friends had died.

Rodney had opened the hood of the 4240 the way an ambulance driver might rip open an injured person's jacket to apply his diagnostic tools. The tractor had had the equivalent of a heart attack. It would cost six thousand dollars to bring it back to life.

"Not worth it," her father said. He rubbed his lips together and looked at the soiled engine as if he were making a practical calculation. "What do I owe you?"

"Not a cent, Albert. Not a cent." Rodney walked to his own Ford 150 with its bright yellow John Deere decal on the door. "Want me to keep an eye out for another good used one?"

"Thanks, but we'll be all right."

Alice's father had another tractor that he had bought at another farm sale in the eighties during the first big round of farm sales, a John Deere 4440, but he had been protecting it, not wanting to start it up just to do chores.

Alice helped her father unhitch the mixer-grinder. He walked to the chewers' pen and retrieved the log chain. He hosed it clean while Alice walked to the machine shed and started the spare tractor, the big 4440. The power of the diesel engine rumbled through her. When she revved it up, the vibrations tingled through her shoulders, relaxing them more deeply. For a moment, she thought of herself as an early woman settler, helping with the work that needed doing even when she was pregnant. She thought of the hard expressions on the faces of the women pictured in her father's old *Atlas*. She could match them in strength and determination. She eased the clutch out, and the tractor stepped forward, slow but confident like an old and stubborn workhorse. Slowly, Alice directed the 4440 to drag its dead brother toward the grove. When they got close to what would be the disabled tractor's final resting-place, her father insisted that he do the driving. In a few minutes she saw why: he was determined to align it with the other machinery so that it would not declare its uselessness.

As they walked toward the house together, Alice opened the conversation that would test his need for alignments. If anything was going to disrupt his notion of clarity and order, what she had to tell him would.

"Dad, I've got something important to tell you."

He still smelled of disinfectant from his work at the dairy. He was stooped and slow. Each foot landed as if it had its own tired life. "What's wrong?"

She could read his hopeless expression: he assumed something was wrong on the farm. First his tractor, and now what—the steers?

"I need to talk to you about what's happening in my life."

He quickly read the seriousness of her statement. "All right, let's go down to my office," he said, "so we won't disturb your mother."

They went to his office, and he closed the door. The old *Atlas* was lying open on his desk. He closed it and sat down. Already he looked like a man of sorrow acquainted with grief.

"What is it?"

Alice stood directly before him, her arms at her side. "I'm going to have a baby."

He pulled his elbows back on the armrests of his chair. "Don't say things like that."

"I'm pregnant."

"Don't tell me that," he said. "That's not possible."

"I'm afraid it is."

He studied her. He looked bewildered. "Are you telling me that you have been having sex?"

"Yes."

He leaned against the back of his chair and shook his head. "I don't believe it," he said. "When would you have time for that kind of foolishness?"

Her mother evidently had told him nothing about what she had witnessed in the haymow. In his bewilderment he looked innocent. And
pathetic. Her wise father was blind to who she was.

"Please. I don't want to go into details. It just happened, but I love
him."

"Who do you love? Who did it?"

"Nickson. Dad, I really do love him. Don't think of me as a bad
person."

"That Hmong boy? You're joking."

"No. I love him."

"You what?" He leaned forward but did not get up.

"I love him. I'm going to have his baby."

"No you're not."

"Yes I am."

"I can't believe this."

"It's true."

"When? When? When could something like this happen?"

"Now and then. Dad, don't ask me that. We have to look to the future. We have to make plans."

Alice was prepared for his anger, but not his bewilderment. She imagined that he would be shocked and disappointed, then angry, but that
he'd quickly become the problem solver. He'd help her figure out how to
finish high school and get ready for college as a young married woman.
He looked at the floor, then stood up and walked to look out the small
basement window that gave a ground-level view toward the barn. He let
out a sigh that sounded as if it had a sob behind it.

If her father was hoping that she might become everything that
David might have been, that hope had just dissipated forever. For her
father, the news of her pregnancy was the last straw: he was ready to collapse like the rest of the farm.

"I'm so sorry, Dad," she said. "I am so sorry about everything. You
don't deserve this. I'm sorry I failed you. I couldn't *not* tell you. I had to
tell you. I'm so sorry I have disappointed you."

Alice sniffed back the tears.

He turned and stared at her. The glare in his eyes was something
Alice did not recognize. She thought it must be his anger, waiting to

break loose from its chains. Alice prepared for the explosion when he walked toward her, but he stopped and stood in front of her, his whole body stiff and erect. His ability to stay in control was giving way as his eyes glossed over and the tension in his shoulders gave way. A vibrating inhalation of air, and his shoulders shook. He put his chin down and turned his head to the side, and wept.

"Why you?" he sobbed. "Why you?"

"I'm sorry, Dad. I was irresponsible."

He paused and swallowed. "We all are," he said.

"Dad?"

"We're all sinners. I was too. Your mother and I were too. Your mother and I were thirty-seven years old," he said. "Do you know what I'm saying? We were thirty-seven years old. We weren't kids. But we weren't married and should have known better. Your mother believes that losing David was our punishment."

Alice understood what he was telling her, and she couldn't repress the fact that some pleasure was warring with her pain. Maybe her parents' first lovemaking was out in pastures and haymows too. Maybe her mother came to catch her and Nickson in the haymow so that she could replay her own good old days.

"I love you, Dad."

"I shouldn't have told you," he said. His composure was coming back. He looked squarely at Alice. "Your mother would kill me."

"I won't say anything," said Alice.

She reached out her arms, but he did not reach out his. She flung her arms around his waist anyhow, and he put his hands on her back and patted her as together they wept with the sorrowful joy of a father and daughter accepting the mutual distress of their lives.

Slowly, he released her and wiped his eyes with the back of his hand. "Does your mother know?"

Alice shook her head. "She knows I've been seeing Nickson. She doesn't know that I'm pregnant."

"Do you want me to tell her?"

Alice shook her head again. "I need to do it," she said. "Please don't listen in."

"I won't."

Alice laid her hand on her father's shoulder before turning to go upstairs. Her mother sat in the living room with a magazine on her lap. She
looked up, saw Alice's face, and must have spotted an imminent crisis.

"Sit down," she said calmly.

Alice sat. She looked directly at her mother. "I am going to have
a baby."

Her mother nodded her head. Not one startled movement.

"Not surprised," she said. "That's what happens. You might have
talked to me about it." She laid her magazine down and put the tips of
her fingers together so that she looked as if she was holding an invisible
cantaloupe.

"I am," she said. "I'm talking to you now."

Her mother dropped the invisible cantaloupe and folded her hands.
"You might have talked to me about how to keep this from happening."

"Right. You would have put me on the pill?"

She looked at Alice quickly. "Of course," she said. "When it was
obvious you weren't going to listen to me about not getting involved
with him. And I warned you about *them*. They're notorious for having
big families."

"You don't know anything."

"I know more than you think I do," she said. "I'm a realist. I look at
the facts and figure out what's behind them."

"Please." Now it was Alice who looked away. She was looking out
the window when she said, "I love Nickson. His family are wonderful
Christian people."

"You have blinders on. Don't you see how it's all coming together?
Don't you see how it's all adding up?"

"Mother, I don't need this. I need your support."

"You had my support when I told you not to get involved.
Remember?" She stood up and walked toward the kitchen. "Where is
your father?"

"In his office."

"You told him?"

"Yes. Mother, why didn't you tell him that I was seeing Nickson?"

"He has enough pain in his life. Now you've really done it. All the bad news at one time. Get out of the house. Just go do your chores. I'm going to talk to your father."

Alice did do her chores and thought of her parents as she worked. She tried to think of moments of affection between them and couldn't think of any: no little hugs, no hand-holding, no kisses on the lips or cheeks. But they had something. They listened to each other and didn't argue. They weren't like hot coals to each other, but they weren't cold ashes either. Even in her mother's darkest moods, her father accepted her, and they were probably having a sane and quiet discussion about her at that very moment. They must have talked to each other when Alice was not around. They might be praying together at that very moment, praying for the future for her and the whole family.

Even if her parents had found a path toward harmony with each other, Alice could not think of one moment when her mother showed pride in her. If she was acting on some notion of child rearing, it was the idea that you'd help your child by holding up so many "nos" that she'd have no choice but to find the "yeses." The only "yeses" Alice ever found by following her mother was the "Yes, you are wrong; yes, you are worse than you think you are." The only thing that made sense was to conclude that her mother was jealous. She didn't want Alice to become something bigger, happier, or more accomplished than she was. If Alice could have been sure that it was simply jealousy that made her mother attack her at every corner, that would have helped. Jealousy would have shown that she was actually proud of Alice, even if it was a warped pride. Now that Alice had been brought down, perhaps her mother would be satisfied.

Alice tried to remember one moment when her mother was in a good mood. She did remember some, but they dated back to when Alice was in grade school. She had good moods back then, so good that the color black looked bright on her and shone like the fur of a happy dark cat basking by a windowpane at noon. When she was in one of those good moods, Alice could see why her father fell in love with her. But then the cloudy years had come. No matter what she wore, it looked like a shroud, and when she spoke, her words did not so much sound as if they were coming from the tomb as from the cold lips of an executioner. When she was in her dark, scathing moods, Alice always felt her own blood fire up and the words that came to her mind were knives that were ready to slash back at the verbal thrusts her mother made.

Before going back to the house, Alice needed a plan that built on her initial resolve that she felt when she was ready to make her announcements. She needed to declare what she wanted and not let them try to define her life the way her parents had defined Aldah's. The plan was sketchy but clear: she would marry Nickson and finish high school. She'd do all the schoolwork and when she was obviously pregnant and not allowed to attend classes at Midwest, she'd have Mai or Nickson deliver her completed assignments to school. She and Nickson could live in the Krayenbraak house: it had plenty of room, and even had a spare room where Nickson could study. If the farm operation collapsed completely, she and Nickson could live in a small apartment. Maybe somebody's basement.

If it was a baby girl, they would name her Aldah. If it was a baby boy, they would name him Albert after her father. If that was all right with Nickson.

38

"Sit," said Alice's father. "Your mother and I have been talking."

Alice sat down.

"You can keep going to school until we see if we can get financial assistance for you to live in a home for unwed mothers."

"You're joking. I'm not a runaway. Knock it off."

"Listen to your father."

This is how a young calf must feel when it's surrounded by farmhands that are determined to lasso it, hold it down, and administer some kind of medicine that is supposed to protect it from the dangers of the environment. They're cornering me, Alice realized. I will not be cornered. I will not.

"I am going to finish high school," she said in a sharp but restrained voice. "I won't have to quit until after the first semester, and then I can do it by correspondence. By e-mail. I'll get the assignments and have somebody take them to school. I'm not dropping out of school."

"You're both children," said her mother. "You will not be going off at night to see him anymore."

"That's right," said her father.

Alice knew this was no time to argue about seeing Nickson. That would only encourage them to build a higher fence to keep her in. She already had extra sets of keys for the 150 and Taurus, but they could get the locks changed—if they could afford it.

She wouldn't argue, but she had found ways of seeing him before her parents knew about the pregnancy. She'd find ways now too. The fetus could sleep any time it wanted to, but her parents couldn't keep their eyes open forever. If you love someone, there is always a way. Always. There was no way on earth they were going to keep her from seeing Nickson.

"Have you even thought about your sin?" said her mother.

Wasn't that one of those have-you-stopped-beating-your-wife-yet questions?

Alice didn't answer her.

Her mother persisted: "Do you have a spiritual life at all anymore?"

"Yes, I do," said Alice. "I'm going to go see Rev. Prunesma right now, and you'd better not try stopping me."

They didn't. She had outmaneuvered them and gotten out of the interrogation corral, but, yes, this was one of those solutions that brought on a new problem: Rev. Prunesma.

As she drove the 150 toward Dutch Center, her greatest distress was in how her father had changed so much so soon. In the basement with his own confession, he had seemed so *real,* so gentlehearted. Her mother had done a Lady Macbeth number on him and now he had joined her conspiracy to do Alice in, to entrap her, to write the script of her life!

Alice's best hope now would be with Rev. Prunesma. She would tell the Rev that her parents were trying to push her out of the house the way they had pushed Aldah out. Aldah in Children's Care and Alice in a home for unwed mothers? Both children cast out of the house? The Rev would have to understand how wrong this whole picture was.

She would start with the clear announcement. She knew where the church stood on out-of-wedlock pregnancy. It fell back on the Big Gun of the Ten Commandments and called it a sin against the Seventh Commandment. It was seen as a public sin, so it needed to be confessed publicly. In her great-great-grandfather's time, the offending couple's confession had to be made by the couple standing in front of the entire congregation. Now it could be made more privately to the minister as Alice planned to do. The confession was usually followed by an announcement of the wedding.

The wedding. She had hardly admitted to herself that she assumed she and Nickson would get married, but her parents hadn't even mentioned the possibility.

Rev. Prunesma would think otherwise. He would be in his office preparing his sermon on a Saturday afternoon. She drove past the large brick parsonage and into the church parking lot. She could see the Vangs' house across the street and the single overhead bulb in Lia's workroom. The simple dwelling of the people who would soon be part of her family.

Alice heard the organist practicing some wretched hymn variations for tomorrow's service as she opened the back door of the church. She walked down the basement corridor past the children's playroom to Rev. Prunesma's office. She knocked lightly.

The reverend himself opened the door, looked slightly surprised, then nodded. Alice was not the kind of person who would interrupt him in his office without a good reason, and he knew it.

"Come in, Alice."

He gestured toward the leather chair next to his desk. It had a serious business look about it and was large enough to hold a person who was carrying all the burdens in the world. It didn't look as if it had been used very often, which made Alice think that her visit was of a rare sort for the Rev.

She sat down. "I am with child," she said.

He nodded and sat quietly for a minute studying her. The arms of the leather chair seemed to rise under Alice's arms to support her.

"You're telling me that you're pregnant?"

"I am going to have a baby."

The Rev showed no alarm. "Who would the father be?"

"Nickson," she said. "Nickson Vang."

He kept nodding and looking at her steadily. His professionalism was comforting. He almost looked serene with the news and at that moment seemed wonderfully different from her parents.

"How are you feeling right now?" He gave her a kind smile.

"I don't have any morning sickness or anything," she said.

"No, Alice," he said, and his kind smile remained. "I mean how are you feeling *spiritually* right now?'"

She nodded vigorously and said, "I feel I need to talk to you."

"This is good," he said. "Do you feel ashamed?"

"I don't want to feel ashamed. I love him."

He paused, looked to the side, and then back at her: "You just met him in September?"

"Yes."

The Rev's chest inflated. For the first time, his look was stern, not comforting. "Child, love does not happen that fast."

"Help me," said Alice. "Help me deal with my parents."

He raised his eyebrows and his eyes opened wide. "Your parents are your parents," he said. "What do they want you to do?"

"You wouldn't believe what they said, Reverend. You wouldn't believe it. They want to send me to a home for unwed mothers—like I'm some sort of runaway kid or something. You should talk to them. They were just awful about this. I feel like they're disowning me. And they already kicked Aldah out. They're just emptying their lives of their children. You need to help them. They're really way off base on this whole thing. They won't listen to reason."

Alice had gotten increasingly animated as she spoke, but she could not detect in the Rev's expression that he was joining her in her dismay with her parents.

"It sounds to me as if they're trying to think of what is best for you in your situation." He did not sound angry, but he wasn't showing comforting concern either. He was on his own autopilot, reciting as if he were reading from a manual.

"Best for me! This is Nickson's and my baby. We love each other. This baby was conceived in love. I will never deny love. I can admit I sinned if that will make you feel better, but I will not give this baby up for adoption. That's what you're suggesting, right? That's part of this whole unwed mother program, right?"

"Not necessarily," he said. "Many unwed mothers keep the child." He was still reading from his manual, and Alice sensed that from this point on, she would be getting standard-issue stuff. She felt deflated with his words: somebody she thought would be her ally sounded more like someone who had chosen to move into the enemy camp. She should have walked out, but she had no one else to turn to.

"Are you really suggesting that I keep the baby and raise it as an unwed mother?"

"This is a time of great decision for you, Alice. You must choose."

"I choose Nickson," she said. "I want to marry him and have our baby. I can finish school. I can get scholarships."

"There should be larger considerations than your own ambitions. You have much larger obligations. You need to start by humbling yourself. I don't see humility. I don't see regret. I don't really see a penitent heart."

"All right," she said, and tried to regain her resolve. "I know you don't approve of our having sex. I'm sorry about that, but I love him. I wish this hadn't happened, but it did and I'm not going to do anything now that doesn't include Nickson. Isn't that what love is about, sticking with each other when the unplanned happens? I want to marry Nickson and have our baby."

"It would be unfair to the baby," he said. "And it would be unfair to your parents. Have you thought of the emotional drain on your mother? The economic drain on your father?"

"It would not be their child! It would be my and Nickson's child."

"So Nickson and the Vangs have the means to provide for a child?"

"Are you saying you don't think I should marry Nickson?"

"Have you even studied the Hmong culture?" said the Rev in a voice that Alice heard as false sincerity. "Do you really want to become a part of a clan? A clan in which the men decide everything? You'd probably have to rely on Nickson's relatives for support. Do you think they'll give support without wanting control?"

"The Vangs are not like that," said Alice. "Nickson's not like that."

"From what I know," said the reverend, "he would be as soon as you married him."

The Rev sat motionless and speechless and slowly shook his head. He had started out by sounding so kind and reasonable, but then he had sunk back into his bunker. A Dweller. He was as bad as her parents. It was still unimaginable to Alice that he would not encourage marriage. She had never heard of anyone in her church not getting married after they found out they were pregnant. It was a natural consequence. One followed the other as certainly as light followed sunrise.

The reverend asked that they pray together before she left. He prayed for wisdom and forgiveness. He prayed for the Krayenbraak family and that they would together find God's will in this matter. He thanked God for parents and the wisdom of parents. Afterwards, he smiled kindly and shook Alice's hand as she left. "Do not underestimate your parents' wisdom," he said.

When Alice left the church, the 150 was one of only two vehicles in the parking lot. People driving by would recognize organist Louise Den Leuwing's old Dodge and they'd probably recognize the Krayenbraaks' 150 too. Folks would assume Louise was practicing organ; they'd probably also assume that someone from the Krayenbraak family was seeking out the Rev for some kind of help. So what? Alice didn't have much to hide. Not anymore.

She got into the 150 and stared through the windshield toward the Vangs' house. She wondered what Nickson was going through and whether it could be half as bad as what she had gone through with her parents and Rev. Prunesma. The light in Lia's sewing room was on, and Alice wondered if she had turned to work as a way of dealing with the news of Alice's pregnancy. Was the Rev right in his supposed concerns about money to provide for the child? I have money, Alice reminded herself. I could provide for this baby by myself, if I had to. She and Nickson could get married and live happily by themselves on her thirty-two thousand dollars if it came to that. She was not about to be corralled by anyone else's agenda. She was not about to let anyone or anything stand between her and Nickson.

39

That Sunday passed in a peaceful vacuum of silence at the Krayenbraak house.

Alice did not mention her conversation with Rev. Prunesma. She did not look at her mother's expression when the Vangs walked into church—looking so normal, looking as if nothing new had come into their lives. Alice's parents went off to visit Aldah at Children's Care after church; Alice went home and did the evening chores.

After supper, Alice studied Emily Dickinson. She saw Nickson in the hallways at school on Monday. He looked sad but gave his warm smile when he saw her. They both knew how much they had to talk about and agreed to meet after school.

Miss Den Harmsel introduced Emily Dickinson by reading "After great pain, a formal feeling comes. / The nerves sit ceremonious—like tombs." She read the lines as if they were self-evident. To Alice, they were. She had gone into the darkness of the tomb and come back out. The formal feeling had come to replace the informal feelings—those scattered feelings of fear and resentment. She felt as if she had gone through all the stages of grief and come to the grand finale of acceptance. Or was she just exhausted from it all?

At the end of the class period, Miss Den Harmsel called Lydia and Alice as they were leaving the room. "Do you two have a minute?"

It was hard to read her expression, which looked apologetic, as if she were afraid that she was imposing on them.

"Sure," Lydia answered for both of them.

Miss Den Harmsel wore her hair in bangs and had recently had the sides cut to curl up under her ears. When her hair was longer, some gray streaked through the glossy dark brown, but the gray was hardly noticeable now that she had cut it short. Alice didn't think it was vanity that led her to cut her hair: it was just a way to allow herself to do her work more efficiently—less time wasted. She wore plain blouses that resembled men's shirts, with the top button open and a gold chain around her neck. That day she wore a sky-blue blouse with a dark blue skirt that came down just below her knees. Little gold bulb earrings. And always those sensible low-heeled black shoes and gray-tinted hose.

"I've been wanting to talk to you two," she said. She closed the classroom door and sat down behind her desk. Lydia and Alice sat down in desks in front of her. Behind Miss Den Harmsel, just above the chalkboard, sat the model of the Globe Theatre which, from the angle where Alice and Lydia sat, looked oddly like a crown on her head.

"I know both of you will be graduating next spring." She paused and swallowed.

"With a little luck," said Alice.

Lydia gave out a nervous giggle.

"Sometimes my best students graduate and I never really have a chance to talk to them."

Lydia looked back over her shoulder, pretending that Miss Den Harmsel was talking to someone behind her.

"Very funny, Lydia." Miss Den Harmsel paused again. She folded her hands and put her forearms on her desk. Alice saw how long and lean her fingers were. Long and lean like her face. She seemed more physical than usual. In her classes, Alice noticed what she wore, but she had a presence that didn't feel physical. Just her energy and the intensity of her mind. Her body was an instrument for knowledge.

The expression on her face became very serious. "Students like you two are a blessing. I want you to know that."

Alice could feel herself blushing. She glanced at Lydia. She was feeling the same way.

"You're a wonderful teacher," said Alice. "My favorite ever."

"Mine too," said Lydia. "We talk about your class all the time."

"I couldn't, I couldn't," said Miss Den Harmsel.

Alice couldn't imagine that Miss Den Harmsel would ever cry, but she looked as if she was going to. Lydia and Alice sat tensely waiting while Miss Den Harmsel regained her composure.

"If I didn't have a few students like you two, I couldn't do this," she said. "It wouldn't be worth it. It wouldn't be worth the time and effort; it wouldn't be worth the love I have for literature, for all the music and beauty of it. For the truth of life that only literature can show us. The way it can lift the human spirit. The way it can be a window into ourselves. A magnifying glass really. I know you understand what I'm saying."

"Who wouldn't love Shakespeare the way you teach it," said Lydia.

"And the way you read it," said Alice.

"I wish all my students felt that way," she said. "It's so hard today. I feel so irrelevant."

"Don't say that," said Alice.

"'To thine own self be true,'" said Lydia.

"Lydia, you'd make a good Polonius," said Miss Den Harmsel.

"'And it must follow, as the night the day, / Thou canst not then be false to any man,'" added Alice.

"See what I mean?" said Miss Den Harmsel. "Oh my, oh my. If all my students could be like you two."

She shook her head slowly and stared off somewhere over their heads. "If it weren't for a few students like you." She kept staring over them and shaking her head. She looked as if she was replaying years of memories. "When I walk into class and look out at the students, if I didn't see some love of literature coming back at me when I teach. . . ."

She stopped again. Alice reached in her purse for a tissue, but Miss Den Harmsel didn't need one.

"There's no way you could know," she went on, "and I don't expect you to know. You don't know what it's like to stand up there and pour your heart out at all those faces and see all these dumb expressions, like 'Huh, where are you coming from anyhow, old fogey?' Good question. If you could see what I see from the front of the classroom—even in the advanced placement classes—all that indifference, all that blankness, all that emptiness, all that sadness that says, 'What good is literature, what good is all this strange language that's so hard to understand? Give me a video game, give me a cheap thrill.' But you two. You two, you're different. I'm sorry for carrying on like this. But I had to tell you. I wanted to make sure you knew that before you graduated and went off to have your own exciting lives."

"Oh, Miss Den Harmsel," said Lydia.

"The world will always need teachers like you," said Alice.

"The only thing I worry about with you two is that your dreams do not have the clarity of boundaries."

This felt like chapter two of Miss Den Harmsel's thoughts to Alice and Lydia. Chapter two, and the terms were changing. She looked troubled with the kind of deep concern that can reach into a person and make them stiffen. It was a look of displeasure, and not the kind that softens and leads to tears.

"As you know very well, this community, we Dutch Calvinists, we know how to set boundaries. There is some freedom in that: if you know the rules by heart—if you've internalized them, so to speak—you can act quite *un*self-consciously. There is some freedom in autopilot." Now she grinned at her metaphor.

"Freedom for Dwellers," said Alice.

"Is that a reference to something?"

"Seekers and Dwellers?" said Alice. "Rev. Prunesma preached about that. Dwellers are comfortable with the restrictions around them."

"Oh, yes, of course," said Miss Den Harmsel. "Actually, I've heard that distinction before. It *is* useful. Personally, if I understand the distinction, I live my external life as a Dweller." She paused.

Alice rarely heard Miss Den Harmsel make reference to anything so personal. "And your internal life?" she dared to ask.

"Yes, you're right: my internal life is the life of a Seeker." She smiled again. "But you're changing the subject, aren't you?"

"I don't know."

"I do have some concern about your dreams. Not that you shouldn't have them, but that you won't be ready for everything they bring."

Miss Den Harmsel could not possibly have known about Alice's pregnancy, but of course she did know about her friendship with Nickson. She no doubt also knew that they had become more than debate partners. "Are you talking about Nickson?" Alice asked directly. "About Nickson and me?"

"Not really," she said, "but that certainly is one indicator. He's a lovely young man. I totally approve of your friendship. Oh, I certainly do wonder if you've looked into a crystal ball of the future. There's no familiar precedent for you. Not among your relatives. Probably not in this whole community. Different cultures. Very different cultures. If your friendship continues, will you be ready for the, well, for the complications that will accompany the friendship? If it deepens."

"I feel like maybe I shouldn't be listening in on this," said Lydia.

"Stay," said Alice. "Please stay. I want you to stay."

"I do hope this is not getting too personal," said Miss Den Harmsel.

"No, no," said Alice. "I need this conversation, and I need both of you here."

"Take the sturdy framework of your culture with you," said Miss Den Harmsel. "Build any elaborate structure you want around it." She pointed to the model Globe Theatre. "The sturdy framework will always hold you up. Use what it has instilled in you. Don't desert it. Use it. And I'm talking to both of you now."

"Yes," said Lydia.

Miss Den Harmsel stood up, a clear signal that she had finished what she had to say. Alice and Lydia moved toward her. Miss Den Harmsel was not somebody a student would hug. Alice couldn't even imagine touching her. Lydia and Alice had a simultaneous impulse: they held out their hands to shake hers. She shook their hands, each separately, a good, formal handshake.

"Thank you," she said.

Later when they talked, Lydia was quiet. "What's the matter?" asked Alice.

"I adore Miss Den Harmsel," said Lydia, "but that 'sturdy framework of our culture' is crap. I hate our culture of money and sports and racism, the whole blind conformity that assumes we have the answers. Answers? We don't even know how to ask the questions."

"You're being awfully abstract, girlfriend."

"You know exactly what I'm talking about."

"I guess. But it's hardly newsworthy. People are people. Nobody's perfect."

"Whoo-hoo! Should I write that down?"

"I think it's impossible for anybody who believes something strongly to be consistent. Believing anything strongly means that you're bound to be a hypocrite."

"Amen. Maybe I will write *that one* down."

Alice knew there would never be a perfect time to tell Lydia what she knew she had to tell her. Alone with her now was as good a time as any.

"Lydia, I've got to tell you something, and, no, I don't want you to write this down."

"Uh-oh," said Lydia the mind reader. "This does not sound good."

They walked to the women's room and waited for the bell to ring.

"Is it so important that we should be late for class?" said Lydia.

"Yes. I think we won't have any trouble being excused just once."

"Shoot."

"I'm going to have a baby."

"You what?"

"It's true."

"Nickson got you pregnant?"

"Don't put it like that."

"Didn't you use protection?"

"Yes. He always used condoms."

"I can't believe you! Condoms are for keeping you from getting AIDS; the pill is for keeping you from getting pregnant! God! I can't believe you could be so dumb."

"Don't, don't. Don't be cruel now."

"You've never listened to me. You always think you're so damn smart. Now look at you: knocked up, and by somebody from a totally different culture."

"Back off, Lydia. At least he's got a brain."

Lydia was not backing down. She leaned into Alice. "You and I, Alice, we used to be smart together, remember? We didn't do stupid things like other people. Pregnant. Good grief, Alice. I still can't believe you could be so stupid."

"You can be the damn valedictorian."

Alice didn't know if Lydia was rejecting her or if she was rejecting Lydia, but this really was the last straw. If Lydia couldn't stand with her now, she wasn't a friend at all. Time to end the pretense. Alice was finished with Lydia for good this time. Totally finished with her. What an insensitive bitch!

40

It had not been a day for meeting in Miss Den Harmsel's room, so Nickson went straight for the 150 after school and hopped in. This was the first chance for him and Alice to talk all day—and now they'd have only a few minutes before she'd have to go home for afternoon chores. So much to talk about and so little time.

"You look angry," he said.

"I am," she said. "Very angry. Lydia."

"Want to talk about it?"

"No, but tell me about your mom and Mai? How did they take it?"

"I didn't tell them yet."

Alice pulled over. "You didn't tell them?" It was the first time she had ever shouted at Nickson, and she quickly checked herself. She'd save that tone of voice for that bitch Lydia. If she ever talked to her again.

"I'm not ready to tell them." He wouldn't look at Alice.

"But you told Mai."

"Didn't tell her either."

"I don't understand," said Alice. "I really don't understand. You two tell each other everything. Don't tell me you're afraid of your sister. She worships the ground you walk on. You could tell her anything and she wouldn't reject you. I know that much. I've seen you two. There's nothing you wouldn't do for each other."

"She's a good sister." He still wasn't looking at Alice, and she could tell how hard it was for him to be telling her what he was saying.

"So tell me. Why haven't you told her?"

"She'd tell my mom."

"So tell Mai not to tell your mom until you're ready to tell her."

"I don't think she could do that. It would come out."

"I just don't understand."

"I know it," said Nickson. "What about your folks?"

"Predictable," said Alice. "My dad took it all right until he talked to my mom. My mother, well, you can guess where she's coming from. My getting pregnant is all part of her idea of how everything is going to get worse and worse as we get closer to the millennium. My dad just caves in to her and does what she says, so now they both want me to go to a home for unwed mothers. They don't want me to ever see you again. And now that bitch Lydia."

Alice drove on to the Vang house. All of her movements with the 150 were stiff and sharp, but when she drove up to the Vangs' house, she said, "I don't want you to get out. You're not even out of the car and I miss you already."

"There's something I have to tell you," said Nickson.

Alice's mind, her heart, were ready for a deepening announcement of his love. The sincerity in his eyes. "What is it?"

"Two things."

Getting ready to tell her showed no struggle in his expression, but he did look serious, with his brow wrinkling and his dark eyes studying the empty space between them.

"I'm older than sixteen. Probably nineteen or so. There were some pretty mixed-up years in there."

Alice nodded. "All right," she said. "You said you might be older, but that's still only two years difference. You're wiser than sixteen."

"Other thing is I've done some pretty bad stuff. Never been arrested, but I could have been. I have some money I shouldn't have."

"Drugs?"

He nodded.

"From around here?"

He nodded.

"You knew those guys who beat you up?"

"No. They thought I was somebody else, just like everybody figured. But I did some pretty big deals in September."

"You're a drug dealer?"

"No. Not really. I just carried money from one place and drugs to another place."

"This sort of thing is happening in Dutch Center?"

"Oh yeah. I'm not doing it anymore. Not going to either. Everything changed when I started seeing you. I'll never do anything like that again. But I've got some money."

"This is hard to believe. This doesn't sound like you."

"I did it for Mom. She's not making much. It doesn't bother her if your church keeps giving us stuff, but it bothers me."

Of course. This sounded like the Nickson she understood and loved. He would never do anything illegal because he was selfish. He did it for the ones he loved. So he had been a drug and drug-money runner, a person who risked his life between two parties, neither of whom could be trusted. He risked his life for his family.

It had all happened in September. Nickson had kept his secret by being the one who bought the groceries and who made the bank deposits. When he bought groceries, he bought far more than the money his mother gave him could have paid for. When he made bank deposits with checks from Variety Paradise, he gave his mother cash and said this had been withheld from the checks he deposited in the bank. He had, in fact, always given her as much cash as he had deposited in their account. The Vangs now had three thousand dollars in the bank and another two thousand dollars hidden in Lia's sewing room.

"And I still have another two thousand," he said.

"My dad put away money for me too," said Alice.

He sat speechless for a moment. Then he told Alice that she shouldn't be bothered by Lydia. She didn't count as much as her parents. He said, "Your parents shouldn't reject you. You're family."

"But you're afraid your mother is going to reject *you*."

"No, I'm not. I just don't want to put any more weight on her shoulders."

"What if your mother did reject you when you told her? Then what?"

"My mother couldn't reject me."

"What do you mean, she couldn't?"

"Mothers don't reject their sons because they got somebody pregnant. It's not done."

"I don't get it."

"I know it."

"My parents don't seem to have any trouble sending me out of the house."

"You don't understand," he said. "We could even live at our house if we wanted to. She'd have to let us if that's what we wanted. She might not talk to us much."

"So you're saying a mother can't punish her son if he does something she doesn't like?"

"It's hard to explain."

"I'll live anywhere with you. But there's my parents. They wouldn't let me."

"I figured that."

"Nickson, what do you want to do? I want to do whatever you want to do."

"You sure?"

"Positive."

"I should talk to my uncles," he said.

"They'd come over here just to talk to you?"

"If they knew it was important, sure. But maybe I should go over there."

"Is this what you meant by needing time to think?"

"Yes," said Nickson. "Yes, it is."

Alice stared out the window of the 150 over the snowless frozen lawns through the stark branches of ash trees into the gray sky. When the whole world was being remade, everything she'd planned and assumed upended, turned over, scrambled, shuffled, when none of the pieces fit together the way she once thought they did.

"Nickson, what do you think we would be doing if I wasn't pregnant?"

"Figuring out how to be together."

"And next year? What would have happened next year when I was in college?"

"Maybe you'd go to Redemption with Mai until I finished high school. Then maybe we would go to the same college somewhere else."

"You've been thinking these things?"

"From the start. When you went with Mai to the pizza place, you know. That was it. I knew you were the one."

"That's when you said you wanted to go out for debate."

"I wanted our minds to come together."

"You went out for debate so you could be with me?"

"So I could be with you. Your mind. Your spirit. You have that fearless thing. I need to be with someone who is fearless."

Alice studied him. His face looked so strong just then. He was the one who looked fearless and determined. "Rev. Prunesma said some things," said Alice. "He tried to tell me Hmong men don't like women in charge."

"Not in charge. Fearless. That night when Mai and I came back from dealing with those thugs, when I saw you at the table, how brave you were, I started loving you. I knew that if a time came like right now, you'd do what we have to do."

She waited to see what he meant.

"I should talk to the elders. Hear them out, you know. I'm going to phone them, but it would be even better if we went to Saint Paul together. I think if the men in my family saw you, they'd approve. They'd have some questions."

"Like whether I really loved you?"

"They'd be curious whether you're expecting a boy or a girl."

"What difference would that make?"

"Never mind."

Alice's mind came into focus. Some things needed to be figured out step-by-step by gathering evidence and coming to a conclusion. Had he really suggested that they leave? Leave their worlds? Leave Dutch Center? Leave everything? Loving Nickson was not a question, but the suggestion to leave was not something that fit her analysis kit.

"You could just take off?"

"You and me. We could just show up. We've both got some money, right?"

"And your mom?

"She'd just have to understand, that's all."

"And Mai?"

"She'd understand, no problem."

"If we just took off, we'd be losers, admitting that we can't deal with things here."

"You run, that's not losing."

"Fleeing is admitting defeat."

"Sometimes you have to flee to get what you need. Pull back. Let the problem fly on by. We're not a problem to each other. Your parents are the problem. And that minister, Rev. Prune."

The idea to pick up and leave came into Alice's mind differently from what she might have expected. All of her fantasies, including the ones before she met Nickson, meant leaving Dutch Center and becoming that new person she could so easily imagine—a woman who was educated, respectable, and sophisticated—free from the stains of farm life, free from the narrow-minded bonds of her church, free from her mother's judgment, soaring off like a beautiful swallow into the infinite skies of possibility.

"I can't think like that," she said. "I just can't."

Alice didn't understand her own fear at that moment. She felt the way she did the first time she walked to the edge of the high diving board at the local sandpit swimming spot. She had thought she would run and cannonball fifteen feet down to the cold spring water; but when she had looked down, an unfamiliar fear held her back. She was there again, inside that sudden, recoiling fear.

"The only world I've ever known is right here," she said. "What problems I have I'm going to have to deal with right here before I move on."

"Sounds like *you* need some time."

"Yes," she said in a whimper, "I need time."

They agreed that they would not talk to anyone about what they might do next. They'd go about living their lives as normally as they could for a few days.

Alice took a different road home, turning down roads that would take her into the least familiar territory she could find between Dutch Center and the Krayenbraak farm, leaving the main highway and sticking to the gravel roads. There was little snow on the ground, and a stiff wind churned dirt up into the air, a mist of frozen black particles that gave a hissing sound against the radiator of the 150.

More than once she came within a hundred yards of a barn or pasture where she and Nickson had made love, and each time had a quick fantasy that she was looking at the very spot where she conceived. She had a moment of confusion when she came to an intersection four miles from home. She remembered the intersection, but a whole set of farm buildings was missing since the last time she had driven by in October. The Steenema place. It had been abandoned for two years, but people had once lived in the house and kept a pony in the red barn. The red barn, the chicken coop, the hog house, the metal machine shed, and the skinny white house were all gone now. She called back the images in her mind: that thick horse-shaped grove gone. It was gone! Even the fences along the road were gone—and there wasn't any rubble anywhere. There weren't any stacks of lumber to be burned; there wasn't even any crippled machinery from the present or the past. She stopped and stared at the absence. It was as if a skillful surgeon had stooped down and removed a tumor and sewn the earth back up without leaving a hint of a scar.

Maybe there was another way of looking at it. The earth was wiped clean for a fresh beginning. A birth instead of a death. A cycle of things. The earth would come alive again and flourish with mile-long rows of soybeans. Mile-long rows of corn. But who would be the new land-owners and where would they live? Who would be the new stewards of the earth? The question shouldn't have bothered her but it did. It shouldn't have been her sorrow but it was.

The sadness of not seeing what once was there entered her as a sadness about what she no longer was. It was a painful embarrassment to admit her own changes: not only had her unbridled behavior brought this pregnancy upon herself, but some part of her must have wished for it. With the admission that this was something she secretly wanted came a second flush, but this flush was not of embarrassment. It was an odd feeling of satisfaction that being pregnant made her safe by having something that her mother could not criticize out of her. Her father couldn't pray it away, Rev. Prunesma couldn't preach it away, and Lydia couldn't mock it away. And if the farm collapsed in a whimper tomorrow with creditors descending like scavenging crows from every direction, she would still hold a whole world with the hope of the future growing inside her.

The nuisance of common sense confronted the defiantly satisfied feeling: How could she be a mother and a college student at the same time? How could she have it all? Couldn't the same brain that gave her straight-As at Midwest show her a way? She wouldn't be the first person to graduate from college with a four-year-old, and Nickson was so smart. He'd do his fair share. And colleges had married-student housing units.

She turned around at the next intersection and drove back to the space where the entire farmyard had been wiped off the face of the earth. She let her feeling of sadness return. She waited it out. As whiffs of frozen black earth rose into the air, she said to herself *Yes*. This is what new beginnings look like.

But when she got home, the thermostat was still set at fifty degrees, and her mother was bent over the kitchen counter dressed in her blue down parka that now had grease stains on the sleeves. Alice walked past her without comment and went to her room to change into her work clothes. She put on a loose sweatshirt, but when she planted herself in front of the electrical panel to feed the steers, she still bumped her swollen left breast on the control lever. She left the churning augers and the feasting steers, walked inside the barn, took off her coat, and removed her bra and put it in her pocket. She wouldn't ask her parents to buy her a larger one. She would wear loose sweaters and go without a bra if she had to.

She went back out to watch the steers finish their dinner. Miss Den Harmsel had told them that most Emily Dickinson poems could be sung to the tune of familiar hymns. She sang to the steers "I heard a fly buzz when I died" to the tune of "A Mighty Fortress Is Our God."

Her parents were waiting for her when she got back to the house.

"You are not obeying us," said her father. "We know you can finish the fall semester. Before you start showing. And then you know what you'll have to do. We've made arrangements."

Alice knew he was mouthing what was really her mother's plan, so she did not answer him.

"We can't stop you from seeing him while you're in school," said her mother, "but we know you're seeing him after school. Give your father the pickup keys."

"What's going on?"

"Your mother will drive you to school in the morning and pick you up right afterwards."

"Whatever you have to do," said Alice. Then she turned on her father and gave him a look that was as frozen as the look he had given her. "Why aren't you in bed getting some sleep? You have to be at work at midnight, remember?"

In some bizarre attempt at bringing the family closer together—or maybe to give them the chance to keep their eyes on Alice more of the time—her parents decided that they would have supper together at five o'clock and her father would put off going to bed until after supper.

They all wore their coats at the supper table. Alice kept her eyes open during family devotions. Her mother caught her at it but didn't say anything because she had been just as guilty as Alice. Her father's opening and closing prayers were rich in pleas for forgiveness and guidance. When he looked up, there was a distant look in his eyes and his complexion didn't look right. When he stood up, the controlled and upright figure was not there as he sluggishly walked toward the living room in a way that was much more like her mother's manner than his. He stopped and put his hand to his face.

"What's wrong, Albert?" asked Alice's mother.

"Pain in my jaw," he said. "Hope it's not an abscessed tooth."

"That's all we need," said her mother.

"Feeling kind of dizzy too," he said.

"You'd better get some sleep."

He made his way toward their bedroom: he'd be getting less than six hours of sleep before going to work at the dairy.

Alice and her mother stood across the table staring at each other.

"Have a good look," said her mother.

"I am." Alice stared her straight on in the eyes.

"This is the mother who has tried to lead you through the darkness of the world," her mother said. Her voice was sonorous. She spoke as if in a trance, as if she were the medium for some otherworldly vision: "God knows I did not want you to be part of the darkness. I wanted you to live in light and to be a light unto others. Please sit," she said.

Her mother sat down on one side of the table, and Alice sat on the other.

"I wanted you to survive it all," said her mother. "I wanted you to separate yourself from the dying world and to give life to whatever remains behind. I prayed that you would listen to me and that I would be the voice of wisdom that prepared you. I prayed that you would be one who would remain standing in the next world, whatever that world might be. But we are what we are," she said and leveled a look that to Alice felt hateful.

She went on for what Alice assumed was her planned conclusion: "Being a realist is not just a matter of seeing things as they really are; it's also a matter of seeing what the outer appearance tells about the inner workings. 'The soul exists and does the body make.' That's not from the Bible, but there's some truth in it. When I first saw your outbreak of acne, I knew that it was a warning that something was deeply wrong inside. With your thoughts and desires. We cannot hide what we are. It comes to the surface. That's true with me too. I know that. When I look at myself clearly, I see an emptiness. I can say it is because I never knew my beloved son David, and his absence leaves a hollowness in me that will follow me to the grave. I can say it is because Aldah has always been outside the possibilities of my guidance. But I don't blame you for what I am. And for what I am not."

Her speech made Alice feel weary and sad. "Thank you, Mother. So just exactly what do you expect me to do? What do you want?"

"Nothing, really. I only hope that you will see who you are, what you have become, and learn humility."

Again, Alice said, "Thank you," but what was she thanking? Her mother's loss of respect for her? Her mother's judgment?

Alice heated a kettle of water and went to the bathroom to give herself a sponge bath. She crawled into bed fully clothed with her journal and *The Complete Works of Emily Dickinson*.

As a true-believing twelve-year-old she had read the Bible every night before going to sleep and had become obsessed with the Proverbs of Solomon, copying down verses in purple and pink ink. Her very favorite she had highlighted over and over in different colors of ink so that it stood on the page like a rainbow of truth: "A word fitly spoken is like apples of gold in pitchers of silver." Other quotations from Proverbs followed in smaller print:

Take fast hold of instruction.

Say unto wisdom, Thou art my sister.

Wisdom is better than rubies.

Go to the ant, thou sluggard; consider her ways, and be wise.

She had also liked the verse that said, "Give not sleep to thine eyes" and thought that it meant that she should stay awake as long as possible to please God.

All God had given her for that allegiance was a habit of sleeplessness.

Now Emily Dickinson looked like a better prospect than either the Proverbs of Solomon or her mother as her new Scriptures of Wisdom. Single lines spoke to her and she wrote them down:

A counterfeit—a Plated Person— / I would not be—
There is no Frigate like a Book.
The Brain—is wider than the Sky.
To undertake is to achieve.
Each Life Converges to some Center.
Of God we ask one favor, / That we may be forgiven.

Emily Dickinson was cold comfort, but after her mother, she was still comfort.

41

Alice was awakened at eleven thirty by her mother's screaming: "Albert! Albert!"

When Alice got downstairs, her mother was kneeling over the motionless figure of her father on the living room floor. She had a rolled-up coat under his head and was staring into his eyes, which looked distant and blank. Alice saw her father's chest moving, though his breathing sounded desperate.

"Call an ambulance and get me some aspirins," her mother said in a harsh but calm voice.

Alice rehearsed her words as she ran into the kitchen for the phone. "We need an ambulance! This is Alice Krayenbraak at the Albert Krayenbraak farm. My father has had some kind of stroke or heart attack. He's barely conscious. We're at fire number 8763. Yes, 8763. North of town, a mile off 75."

"Stay on the line." After a few seconds the voice was back with quick questions: Was there a regular pulse? What color was his face? Was his breathing steady?

Alice didn't know the answers to any of the questions, and could only tell her that he was breathing. The dispatcher said an ambulance was on its way but she'd stay on the line while Alice checked to see if she could give more information.

"He's still breathing," said her mother.

"Dad, can you say something?"

He didn't say anything.

The reality and unreality of the moment, its haziness and its clarity, the slow motion of it, the long image of her father lying faceup on the living room floor, the disinfectant smell from the dairy that never left his clothing, his strange breathing, the stern resolve on her mother's face, but its wrinkles, her aging, the shape of her loose breasts under her shirt, her blue anklets and black denim pants, and her father—the way his eyelids were not quite closed—like somebody faking sleep.

Alice told the dispatcher that he was breathing and had a pulse, and that he looked awfully pale.

Alice's mother was softly slapping her father's cheek. "Albert," she said, "can you swallow? Can you take these aspirin?"

She lifted his head and he swallowed the two aspirins with a few sips of water.

Within an hour they knew that her father had suffered a heart attack. The doctor came into the waiting room to tell Alice and her mother that Albert was in the intensive care unit but was going to live.

"There was significant physiological impairment," said the doctor, "but he is stable."

They would not be able to see him for several hours and they had better not leave the hospital, "in case there were new symptoms of complications."

The dairy operation would have to function without her father's supervision that night. He already had reached coherence and told the doctor about his work duties. "It will be all right," he said. "Those Mexicans are never sick. Moses will take over."

The doctors would be doing a surgical procedure that involved putting a stent in her father's heart, and he'd be able to go home in a day or two if the procedure went well and he showed no other threatening signs.

In the meantime, Alice at least had the keys to the 150 again, and she used them to leave the hospital and to drive to Children's Care to get Aldah. She didn't bother telling her mother, but when she returned with Aldah forty-five minutes later, her mother looked furiously displeased for only a second, then nodded as if to say, "Yes, of course, this is only right."

Alice was convinced that it was the right thing to do, but she had no idea how Aldah would react. She had warned her on the way to the hospital that their father was sick, and Aldah nodded as if she understood fully why they were going to see him, but she seemed in no way distressed by the news.

Aldah looked at the tube running into her father's nose and at the needle taped to the top of his hand. She slowly approached her sleeping father where he lay, dressed in a white hospital gown.

"Don't touch him," said their mother, who stood up and walked to the bedside as if to protect her husband from their daughter's possible misbehavior.

"Don't touch," Aldah repeated but walked up closely and stared at her father's face. Then, disobeying her mother, she did reach out to his hand, but so slowly that her mother must not have seen a need to stop her. Aldah touched, then rubbed her fingers lightly over his.

"Touch gentle," she said.

Alice stood beside her, then reached to touch their father's hand too.

"Gently," said Alice and touched his hand.

Aldah imitated her. "Touch gentle, David," she said.

Their father's eyes opened and he turned his head slightly in their direction. His face remained expressionless, and Alice could not determine if he was seeing them. His hand reached to rub the dry spittle in the corners of his mouth.

"That's enough," said their mother. "Let him rest."

As they prepared to leave, Alice waited to see if her mother would try to have a sweet moment with Aldah. She watched both of them, Aldah to see if she would make an advance toward their mother, and their mother to see if she would make an advance toward Aldah. They both did say good-bye but they said it in the way a person might say good-bye to someone they saw casually every day—and these two had not seen each other for two weeks.

Alice drove back to Children's Care, assuring Aldah all the while that their father would be all right and that he'd come to visit her as soon as he was well.

"I visit him," said Aldah.

"Yes, and he will visit you. When he's all better. All right?"

"All right," said Aldah, whose eyes lit up as they drove up to Children's Care. Aldah was happy to be back at her new home.

There had been the sound of the ambulance siren going down Main Street of Dutch Center, so Alice assumed the grapevine would have told everyone about her father's heart attack and that many people at Midwest would already know about it.

She assumed she'd talk to Nickson first and tell him what she knew, but it was Lydia who was waiting for Alice when she drove up to Midwest. She ran out to the 150 as Alice got out. Alice knew that her heart had already forgiven Lydia for being such a total bitch the last time they had seen each other, but the look on Lydia's face was neither a look of apology nor happiness. It was a desperate look.

"So sorry to hear about your dad," said Lydia. She held Alice's arm and looked intensely into her eyes. "But there's something else I have to tell you. It's terribly important and I'm so sorry to tell you after what you've been going through with your dad."

"What? What is it?"

"Let's get inside the pickup," she said.

When they did, Lydia took her arm again. "The acne medication!" she said. "You've got to stop taking it right now!"

In a desperate apology, Lydia explained to Alice that the medication was dangerous for pregnant women and that it could do terrible damage to the fetus.

"Why didn't you tell me?" asked Alice. "You just gave them to me in a baggy. There weren't any warnings on a baggy!"

"Because the package they come in has these ugly pictures with an ex over a stick-woman's pregnant tummy. Never in a million years did I think you'd get pregnant."

They cried together and the windows of the 150 steamed up.

"You'll probably be all right," said Lydia. "Just stop taking them."

"I will," said Alice, "even though my acne isn't totally gone. Look at these ugly lumps."

"They've faded a lot already," said Lydia. "I was going to tell you how good you were looking."

"If I did something to the baby, I'll never forgive myself. I couldn't do that to Nickson either. He doesn't deserve that. I just can't think about this, Lydia. I just can't."

"You could get an abortion and tell people you had a miscarriage," said Lydia. "You've just had to deal with your dad's thing. You don't need any more problems."

Lydia's suggestion was not as biting as it might have been because the thought of an abortion had actually crossed Alice's mind before Lydia's news about the medication, but only briefly. She had weighed the idea, but she also had come to a quick conclusion. "No," she said. "I couldn't do that."

"Because you think it's murder?"

"I don't know if it's murder, but I do know the fetus is something different from me. We don't even have the same blood type. I couldn't do it."

"Because of your parents?"

"Because of Nickson. I wouldn't throw away his baby."

"His baby?"

"Our baby."

They left the 150 and headed for the front door of the school. "I'm not going to tell Nickson about this," said Alice.

"I wouldn't," said Lydia. "You'll probably be all right."

"It's not me I'm worried about."

Nickson had also been waiting for Alice and they quickly slipped off together into the math classroom before the others got there. "Sorry to hear about your dad," he said.

"He's going to be all right."

"Don't blame yourself," he said.

What a strange thing for him to say, Alice thought, especially since she now had a much bigger worry for which she might have to blame herself. They had only a few minutes together, and this was no place to ask him whether he'd told his mother and Mai that she was pregnant. She wanted to embrace him, and she could see the same desire in his eyes, but every moment had a new seriousness to it. Everything in her life fought against the quick urges that once had seemed so simple and sweet.

"I have the keys to the pickup again," she said as they parted, but she couldn't think of what to add. He simply nodded, as if knowing that seeing each other would be a possibility again.

Miss Den Harmsel's class was starting in a few minutes, and Alice converged with Lydia as they walked toward the classroom. "Let's be great for her today," said Lydia.

"I'm ready," said Alice.

Miss Den Harmsel was there, but so was a "practice teacher," a young man named Vic Uitenboomgaars. He was young and slick, a Redemption

College senior education major. Miss Den Harmsel introduced him as "one of Redemption's best" and someone who had a double major in English Education and Speech/Drama.

He swirled around the classroom and spoke in a loud effeminate voice and acted as if he was born to be in the classroom, or on stage. By the end of the class they knew that he would be leading the class twice a week.

In her generous way, Miss Den Harmsel was allowing Mr. Vic to give his touch to the curriculum by teaching contemporary fiction on his two days each week. The class would return to Emily Dickinson on Miss Den Harmsel's days.

"I need you as my friend more than ever," Alice said to Lydia after class.

"Nothing can happen to change that," said Lydia. "I just hope that you'll figure out a way to go to college and become everything you can become. You've got it all, Alice, you've got it all: brains, wit, ambition, looks, personality—you name it."

"Stop describing yourself."

"Why do we sometimes say such cruel things to each other?"

"We're still birds of a feather."

"'We're still birds of a feather,' Nancy chirped." That was Alice, and the cleverness of it made her feel happier than she had all day.

"I'll babysit for you if it comes to that," said Lydia. "You know that, don't you? I really will."

"I know. Until you leave for college."

"Until *we* leave for college?"

"Whatever."

"We can handle anything."

"I know."

Miss Den Harmsel's praise of them did boost Lydia and Alice's opinions of their intellectual superiority, but they knew they were big fish in a little pond. If they were in a big urban setting, they doubted that they would stand out the way they did in Dutch Center.

"One way or another, I'm going to be part of the Vang family," said Alice.

"Are you ready for that?"

"I'm ready for anything. Are you?"

"I mean, can you accept them as part of my family? It would mean Mai too."

"Of course," said Lydia. "What I've heard about Mai, she's burning a hole at Redemption. I hear she's a straight-A student there. My mom told me she comes to the library to read poetry and literary magazines. I guess she's the editor of Redemption's annual literary publication."

"That girl moves fast," said Alice. "Want to get to know her better?"

"I'd love to. How does she feel about your being pregnant?"

"I'm not sure she knows yet. Nickson is working through the whole family thing."

Lydia telephoned her mother at the library to learn that Mai was there at that very moment. A twenty-second conversation between Mai and Lydia and the arrangement was made—and it was immediate, right after school that very day. Alice would have one precious half hour before she'd have to go home for chores.

"Maybe we should talk politics," said Lydia as they headed off for their meeting with Mai at the Redemption coffee shop. "We could ask her if she knows why President Clinton put the Oval Office mistletoe under his desk."

"Stop it," said Alice. "We promised we weren't going to tell any Monica jokes. And what does President Clinton have to do with those books that Miss Den Harmsel gave you for the summer, *The Federalist Papers*?"

"That's right," said Lydia, "and Jefferson's book on Virginia. Now Jefferson and Clinton, those two had a few things in common in the woman department."

When they met Mai, they immediately started talking literature.

"When I first learned how to read English," said Mai, "I told my mom that I wanted to read every book that was ever published in English."

"How are you doing?" asked Lydia.

"I have three to go," she said.

That was the icebreaker. They all laughed so loudly that other students turned to stare at them. Mai really was a bird of the same feather, and Alice was almost ready to introduce her to Nancy Swifties.

Mai had sat down beside Alice, and Lydia across from her. When they set their coffees down, Mai said, "I need the bathroom first."

"I'll go with you," said Lydia.

Alice stayed behind to guard their purses.

Mai had left her purse open, and it was easy to look inside. Alice wasn't going to steal from her, but she did wonder how much cash she carried around. Mai's purse was as organized as Alice's father's filing cabinets. Alice quickly shuffled through it, and in the bottom of the smallest compartment she saw them, those little wrapped packets with the words "For prevention of disease only." Mai carried the same brand of condoms as Nickson used. They must have been a family favorite.

Lydia's purse was in reach of Alice's foot, so she pulled it over to her chair, picked it up and opened it. It was a mess. Alice started scratching through the bits of paper scraps and came upon a note that looked like something she had been writing to Alice. No, it was a poem for Alice, written in the manner of Emily Dickinson. She was rhyming words like *confusion* and *delusion*—and then, out of nowhere, there they were, back from the restroom after what must have been the fastest pee on record. Alice had Lydia's purse open on her lap.

"Why are you looking in my purse?" said Lydia.

"I don't know, I don't know," said Alice.

"What on earth are you looking for?"

"I don't know, I don't know."

"You two stop it," said Mai in her familiar cheerful way. "We're here to talk about literature, remember? Not about the secrets of our purses."

"You're weird," said Lydia.

"As if you didn't know," said Alice. "Want to see mine?"

"Here's mine," said Mai. "Maybe we should all switch purses!"

Mai had saved them—or at least she had saved Alice, and now they really were ready to be three serious young women talking about literature. Alice and Lydia didn't tell Mai that they already knew she was acing all of her classes at Redemption, but they quizzed her on her love of literature.

Mai's favorite teacher at Redemption College was a published writer by the name of James Schaapsma. Mai had read a collection of his short stories and said she thought he was one of the best Christian writers she had ever read. "He doesn't try to make things easy," she said. "He isn't one of these phony, easy-answer writers."

Lydia and Alice were in luck: Mr. Vic was only interested in teaching contemporary authors, especially the Dutch American ones—people like Peter De Vries and Feike Feikema who for some reason had changed his publishing name to Frederick Manfred, but most of those Dutch American authors had fallen away from the faith. Like Mai, Mr. Vic liked James Schaapsma because, he said, he showed that you didn't have to be a sheep going "Baaa, that's nice, baaa, that's wholesome, baaa, isn't that pretty?" You could actually tell the truth and still be a believer.

Mr. Vic also had them read stories by an older guy who grew up around Dutch Center and wrote stories about farm boys. Little tiny stories that were about as long as a sneeze and that some people thought were funny. Mr. Vic said he was the "Hemingway of farm life." Ho hum. Alice didn't have much use for this guy's work. Too much animal cruelty. In one of his stories, his farm boys threw live cats from the top of a windmill with homemade parachutes on them.

"Cats died in that story!" Alice proclaimed. "That was supposed to be funny? What redeeming value could anyone find in a story that kills cats!"

"You never eat cats or dogs in America, do you?" asked Mai. She didn't sound like she was teasing.

"Hey, I'm a farm girl," said Alice. "I've seen lots of dead animals. I once held the head of a steer as it died. It's not as if I was freaked out by animal deaths. But why on earth would anyone kill cats in fiction?"

"How about tigers?" said Mai.

"That's different," said Alice. "But if I wanted something gruesome, I'd read *The Godfather.*"

"You ought to eat more cats in America," said Mai. "You people spend more money on cat food than on baby food."

"And cats kill millions of birds a year in this country," said Lydia. "Millions and millions."

"That's still no reason to throw them off a windmill in parachutes," said Alice.

"My mom prefers parachutes to cats," said Mai. "There's more money in parachute material than cat hide, I'll tell you that."

"How about Shakespeare and Emily Dickinson?" Lydia broke in.

"Shakespeare, of course," Mai said. "I love Shakespeare's Histories. Falstaff is my favorite character."

Miss Den Harmsel had not assigned any of the Histories. Mai had one-upped them there, so they pressed on to Emily Dickinson.

"She's great," said Mai, "but have you read William Butler Yeats?"

They hadn't.

"My favorite, though, is William Blake," said Mai.

Once they'd gotten off the subject of dead cats, their first session of talking literature with Mai was more a session of listening to her tell about authors they had not read—and in most cases, not even heard of. Miss Den Harmsel's two-person repertoire was starting to look pretty limited.

"Would Shakespeare ever kill a cat?" asked Lydia. She had that smart-aleck smirk. "Would Emily Dickinson?"

"William Blake would see a whole world in a dead cat," said Mai. "You guys have got to read Blake."

They promised they would.

42

When Alice offered to drive Mai to the Vangs' house, Mai said, "I've got something to tell you."

"Should I be afraid?"

"Not of me," said Mai. "Nickson told me that you're pregnant."

Alice watched Mai's face. She watched for the anger, the disappointment, the disgust. Instead, she got open arms and Mai's infectiously happy face, and all of the pains and fears of the day were, for a wonderful moment, taken away.

"We need more talk time," said Alice. "Hop in."

When Mai got into the 150 Alice whipped it around and headed toward the farm.

"I want time with you before I see Nickson again. Talk to me. Tell me everything I should know."

Mai did tell her everything, or as much as could be told in a ten-minute ride. Nickson had spilled the big news to Mai first and then their mother. Mai had gone with Nickson to tell Lia.

"She took it the way I thought she would," said Mai. "She's a little bit like Nickson, you know. Nickson's a bamboo man: hard on the outside and soft in the middle. She doesn't drip her feelings over everybody, but she's harder on the inside than Nickson is. She thinks America does strange things to people. Makes them act like this. Kids getting pregnant. If she had known that you and Nickson were seeing each other by yourselves, she wouldn't have been surprised at all about what has happened."

"Nickson told me that's what you people thought. But does she know how much we love each other?"

That question was tougher. Mai said the Hmong distrusted teenage romance even more than Rev. Prunesma did. Romantic feelings between any male and female, no matter what their age, were just the silliness of the heart.

Eros unbridled and on the rampage, Alice thought.

Lia's concern was not whether Nickson and Alice loved each other. She was worried about the bigger marriage, the marriage of their families.

"I know about the bride-price thing," said Alice.

"You're white folks, Mom knows that. The whole family in Saint Paul would know that too, but still. . . ."

"I can't believe you and Nickson would ever live by those rules."

"That doesn't mean we don't know them."

Alice drove Mai to the silo. Together they went into the switchboard room and Mai watched as Alice set the augers in motion. This drew most of the steers from across the feedlot and out of the barn.

"I want you to see the barn."

When Alice opened the door, a few steers were still lounging around and showing little interest in the feed that was being augered into the bunks outside. "Haii-ee! Haii-ee!" Alice yelled and waved her arms. One trudged toward her as if expecting a free handout.

"Go eat," said Alice, and shoved its wet nose away from her.

"They're not scared of you," said Mai, though she looked scared of them.

"They're just fat and content," said Alice. "Come on, come on, move along." She moved past them, slapping rumps. "Out of here. Out of here."

With the barn cleared, they walked toward the ladder leading up the haymow. "Follow me." Mai fidgeted uneasily, but when Alice reached back and took her hand, Mai trusted her and followed her up the wooden ladder that consisted of one-by-four slats nailed to parallel two-by-fours that extended up the back of the barn and through the floor opening into the haymow.

Mai looked around at the grand expanse of baled hay and open space. She stared in the same way Nickson had stared at the angled rafters and at the long metal rail running the length of the barn just under the peak, and the draped barn rope that hung like a one-braid hammock beneath the rail. A few sparrows startled at their presence, flew around, then

landed and watched them to see if they were a threat. Mai pulled her
sweatshirt hood over her head.

"I don't want any birds pooping on my head," she said. "That's really
bad luck."

"So I've learned. Of course, it all depends on what you mean by 'luck.'"

Mai looked around. "This is beautiful," she said. "It smells so good,
and it's so big." Her voice sounded warm and melodic in the cushioned
world of hay. "And private," she said. "It's so peaceful and quiet. I've
never been upstairs in a barn before."

"It's called the haymow."

"I love it. I just love it up here." Then a terrible seriousness swept over
her face. "Let's sit," she said. "I have something important to tell you. I've
been putting it off."

Alice sat down. Mai told Alice that Nickson was the one who worried about the whole bride-price thing, and that he was going to appeal
to their relatives. "You have to help me stop him. All right?"

"All right," said Alice. "I am Nickson's free of charge."

"Bride price isn't really about buying a woman, it's about connecting
two families."

"I get that," said Alice. "I'm starting to get a lot of things."

When Alice returned to the farm after dropping Mai off, her mother
was home. She looked sad but not angry. She had either given up on
Alice or given in to the weight of the world. As soon as she went to bed,
Alice walked out of the unguarded front door of their house and drove
off to see Nickson.

"Thank you for breaking the news to Mai and your mom," she said
when she picked him up.

He swallowed. "It was so hard, you know," he said.

Bamboo man: he hid his troubles. His tears went inside instead of
out. He felt pain and sorrow, all right, but none of it spilled out on other
people. They rode around town, comfortable in each other's company
and comfortable with the fact that they would soon be a public couple
with nothing to hide from anyone.

"I should be helping you pay for the gas," said Nickson.

The suggestion struck Alice as funny, and she almost reminded him that she had never helped pay for the condoms, but somehow that little joke would not have seemed all that funny at the moment.

Alice should have driven to the mini-mall where they could have taken a table in the food court and continued their serious talk. Since they had nothing to hide anymore, they could have sat there and talked until the place was ready to close up. And by then they could have ridden around until after midnight.

The mistake she made was accepting Nickson's offer to pay for some of the gas, an offer she was willing to accept because the 150 gas tank was still over half full, and filling it would not be a big money burden on Nickson.

Under the bright lights of the service station, the 150 stood out like a cherry on ice cream. While Nickson was standing next to the 150 with the gas nozzle in the gas tank, Alice saw the car go past with three male figures in it. She saw them glance, then jerk their heads in the direction of the 150 and Nickson pumping gas.

She rolled down her window. "Nickson, stop pumping and get in."

"We're only up to five dollars' worth," he said.

"Stop and get in," she repeated. "We're in trouble."

"Our troubles are over," he said calmly and kept pumping gas.

Then his head jerked up and looked to the street. The car with the three males had turned around and was driving slowly past the gas station, all three heads aimed in their direction as it cruised by. If it really was them, all three heads had found new crowns in the forms of black stocking caps.

"See them?"

"I see them," said Nickson.

"Get in!" yelled Alice.

"I haven't paid," said Nickson.

"Get in!" she yelled again.

This time Nickson listened, pulled the gas nozzle from the pickup, hung it up quickly, and jumped into the 150. Alice gunned the 150 away from the gas pump, and as she did, she saw the startled face of the gas station attendant staring at her in disbelief as the 150 bolted toward the street.

"That gas station guy thinks I was stealing," said Nickson. "I owe them seven dollars and fifty-six cents!"

"We have bigger worries," said Alice.

And they did: the car with the three thugs had made a U-turn and was only a city block behind them. Alice saw the front end of their car lift up with a little jolt when the driver must have given the car quick acceleration. It was a huge gray sedan, maybe a 1990 Buick, and even its headlights had a menacing look, with one light brighter and pointing higher than the other. Their car was as screwed up as they were. So let it be a battle between their sick monster and the pure energy of the 150! Alice put her foot to the floor, and with the surge of the 150's energy both her and Nickson's shoulders jumped back against the seat back.

Alice glanced over at Nickson and saw him reach for his backpack, and it was the first that Alice had noticed that he had brought it.

"It really was them, wasn't it?" she asked.

"Oh yes," said Nickson.

"How do they dare to hang out around here again?"

"Why not?" he said. "They didn't get arrested the last time, and they looked pretty comfortable dealing in that little South Dakota town. They're the same guys, I know it."

"The driver has a beard."

"I can see through beards."

"What are you doing in your backpack?"

Then she saw what he had. "Not the gun, Nickson!" she yelled, even as she saw the 150's speedometer reach sixty-five on Main Street. "Not the gun!"

It was like watching the birth of a serpent as the big L-shaped thing slithered, shining, from his backpack. He held it by its handle with his left hand, and with his right hand he slipped the sleek cartridge clip into the handle. As Alice refocused her eyes on the road, she heard a sliding and snapping sound of a cartridge going into the chamber.

She stepped on the gas. "They're not going to get close to us. Put that gun away."

"Be careful. These streets look slippery."

In her peripheral vision Alice could see the gun and could see Nickson ease the hammer down.

Alice looked in her rearview mirror and saw that the gray sedan was still a city block behind them.

"Nickson. Put. That. Gun. Away," she said. "I'll ditch them."

The 150 was hardly warmed up when she took the corner of Main Street and onto the blacktop leading out of Dutch Center. She saw the gray sedan take the same corner, hard, almost skidding out of control. No doubt about it: they were serious about chasing them.

Alice put the spurs to the 150. The Buick was not a lazy car: it was gaining on them even as the 150's speedometer reached seventy-five, then eighty-five. The blacktop road was narrow and had icy spots behind groves. She eased back in tight, controlled pressure on the accelerator, still holding a steady speed on the ice, always keeping two tires on dry pavement when she could. At this speed she expected the sedan to skid, but so far it hadn't. She kept pushing the 150 as the spaced white lines down the center of the road flashed by faster and faster and the hills got sharper, making her stomach leap as she crested them, a roller coaster of sharp hills that made the headlights behind them disappear and pop up again like frog eyes out of a pond. Nickson had his gun pointed at the floor and tried to take quick glances back, but he was becoming more concerned with their speed and stared out the front windshield as the little patch of light in front of the headlights got shorter and shorter and darkness beyond the light kept coming at them faster and faster.

The 150 was going ninety-five when Alice knew they were only a mile from where she was going to turn. She should have lost them by now, but since she hadn't, she would lead them into a testing area that she was sure only she would be able to handle. The 150 reached 105 before Alice lifted her foot, and she didn't touch the brake until she saw the flash of the green street sign where she'd make her turn.

When she did turn, Nickson shouted as if warning her of something she didn't know: "Dead End!"

"It's all right," she said in a voice that was much more controlled now. "Put the gun away. You're not going to need it."

Alice planned to lead that hulking gray sedan onto the frozen sandpit that waited for them a mile down the road. If they liked speed so much, she'd see how they liked speed on a really slippery surface. Her confident hands on the steering wheel were those of a wife protecting her husband and unborn child.

The sandpit, what the community named Crystal Waters, was ten acres of fresh spring-fed water and the favorite and only outdoor swimming area within ten miles of Dutch Center. The temperatures had been so cold that Alice knew the ice was thick, and snow had been so scarce that it would not be deep enough to keep the 150 from getting onto the ice.

The final stretch was bumpy and narrow with packed snow that might make the car behind them lose control, but it didn't. The headlights of the sedan lunged over the bumps, but the driver knew something about driving on ice. The car kept coming, fast and aggressive. The driver probably thought he'd trap them in this dead end.

"Nickson. I really need you to put that gun away."

"They'll try to kill us."

"They won't get a chance. Please put that gun away."

The picnic tables and cement-block dressing rooms came into view— and beyond them the snow-covered bed of ice. Alice aimed the 150 down the gradual slope of the beach next to the dock. They hit Crystal Waters at thirty miles an hour, with the confident sedan a hundred yards behind.

Alice gunned the 150 over the snow-covered ice. When she saw a glaring snow-free area of ice, she headed toward it. Just before she got to the bare ice, she turned the wheel and put the 150 into a skid that sent them gliding sideways down snow-free ice. The driver of the sedan did not try to slow down until he came onto the pure ice, then he put on his brakes, but the car slid straight and went sledding helplessly past them.

She eased the 150 back to the snow for traction, accelerated and pulled away from the sedan before the driver regained control and came back at them. Alice turned the 150's headlights on bright so they'd blind the driver of the sedan if she ended up facing them. What the 150's bright headlights did was light up the limestone embankment on the far end of Crystal Waters.

When the sedan accelerated toward them again, Alice accelerated too, but she put the 150 into a long arcing skid. She did not know if it was she or the 150 who designed the skid, but they were accelerating even as they angled, skidding but moving in a big calligraphic C across the snow-covered ice, the speedometer reading seventy as they moved at twenty miles per hour across the snow-packed ice. Like a dog trying to cut catty-corner through the arcing pattern of a fleeing rabbit, the driver of the sedan aimed his car to catch the 150 broadside. The unmatched eyes of its headlights came closer and closer before the 150 pulled out of the skid and accelerated ahead fast. The sedan whizzed past. Alice looked to see the brake lights go on and its unlevel lights shining against the embankment just before the sedan crashed headlong into it. The sedan's rear end rose quickly into the air and came down hard on the ice.

"Yes!" screamed Nickson.

The door of the 150 flung open. "Alice! Alice! What are you doing?"

Alice saw the door on Nickson's side fling open too and she saw the gun in his hand. But she was running, running hard toward the sedan. "Alice! Alice!"

Alice grabbed the door handle of the sedan on the driver's side and yanked at it. Inside were three people coughing in a thick cloud of dust.

Nickson was beside her now and pulled at her arm.

"Give me that gun, Nickson! Give me that gun!"

"Alice! No!"

Alice saw the dark handle sticking out of his coat pocket. She shoved and grabbed at the same time and sent Nickson sliding away from her on the ice. The gun was in her hand. She pulled the hammer back.

"No, Alice! No!" yelled Nickson as he struggled to his feet.

The sight down the barrel was so easy to follow and the weight of the gun seemed to steady her hands. She stood next to the driver's side window and aimed inside. Two of the occupants were barely visible through the dust but looked as if they had their noses buried in their armpits. The driver was the only one who was clearly visible with his face next to the window, looking at her.

Those frightened eyes. That broken front tooth. That flimsy beard. The slim beak of a nose. The black stocking cap, frayed and grease stained. Pointing the gun at him was as easy as pointing a finger.

And then the driver screamed: "Do you know me? Do you know me?"

Alice stared at him over the barrel of the gun.

The stupidity of his frightened eyes.

Nickson was now standing beside her but didn't touch her arm.

Alice lowered the gun. "You take this," she said.

Nickson took the gun, pointed it at the ice, and eased the hammer down.

"They're not going anyplace," he said. "Let's go."

43

Alice stopped at the gas station when they got back to Dutch Center.

"We knew you'd be back," said the attendant. "Seven fifty-six please."

Alice asked to use the phone. The attendant pretended not to listen as Alice called the police and told them what to look for, and why.

Within a day, news of the sandpit event was so widespread around Dutch Center that no one spoke openly about it. How could they? What the Krayenbraaks were going through was so far outside of everyone's experience that the would-be gossipers could not come up with anything surprising. It was all so obvious that the Krayenbraaks were going broke that it was hardly worth talking about. Their financial woes were just a drop in the bucket of their misfortunes. Then the head of the household had a heart attack. One daughter was in an institution and the other dating a foreigner who led her into that frightful event with those criminals. Those criminals. At least they weren't Dutch. Of course they weren't Dutch. And the mother, what could be said about the mother that hadn't already been said? No matter how strange she was, she had to be strong. There had to be a rock beneath that sea of strangeness. All that could be done about the whole unspeakable situation, really, was to pray and hope for the best. Trust in the Lord. *Zeg maar niks.*

The reality at the home of the Krayenbraaks was strangely unremarkable. Her father's surgery was successful and he was recovering nicely, getting a little exercise, and spending a lot of time in his study. Where was money coming from to buy groceries? Alice didn't know. What were her parents planning for her now that they really couldn't stop her from seeing Nickson? Alice didn't know. How was her father's heart attack actually affecting Aldah? Alice didn't know. What did the Vangs know, and what were they thinking? Alice didn't know. If she could have described

her own state of mind, Alice would have called it oddly tranquil. She
didn't analyze the feeling. This may have been what people meant by "a
state of shock." It felt more like a state of invulnerability, a peace that
came with sinking to the lowest depths and knowing you were there.

Her father's face was a quiet sheet of acceptance. Still, Alice knew
his assumptions: he assumed she would be going to live in the home for
unwed mothers at the beginning of the new year.

Like everyone else from Dutch Center, he heard about the sandpit
scene. It was all over the news and it rippled through the grapevine. But
he didn't talk to Alice about it. Some part of him was letting go, and he
demonstrated no need to control anything.

His only comfort was his office, and Alice did snoop around in it
when he walked around the farmyard slowly to check on what Alice had
done with the animals. He didn't have quick-money brochures or tables
of profit and loss on his desk. He had history books, not only the old
Atlas but also particular ones about the Dutch in America. Her mother
had gone to the library for him and had come back with a stack of books
that Lydia's mother had selected and which he now had laid out in his
study. He also had pages and pages of material that he had run off from
his Internet searches. Alice was not sure what exactly he was looking
for—some solace in the past? Some echo of Dutch character that might
sustain him in the present? He was taking notes and highlighting whole
passages. He reminded her of herself.

"Dad?" she said as she approached. She did not want to catch him off
guard in the middle of his private escape. He had the *Atlas* open again,
but right now he seemed less interested in the grim legacy of the faces
than in the optimistic advertisements that appeared every few pages—
implement dealers, furniture merchants, grocers, druggists, carpenters,
and an auctioneer who advertised "Public Sales Cried in Dutch or
American." Most of the advertisements were for horses and livestock:
Percheron Horses, Clydesdale Horses, Hamiltonian Horses, Shorthorn
Cattle, Hereford Cattle, Aberdeen Angus Cattle, Polled Durham
Cattle, Holstein-Friesian Cattle, Poland China Swine, Duroc-Jersey
Swine, Chester White Swine, Berkshire Swine, Silver-Laced Wyandottes
and Silver-Spangled Hamburg Fowls, Barred Plymouth Rock Chickens,
Brown Leghorn Chickens, White Pekin Ducks.

The pictures of the feeder cattle showed box-shaped animals on short legs and with low full briskets. The pigs, too, were bulky and rectangular and appeared to have more fat than pork. All the meat animals looked so different from the long-legged lean creatures that they were feeding.

Alice sat next to her father and looked at page after page of advertisements with him. The names attached to the advertisements were only family names. There did not seem to be one corporation name in the entire county.

"Things sure aren't what they used to be," said her father.

"And the family portrait section," said Alice, "those days didn't look so hot either."

"No, they probably weren't."

Alice felt like a first grader sitting down with her teacher for story time. Her feelings were not quite that simple. She felt despair about the Krayenbraak farm and yet free from it. She felt emptied of grief and yet sad. Was this the freedom one feels when hitting rock-bottom or when one has been totally transformed by love? Nickson's love? God's love? Maybe even her stern father's love?

"Dad," she said, "tell me about your work at the dairy. Did you have time to think or anything like that?"

"All I did when I was at the dairy was think," he said. "Putting on eight hundred teat cups a night is a little bit like cultivating corn back in the days when they had checked corn. You know, every corn plant perfectly spaced from the next one?—blip blip blip, those plants would click by all day as you cultivated a big field. Thousands and thousands of times a day. Hypnotic. Makes you daydream. Makes you think."

"I thought your job was supervisory."

A rare little grin crept across his face. "Right." He sat smiling and shaking his head. "What a laugh. After I spent a few hours putting on teat cups I'd go to the boss and report how the Mexicans were doing—like whether they were putting on the teat cups too soon after the disinfectant spray had been put on."

He made exact gestures with his hands. He was trying to give a clear mental picture.

"You see," he said, "one person walked ahead with the disinfectant spray, but timing was crucial. The disinfectant was supposed to be on thirty seconds. If the milker was too fast or the disinfectant man too slow, the timing got off. My job was to notice all these things. They called me their time-and-motion-study man. But I did all the other work too. I was supposed to be the brain and the grunt. I was a grunt more of the time than I was a brain."

"Did you go the whole night without anybody to talk to?"

"Not much talking," he said. "The Mexicans talked to each other and I talked to the boss about how the operation was going."

"You always were good with details."

He pinched his chin, then looked back at her. "Putting on teat cups wipes the mind clean. Like a blank slate. That blank slate of my mind," he said. "I kept waiting for God to write something on it."

She looked at this quiet, resolved man sitting there. The system, the world, the weather, the prices, his own wife, his pregnant daughter—everything had defeated him. He was losing the family farm, but he didn't look beaten. He really didn't.

"Dad," she said, "did I make you have a heart attack?"

Without hesitating, he shook his head. "No," he said. "God's message in this is to me, not to you."

"You mean that?"

"I mean that," he said. "What about you? Are you praying? Are you ready for the future?"

"I'm working on it," she said. "When you're down here by yourself, what are you really looking for?"

He told her. For the next hour he told her.

Alice's father liked to talk about "our people" as if they were still some kind of distinct group. On the surface, they weren't. The Dutch descendants might have kept a trace of the stone-facedness that she saw in the portraits of the early settlers, but in most settings they blended in. Until that telltale saying grace in public places.

Her father's interest in history was a mystery, but she was trying to understand it. For a while, she thought he believed that connecting to their roots would somehow bring them out of the financial disaster that had come upon them. She was wrong. That was not it at all.

When her father looked at the history of the Dutch in Iowa, he saw the history of humble country people seeking lives of piety in a sinful world that forever tempted God's people with the frivolous lures of "*spelen, zuiperijen en zwelgerijen*"—gambling, boozing, and sensual indulgence.

He seemed to relish those Dutch words, though Alice did not know how good his pronunciation was. Alice knew that what her father was reading was the real stuff. This was the thinking that made its way down through the generations. Phony and godless optimism of the Enlightenment? No wonder such indulgent attitudes toward the self led to *spelen, zuiperijen en zwelgerijen!* Still, her father could talk like a scholar, like a learned philosopher or historian. Alice knew how rare he was. He was an old breed: the thinking, learned farmer. But right then, it occurred to Alice that her father's study of history was his way of accepting the worst.

One thing that attracted Alice to the Vangs was that they didn't seem to have the same sense of sin that the people of her tradition had. Mai could date wildly but clearly took all the precautions against sexually transmitted diseases and pregnancy and gave no indication that she thought she was doing anything wrong. Alice still puzzled over how easily she could move beyond the scene at Perfect Pizza, and to move on without guilt for slapping those guys and without fear of their retaliation. Nickson didn't show much remorse about his drug life either. He simply accepted what he had done as something he had to do at the moment. If either of them ever experienced guilt, it was more over whether they measured up to the needs of their family than to the demands of God. It seemed to Alice that they were more afraid of offending their ancestors than of offending The Almighty. She sometimes both admired and resented Mai and Nickson's freedom from guilt. They just didn't have it. Things happened and they moved on.

Nickson and Mai didn't worry about money either, maybe because they never knew what it would be like to lose what the Krayenbraaks were losing. Alice tried to imagine explaining to Nickson what this loss meant. If the past followed the Vangs through ancient wars with China, through war with the Communists in Laos, through the hard life in refugee camps, something of the distant past was living in Alice's family too. Perhaps her father's interest in history was his way of finding out who they once were so that he would find even one reason to have hope in the present.

Some of the Krayenbraak troubles must have looked silly to the Vangs. The Hmong had known starvation hundreds of times. They had had to move to survive hundreds of times. The idea of feeling that everything was at stake just because of losing the family farm must have seemed to them self-indulgent. Who did the Krayenbraaks think they were—so privileged that ownership of land would forever be a given? Even if they lost the farm, Alice couldn't imagine that they would starve—or even have to go on food stamps. This wasn't the Great Depression, and they would not be that destitute. The very worst thing that could happen would be that they'd have to live on her mother's hoarded supply of Spam and pork and beans for a year and continue to bathe in cold water.

Alice never thought they were people in a high place. They were just an average farm family with the average conveniences of a nice house with all the amenities, a pickup, a car, and all the farm equipment necessary for working the fields and feeding the cattle and pigs. Nothing out of the ordinary. But she also knew that to her father, losing the farm wasn't just losing the land and equipment. Losing his money wasn't losing money. To him, the loss was bigger and deeper than that. Material loss was no more significant than the loss of his hair, just a superficial thing. Nor was it anything so simple as pride. He, like thousands of other farmers, had lost face years ago when it was becoming clear that sooner or later corporations, not individuals, would own most of the land in Iowa, even Groningen County. To her father, losing the farm was losing everything that history bequeathed to a person. It was losing the gift of the past. Memories of his father and grandfather were painful to him, as if he felt they were looking down from heaven with disappointed eyes. He had failed to uphold their legacy. So much had been given to him, and now he had not earned the gifts of the past. For a poor man to fail was one thing. For a person who had been so blessed to fail was quite another. She was confident that she understood her father and what he was going through.

"We'll never lose everything," she said to him.

"No, no," he said, "of course not." He held up the old *Atlas*. "This is what we are losing," he said. "All of it."

"But you don't seem troubled. You seem so accepting of things."

"I'm trying," he said.

Through the entire conversation, he had not said one word about her pregnancy and what he wanted her to do next.

44

Lydia was scheduled to give a chapel speech. Alice couldn't imagine why Lydia had been asked, though it occurred to her that it might have been Miss Den Harmsel's suggestion. Or it may have been the principal's way of warming Lydia up for giving the valedictorian address next spring. In some ways, it was a relief to think that Lydia might be the valedictorian: it would save Alice from the embarrassment of being denied the role because she had gotten pregnant. Alice still felt some jealousy: she could easily have been the one to give a chapel speech before news was out that she was pregnant.

Lydia was dressed in bright green and red Christmas colors as she walked up to the lectern. She looked brilliant. She looked beautiful. She smiled brightly as she adjusted the direction of the microphone. She looked as if she had practiced in front of an adoring mirror!

"This is a privilege" were her first words. "I am honored to share some thoughts with all of you this morning."

Please, Lydia, Alice thought to herself. Don't give a political harangue.

Lydia had chosen two short Scriptural texts, Matthew 6, verse 24—"Ye cannot serve God and mammon"—and Proverbs 11, verse 28—"He that trusteth in his riches shall fall: but the righteous shall flourish as a branch."

"The rich are inheriting the earth," she began. "I apologize for sounding so political, but I have prayed about this. I believe we are at a crossroads in this country as the millennium is upon us, and I believe this is especially true for us at Midwest Christian and in the Dutch Center community. As some of you know, my parents were born in the Netherlands. Dutch was my first language. My mother's favorite expression is '*Hoge bomen vangen veel wind*—'tall trees catch a lot of wind,' which in Proverbs reads, 'Whoever trusts in his riches will fall.'

"My friends, I believe money and the use of money to control our minds is the biggest threat to the well-being of our country as we enter the twenty-first century."

Lydia, you big hypocrite, Alice thought. Everybody here knows your parents are rich!

Lydia didn't stop. She went on to talk about corporate power and greed. She attacked Rush Limbaugh. Alice's last hope was that Lydia would not start naming politicians like Steve Forbes and George W. Bush. But she did—both of them. And not in a very respectful way. She called George Bush a bumbling rich boy who was born with a silver foot in his mouth. Alice could feel tension growing in the students around her. Lydia was building a wall of alienation around herself.

Her finale was the hardest to listen to:

"I know we Dutch Calvinists are just a small speck in the larger culture," she said, "but we could easily become a shot of adrenaline into the bulging greedy veins of corporate America. We are being swallowed by the ruthless Right Wing with all of its corporate clout and in return we are giving it legitimacy with our quiet but seasoned religious fervor. I fear that when Jesus said, 'Get thee behind me, Satan,' Satan said, 'All righty' then slipped behind Jesus and went straight into the first Dutch Reformation Church he could find. That clever Evil One started in the church basement, helped himself to some Christmas candy, and sauntered up to the pulpit on a sugar high with his smiley devilish face and started preaching distrust and suspicion of anyone who was not aligned with corporate America. Ignorance was the Evil One's pal. The only thing worse than ignorance is confident ignorance—and that's what we see today: people brainwashed into a state of ignorance. Keep them distracted with sports and television and feed them hate-filled drivel on talk radio, make them suspicious of legitimate newspapers, get them all thinking in the same direction so that their ideas are so uniform that nobody questions their nonsense!"

Oh Lydia, Oh Lydia, Oh Lydia, Alice thought inside her blushing head.

"Make immigrants the enemy! Make the *New York Times* the enemy! Make science the enemy! Oh, those evil scientists with their global warming theories. Evil, evil science! Get folks so scared that their only refuge is the gospel of American Capitalism and Militarism. The Mighty Dollar and The Mighty Sword! And when the Evil One had polluted everybody into greed and hate-filled conformity, he went up into the steeple. That's where he is today, in the highest church steeples, surveying his kingdom."

Lydia stopped, her face red with excitement. She smiled. "But with God's grace," she concluded, "we will not lift our faces to the false god of Mammon this Christmas. Instead, we will worship the Prince of Peace and be among the righteous who flourish like a green leaf."

Several teachers went up to Lydia and shook her hand after chapel. Some of them were even smiling. Alice was the only student who approached her.

"Wow," said Alice, "that was something."

"Too much?"

"You were great, but what did you think you were doing?"

"I was trying to be real," said Lydia.

"I love you for that, but don't you think some students will think you're a hypocrite in your talk about Mammon? It's not as if your family is poor."

"*Van zij die veel krijgen, wordt veel verwacht,*" said Lydia. "That's my father's motto. It means, 'To whom much is given, much is expected.' Can you keep a secret?"

"You know I can," said Alice.

"My father is a big anonymous donor. He's paying for the Vangs' house rent. He's paying Mai's tuition. He subsidizes the housing expenses for Mexican immigrants. By the time he's finished giving, we don't have all that much left."

Alice was speechless for a moment. "I had no idea," she said. "That's wonderful. But I wonder if some students will still think you're a hypocrite."

"Let them. I don't care."

"You really don't, do you?"

"I really don't."

Alice went looking for Nickson, hoping to ask him what he thought of Lydia's chapel speech. She couldn't find him. She looked for him again at lunch, but Lydia told her that he wasn't in the class they had together. Nickson wasn't in school. Alice told the principal she needed to miss her afternoon classes, and, as a model student in his eyes, he immediately gave her permission. Alice drove straight to the Vangs, hoping that Nickson had stayed home to think about what they should do and that he would answer the door when she knocked. It was Lia who answered the door. She started to bow, then gestured Alice inside. She gave Alice the kind of look that needed no translation.

"Nickson not here," she said. "He back to Saint Paul."

"Thank you," said Alice and went back to the 150, drove one block, pulled over and parked. Numbness. I'm in shock, she told herself. This doesn't make sense. This isn't possible. No, he couldn't leave without telling me what he was going to do. Impossible. But he was gone. Nickson was gone.

She tried to hold the rage back, pushing at it with reason. He must have had a good reason to leave, but why didn't he talk to her first? Why didn't he explain? Reason kept struggling for a foothold, but rage kept shoving itself forward, relentlessly, a force that would not be stopped until it burst through to the surface.

"Why!" she screamed at the windshield of the 150.

She drove away, fast. I am beside myself, she reasoned with herself. I need to think, but some other part of her had taken over and she pushed the 150 seventy miles an hour down the gravel road. She hit the railroad track at sixty and came down hard enough to make dust puff down from the ceiling. The 150 made an awkward front-end bounce but did not betray her with swerves or skids. She took the puff of ceiling dust as a call back to reality and slowed down, but not by much.

She drove straight to the cattle feedlots over the frozen knobby ground and skidded to a stop in a spray of icy dust. She was going to do chores in her school clothes. So what? And she'd wear these same clothes to school tomorrow smelling like a manure pile. That would make people keep their distance.

Did she spook a few skittish Limousins when she fed the cattle? She spooked a few skittish Limousins.

She yelled at the steers as they crowded up to the bunks. Those four-legged chunks of fat. "Here, gain four pounds a day!" she yelled at them when she threw the auger switch. As she watched them bump and shove to get at the feed troughs, she thought that if these useless fat blobs weren't castrated already, she'd castrate them now. With her bare hands and a tin-shears. A dull tin-shears.

When Alice was finished with chores and walked in the house, her mother looked pleased, probably because she could see how distraught Alice was. Then the phone rang, and her mother answered.

"It's for you," she said. "It's that Hmong girl."

Alice almost refused to take it, but when she did she wanted to scream into the phone. Mai spoke before she could say anything: "I hope you didn't misunderstand Mom this afternoon. She said you looked upset when you left."

"Upset? Upset?" Her voice was rising. "Mai, how could he just up and leave like this?"

For the first time since she got the news of Nickson's departure, she felt like crying—and she did: "Mai," she sobbed. "How could he? How could he?"

"Just listen," said Mai. "I was afraid that's what you were thinking."

Alice listened while Mai gave the story: Nickson told the whole family what was happening, that Alice had gotten pregnant. Lia was angry, really angry at first. Then she had gotten on the phone with their Saint Paul relatives, and one of the uncles had calmed her down. Calmed her down and then jumped in the car and drove nonstop to Dutch Center.

"Nickson needed to spend some time with the men of the family," said Mai, "and my mom agreed."

After that, Mai explained a lot of things. Lia needed a man in the household too, and Nickson had played that role. She explained why the whole family had come to Dutch Center, rather than just Mai by herself to go to Redemption. Nickson had been on the edge of "big trouble," in Saint Paul, whatever that meant—and Alice didn't ask. Mai's getting a scholarship to Redemption had solved several problems at once: if the whole family went together, it was a way of getting Nickson away from the people who were getting him into trouble, and Lia would still have a man in the household.

Nickson had gone back to Saint Paul to talk with his uncles, one of whom was the clan leader.

"Nickson really does need his uncles to be involved," said Mai. "It's our families that aren't married yet."

Alice couldn't think of any quotations from Shakespeare or Emily Dickinson to fit that moment. She did know that she was falling totally back in love with Nickson as quickly as love had evaporated at the thought that he had simply deserted her without warning. He was exactly what she thought he was: a noble and honorable person, a beautiful man. Here she was—seventeen, unwed, and pregnant—and she felt incredibly happy. How could she ever have doubted him, even for a horrible second? She felt foolish. Never again, she said to herself, never again will I question this beautiful man.

When she got off the phone, she walked back into the kitchen where her mother was standing.

"I heard part of that conversation," she said. "He's already run out on you, hasn't he?"

"He's coming back," said Alice. "He went to Saint Paul to talk to his uncles."

Alice did not tell her mother about the marriage of families.

"If he left once, he'll leave again," said her mother. "You don't want to stay connected to him. It will ruin your life. Are you listening to me?"

"I am always listening to you, Mother. Always."

That night Alice woke up at 2:00 a.m. from what she thought was a bad dream, but it wasn't: it was an aching pain in her abdomen. She knew this pain: it felt as if she was starting her period—but that could not be. She went down to the bathroom. There was blood, but she already knew about breakthrough bleeding. She had heard that this was not uncommon, and she was not alarmed. She would take several deep breaths and let her body relax. She would rest peacefully until the bleeding stopped. This was probably a response to the strain she had been under. The pain turned up its volume as she waited in the bathroom, and then the pain became excruciating, but only briefly. In a minute, it was over, a dark red blob floated in the toilet bowl.

"'When sorrows come, they come not single spies but in battalions,'" she said aloud to herself. She stared at the fetus that turned over like a small bloody fish in the toilet bowl. She stared at what might have been her child. She thought of fishing it out to see if she could determine its sex. Instead, she said aloud, "It's over."

Numbness was her body's way of holding back the feelings of sorrow and relief that came together in her chest, and when relief stepped forward it was countered by shame with its taunting proposition that she never cared about the fetus in the first place which meant that her love for Nickson was not real which meant their baby would not have been the product of love but of foolish lust which meant that she was a terrible person which meant that her mother was right all the time and that her pride had produced everything else that was happening which meant that she deserved both the pregnancy and the loss she was staring at right now. She deserved it all, and she wasn't sure whether the Evil One or Almighty God was smiling at her predicament or if she had been their joint project. Either way, she was getting what was coming to her.

She thought of the moment in the drugstore when she had learned that she was pregnant. The horror of the realization had been so simple; it had only one dimension. This was different. Now she felt a condensation of all the emotions that had followed: after the shock and pain of knowing had come the blessing of knowing. The creation of life was the greatest miracle on earth, and she had become part of that miracle. The hard part of telling the world was already behind her, and the hardest part now would have been preparing to care for the miracle that had been growing inside her. She was even ready for the scorn and mockery of classmates who didn't like her: the ones who would enjoy the fact that the mighty honor-student Alice had been brought down. She had moved beyond the fear of embarrassment and become more of a realist than her mother could ever have been. The baby would have been a blessing to her—and to Nickson, and to Aldah. She had fantasies of Aldah holding her baby and loving her. She imagined a baby girl with dark hair like Nickson's and a sharp chin like her own. All of the memories, all of the scattered experiences, compacted themselves into a clenched fist. She thought of her mother's dire predictions for the millennium. It was starting to make sense: December 31 stood there like a dam against which her whole life was pressing. December 31 was a sign that read The End, because, for Alice, it was—and she was the single cause.

The cramping returned, and she quietly groaned through the last of it. She stared once more at what might have been, and then flushed it down the toilet. Her legs were shaky as she climbed the stairs back to her bedroom. She stood in front of the mirror and stared at herself. She saw her mother's sad eyes, she saw her mother's slack jaw, and she saw her slumping shoulders.

She had occasional spasms of pain throughout the night, but she did manage to get some sleep. In the morning she felt exhausted. And hopelessly sad.

Lydia, she thought, you were right: I should have gotten an abortion. If I had, all I'd have now is guilt, and I know how to deal with guilt.

The Vangs were early risers, so she called Mai before seven.

"Mai, I had a miscarriage. It's over." Mai didn't respond. "Mai, it's over," said Alice. "I'm not pregnant anymore."

"I heard you," said Mai. "Did you save the placenta?"

"Mai, it was much too early for a placenta. Just a blob. Have you talked to Nickson?"

"Yes," she said. "He told me to tell you he loves you."

"He did? He called you to tell you that? Why didn't he call me?"

"He didn't think it would be all right to call your house."

Alice asked Mai for Nickson's number in Saint Paul. As soon as they hung up, Alice called the Saint Paul number. Someone answered who barely spoke English, but she recognized the name Nickson when Alice repeated it. "Not here, not here."

She called Mai back to explain what had happened and to ask her to please please try to reach Nickson and tell him everything.

"Tell him it's all over. There is no baby. Tell him to hurry back. Tell him I love him too."

"Should I tell him you're going on the pill?" Alice had never heard sarcasm in Mai's voice before, and she tried not to hear it now. Perhaps she was simply trying to be a realist.

"Yes," said Alice, with no sarcasm.

Alice phoned the principal's office at Midwest and told them she was sick and wouldn't be in school. She still had to do the chores. Would she have the strength after what just happened? Yes, she would have the strength. She had to have the strength, and she did, and as she worked she thought of the women who had come before her, women who did what needed doing in the world even after a miscarriage. There were women who would be able to do what she was doing if they had just had a baby. Women who could do what she was doing if their husband had just died. She worked with the energy of what she imagined to be the energy of every strong woman who had come before her—the Dutch women, the Hmong women.

When she finished chores, she knew she needed a different kind of strength now that she had to tell her parents that she had miscarried. Yes, she told herself, she had the strength for this too: just another tough announcement in a life of tough announcements.

She told her parents over breakfast.

"I had a miscarriage last night," she said.

Her mother showed no reaction. Her father's shoulders tightened and then relaxed. Then her mother said, "That will make some things easier, but you still did what you did. Don't you ever forget it. You still did what you did."

"I know, Mother, I know," she said.

Her father's expression was blank. He probably had resolved not to be disturbed by either good or bad news. Perhaps he was most relieved that they would not be forced into following through on their plan to have Alice go off to a home for unwed mothers.

"I'm tired," said Alice. "I need to rest."

Her father closed with prayer, a safe prayer that thanked God for the food they had eaten and asked for his guidance. Her father rose from the table and started toward his basement office.

"Are you all right, Albert?" her mother asked.

"Yes, yes," he said. "I'm fine."

Her mother turned slowly toward Alice. A little smile made its way onto her face, but her words were not cheerful: "You didn't get away with anything," she said.

"I wasn't trying to," said Alice.

"You'll need to see a doctor."

Alice assumed that she meant she needed to go on the pill immediately, but that was not what her mother meant.

"This won't happen again," said Alice.

What Alice meant was that she thought when Nickson returned from Saint Paul they would stop having sex and change their relationship to one that could withstand scrutiny—even her mother's. She honestly did imagine that she would never have sex again until she was married and that her marriage would be to Nickson—in a few years, while they were both in college. That is, if she, or anyone else, survived the millennium.

"You can't put toothpaste back into the toothpaste tube," said her mother.

"What on earth are you talking about?"

"Progression is progression," she said. "You can't go back to something you no longer have. You've gone too far. There are some stains you can't bleach out. You are what you are."

"Please, Mother."

"I was a virgin when I married your father."

That was good! Having her mother tell a blatant lie was delicious, and it quickly changed the chaotic world of her feelings. Her mother a liar! Alice wouldn't even call her on it. She'd just savor it.

The idea that her parents might have been practiced lovers when they met was not an unpleasant thought to Alice, though she had never given it much thought before. Now she would. Her mother didn't have to volunteer that information about her virginity. She didn't have to lie, but she did, so there must have been some guilt there too. This was very good.

45

Alice did see a doctor that day—and it was not to get a prescription for the pill. Her mother made the appointment and made Alice go by herself—"to tell the truth and to face the truth. Your body has been through some trauma."

"Reason for seeing Dr. Jungeweerd?" asked the perky but suspicious receptionist.

"Personal," Alice said soberly—and made sure she didn't show an inkling of embarrassment or fear. The receptionist was irritated, but she must have heard this one before: she thought that Alice had come in for some kind of venereal disease and that she'd get her perverse pleasure when she saw what drugs the doctor prescribed. Alice didn't see what the receptionist wrote down, but she didn't push Alice any further.

Dr. Jungeweerd's face was the kindest face Alice had seen in days. She would like to think that this was what the face of Jesus really looked like, even though Dr. Jungeweerd was a fat and jowly bald man. His wrinkled cheeks bulged when he smiled. His squirrel-tail eyebrows rose over large, gentle eyes.

"Alice, is it?"

"Yes, thank you."

"What can we do for you today?"

Alice looked at the examining table over his shoulder and imagined for a split second what it would be like to be lying on that table to have her baby delivered.

"I had a miscarriage."

He nodded his head. "I see," he said. His kind professionalism reminded her of Rev. Prunesma, but his kind eyes did not. "Do your parents know about this?"

"Yes."

"And how long has it been since you aborted?"

"Two o'clock this morning?"

"And did you see what you passed?"

"Yes," she said. "I looked."

"How long had it been since your last period?"

"Eight weeks."

"Did you have a pregnancy test?"

"I bought a kit. I gave myself one. It said I was pregnant and it was right."

"When you passed the fetus, did you also see any tissue?"

"Yes," she said. She paused for a second and then she said, "It looked like pieces of pig lungs."

He looked up as if he were trying to imagine what Alice imagined. "Good," he said. "Has the bleeding stopped?"

"Pretty much," she said. "I did chores this morning and didn't come back bloody. Maybe just a spot."

"Good," he said. "I think you will be fine, but I want to do a D and C just to make sure the uterus is clean and healthy. All right?"

"All right."

"We can do that procedure right here. Dr. Vander Wheele will see you. She is excellent. I think you'll like her."

"Thank you."

"Before Dr. Vander Wheele sees you, would you like to discuss contraception?"

"That won't be necessary."

He studied Alice kindly. "You do know that everything that is done or said in this office is private information. It's confidential."

"Even with the receptionist?"

"With all of us," he said.

"Would my parents have to know?"

"No."

"Are they expensive?"

"You'd have to call the druggist. They're not prohibitively expensive."

"Could I get them at Walmart?"

"That would be fine."

"I'd better not," she said. "I'm not going to have sex again until I'm married."

"If you change your mind, call me. Just leave a message with the receptionist. Just say, 'I'm calling about the prescription Dr. Jungeweerd recommended.' That's all I'll need."

"Thank you."

"Is there anything else you would like to talk about?"

"I think that's it."

"All right, I'll have the nurse come in and help you get ready for Dr. Vander Wheele. And you let me know if you have any unusual pain or bleeding, all right?"

"All right. Thank you."

"You won't be able to drive a vehicle after this procedure. Would it be all right if we called your parents to come and drive you home?

"Yes, please."

"I forgot to ask one important question," said the doctor.

"Yes?"

"Were you using any drugs?"

"Drugs?" Alice thought of Nickson's marijuana and her mother's Valium.

"Not really," said Alice.

The doctor's face showed that he knew he had opened a door that Alice was reluctant to open. "I told you everything you say is confidential."

"Well, I smoked marijuana a couple of times."

"Anything else?"

"I took a couple of my mom's Valiums. Did that cause the abortion?"

"Probably not. Neither of those things would be likely to cause a spontaneous abortion. Any other drugs? Acne medication, or anything like that?

"Acne medication? No, certainly not."

The doctor's eyes roamed her face. He was looking at her cheeks and probably seeing her blush.

"How have you been treating your acne? It looks like it's fading."

"Luck, I guess," she said.

"I see," he said. "Well, if you are ever pregnant again, be sure to see me before taking any kind of medications, all right?"

"All right," said Alice.

The doctor touched Alice's shoulder with his gentle hand. "See you in church," he said, and left.

After the procedure, Alice's parents were waiting outside. Alice had lost track of time, but she thought it was midafternoon. Her father drove the 150. Alice rode in the front seat of the Taurus while her mother drove.

What Alice could not tell her mother on the way home was that it was not until after the D and C, in that strange zone of pain and total medicated relaxation, that she felt the impact of the loss. A child had begun inside her body, a whole potential life was there—its future sorrows and future joys—all of it was potentially there. She did not even know what sex it might have been, but she believed it was the makings of a boy, and, yes, instead of naming him after her father, or after Nickson, she would have named him David and given her parents the son they never had—and little brother, no, nephew for Aldah.

These were the thoughts she could not share as her mother drove the Taurus, with eyes straight ahead, hands at eleven and two o'clock— these were the thoughts that roamed freely through Alice's mind, and then, without warning or forethought, her lips and tongue erupted with the words, "I'm sure it was a boy, and his name was David."

The words hung in the air, and after she had said them, Alice thought the sound of the heater's blower had either distorted or obliterated them. She looked out the window as they moved through the outskirts of Dutch Center at the shoestring factory that was being built, a single-level brick building whose construction had been started and then abandoned until spring. Its flat roof was in place and its lines of blank, black windows looked hopeless and expressionless, a hollow, useless structure like herself.

"Our David was a real person," said her mother in her unemotional voice. "Don't use his name like that."

Alice felt neither a reason to respond to her mother, nor to regret the words that had sprung uninvited from her own lips. Two miles passed in silence. Not responding to her mother gave Alice an odd feeling of relief, as if she had truly begun the process of letting her mother go.

And did it really matter what a person thought about a fetus anyhow?

It was too private and personal for judgment or generalization. She remembered Mai's response when she had told her about her miscarriage: "Did you save the placenta?" she had asked. She must have believed that the fetus had a spiritual life that went on. Because a spirit was intangible, it really was a personal thing. Maybe Mai could believe that the fetus could carry on in the septic system of the Krayenbraak farm, its spirit joining those of its ancestors. If Nickson believed that, Alice did hope for the eternal life of her and Nickson's fetus, living forever with Mai and Nickson's ancestors, if not with her own.

"It is time to move on," said Alice's mother as she turned down the driveway of the Krayenbraak farm. "You have a whole life ahead of you."

It was the most hopeful thing she could remember her mother ever saying.

In her own heart, Alice heard herself saying, Amen.

Alice went to bed and slept through chores, which her mother helped her father finish before he went to bed at six thirty. He was returning to his work at the dairy and would be getting four and a half hours of sleep before he'd have to get up.

At eight o'clock that night Alice's mother called her down from her bedroom. She had a visitor, Mai, who had driven over to talk. Disapproval bordering on hatred burned in Alice's mother's eyes. If she could have had her way, the entire Vang family would be sent back to Saint Paul.

Mai was not bubbling. She was a small statue of intense seriousness. A frozen face, her usual animation gone. She wore a gray hooded sweatshirt that she had pulled up over her head. She looked like a little nun. Alice walked outside and opened her arms to her. With that, Mai came to life, opening her arms too. They stood on the cold gravel driveway next to the Vangs' station wagon holding each other. Alice didn't realize how tense her body was until she felt Mai's small strong arms around her and almost melted into them.

"This day has been too much," Alice sighed. "Just too too much." Mai rubbed her hand soothingly between Alice's shoulders. She was no longer her sister-in-law. They were back to being friends.

"It's not over," she said. "Where can we go and talk?"

"We could go to the barn again, if you feel comfortable there."

"Perfect," said Mai. "That is one magical place. It made me feel very comfortable the last time."

In the great expanse of the haymow the two sat down. Mai folded her legs under her in a Buddha position and took a deep breath. Then a terrible seriousness swept over her face. "Sit down with me," she said. "I have an awful lot to tell you."

Alice sat down. That's when she told Alice that Nickson was essentially in the custody of one of their uncles.

"But," she went on, "the uncle he is staying with is very respected in Saint Paul. He's a very successful public accountant. That uncle also has a very stiff head. He's bossy, big-time patriarchal bossy. When I talked to him on the phone this morning, he said that your miscarriage was a message from our ancestors and that Nickson should stay in Saint Paul to be close to the strong men of our clan."

"You're not saying that Nickson's not coming back, are you?"

"I'm sure he loves you," said Mai, "but he's not coming back right now."

"When can I see Nickson?" Alice interrupted. "I have to see him."

"My uncle wants Nickson to stay in Saint Paul and finish high school there. You probably know that Nickson wants to become a lawyer. He already has one uncle who graduated from William Mitchell College of Law and one who was admitted to University of Minnesota Law School. Law and accounting seem to be the direction of the men in our family. And then there's the fact that all the men in the clan believe Nickson needs a strong man in his life right now."

"Mai, what do you think?"

"I think so too," she said. "You could always go see him."

"I couldn't afford to do that."

"What happened to all that money you said you had?" she asked.

Alice did not like the way the conversation ended, but Mai had not said anything that would end their friendship.

46

When Alice saw Lydia in the hallway at school, the anger she might have had about the dangers of the acne medication simply was not there. Her anger had been so intense just yesterday, and now it was like a car that wouldn't start. Her anger had a dead battery.

She circled around her heart with her mind. It had submitted to realities that were larger than her scrambled emotions, and now it was sealed in a container that was no longer vulnerable. It had spent itself. Her heart was bankrupt and had nothing left with which to pay or repay anyone or anything. Her heart had achieved a hard-edged but comfortable neutrality.

When Alice looked at Lydia dressed in another red holiday dress, she looked like a stranger for whom Alice held neither good nor bad feelings. She looked like somebody from a life that she no longer lived.

"There are some things you need to know," she said to Lydia. "Let's go for a ride during noon hour and talk."

"Important?"

"What do you think?"

At noon they left school together and rode around town in the 150.

"I had a miscarriage," she told Lydia.

"Miscarriage or abortion?" asked Lydia.

"Miscarriage. Dr. Jungeweerd as much as told me the acne medication caused it." The words came out of her mouth easily, with no indication of malice.

"Oh, God." Lydia was not one to gasp, but she came close to it. Alice looked over at her briefly and kept driving.

"It's all right," said Alice. "It's all right. I'm sure everything is working out for the best. It wasn't your fault, Lydia. There's something big out

there that allows things to happen that are not in our control. I don't
ever want to blame anybody for anything ever again. Maybe myself, but
even that seems kind of stupid to me right now. Things happen, and we
just need to accept them."

"You don't sound like yourself. Are you sure you're all right?"

"I'm all right. We're having a farm sale first thing in the new year. The
millennium is here, Lydia. The world as I once knew it has ended."

"You're depressed. I don't blame you, after everything you've gone
through."

"Just taking what comes."

"What are you doing for New Year's?"

"Getting ready for the farm sale. We're selling everything."

The Sunday after Christmas Alice called Rev. Prunesma in his
church office where she knew he would be before the service. He
needed to call off the public confession of transgression of the Seventh
Commandment. That sin had been washed away by the blood of a miscarriage. She wouldn't put it to him like that, but she did want to get
a few things straight in her life. This was no longer a public sin. It was
private! Already she regretted telling anyone. If she hadn't told Nickson,
he would still have been right there in Dutch Center and in her life.

"Rev. Prunesma," she said, "sorry to interrupt you but I have something important to tell you."

"Yes, Alice, of course."

"The Lord decided to take my child away."

"So you are going to give the baby up for adoption? That may be
a good decision, Alice. There are many Christian agencies that place
babies with Christian families."

"No no," she said. "I aborted."

"No, Alice, please don't tell me that. There was no reason to do that.
Why didn't you call me sooner?"

"I didn't abort on purpose. I had a miscarriage."

"I already told the consistory, Alice."

"But it's not a public sin anymore, right?"

"Are you ready to change your ways? Do you feel that you've been
forgiven?"

"Pretty much," said Alice. "I'm pretty clear about most things."

"Are you willing to come in for spiritual counseling for several months?"

"You name the time, Reverend, and I'll be there Johnny-on-the-spot. Just don't announce it in church, all right?"

"Very well, then," he said. "Your sin will be private. I'll talk to you next week, but stop by right after church today. I was going to call you if you hadn't called me. I have something I need to give you."

Mai and Lia were not in church that morning. It seemed strange, but Alice assumed they needed a break from everything too.

Her mother knew better, and chose to tell Alice when they had settled in their pew. "All the Vangs left yesterday," she whispered. "They've all gone back to Saint Paul. They are out of your life. Do you have collection money?"

Alice held out her hand for the dollar her mother gave her. She went into hibernation through the sermon and walked calmly to Rev. Prunesma's office after the service.

The Rev handed her an envelope.

"This is about the Vangs, isn't it? They've all left, haven't they?"

"Yes," he said. "We all prayed together yesterday and decided it was best for everyone. Mai will be coming back next semester. I convinced her of that. Goodness. We have invested so much money in her, she'd better honor the bargain. But the mother and Nickson, yes, they will be staying in Saint Paul."

The envelope had a printed note from Mai:

"Alice, I know you may find all of us strange, but we are doing what we have to do. I admire you so much. I know Nickson loves you, but we feel we really don't have a choice. Nickson needs to stay here. He needs a dad. I'll be back at Redemption in January, but all the dorms are full, so I'll be staying with Lydia's family. I hope that is all right with you. You are a wonderful person and somebody I will always admire. With much love, Mai."

When Alice finished reading, the Rev waved her to the large leather chair that she remembered all too well.

Alice sat in the chair, and the Rev sat behind his desk.

"I don't pretend to know everything," he said. "Sometimes I feel quite unqualified in my role as a spiritual leader. I am weak. I am a sinner too."

He wasn't looking at Alice as he spoke. He had relinquished the power of direct eye contact by looking down at his desk. He moved his hand across it as if he were smoothing an already smooth and shiny surface.

"I admire you," he said. He turned his head and looked at Alice. "I've watched you through these last difficult months. I can only pray that God will give me your courage."

"I don't understand," said Alice. "Courage? I don't think so."

"I understand how difficult your family is," he said. "And then all the rest. You've held up amazingly well."

"I don't think so," said Alice.

"I'm not the only one who thinks so," said the Rev. "You have many admirers. I realize your life has brought you pain. Shame. Remorse. But you have come through bravely. You are an inspiration to others."

"Me? Who? Name one."

"I'm not free to name names. Well, maybe one. Miss Den Harmsel."

"She doesn't even go to our church."

"We talk," said the Rev. "I believe the Lord has blessed you with strength."

Alice didn't say anything.

"You don't have to say anything," said the Rev. "Let's offer some thanks together and then you'd better go take care of your mother."

The Rev gave a simple prayer of thanksgiving, and Alice left the church.

When she was free of the Rev's presence, free from his judgment, and free from his assurances, she waited for her chest to explode with rage. In her mind she watched her own anger. She saw herself shaking her fist at God! Shaking her fist at her parents! Shaking her fist at Nickson and the whole stupid Hmong patriarchal nonsense that pulled him away from her! That code was even worse than the hellfire and brimstone code of her own tradition! She watched her anger in her mind, but it was only an act of her imagination. She didn't feel real anger, but she did feel a deep and sad relief. It was over. The horror show of her own life and foolishness was over. And in that relief she did not feel thankful; she felt guilty. *I am a worthless piece of crap, and I have gotten what I deserve.*

Nickson was gone. Like her mother said, everything was coming together—or falling apart. But they probably meant the same thing.

After the farm sale, the Krayenbraaks would be able to continue living in the old family house—renting it—and caring for the animals. Alice's father would be the manager—the current nice word for displaced farmers who had become farmhands. Appearances would remain the same. Anyone driving by would think the Krayenbraaks still owned everything and that dear Agnes and Albert no longer had to work away from home. They were not alone in this gradual fade-out. Other farmers around Dutch Center had met the same fate. Staying on the farm they once owned was one way to save face because the surface of things remained the same. It had almost become a standard procedure, a way of whitewashing failure. The big guys were just absorbing the little guys, allowing them to look as if they still were independent when, in fact, they were anything but. The steers would be sold, and they'd have only the hogs to look out for. No strenuous work for Albert: his heart, after all. Who ever said corporate owners didn't have any compassion: they would go easy on him.

Alice thought her father would be like a pheasant mounted to the landscape, with its beautiful surface—a lifelike plastic eye and the wings set to imitate real flight—but beneath the feathers there was nothing but stuffing.

The weather had been blusteringly cold, but Alice helped her father get everything ready for the January 2 sale. Her father's habit of keeping everything in order made the task of getting ready for the farm sale easy: he had the farm equipment lined up in the grove and had painted a little sign for the 4020—"As Is." Her father would not try to deceive anyone about the condition of anything.

"Let me lift that," said Alice as they stacked old pipe and electrical fixtures, some of the wrenches and hammers, the grease guns and screws and nuts and bolts, into separate boxes and set them on wagons where buyers could examine them. Everything was ready before New Year's Eve Day, a Friday, which they both knew would be a busy day.

Friday, December 31, Alice's mother served Spam and pork and beans for lunch but she was dressed up in her Sunday clothes.

"I want to look good today," she said. "This is it, then. We've reached the millennium."

"It's already started, Mother. It's already the year 2000 in China."

"I know," she said. "I have been preparing for this for a long time."

"And airplanes are still flying and computers are still working."

"I know."

"So you were wrong about those things."

"Not really."

"Not really? Mother, I know it's been an awful year, but the world is not coming to an end."

"Do you study metaphors in school?"

"Of course. 'All the world's a stage.'"

"For me, accepting the end of things, metaphorically—do you know that word?"

"Are you trying to insult me?"

"Metaphorically, the old world has ended. It has collapsed. I accept the death of things, even if it's just a number, a year we record in history. We need to die to live, don't you understand that?"

"You mean you've been teasing, just pretending, with all your doomsday talk?"

"Not at all. Not at all. Unless we live the doom, truly accept it, we cannot be ready for the new light. I once hoped you would be a harbinger of the new light, but I've come to realize the light didn't need you—or me, or anyone else."

"I have been living the doom," said Alice.

"Maybe you've learned something," said her mother. "So have I. I had to go there. I had to live the ending. Oh, the Spam and pork and beans. You probably looked at the books I had."

"You were taking Valium."

"Except for the dozen you stole from me."

"You were fighting anxiety or something. You weren't constructing a metaphor. Let me tell you straight-out, Mother. You are a weird person. I am not the only person who thinks so. Everybody knows you're not normal. You always say you're a realist? Does a realist fantasize the end of the world?"

"Fantasize?"

"Isn't that what you were doing? You're not stupid like some of the wackos around here, but don't pretend you're normal. You're not, Mother. You're not a normal person."

"As you wish. I see humility has not exactly slapped you across the face yet. I'm not sure what it will take."

"Why are you all dressed up?"

"To welcome the new millennium. And to welcome Aldah for the weekend. She has shown so much improvement. That was one of the best ideas we ever had. She has shown so much progress after the years of darkness. This is a dawning for her too."

Alice's need to confront or challenge her mother was gone. If this new freedom she was feeling was really a hardening of her heart, was this hardening a breastplate of security? It didn't feel like a breastplate of faith, but perhaps faith was nothing less than an absence of fear.

47

Lydia was getting responses from the many colleges where she had applied—including Princeton, Stanford, Yale, and McGill in Canada—and she had already gotten one notice of early admission. Her scores on all entry tests "were off the charts." Lydia was hoping to have a double major, one in history and one in political science. Miss Den Harmsel seemed to know what direction Lydia would be heading before Lydia realized it herself.

Alice had applied to the big places too, but she hadn't followed up on any of them. Some letters that might have been acceptances were lying unopened in her room. She had not yet admitted to herself that by not making any decisions, circumstances would make them for her. If she waited until spring, there was really only one place where she could be assured of acceptance at such a late date, and she knew that place was Redemption. Alice knew that her academic achievements were not a secret and that she could probably be admitted to Redemption with little more than a phone call. She had looked at their catalog and found her eye moving to their major in elementary education.

Alice looked for her mother's Valium but couldn't find the bottle. Her mother was certainly still taking them, and hiding them was probably one more way that she could torment Alice.

The direct approach might set a new precedent, so Alice simply asked her: "Mom, I'm sorry I took those Valium without your permission but I sure could use some."

"You're addicted," said her mother.

"Me? You're the one who's addicted."

"I'll give you one, but if you think you need another one you'll have to see a doctor."

She had the bottle of Valium in her pocket. She deposited one in Alice's outstretched hand and put the bottle back in her pocket.

Alice split the Valium in half and washed the half tablet down.

When she felt the tension leaving her shoulders and neck, it scared her. Not feeling pain at the absence of Nickson was an insult to their love. She should have been weeping and beating the walls. She didn't feel like weeping and beating the walls. She should have been planning a way to withdraw her money and go off to Saint Paul. She didn't feel like withdrawing her money and going off to Saint Paul. She lay in her room staring at the ceiling. Still no anger. Maybe the anger will come as an aftershock when I least expect it, she thought.

Then she had a feeling that she could only think of as admiration for the Vangs. Those people know how to make a decision and stick with it, she thought. They've been through so much, there's probably nothing on earth that can hurt them.

Was Nickson lying on a bed in Saint Paul, weeping because he was not with her? She didn't think so. Did she love him? Yes, and he probably loved her too, but something even bigger than their love had a grip on him now. There's something ruthless about that, she thought.

When Alice pondered her own life of the past few months—starting with the hailstorm through the steadily dripping news of their farm's problems, through her love for Nickson, the pregnancy and loss of it, through her father's health and the dead end to which her life had come, she wondered why she was not feeling total despair. If anything, the pain of it all was diminishing as fast as it had come upon her. It was not as if she thought that Rev. Prunesma might have been right when he told her that "love doesn't happen that fast." If the love she had felt for Nickson wasn't the real thing, what would the real thing look and feel like? She couldn't picture it, and within that emptiness there should have been waves of profound sadness, but there weren't. Even as part of her mind told her she should be feeling worse, she could feel an optimism hatching like a mayfly from the dark waters of her heart and whispering gracefully into the air. She did not know where the good feeling came from, and she did not know how to name it. It was bigger than anything Valium or marijuana or Shakespeare or Emily Dickinson could ever give.

As she imagined her own future, she saw a grade school teacher. She saw the earnest face of Miss Den Harmsel in her own face. She saw a room full of delighted faces.

When Alice picked up Aldah from Children's Care, the sight of her dear sister's face did awaken an old and tender feeling. Yes, she thought, the breastplate of love. Aldah would be a good beginning to the new millennium.

When Alice and Aldah got home, Aldah looked at her parents as if they were strangers and promptly asked Alice to take her back outside. Her father seemed to understand that Aldah was moving toward an independence that made him less necessary for her welfare or happiness. He walked over to her, bent down, and told her how big she was getting—which was a strange kind of lie because she had lost weight. Still, her father probably knew that the compliment was appropriate because Aldah had clearly grown in other ways.

Their mother looked at Aldah too but in no way showed any disturbance over the fact that Aldah showed no interest in her.

Aldah was eager to tell Alice about what she had been doing in Children's Care.

"I can read words," she said.

"Of course you can, my special person."

"I can fold clothes like this," she said, and placed one hand over the other.

"Of course you can," said Alice. "I am very proud of you."

"Yes," said Aldah.

Aldah didn't have anything she needed to tell or demonstrate to her parents.

"Come," said Aldah, and coaxed Alice to go outside with her. It was freezing cold, but they walked around the farmyard looking at the items that had been prepared for the sale.

Aldah understood that all the items on display, from the tractors and wagons to the hoses and wrenches laid out on flatbed wagons, were going to be sold, and that they wouldn't be on the Krayenbraak farm any longer.

"Good-bye," said Aldah to the John Deere 4440.

"Yes, good-bye, tractor," said Alice.

Aldah turned to the hog house. "Good-bye," she said. Then she looked at the Krayenbraak house and waved at it. "Good-bye," she said.

"No, not the house," said Alice. "Mother and Father and I will still live in the house."

"Good-bye," said Aldah.

"The 150 will be here!" said Alice. "Don't you think it needs some cleaning up, our 150?"

Her father was not required to sell it as part of the farm sale, but he didn't want it standing out there like a dirty sore thumb, indicating to buyers that they were sloppy and therefore not worthy of their serious attention on all the items they did have for sale. Aldah understood that washing the 150 on that terribly cold day was something she could do with Alice and Alice only. They were going to "make it shiny." It was so very cold, but Aldah was also so very brave, setting to work with Alice, all bundled up with her thick mittens on, the yellow leather ones with the furry insides. She loved those mittens because when she held up her hands her fingers weren't there, just these two big paws.

"Paws! Paws!" she shouted as she waved them in the air.

She watched as Alice scrubbed down the 150—and there it was, like a bright red tulip blooming in winter, made brighter by the conspiracy of sunshine and cold—cold to give it the polish of a thin layer of ice, and sunshine to magnify the luster of everything. Aldah wanted to go for a ride when they had finished the job, go for a ride in "shiny one-fifty."

"Yes, we'll go for a ride," said Alice.

"Far away," said Aldah.

"Not so far," said Alice.

"I am your mommy," said Aldah.

"No, no, Aldah, you are my sister. I am your sister. We are sisters."

"You are my sister, I am your mommy," she said.

"No, Aldah, our mommy is your mommy."

"I am your mommy," said Aldah and stamped her foot.

"Let's get in the pickup," said Alice, but when she tried to open the door, it was frozen shut. She walked around to the door on the other side, the side that had the full exposure to the sunlight on the south, but even there the ice had a firm grip.

"All stuck," said Aldah.

"All stuck."

"Come," she said, and reached out her big-mittened paw. "Read to me."

"All right," said Alice. "One story."

"I am your mommy," she said.

"No, no. I am your sister."

"No, I am your mommy," she said in a sassy, defiant voice.

They returned to the house and Alice did read to the smiling pleasure of her sister. In a few moments her eyes closed and her gentle snoring began. Alice was about to get an extra blanket for her sister, but then realized someone had turned up the thermostat and the temperature was a toasty seventy-four degrees.

No one, especially Rev. Prunesma, had ever told Alice that when Seekers stop seeking and try to become Dwellers they plunge into another desperation and another struggle. Alice felt that desperation now when she admitted to herself that she would not be joining Lydia in a grand intellectual journey in a prestigious university. She would not have that struggle, but she would have this one.

Her mother stood in the living room door dressed in her sleek and tight black dress, one that looked too feminine for church and too formal for home. A silver necklace glistened around her neck, her hair had been carefully coifed, and she had a slight smile on her face, one that Alice recognized as the grin her mother wore when she thought she had won an argument.

Acknowledgments

Special thanks to Mai Neng Moua, Blong Yang, and Chao Xiong for their patient and thoughtful assistance on Hmong culture and language. Any errors or misrepresentations are entirely mine. Special thanks also to Professor Herman De Vries, Stacey Knecht, and Maikel van de Mortel for their help with the Dutch language.

I want to thank Sarah T. Williams, Eric Goodman, and Josip Novakovitch for reading and critiquing early drafts and to the many other people who offered advice and encouragement along the way or provided crucial information, especially Cleo Granneman, Rob De Haan, James Schaap, Tobias Wolff, Bill Ransom, Willie Heynen, Dan Buyert, Owen Petersen, Daryll Vander Koii, Steve Mowry, and Drs. Jim McCarron and Doug Kurata.

Thanks to Dykstra Dairy for the informative tour of their facilities and to the Sioux Center, Iowa public library and librarians for directing me to historical materials on the early Dutch inhabitants of Northwest Iowa. Thanks also to the highly informed members of the Iowa Environmental Council.

For providing me residencies with space and time to write, I want to thank Robert Hedin and the Anderson Center in Red Wing, Minnesota, and Centrum Foundation at Fort Worden in Port Townsend, Washington; I am grateful to Greg Booth and Vickie Kettlewell for the use of the ranch-hand house at Sunup Ranch and to the Williams family for use of the "Writer's Cottage" on Lake Fredenberg.

Jim Heynen was born on a farm in Northwest Iowa. He currently lives in St. Paul, Minnesota, with his wife, Sarah T. Williams.

More Fiction from Milkweed Editions

To order books or for more information, contact Milkweed
at (800) 520-6455
or visit our Web site (www.milkweed.org).

Vandal Love
by Deni Y. Béchard

The Long-Shining Waters
by Danielle Sosin

American Boy
by Larry Watson

Vestments
by John Reimringer

Driftless
by David Rhodes

Milkweed Editions

Founded as a nonprofit organization in 1980, Milkweed Editions is an independent publisher. Our mission is to identify, nurture and publish transformative literature, and build an engaged community around it.

Join Us

In addition to revenue generated by the sales of books we publish, Milkweed Editions depends on the generosity of institutions and individuals like you. In an increasingly consolidated and bottom-line-driven publishing world, your support allows us to select and publish books on the basis of their literary quality and transformative potential. Please visit our Web site (www.milkweed.org) or contact us at (800) 520-6455 to learn more.

Milkweed Editions, a nonprofit publisher, gratefully acknowledges sustaining support from Maurice and Sally Blanks; Emilie and Henry Buchwald; the Bush Foundation; the Patrick and Aimee Butler Foundation; Timothy and Tara Clark; Betsy and Edward Cussler; the Dougherty Family Foundation; Mary Lee Dayton; Julie B. DuBois; Joanne and John Gordon; Ellen Grace; William and Jeanne Grandy; John and Andrea Gulla; Elizabeth Driscoll Hlavka and Edwin Hlavka; the Jerome Foundation; the Lerner Foundation; the Lindquist & Vennum Foundation; Sanders and Tasha Marvin; Robert E. and Vivian McDonald; the McKnight Foundation; Mid-Continent Engineering; the Minnesota State Arts Board, through an appropriation by the Minnesota State Legislature and a grant from the National Endowment for the Arts; Christine and John L. Morrison; Kelly Morrison and John Willoughby; the National Endowment for the Arts; Ann and Doug Ness; Jörg and Angie Pierach; the RBC Foundation USA; Deborah Reynolds; Cheryl Ryland; Schele and Philip Smith; the Target Foundation; the Travelers Foundation; Moira Turner; and Edward and Jenny Wahl.

Interior design by Connie Kuhnz
Typeset in Garamond Premier Pro
by BookMobile Design and Digital Publisher Services
Printed on acid-free 100% postconsumer waste paper
by Friesens Corporation

ENVIRONMENTAL BENEFITS STATEMENT

Milkweed Editions saved the following resources by
printing the pages of this book on chlorine free paper
made with 100% post-consumer waste.

TREES	WATER	ENERGY	SOLID WASTE	GREENHOUSE GASES
69	31,561	28	2,001	6,999
FULLY GROWN	GALLONS	MILLION BTUs	POUNDS	POUNDS

Environmental impact estimates were made using the Environmental Paper Network
Paper Calculator. For more information visit www.papercalculator.org.